SUPREME BETRAYAL

Mark M. Bello

A Zachary Blake Legal Thriller

Published by 8Grand Publications
Printed in the United States of America

ISBN: 978-1734548921

Dedicated to the *Me Too* Movement

Prologue

August 1997

Teenagers in various states of inebriation and consciousness packed the Walnut Lakefront home in West Bloomfield. Hayley Larson had a couple of beers but was among the soberer of partygoers. She needed a bathroom for a variety of reasons related to her drinking and partying. She climbed the stairs of the beautiful lakefront residence, more mansion than home, looking for a bathroom.

Hayley wasn't a *bad* girl—hell, she wasn't even a *party* girl. She was tired of her friends accusing her of being a 'pussy' and always doing anything and everything her parents ordered. Her parents certainly would disapprove of her being at a party where kids were engaged in various sex acts or where alcohol, drugs, and marijuana were being used and abused.

This is my coming out party! I'm going to college next year!

Hayley reached the landing, looked left and then right. She decided to go right.

Good choice!

She found herself in the master bedroom. *There must be a gorgeous master bathroom.* She breezed through the enormous bedroom and found herself in the most beautiful bathroom she'd ever seen. It was *huge*, perhaps larger than the *bedroom* she just passed through. The bathroom featured beautiful black and white marble with gold accents.

Is this solid gold?

As she walked to the commode, the seat cover automatically rose, and an electronic robotic voice chirped 'welcome.' An automatic fan began to hum, activated by her entry through the bathroom door.

She sat down on the toilet and did her business. She realized there was no visible toilet paper. As she looked around, Hayley noticed a panel of buttons where one would expect to see a toilet paper holder. She pushed the top button. A panel opened and dispensed a toilet seat cover. Hayley laughed out loud.

Too late for that!

She crumbled the seat cover, spread her legs, and dropped the crumpled paper into the toilet.

There were two more buttons. Naturally curious, Hayley pressed the second button. A gold metal flap opened, and a toilet paper dispenser roll immediately projected through the opening. She did what one does with toilet paper, and when she finished, Hayley disposed of the used paper into the toilet. She pressed the third button, and the toilet flushed underneath her. She smiled to herself, stunned at the wasted extravagance.

The home belonged to the parents of a classmate and his older brother. It was a popular party spot because the boys' parents were always traveling without them, more than willing to leave their two sons alone in the house. Mr. and Mrs. Orville Wilkinson were narcissistic and obscenely wealthy. Both unplanned boys, Oliver and Jared, were nuisances who cramped their parents' active lifestyle.

To assuage their guilt, they spoiled the boys rotten. Oliver, a freshmen law student at Wayne State University Law School in Detroit, was the older brother of Hayley's classmate, Jared. Oliver sported a Rolex watch on his wrist and drove a Mercedes convertible, both purchased by his father.

The two boys possessed all of the latest and greatest electronic gadgets of the time. They had everything a high school or college student could want except for caring and loving parents. Jared and Oliver loathed their parents for their neglect. To get even with their neglectful parents, the younger Wilkinsons threw parties entertaining hundreds of partying teenagers and college students in their parents' expensive lakefront mansion every time the elder Wilkinsons ventured out of town.

The boys' entitled lifestyles, wealth, and party man images were chick magnets. Girls of all ages flocked to their parties. Drugs, booze, and wild sex orgies ruled these events. Jared and Oliver were famous for these get-togethers, excessive use of drugs and booze, and, especially, for their sexual conquests. High school-aged girls considered sex with a Wilkerson, especially Oliver, a badge of honor.

Jared was somewhat of a gentleman. Perhaps it was because he was younger. On the other hand, Oliver rarely waited for an invitation—he simply *took* what he wanted. Young girls in various stages of inebriation would be swept off their feet and carried into a bedroom. Whether previously deflowered or not, they became willing participants (so they all claimed) in wild moments of sex and drugs. Not a single girl ever pressed charges or uttered a word of complaint about Oliver's behavior.

While Hayley Larson was undoubtedly impressed with the house and its extravagance, she was not especially enamored with her hosts. She thought both Jared and Oliver were gross, obnoxious, immature, entitled, and spoiled brats.

Her parents had nothing to worry about. Though under the drinking age, Hayley didn't mind a beer here and there. However, she did not do drugs and was not sexually active. Hayley was no puritan, but, at sixteen, she had never been in a serious relationship. She was saving her virginity for her first loving relationship and would never engage in gratuitous sex.

Hayley rose from the commode, and the toilet seat descended and closed—automatically, of course. Suddenly, a sweet-smelling room deodorizer sprayed from a ceiling fan. She surveyed the room, taking in various gadgets and gizmos, shaking her head from side to side, and wondering about other hidden devices the boys' parents might privately enjoy using in this bathroom of all bathrooms. She chuckled at the thought and then studied and primped herself in front of a massive gold-trimmed mirror.

Hayley was a very attractive young lady with long, straight auburn-colored hair and large greenish-blue eyes. A few light freckles dotted her face. Her skin glowed like porcelain, almost like the skin of a doll. She was tall, about five foot nine, athletic (she played varsity soccer), and dressed impeccably, tastefully accenting her long smooth legs and ample breasts. In short, Hayley was a stunning young woman.

Hayley adjusted her clothing, freshened her make-up, and opened the bathroom door to leave. She took a step, looked up, and was startled to see Oliver Wilkinson standing at the door, blocking her exit. Shane Marbury, Oliver's best friend, stood by Oliver's side.

"Shit, guys! You scared the hell out of me! How long have you been standing there?" Hayley uttered with a stunned smirk.

The young men were barely coherent, incredibly drunk, stoned, high, or a combination of the three.

"Hey, baby. We saw you come up here and thought you might want to party. Jared's told me all about you. You're Hayley, right? How about this bathroom?" Oliver's speech was slurred. He turned three hundred sixty degrees, taking in his surroundings.

"We *are* partying, Oliver. I needed to use the bathroom, and now I'm ready to go back down. You coming?"

She tried to push by them, but they continued to block the bathroom exit.

"Let me show you all of the clever gadgets my parents enjoy using in here." Oliver gyrated and made lewd gestures.

Hayley expelled a nervous laugh. She felt trapped, threatened, and unsure where this was going.

"From the gadgets in here, I can imagine, but I'll pass, thank you." She was very anxious to leave.

"Come on, Hayley. Don't be like that," Marbury stammered.

"We can have a lot of fun in here. Stop being so high and mighty. Do you think you're better than us? You're nothing but a pompous bitch," Oliver added, turning to Shane. "I think our girl Hayley needs to be taught a lesson, don't you agree, Shane?"

Oliver waxed hurt feelings. The two young men pushed forward, backing Hayley further into the bathroom. She tried, unsuccessfully, to push by them, but they held their positions. Oliver closed the door behind him.

Hayley's nervousness now escalated into full-blown panic. She tried to maintain her composure.

"Cut it out, guys! This is not the least bit funny. If you two want to play in the bathroom, be my guest, but find another play toy. I'm not interested."

Hayley was now experiencing a complete loss of composure. She again tried to push by the two men but was again blocked from leaving. They continued to push her back into the bathroom.

"Let me show you the whirlpool," Oliver urged. He staggered to a panel on the wall closest to him. He hit a button, and the whirlpool activated.

"My parents have all kinds of fun in here. See this panel?"

He walked over to another gold-plated panel and pushed a button. The panel opened, and a tray of sex toys, lubricants, and oils shot out from the opening behind the panel door.

"Pretty cool, huh? Have you ever had sex in a whirlpool? It is the absolute shit!"

"I've never had sex in a whirlpool," Shane exclaimed, gyrating his pelvis. "I'm looking forward to it."

"I've never had sex anywhere. I'm a virgin, and I plan to keep it that way. Now, get out of my way, or I am going to call 9-1-1," Hayley threatened.

She pulled out her phone and began to dial. Oliver raced over to her, pulled the phone from her hands, and threw it into the filling whirlpool.

"Not so fast, bitch," Oliver snarled.

"If you really are a virgin, which I don't believe for a fucking second, prepare to lose your virginity. You have two choices: Relax, enjoy the experience, and have fun with two great guys. Or fight, scream, scratch, and resist. Either way, we always get what we want. No one ever says no to us, and no one has ever been sorry."

The disgusting young men stood in front of Hayley, blocking her exit, gyrating their pelvises and hips back and forth. They unzipped their pants and grabbed their crotches.

"You assholes ruined my phone. You're drunk or high, maybe both. You're out of your damned minds. Let me out of here, now! I'll fucking scream!" Hayley raged. She was officially terrified.

"Language, Hayley, language, shame on you. Everyone's wasted. Scream all you want. No one's coming to help you, Oliver rumbled and sneered at her. He reached his arm toward her, grabbed her blouse, and ripped it open, revealing a scant bra and ample cleavage.

"What beautiful tits you have, my dear," he marveled, imitating the Big, Bad Wolf character from the ancient children's story.

"The better to suck on," laughed Shane.

Hayley stepped back, helpless, stunned at their escalating criminal behavior.

Have they done this before?

Hayley screamed at the top of her voice. Her screams had the opposite effect of what she intended. It triggered action from the two men. The young men cornered her and began to rip at her pants, tearing them from her body and leaving her standing in bra and panties. They stepped back and admired their handiwork and her body.

"Beautiful specimen, Dr. Marbury, wouldn't you say?" Oliver marveled, studying Hayley, one arm crossing his chest, the other supporting his chin like *Rodin's* famous *The Thinker.*

"Stunning, Dr. Wilkinson," Marbury concurred, adopting a similar pose and glaring salaciously at Hayley's body. His eyes darted up and down. He reached out and ripped at her bra, attempting to yank it off her body. Hayley screamed again and lashed out at Shane, deeply scratching his left cheek. He recoiled in pain. Blood began to run down his cheek.

"You fucking bitch!" Shane snapped. "You cut my face."

He turned to Oliver and then to the mirror, studying his torn cheek.

"That's going to leave a scar."

He turned back to the terrified Hayley, now cowering in the corner, screaming at the top of her voice.

"Stop that fucking screaming! Look at my face. What the fuck? You are going to pay for this. No more mister nice guy."

Shane and Oliver pounced and began tearing at Hayley's bra and panties. Someone knocked loudly on the bathroom door.

"What's going on in there?" A female voice screamed. "Open the fucking door!"

Hayley continued to scream as loud as she could. Oliver placed his hand over her nose and mouth in a vain attempt to shut her up. His actions prevented her from breathing, and Hayley began to thrash and kick violently. Oliver held on for dear life while the girls outside the bathroom continued to shout and pounded on the door. Shane was no longer interested. He continued to peer into the mirror, studying his injury.

Hayley mustered all of the strength she could and finally pulled one arm free. She poked Oliver in the eye and then swung her fist as hard as she could, hitting him squarely on the chin. Oliver tumbled backward and fell into the whirlpool. Hayley raced for the door and pulled it open. Four classmates, three girls and Oliver's brother, Jared, were standing outside the door.

"Oh my God, Hayley! Are you okay? What happened in there?" One girl cried.

Hayley didn't answer. She was hysterical. She lowered her head like a charging bull and charged out of the bathroom, leaving her four classmates stunned at her appearance and demeanor.

They peered into the bathroom and saw Shane Marbury staggering around, tending to his bloody face. His penis was exposed. Oliver was fully clothed and lying in the whirlpool. His arms were on the side railings, and he was trying, without much success, to extricate himself from the whirlpool tub.

Two girls ran down the hall to check on Hayley. They reached the top of the stairs and observed Hayley running down the stairs. She was almost to the bottom. They watched her run toward the front door and called out to her, urging her to wait, to let them help. Stunned partygoers turned to watch Hayley Larson run out of the front door in scant undergarments.

"Holy shit!" One jubilant and inebriated college boy shouted.

"That bitch sure knows how to party!"

Chapter One

April 2020

Democrats and the Democratic Party were counting down the months before Stephen Golding's presidency was history. Many Dems opined Golding was a decent man (for a Republican). Still, most Democrats and Independents wanted a permanent end to the government stain that began with Ronald John's election. Much happened since John's election.

John's politics were repugnant to most American citizens. His first act as *POTUS* was to institute a ban on all Muslims trying to enter the country. He sought billions in taxpayer money to build unnecessary barrier walls between Mexico and the United States and Canada and the United States. He became a champion of white nationalists and racists everywhere.

He cut taxes for millionaires and billionaires and left the middle class with the huge bill. He cut critical environmental regulations, which allowed polluters to self-regulate. Many social programs for America's poorest citizens were drastically cut or eliminated. America was reeling as a direct result of his policies.

His ethics were worse than his politics. John was a self-proclaimed, self-made billionaire. When he was elected president, he was supposed to sever ties with all of his business interests. A president must avoid conflicts of interest or the *appearance* of such. However, while the arrogant and narcissistic John *purported* to sever ties with those interests, he never actually did so. One such interest was his partial ownership of the Barrington Arms Corporation, an international gun manufacturer.

A short time ago, a troubled young man named Kevin Burns, brandishing Barrington Arms weapons, walked into a suburban Michigan high school and opened fire, killing nine students and injuring several others. At the same time, a special prosecutor investigated the president. His report found evidence of President John's participation in a conspiracy to commit murder and obstruct justice. The House of Representatives impeached him. The Senate convicted him and removed him from office. Ronald John was currently under house arrest awaiting trial on multiple charges. His co-conspirators, facing significant prison time, were happy to turn on John and testify against him and for the government.

Stephen Golding was Ronald John's vice president. His claim to fame was his refusal to pardon President John for his multiple crimes. That one act made Golding enormously popular with many Americans, albeit for a short period of time. Despite immense political pressure from the right-wing of the party, Golding stuck to his principles. In his opinion, John's crimes, if proven, were too egregious to pardon.

Golding squandered the goodwill he created by caving in to his party's strictest conservative policies and those of his predecessor. He was far less bombastic or controversial than John, but his partisan policies were not much different. He supported immigration restrictions, drastically reduced taxes for the wealthiest one percent, and deregulated various business interests. He also supported virtually all of President John's draconian cuts to, or elimination of, social programs for the poor.

Golding's embrace of a right-wing conservative agenda caused rapid erosion of his support from centrist Democrats and independents. Stephen Golding was simply too extreme for them. His poll numbers dropped dramatically. There were rumors he would withdraw his name from consideration for the upcoming presidential election. While the party persuaded him to continue, he seemed disinterested. The polls showed him trailing virtually every Democratic candidate.

Zachary Blake was a prominent Michigan trial lawyer and a staunch advocate of the Democratic Party and democratic values. While he appreciated Golding's position denying a presidential pardon for Ronald John, he opposed his stance on every other policy.

Zack was ecstatic with polls predicting a proverbial blue wave in the next election. However, he remained cautiously optimistic. Three short years ago, Ronald John trailed by five to seven points in every poll leading up to the 2016 election. John won three Democratic-leaning states by a total of seventeen thousand votes and became president, despite losing the popular vote by almost ten million votes.

Zack played a huge and happy role in bringing Ronald John to his knees. He represented several of the Michigan school shooting victims, the families of those killed, and a number of those injured. Among the injury victims was one of Zack's sons, Kenny Tracy, who became a student advocate against gun violence and a political activist in the battle for gun control.

Zack's recent exploits in relatively high-profile criminal and civil cases made him a multi-millionaire and caused clients everywhere to seek out his firm's legal services. Business was booming. Zack was rather young, considering his success. While short in stature, about five feet, seven inches tall, he was very nice looking, with a dazzling smile, deep blue eyes, and jet black hair with a gray touch at the temples. His combination of skill, looks, and quiet confidence made Zack a sought-after local and national talking head on all legal topics.

On this day in April, Zack was enjoying a rare quiet moment at home with the love of his life, his wife, Jennifer. The couple was watching *All in with Chris Hayes* on MSNBC. The show and its host were highly critical of Ronald John, Steven Golding, and the Republican Party in general, which is why Zack enjoyed the program and the network.

A 'breaking news' bulletin scrolled at the bottom of the screen, and Hayes interrupted a story about chaos at the southern border. Instead, he began reporting the 'breaking news.'

"This just in—the United States Supreme Court has announced the sudden retirement of Justice Noah Fitzgerald, an important moderate and the so-called 'swing vote' on the court. The prospect of Steven Golding appointing our next Supreme Court Justice and solidifying a conservative majority on the high court is a positively chilling development," Hayes reported.

"Justice Fitzgerald is quoted as saying it has been his honor and privilege to serve on the nation's highest court for the past twenty-seven years, and he has the utmost confidence President Golding will appoint a worthy and competent successor."

Hayes looked gravely into the camera and shook his head from side to side.

"We all know Justice Fitzgerald's role as a centrist jurist has been the crucial balance between the conservative and liberal-leaning justices on the high court. He was probably the most important member of the modern version of the Supreme Court."

Zachary Blake could not believe his ears.

Why can't Fitzgerald wait a year for the good of the country? Why would this decent man and fair Justice retire now and permit the likes of Golding to nominate his successor? Is Fitz in poor health? Perhaps I was wrong about his integrity.

Zack cringed at the prospect of lame-duck President Golding appointing a young right-wing Supreme Court justice. After all, the pick would impact the high court for the next thirty to forty years, long after the country forgot about the short presidency of Stephen Golding.

The mid-term elections heavily favored the Democrats, but because of substantial Republican gains resulting from Ronald John's sweeping victory two years earlier, the Republicans still managed to hold onto a slim majority in both houses of Congress. Thus, there was very little the Democrats could actually do to prevent a Golding appointee from becoming the country's next Supreme Court Justice.

The rest of the "All In" program speculated on and discussed that very issue. Hayes and his left-leaning guests addressed the type of jurist Golding might nominate. They sarcastically urged Justice Fitzgerald to reconsider, to delay his retirement to permit Golding's successor the opportunity to nominate Fitz's replacement on the high court.

This was folly, however. Fitzgerald's retirement was a done deal. Zack and every other pro-justice lawyer would have to acclimate themselves to a Supreme Court shift to the right. Zack could only hope Golding would ignore conventional wisdom and the will of his party's leaders.

Might he choose a moderate?

Hayes' guests began to toss some names around. Zack listened to various suggestions from all over the country. None of the names being bandied about were familiar to him. These men and women were from other states. He assumed they were very conservative, but none of them rang his alarm bell.

Alarm bells sounded when Hayes suggested Sixth Circuit Court of Appeals Judge Oliver Wilkinson as a potential nominee. Wilkinson was part of a group of extremist judges appointed to Michigan's state court appeals bench by a conservative Governor in 2010. After Ronald John was elected *POTUS,* one of his first judicial appointments was Oliver Wilkinson to the Sixth Circuit Court of Appeals.

The Sixth Circuit Court of Appeals serves parts of Michigan, Ohio, Kentucky, and Tennessee. Wilkinson was its most extreme, conservative member. Zack knew Wilkinson from his days on the Michigan Court of Appeals and was appalled by the suggestion. He glared at the television screen and cursed Chris Hayes for mentioning Wilkinson in the context of a United States Supreme Court appointment.

Judge Oliver Wilkinson was one of the youngest people ever appointed to the Sixth Circuit Court of Appeals. He was responsible for many decisions that moved Michigan jurisprudence far to the right of its citizens. Wilkinson's judicial philosophy was decidedly anti-justice. His opinions sided with insurance companies and large corporations over 97% of the time. Severe restrictions on Michigan Malpractice cases, Premises Liability cases, and Auto Accident cases resulted from concepts first offered by and from opinions or decisions originally penned by Judge Oliver Wilkinson.

Michigan elects its state judges. After his initial appointment, Wilkinson was supported by and received millions in PAC money from pro-insurance and large corporate interests. The local trial lawyers' associations, voices of the people, always supported his judicial opponents but lacked the funding to compete with large corporate donors.

These very same interests and donors recommended Wilkinson to Ronald John for a federal judicial appointment. The donors especially liked Wilkinson because of his extremism and

youth. He would be wreaking havoc on liberals for decades.
Federal judges are not elected and not subject to the will of the
people, but Ronald John *was* an elected official. Pro-corporate
and pro-insurance donors helped him become president of the
United States, and he was more than happy to oblige his donors.
In turn, Wilkinson rewarded President John and his ilk for their
support, issuing extremely conservative opinions on various
federal issues.

The thought of Oliver Wilkinson on the United States
Supreme Court made Zack physically ill. At his age, forty-four,
Wilkinson could be penning terrible decisions on the Supreme
Court for almost half a century. If Wilkinson became the final
candidate, Zachary Blake vowed to do everything in his power to
prevent the nomination. Civil rights, human rights, women's
rights, affirmative action, campaign finance, capital punishment,
and social, civil, and criminal justice reforms all hinged upon the
next nominee to the high court.

Chapter Two

Over the following days and weeks, the news media and social media sites were falling over themselves, predicting and vetting the various candidates being considered by President Golding. One week earlier, because of all of the hoopla surrounding the pick, Golding released a list of nominees and the criteria he would use to select or eliminate candidates.

The finalists read like a who's who of conservative judges, and the criterion completely followed the right-wing playbook. The list of six potential candidates included two women and four men. The candidates were Amanda Paget, Ninth Circuit Court of Appeals Judge from Arizona, Stewart Shapiro, Tenth Circuit Court of Appeals Judge from Utah, Terry O'Donnell, Eighth Circuit Court of Appeals from North Dakota, Oliver Wilkinson, Sixth Circuit Court of Appeals Judge from Michigan, Emily Gordon, Fifth Circuit Court of Appeals from Texas, and a wild card pick, the current Attorney General, Julian Bell.

Bell was an extremely unpopular choice. He was not expected to make the final cut. He was an assistant under the previous AG, forced to resign for his part in the Bloomfield School shooting scandal that brought down President John. Politically, Bell was tainted by the scandal and was unlikely to pass the full Senate.

Golding, the current *POTUS,* was equally tainted and, worse, a lame-duck. But the fact that the present majority in the Senate and the House was narrowly Republican trumped the stench of scandal. The current majority could not let this pick wait. The next president was very likely to be a progressive Democrat. Many Washington insiders were surprised Bell was even nominated.

The other five picks had solid reputations but extreme right-wing views. None of the choices were acceptable to the Democratic minority, but there was little they could do about it. Prominent Senate and House members promised a thorough investigation and vetting of whomever the final candidate turned out to be. Still, unless there was a serious skeleton in the winner's closet, that person was going to be the next Supreme Court Justice.

Stephen Golding was an attorney and a member of the FedRight Society. President John chose him as his Veep because of his political ideology. Since John was unable to hang around long enough to appoint a Supreme Court Justice, his final 'fuck you' to the Democrats was a successor who was, likewise, a right-wing extremist. Stephen Golding would appoint a right-wing justice to the Supreme Court, and the Democrats were powerless to prevent the confirmation.

To assure the right-wing part of that legacy, Golding turned to Leo Lenard, President of the FedRight Society, and Daniel McGinnis, White House Counsel (and member of the FedRight Society) to help narrow the field. Lenard and McGinnis immediately eliminated the two women. While both were decidedly conservative in most of their rulings, they were wild cards on abortion and other core issues. Golding, Lenard, and McGinnis wanted this pick to swing the Supreme Court so far to the right that *Roe v. Wade* would be in jeopardy.

Gordon cast the swing vote in a Texas case that sought to require a doctor performing an abortion to have admitting privileges at a nearby hospital. The proposed law, struck down by the conservative Fifth Circuit, would have required clinics providing abortions to be the equivalent of small hospitals, with wide corridors and specific (and costly) equipment. The Court ruled that neither requirement was needed to protect the mother's health, and both imposed a substantial burden on a woman's right to have an abortion.

Page was a member of the Ninth Circuit, which included California. She hadn't made any controversial rulings on abortion or any other key FedRight issue, but for McGinnis and Lenard, her venue was a problem. Why take a risk on someone from the Ninth Circuit when there are other conservative candidates?

Lenard and McGinnis were also successful in persuading Golding to withdraw Bell's name from consideration. While he was solidly Conservative and extremely loyal to Golding,

President John, and the FedRight group, the school shooting scandal might hold up the pick and play right into the hands of the Democrats. Thus, Bell was out.

Three candidates virtually eliminated, left only three others for Golding's consideration: Michigan's Wilkinson, Utah's Shapiro, and North Dakota's O'Donnell. Of the three, Wilkinson and Shapiro belonged to the FedRight society.

In 1990, a small group of conservative law students at prestigious Ivy League schools came together to protest that their respective faculties tended to lecture from a liberal point of view. This initial focus was very successful in attracting new members. The group decided to organize the FedRight Society. Their faculty advisers included a veritable who's who of high-profile professors and judges, including some past and future Supreme Court Justices.

The Society was an immediate smash hit and soon spread to other campuses across America. Its rapid growth was also stimulated by enormous contributions from ultra-wealthy conservative donors and by the creation of professional chapters focused on networking opportunities for experienced, conservative lawyers. At present, the Society had well over one hundred thousand members and growing.

Once it became a force in conservative legal and political circles, the Society began to sponsor talks and events around the country. The primary purpose of these events was to spread the doctrine and coach young conservatives in FedRight ideology and judicial philosophy.

Members began filling senior jobs in business, government, and, most important, in the judiciary. The Society's vast network now extended into the White House, as the former president, vice president (now president), attorney general, and white house counsel were all members. FedRight members filled multiple federal judicial vacancies. The impressive list included two current Supreme Court Justices.

The group strongly believed in the separation of powers. While its ideology is mostly conservative, it does not identify exclusively with the Republican Party. The members consider themselves to be constitutionalists. Only the judiciary can

interpret the Constitution and the law of the land. Potential
judicial nominees must prioritize traditional values, the rule of
law, and individual liberty. The Society favored small
government, opposed government regulation on businesses, and
valued privacy. The group believed citizens should be free to do
whatever they want to do on or with their property. FedRight
members also believed strongly in religious freedom, but not to
the extent a citizen could use religion to justify bad conduct. For
instance, the group considered Islam and Muslim fundamentalist
views to be particularly abhorrent. The fact this bigoted notion
clashed with the group's own widely held views on religious
freedoms escaped its collective consciousness.

The FedRight Society was more powerful than it was before
the Ronald John and Stephen Golding administrations. When
John took office, one of the first and most important items he
was made aware of was many judicial vacancies in the federal
court system. This lethal combination allowed the group to
remake the courts. John—now Golding—granted Leo Lenard
and his minions the unprecedented power to recommend all
likely-to-be-appointed judicial nominees.

This power was the genesis of the so-called final 'list of six,'
the nominees to fill the now-vacant Supreme Court seat. Since
Golding was a virtual lame-duck president with no future skin in
the game, he was more than willing to outsource this
appointment and others to assure candidates appealed to the
extreme wing of the president's base. This pick was vitally
important to conservatives because Golding and the current
majority in the House and Senate were likely to be voted out of
office in the next election. An enormous 'blue wave' was likely
in the country's future. As such, this was the FedRight Society's
last best chance to steer the future judiciary to the right. While
conservatives held the presidency and both houses of congress,
their mission was to appoint and approve as many judges as
humanly possible, including a Supreme Court Justice.

In recent years, an independent judiciary prevented many of
President John's initiatives to eliminate environmental
protections, institute a Muslim ban, increase border security, end
protections for a woman's right to choose, increase military

capabilities and trample on LGBTQ rights. The FedRight Society
was implementing emergency measures to imitate this strategy.
The group considered this to be of vital importance going into
the next election cycle. Going forward, facing a government
controlled by liberal Democrats, the only real check and balance
on the out-of-control liberals would be a conservative judiciary.

Lenard and McGinnis poured over the previous lower court
and appellate decisions, speeches, personal appearances, and
writings of the three men. All three were exceptionally well
qualified and *very* conservative. The only chink in anyone's
armor was Shapiro's speech criticizing *Citizens United v. Federal
Election Commission*, a 2010 landmark case. The Supreme Court
ruled wealthy people and PACs had a First Amendment right to
contribute as much as they wanted to the candidate of their
choice. Restrictions on language or contribution size were
unconstitutional.

Justice John Paul Stevens wrote a blistering dissent, famously
arguing 'a democracy cannot function effectively when its
constituent members believe laws are being bought and sold.'
Stevens also opined that Congress always possessed the power to
prevent the improper use of money to influence election results.
To allow 'the improper use of money to influence the result is to
deny to the nation in a vital particular the power of self-
protection.'

In a speech following the publication of *Citizens United*,
Shapiro praised Stevens' dissent and criticized the majority. He
believed in an independent judiciary and feared the unlimited
financing and politicizing of candidates could lead to corruption
and step on the separation of powers. "That genuine possibility,"
Shapiro opined, "trumps free speech."

Citizens United has resulted in unprecedented amounts of
money being poured into political and judiciary campaigns. It is
no secret that wealthy Republican donors have more money and
are far more organized than any Democratic-leaning
constituency. Money and organization resulted in substantial
judicial gains for the extreme right, especially since the left had
no liberal alternative to the FedRight Society. *Citizens United*
was a crucial decision to the FedRighters, and Shapiro's criticism

of the decision was inexcusable. Based on this speech alone, the list was narrowed to two candidates.

In the final analysis, there was virtually no ideological difference between Wilkinson and O'Donnell. Their writings and public speeches were virtually identical, and previous lower court and appellate decisions were remarkably consistent and very conservative. Both candidates fulfilled Golding's right-wing agenda. Only two factors swung Lenard and McGinnis from one candidate to the other. Wilkinson was from Michigan, a swing state, and he was a member of the FedRight Society. The candidate Golding would put forth for the Congress' advice and consent was Oliver Wilkinson, Judge of the Sixth Circuit Court of Appeals. If Wilkinson were confirmed, the Republicans would have a five to four majority on the high court and an unprecedented five Supreme Court Justices who were members of the FedRight Society. Lenard and McGinnis were ecstatic.

Chapter Three

All the major networks broke into regularly scheduled programming for a special report to announce the breaking news of President Golding's nomination of Oliver Wilkinson to the next Supreme Court Justice of the United States. As expected, criticism or praise for the pick was sharply divided along party lines.

Prominent Democrats condemned the pick and warned citizens their precious constitutional rights were being eroded by what they called the secret, silent invasion of right-wing zealots. They argued big business, big insurance, big pharma, and wealthy industrialists were buying themselves a Supreme Court Justice.

Republicans, naturally, argued the opposite and were delighted with Golding's choice. If citizens wanted a true separation of powers, smaller government, less regulation, and a Supreme Court that doesn't legislate from the bench, Wilkinson and the others who would form the new conservative majority on the Court were excellent jurists. On top of all that, the appointee was only forty-four years old and could be issuing ultra-conservative opinions for decades.

Zachary Blake watched the breaking news report with profound dismay. Wilkinson was a destructive force against civil liberties and fundamental fairness in Michigan. There was no reason to believe he would judge cases any differently on the United States Supreme Court. Zack also knew that, short of a scandal, there was very little the Democrats could do to prevent his nomination and elevation to the Supreme Court.

Unless one of the current right-leaning Justices took a sudden swing to the left, Wilkinson would be the swing vote on many pending issues before the high court. Zack expected virtually all cases in which a citizen was suing a corporate entity on issues like pollution, discrimination, unsafe work environments, health insurance, or hospital care were in jeopardy. Wilkinson was solidly anti-citizen and more solidly pro-business. Zack knew the same obscenely wealthy corporate donors who purchased the presidency for Ronald John—thanks to *Citizens United*—were jumping for joy and waiting to reap the benefits of their massive contributions. When Zack first heard Wilkinson was a possible candidate, he vowed to do everything in his power to fight his elevation.

What can anyone do? He's extremely successful. He doesn't appear to have any skeletons in his closet. He's been vetted for appointments to the Michigan Supreme Court and the Sixth Circuit Court of Appeals. Nothing prevented those appointments. I don't like his judicial philosophy or temperament, but he has solid credentials and writes well-reasoned opinions opposed to almost everything I hold sacred. He has to be stopped, but how? I need to talk to Micah.

Chapter Four

Hayley and Joel Schultz were very happily married and lived in the beautiful Detroit area suburb of Huntington Woods. Originally developed in the early 1900s, Huntington Woods is a tree-lined subdivision of elegant English-style homes similar to those in the historic Palmer Woods and Sherwood Forest Subdivisions of Detroit. Yuppies and Millennials flock to 'the Woods' because of its old feel beauty, central location on Detroit's historic Woodward Avenue, proximity to Downtown Detroit, and easy access to all Detroit suburbs.

Hayley and Joel maintained busy careers while raising two beautiful young children. This was sometimes a difficult balancing test, but both parents were dedicated to making things work. When Hayley was busy, Joel found a way to be home for the children. The opposite was true when Joel was busy. Both sets of parents lived nearby, and the kids' two grandmothers were happy to watch their grandchildren when needed, even at a moment's notice.

Joel was a Physiatrist with hospital privileges at nearby Beaumont Hospital in Royal Oak. He earned a bachelor's degree in Physics and a medical degree from the University of Michigan in Ann Arbor. His medical practice specialized in enhancing and restoring functional ability and quality of life to people with physical impairments or disabilities affecting the nerves, bones, spinal cord, ligaments, muscles, and tendons. His specialty was primarily non-surgical. Unlike an Orthopedic Surgeon, who focuses on curing a patient through surgical techniques, Joel's specialty and practice focused on managing a patient's pain and maximizing his or her independence in performing daily activities. His primary goal was to improve a patient's quality of life without surgery. Most of his patients were trying to recover from some type of injury or disabling condition. Joel was the popular choice of internists and general practitioners whose patients wanted to avoid surgery. He also received a significant number of referrals from personal injury attorneys on both sides of a lawsuit.

Hayley also attended U of M, earning a master's degree in Social Work from the prestigious university. Her practice specialized in counseling victims of sexual assault and domestic violence. Despite her relatively young age of 37, Hayley had vast experience in the field. She worked at the Tri-County Rape Crisis Center, serving multiple roles. She was an Assault Prevention Intervention Specialist, acting as a legal advocate and peer counselor. Afterward, she worked as a prevention coordinator, managing sexual assault prevention education programs, and a client services coordinator, managing crisis intervention and legal advocacy programs. She worked with all age groups and provided prevention education and counseling on sexual violence of all types.

When Hayley decided to go out on her own, opening a clinic in nearby Pleasant Ridge, she chose to concentrate her practice on younger and college-aged females, from elementary school children to graduate college students. She specialized in date and party violence and sexual harassment and participated in a host of education services. Her goal was to educate the tri-county community about these issues and to raise awareness of the topic. She coordinated and delivered presentations to the community and became a powerful public speaker on these issues. She donated her time to develop a curriculum and provide professional training to students and interns interested in her field. She helped write grants and did considerable fundraising for free service programs for people who could not otherwise afford treatment.

Despite a busy practice and home life, Hayley found time to create a twenty-four-hour hotline, fundraise to populate the phone banks with caring and competent people, and even contribute her own time to covering shifts. She answered crisis calls and responded to hospitals looking for support for victims of sexual assault as they underwent medical and forensic exams.

Hayley was also part of a sexual assault response team that included responding police officers, nurses, and physician's assistants trained in sexual assault forensics and as rape crisis advocates. Her role on the team was to provide support for the survivor and their decisions moving forward. She notified survivors of their rights as victims and explained those rights as thoroughly as she could. She made sure all survivors knew of their right to have a confidential sexual assault advocate accompany them through every step in the process, providing information and vital emotional support along the way.

Hayley also used her position and influence to provide legal advocacy services for survivors of sexual violence, something sorely lacking in the criminal process. She was part of a group of specialists who provided case status updates and criminal justice system counseling. Since the criminal process is often confusing, scary, and daunting, Hayley used her strong relationships with the law enforcement communities in the tri-county area and the three district attorney's offices to assure victims were kept well informed and understood the process. She and others accompanied survivors to interviews with police officials and the district attorney's office and to court whenever a victim had to testify. Her goal was to minimize or prevent the re-victimization or re-traumatization that survivors often experience when exposed to the criminal justice system.

Her practice also included peer counseling for victims of sexual violence and their loved ones. The advice provided by her office gave survivors a safe place to begin working through their traumatic experiences. Hayley also handled all the administrative responsibilities that fell to the owner of the clinic. She was responsible for clinic and staff management, accounting and bookkeeping, medical billing, and client and program coordination.

Hayley and Joel were quite the power couple around town. They met in a coffee shop eighteen years ago when both were students at U of M. Hayley was a tough nut to crack. She did not seem interested in boys, had very few friends, and refused to attend any of Joel's fraternity parties or any other college parties, for that matter. She was somewhat indifferent to his advances.

Joel was a gentleman, tall, well-built, and very nice looking. While popular with the ladies, he was *enamored* with Hayley.

Perhaps it was her initial indifference. *Is she playing 'hard to get?'*

He assumed Hayley was shy, perhaps not sexually experienced, and he did not want to put any pressure on her. She was very bright, had a pleasant way about her, and possessed a great sense of humor. She was also drop-dead gorgeous. He adored her green-blue eyes, the prettiest eyes he'd ever seen in his life. Hayley wore no make-up and had flawless skin. Hayley's reddish-brown hair accentuated her face, dotted with cute little freckles. Her full lips gave way to a marvelous smile that, when she laughed, revealed perfectly white teeth. And it didn't hurt that Hayley was five foot nine inches tall with a perfect hourglass figure and beautiful long legs.

Hayley was not interested in a relationship. She was interested in getting an education. She had a plan and was driven to implement her plan and begin her career. Dating only got in the way. But Joel was quite the force. She'd never met anyone like him. He was about to begin medical school and was quite the specimen at six foot three inches tall and built like a finely tuned athlete, with a chiseled body, a square chin, beautiful hazel eyes, and jet-black hair. He dressed and looked like a Gentleman's Quarterly model. Slowly, indeed, and very patiently, he courted her until they fell in love. Still, their sex life was a problem. Hayley seemed emotionally numb sometimes, as if she was going through the motions, disinterested in sex. When they slept together, she never initiated sex and often declined to have sex, claiming she was tired or not feeling well.

Joel sometimes watched her sleep. She'd toss, turn, awake with a start, or begin to cry. He'd hold and implore her to open up, but she'd only cuddle closer and promise to explain everything someday. She was the love of his life, and he was willing to wait as long as necessary. His patience and genuine kindness were sincerely appreciated and rewarded over time as Hayley became more and more trusting and comfortable in his embrace. In time, Hayley, too, fell madly in love. Finally, she shared a delicate secret, and everything made sense. Joel couldn't love or be prouder of her as he was at that moment.

After finishing college and starting their careers as social worker and physician, they married in a quiet family ceremony at Hayley's family synagogue.

Their specialties were chosen, and their careers blossomed. After Hayley gave birth to their second child, they bought their Huntington Woods dream house. It was a 1930's four-bedroom English Tudor, renovated and updated by a previous owner. The home, close to work for both Hayley and Joel, had plaster moldings, chestnut and mahogany wood finishes, and a beautiful lower level whose construction—according to the seller—cost more than most homes in the area.

The prior owner was a wealthy auto executive who invested heavily in craftsmanship and materials. He spent the past twenty-two years making improvements. Tradition demanded these improvements be made to the high standards of those who came before him. And this guy took tradition *very* seriously.

Each renovation duplicated styles and shapes of what was being replaced. The lower level featured an elaborate home theatre. Still, it maintained its living room motif, with sofas and chairs around a fireplace made of Pewabic tile and built-in solid white oak bookcases. A hidden door opened to an elaborate 1930's elegant vintage wine cellar. But the crowning architectural achievement was the master bedroom. It was huge, as it included the original master bedroom and a former fifth bedroom or sitting room. After the seller renovated the master and seamlessly broke through the wall to the sitting room to make one enormous master bedroom, his finishing touches included original mahogany and white wood and moldings with a gorgeous marble tile dressing room and master bath.

The home sat on a beautiful corner, treed lot on one of the most sought-after streets in Huntington Woods. It was way out of their initial price range, but they had to have it and stretched and borrowed their way into ownership. They were never sorry; the home was beautiful, close to work, with good schools and great neighbors.

On this night, Hayley was putting the kids to bed when her husband called out from the other room.

"Hayley, honey, you've got to see this!"

"What is it, Joel? I'm putting the kids to bed," she called. She smiled at her daughter, Emily, leaned down to the bed, and gave her a peck on the forehead. Her son, Jason, was already in bed for the night.

"I'll be right down."

"Hurry! Brace yourself."

Hayley blew Emily another kiss and eased out of the bedroom. She left the door open and the hall light on, as Emily preferred. She raced down the stairs and into the great room where Joel was watching a breaking news report. Lester Holt was reporting for NBC News.

"The prestigious list of candidates for the United States Supreme Court's vacancy is now down to one. Sixth Circuit Court of Appeals Judge Oliver Wilkinson has been tapped by President Stephen Golding to fill the vacancy left by the retirement of Associate Justice Noah Fitzgerald, a centrist jurist who was considered the critical swing vote on an increasingly conservative court. Many believe his seat is the most important seat on the high court.

"Political pundits are wondering aloud what caused Justice Fitzgerald to retire at this particular time, with less than a year to go in the Golding Administration, with his successor likely to be a Democrat. Court watchers now speculate Fitzgerald is ideologically less centrist than most people initially thought. These experts believe he simply decided to take one for the team and deny the Democrats the opportunity to appoint his successor. Wilkinson, if confirmed, will control the balance of the court for years to come.

"Wilkinson is only forty-four years old and will be one of the youngest Supreme Court Justices in American history. Assuming he is confirmed, which is very likely, Wilkinson has the opportunity to shift High Court decisions for decades, perhaps for a long as a half-century. Democrats promise a tough confirmation battle in the Senate and will do everything they possibly can to vet the candidate. Things are about to get very interesting in Washington, D.C. Please stay tuned to this NBC station for further updates. We now return you to your regularly scheduled programming. This is Lester Holt reporting. Thanks for watching. Have a good evening."

As NBC returned to the program Joel was watching, Hayley stared at the screen in stunned silence.

How is this possible?

She tried to put the events of twenty-two years ago behind her. She had a wonderful husband, two beautiful kids, and a successful career. She followed the career of Oliver Wilkinson over the years. When he graduated from Wayne State University Law School and began a successful career as an appellate lawyer, she held off notifying the Bar to question his suitability to be an attorney. When he was appointed to the Wayne County Circuit Court bench, she almost contacted the State Bar's Judicial Qualifications Committee to advise that this man should not be a judge. When President John appointed Wilkinson to the Sixth Circuit Court of Appeals, Hayley could be silent no longer.

She wrote a scathing letter of opposition to the nomination and sent copies to the American Bar Association Committee on the Federal Judiciary, the Senate Judiciary Committee, and various news outlets. Not a single news source ran the story, and Hayley never heard back from either committee. Wilkinson was easily confirmed. Hayley focused on her family and career and was able to forget for a while.

But like a terrible, addictive habit, here he was again. This time he was a candidate to become a Justice on the highest court in the land. His vote was to be *the* vital swing vote for a divided court. His sense of entitlement, narcissistic attitude, and political ideology was repugnant to her. On top of all of this, he was a *criminal*. Hayley was beside herself.

What should I do? What can I do after all of these years? Who would believe me? Would I be wasting my time—causing myself unnecessary pain and aggravation? How can such a man be qualified to serve on the United States Supreme Court? Has he done this to anyone else?

"Honey? Are you okay?" Joel snapped her out of her thoughts. She didn't even realize he was holding her.

"Joel, Oh my God! How can they even consider this guy? Did they get my letter? Do they know what kind of man he is?

What kind of predator he is? How can they do this?" She looked into his eyes, pleading for words of comfort, understanding, and, perhaps, wisdom.

"Hayley, sweetheart, maybe they don't know."

"The committees must have gotten my letter."

"You never heard from either committee or the press, for that matter. These committees must sort through a lot of bullshit. Maybe the letter got buried in bureaucracy."

"And the press? What's their excuse?"

"Who knows, Hayley? They get thousands of tips, leads, and story ideas every day, the same type of bureaucracy issues in a different setting. It's not some right-wing conspiracy—maybe it just got lost, ignored, or deep-sixed somewhere."

"Maybe . . ." Hayley drifted off in thought.

"Hayley?" Joel squeezed her hand, bringing her back.

"Oh Joel, how many times must I rehash this? I can't keep going back."

"Who says you have to? Wilkinson certainly has the legal and judicial credentials to be a Supreme Court Justice. Maybe we just leave well enough alone and mind our own business."

Joel didn't really mean what he said. He was brilliantly leading her to the only choice she had—she needed to expose this asshole for the predator he was. His strategy worked almost immediately.

"And what happens when a rape victim needs an abortion? What happens when the Court looks at issues of government funding for victim programs? What happens to a wide variety of social issues a guy like Wilkinson couldn't give two shits about? David won't have any chance to beat Goliath for the next forty years!"

"I understand that sweetheart, but those are issues of political and legal *ideology*. Do you oppose him because he's a criminal or because he's an extreme right-wing appointee?"

"Both. What's wrong with that?"

"Nothing. If you're going to do something, though, whatever that might be, I want you to do it for the right reasons. Would you go after Wilkinson if he was on *your* side of the issues?"

And there it was. Leave it to Joel to wrap this up into a neat little one-sentence package.

Would I?

She paused, staring into outer space again. Joel squeezed her hand.

"Damn straight, I would!" Hayley growled. "He's a criminal! He should be in prison! He should never have been granted a law license, let alone a seat on the circuit or appellate court. United States Supreme Court? Oliver Wilkinson? Joel, that is a bridge too far!"

"So, what do you propose to do?"

Hayley was in agony. She wrinkled her nose, tightly closed her eyes, and dropped her head into her hands.

"I don't have a clue. What do you propose, my knight in shining armor?"

Joel was developing a germ of an idea.

"Are you ready to go public with this?"

"Your idea is to go *public*? What about the kids?"

"How would the kids feel as adults in twenty or thirty years if this guy is still a Supreme Court Justice? How would they feel knowing their mother could have done something to prevent it and did nothing?"

"Boy, you don't pull any punches! What happened to my patient, loving, and supportive knight?"

"He's right here, Hayley. He's watched this guy occupy an important space in your head for years. This asshole has affected your relationships, career choices, moods, and even how you sleep and dream. Your loving knight in shining armor says it is time to fight back."

"What do you propose?"

"You remember Zachary Blake?"

"The lawyer? The one with all the large verdicts and the big ego?"

"That's the one. The ego is well-deserved because Blake is the best in the city."

"Okay, what about him?"

"Zack sends me patients from time to time—we work together on serious accident cases."

"I guess I knew that. What does that have to do with Wilkinson and me?"

"Zack is a powerful guy in Michigan politics. He's a large donor to the Democratic Party in Michigan and nationally. He's well connected and *very* politically active. He can't be happy with the Wilkinson appointment."

"So?"

"I think we should make an appointment to see him, tell him the whole story, let him investigate and expose this guy. No one knows how to play the media better than Zachary Blake. He's the master. If there are legal issues, or if you are called to testify before the Bar or the Senate, Zack can provide legal advice and representation."

"I don't know, Joel. Other than my original complaint and my letters, the only person I've ever talked to about this is you."

"What original complaint? You never mentioned that before."

"When this first happened, I filed a police report and told the West Bloomfield police the whole story."

"What happened?"

"Oliver's parents intervened. They were wealthy, powerful people—very politically connected. That's probably how Oliver became a judge in the first place. Anyway, West Bloomfield PD conducted a brief investigation. I was told it was my word against his. He never actually did anything to me, they argued, so why ruin his future? Higher-ups in West Bloomfield put pressure on me to back off. My parents were embarrassed about the whole thing. Eventually, the case was discontinued for lack of evidence. Never sat well with me, as you well know."

"That's good to know. That means there is an original record that may come in handy. If we decide to go forward, make sure Zack knows about that report and investigation."

"Oh, Joel! What about our careers? This could be a huge media and political spectacle. Press could descend on our front lawn. What about the kids, the school, the neighbors? What about our *privacy*?" Hayley squinted in anguish and buried her face in her hands.

"All good points. Again, we don't have to do this. But I am tired of seeing this space Oliver Wilkinson continues to occupy in your brain. It's your choice and yours alone. I won't force you to do anything you don't want to do. But, I say, go for it! Yes, there will be short-term pain, but the long-term gain, if you are successful, will be well worth it. I can handle it. I'm sure the kids can too. And I know Zack will help us make this as painless as possible. He really is the master. The more important question is, can *you* handle it? Are you up for this, Hayley?"

Again, Hayley Schultz paused, reflecting on what might be a life-altering decision.

"Let's do it," she finally decided with determination.

"Call Zack—let's expose this bastard and let the chips fall where they may."

"That's my girl. I'm on it, sweetheart."

Joel and Hayley Schultz stood and embraced. Joel hugged the love of his life as if he would never let go. Hayley felt so comfortable in his embrace. When they finally separated, they gazed into each other's eyes, perhaps second-guessing their decision to move forward. Joel took Hayley's hand and led her upstairs to the master bedroom. Their lives were about to change, forever . . . *for better or for worse?*

Chapter Five

"Zachary Blake and Associates, Kristin speaking. How may I direct your call?"

"Zack Blake, please?"

"Who's calling?"

"Dr. Joel Schultz."

"Let me see if I can track him down, Dr. Schultz. New case? Something about the medical on an old one?"

"No, more of a personal matter . . . well . . . I guess you could call it a new case . . . I'm not sure what to call it."

"That's all right. I'll find him. Please hold."

"Thanks, Kristin."

Joel was treated to some music on hold, which was abruptly interrupted by Zachary Blake.

"Joel, nice to hear from you. What's up? Calling about any particular client? I can have someone grab a file if necessary."

"I'm not calling about one of our cases, Zack. This is more of a . . . personal matter," Joel hesitated.

"Don't like the sound of that, man. What's wrong? Malpractice issues?"

"No, nothing like that, thanks. Besides, I wouldn't be calling a *plaintiff* lawyer. I'd be calling my carrier."

"True. So, talk to me. What can I do for you?"

"Oliver Wilkinson is about to become a Supreme Court Justice."

"Tell me something I don't know. I'm tearing my hair out over the prospect."

"Are the political heavies on the left currently vetting this guy?"

"You know they are, Joel. Why? What going on?" Zack was getting somewhat impatient.

"What if I have some dirt on Wilkinson but don't have the resources to vet it myself. Do you have the time, resources, or influence to do it for me?"

"I'm listening . . ." Joel now had Zack's undivided attention.

"Back in the late '90s, Oliver Wilkinson committed a sexual assault."

"Whoa! That's quite an accusation. Where does this come from, and how do you know about it?"

"I'll answer those questions in a second, Zack. Assuming I'm telling you the truth and the source is reliable, what would you do with the information?"

"I would get in touch with my PI, Micah Love, independently investigate the allegations, dig up everything I can find, and bring it to the press and my Democratic contacts on the Senate Judiciary Committee. Is that what you're looking for?"

"That's part of it. The lady in question would need someone by her side, legal representation, and a friendly face to help through the process. She's terrified but determined. Would you be interested in doing that for her?"

"One hundred percent, Joel. Who's the lady?"

"Zack, it's Hayley, my wife."

"Holy shit, Joel, Hayley?" Zack was shocked.

"Yes, Zack, Hayley—can we get more credible than that? When she was in high school, Oliver Wilkinson and a buddy of his trapped her in the master bathroom of the Wilkinson mansion and tried to rape her. Apparently, Wilkinson and his little brother were famous for throwing these wild parties whenever their parents were away. Lots of booze, drugs, and sex. Hayley went with a friend. She wasn't on drugs, maybe did some underage drinking, but definitely was not interested in casual sex and certainly not with Oliver Wilkinson. She was *sixteen,* for Christ's sake! He was twenty-two and recently started law school. That's statutory rape, isn't it? She was underage. She only went to the party because all of her friends were going. Peer pressure and all, you know what I mean?"

"Oh my God, Joel, how is she doing? She's been living with this for *twenty-plus years*? That's awful! Is she seeing anyone professionally? I have some good people. Oh, stupid me . . . you're a *doctor!* I'm sure you have plenty of good people." Zack rambled on, searching for the right words.

"Did Hayley report the incident to the police, Joel? If I recall correctly, the Wilkinson family lived in West Bloomfield, right?"

"Hayley's a strong, independent woman, Zack. I'm not going to lie. It hasn't been easy for her. That's why I want her to pursue this. She needs to exorcise this demon. And yes, the Wilkinson family lived and still lives in West Bloomfield. Oliver's parents still own that mansion on Walnut Lake. I hear it's quite a place. Professional help is a great idea if I can persuade her to seek help."

"The Wilkinson family has a lot of money and even more power around these parts. But so do I. I can't believe this happened to *Hayley.* I'm on board. I will do anything and everything I can to help you guys. What do you have in mind?"

Joel spilled his guts. He told Zack all of the gory details of the assault, Hayley's attempt to press charges, and the pressure applied to persuade her to drop the case. Eventually, she succumbed to the pressure, and police and prosecutors declined to pursue an indictment.

"As Wilkinson climbed legal, judicial, and political ladders, she wrote a letter to the Judiciary Committee, the press, and the American Bar's vetting committee telling them about the incident. The letter was ignored and deep-sixed in all three places. Hayley never heard a thing. This attempted rapist became a federal appeals judge! I want this whole thing made public. I want to find people who were at the party and witnessed her coming out of the bathroom. I want to find the brother, what's his name? Jared? But most of all, I want to find his buddy and partner in crime."

"What was his name again?"

"Shane Marbury."

"I don't believe this shit. How could the cops allow this guy to slide? How could committees and the press ignore an attempted rape? Wouldn't they at least investigate and see what the story was? What's the matter with these people? I guess money and power can buy anything these days, even a seat on the Supreme Court."

"Not if Hayley Larson Schultz has anything to say about it, Zack."

"I read you loud and clear, my friend. I'll get the best private investigator in America to investigate the original incident and see if they left any kind of paper trail. These kinds of people hardly ever do a 'one and done.' There should be other women he's assaulted. Let's find them and see if they're willing to come forward. And we'll locate this Marbury character and see whether he's willing to come clean. Maybe he's got a conscience. Then, I'll take the entire thing to the committees and the press. We'll also take this to the public through town halls, personal appearances, and even door-to-door campaigns. The *Me Too* Movement has changed a lot of minds in these situations."

"That would be wonderful, Zack. I had a germ of a plan, but you have already taken it to the next level. I knew you were the right man for this. Thanks a lot, man."

"No, Joel. Thank *you* for bringing this to me. You and Hayley are a Godsend. I've been racking my brain for a strategy to prevent this appointment. Now, I get to prevent the appointment and bring a sexual predator down at the same time. One last question, though—this will not be a walk in the park. This guy is ruthless. A seat on the Supreme Court probably fulfills his ultimate narcissistic dream. He and his family have money, power, and vast political connections on both sides of the aisle. Hayley is going to be dragged through the mud and back. She must be ready to sling the mud right back in their corrupt faces. She's in for the fight of her life. You think she's up to it?"

"Storm clouds have been gathering for twenty-two years. Hayley is ready to fulminate over this. She's educated herself, raised a family, and built a business helping others who have gone through the same type of trauma she went through. And all the while, she's had this assault hanging around like a bad habit. She is the strongest person I know. Do I think she's up to it? I *know* she up to it."

"Let's set a meeting."

"Thanks, Zack. I knew I could count on you."

Chapter Six

A few days later, the meeting took place in the executive conference room of Zachary Blake's law office building on Woodward in Bloomfield Hills. Present were Zack, Joel, Hayley, Micah Love, Zack's private investigator, and Sandy Manning, the firm's chief associate. One of Zack's favorite court reporters, Merrill Bass, was also present to record every word, so there would be no confusion coming out of the meeting.

Hayley was immediately discomforted by the presence of several men in the room who she barely knew or didn't know at all. She was the only woman other than the court reporter. She was strangely comforted by Merrill's presence, although she couldn't understand why. She knew the meeting had a higher purpose. This was only the first of multiple uncomfortable days and moments ahead.

Am I making a mistake?

Zack Blake was charming and comforting, introducing everyone at the table and offering a variety of drinks. A woman named Kristin entered with the drinks and a plate of snacks. After everyone grabbed what each requested and more, Zack began the meeting.

He re-introduced Hayley and broadly described why each person was present. Afterward, he turned to Hayley and invited her to regurgitate her entire story. For Micah's benefit, he told her to be as detailed as possible. Micah needed names, dates, locations, investigators' names and departments, people, stations, newspapers or committee members, and departments to who the letters were sent. Did she keep copies of anything—the original report, the letter, anything? Did she keep a diary or retain any contemporaneous notes or statements?

Hayley struggled through the process but was able to repeat the entire course of events, gathering strength, growing stronger in her presentation as she went along. Telling the story again was, in some ways, cathartic, and she felt better when she was finished. The men listened in stone silence, stunned by

Wilkinson and Marbury's casual cruelty and sense of entitlement. As the story droned on, they eagerly became part of the team, ready to go wherever and do whatever it took to expose Oliver Wilkinson for the sexual predator he was.

Zack carefully watched Hayley deliver her oratory. His focus was exclusively on Hayley for the entire narration. Was the story plausible? Were there any glaring holes? Did she do anything to encourage these boys? Was she entirely truthful? Could she pass a polygraph examination? He noticed her husband sat by her side, riveted to her words, holding her hand and rubbing his thumb back and forth on the back of her hand for comfort. Zack could see how much Joel loved and supported Hayley and how worried he felt about encouraging her to come forward. Would this turn out to be a grave mistake?

Both Zack and Joel could see the determination on her face, the fear in her eyes as she told the riveting story of a high school and college kid party gone mad. Gradually, Joel, too, began to calm.

When Hayley finished her narrative, Zack thanked her. Micah and Sandy offered words of encouragement, complimenting her on her guts, memory for detail, and her determination to push forward. Zack reintroduced Micah Love, and the two men discussed the investigatory portion of the plan.

Micah's assignment was to use his police connections to obtain any and all material that still existed from the twenty-two-year-old charge and investigation. He also was charged with finding and taking statements from witnesses, including Marbury, classmates who knocked on the door during the assault, and anyone who saw Hayley run down the stairs and out the door.

Micah needed to run in-depth background checks on Wilkinson and Marbury to determine whether either man did anything like this to other women, either before or after Hayley. This included cases similar to Hayley's, where the paperwork may have consisted of an allegation or a complaint of sexual misconduct summarily dismissed for no reason in particular, by any arresting authority, whether state or federal. Finally, Micah was also tasked with locating the investigating officers, either on active duty or retired, and finding out what leverage was used to persuade them to back off the investigation.

Sandy Manning would perform the legal legwork. He was to visit a judge and obtain the freedom of information requests. If he needed the power of a subpoena, Zack instructed him to file a brief lawsuit against the City of West Bloomfield or the police department, anyone named Wilkinson or Marbury, or anyone who was at the party. The lawsuit did not need to be served on the defendant. It could be dismissed as soon as the judge issued the subpoenas and Zack or Sandy executed them. Sandy was also responsible for setting Hayley up for a psychiatric examination with Zack's favorite psychiatrist, Dr. Rothenberg, who'd been treating Zack's sons, Kenny and Jake, since their incident with the priest. Finally, Sandy was also expected to set up a polygraph exam for Hayley so that the results could be presented to either the Judicial Fitness Committee, the press, or any other interested party.

Zack's role in the plan was to be at Hayley's side every step of the way. He would be her frontman and mouthpiece, attend every exam and public or private hearing, provide advice and counsel. He was also the plan coordinator. Everyone reported to him and cleared their findings with him before releasing them to anyone else.

Hayley and Joel approved the plan and were extremely relieved and grateful Zack and his team were on board. They especially like the part where Zack would be at Hayley's side for every interview, hearing, or appearance. This couple and their young children were in this battle for the long haul. This would be the most challenging few months of their lives, but Zachary Blake would be there to steer events and make sure Hayley would be treated with dignity and respect. The most controversial Supreme Court nomination process in American history was about to begin.

Chapter Seven

The vetting process for Oliver Wilkinson's appointment to the United States Supreme Court began with an off-the-record, private 'friends only' interview of Judge Wilkinson by key Republican Judiciary Committee Members and Martin MacDonnell, the Senate Majority Leader. The purpose of the meeting was to have a frank, pre-hearing conversation to discover whether there were any skeletons in Wilkinson's closet serious enough to derail his appointment.

Attendees expected Wilkinson to come clean about *anything* that might remotely be considered a negative. That way, an issue would be dealt with before the hearings process. If minor, it might be discussed and discarded. However, if an issue was serious enough to cause Wilkinson to be voted down, the group would still have time to persuade President Golding to withdraw Wilkinson's name.

Honesty at this meeting was sacrosanct. There was too much at stake for Wilkinson to withhold information, even if it was some obscure lapse from his remote past.

Oliver Wilkinson was a party loyalist. He absolutely understood the reasons for the meeting and the need for full disclosure. If there was something in his past, now was the time to disclose it. His friends could suppress the information, but they could also punish him and withdraw his nomination. The greater good of the Party was more important than any one candidate's success, wasn't it? After all, the next Supreme Court Justice would shape American jurisprudence for decades to come. Yes, Oliver Wilkinson knew the right thing to do, but he was too damned narcissistic and arrogant even to consider doing it.

Besides, I've been vetted and investigated by the State Bar of Michigan to get my law license, by the Michigan legislature and governor for my state circuit and appeals court appointments, and by the feds and the American Bar Association for my federal court of appeals appointment. When these issues came up, we

had them quashed. Only one person tried to come forward at any
previous appointment hearing. Would anyone come forward
now? This was so long ago . . . I was just a kid . . . and the girls
were even younger. These things have all been forgotten, haven't
they? Silence is golden here. Why create problems?

"Thanks for coming, Oliver. We are tremendously pleased
with the President's appointment and look forward to working
with you in the years to come." Senator MacDonnell opened the
informal discussion.

"My pleasure, Senator. I'm happy to be here and honored by
the President's and the party's faith in me. This is a very
humbling experience," Wilkinson lied.

Oliver didn't like MacDonnell. He thought he was weak. The
Republicans had a majority in the House and the Senate for the
entire three-year period of the John and Golding administrations
and produced no valuable conservative-friendly legislation.
There were unsuccessful attempts, but still no Muslim ban, no
wall, no immigration reform, and no alternate health care plan.
There was nothing. The only muscle-flexing was a few anti-
environment executive orders issued by Ronald John. Dedicated
and true conservatives could have and should have gotten a lot
more done.

Who the fuck is MacDonnell to judge me?

"You can appreciate the purpose of this meeting. This is
probably our last chance for a while to place a conservative on
the Supreme Court. In fact, this is probably the most important
Supreme Court nomination in this century. If you are confirmed,
conservatives will control the Court for years, maybe even
decades, if our older Justices stay healthy."

"I understand, Senator."

"So, we want to know what no one else knows. Can you
think of anything, anything at all, past actions or rulings that
would derail this process and prevent your confirmation as
Justice of the United States Supreme Court?"

"Senator, I have searched my memory and my writings. I
suppose we've all done something stupid in our youth—
excessive party behavior, getting drunk, smoking a little weed.

However, I know of nothing that could derail my appointment to the Supreme Court."

"Tell us what you mean about the drinking and smoking."

"No big deal. Like Clinton—I didn't inhale? I've tried pot here and there, and I drank beer in college. Some people like water or soda. I like beer."

"In moderation?"

"Not always."

"We can say the use of alcohol and cannabis was casual or recreational?"

"Absolutely."

"You have no substance abuse problems?"

"Of course not."

"Happily married, three kids in private school, correct?"

"Right. Married for twelve years to the same woman, Jodie, the love of my life. Three wonderful kids, I've been blessed."

"Any problems in college or law school? Discipline? Not following rules, complaints from the ladies?"

And there it was, Oliver's status as the preferred conservative candidate hinged on his response to this question.

Dad slapped a tight lid on the cops and any records of complaints or investigations. I don't see anyone getting a hand on this stuff. The girls have been silent . . . even the bitch . . . for the past several years.

"Not that I recall, Senator. I am a gentleman. I have always treated ladies with the respect they deserve."

Some simply didn't deserve any . . .

"No cheating scandals, high marks in high school and college, solid law school credentials, fine work as a judge on multiple benches, right? Any career issues?"

"Nothing like that, Senator. I had very strict parents, so I had to toe the line. Plus, Dad was well connected. We couldn't embarrass the great man, now could we?"

Wilkinson lied. His father and mother cared less about him and more about travel, prestige, and wealth. Kids were an inconvenience, except as keepers of the legacy. Suddenly, as a potential Supreme Court Justice, Oliver was important to 'Daddy.'

"We know your dad well, Oliver. He *is* a great man. I'm sure he's very proud of you."

"And I'm proud to be his son. The feeling is mutual." Oliver almost gagged.

"Does anyone else have a question?" Senator MacDonnell looked over to his colleagues. No one had a question—they were more than satisfied, hungry for a Supreme Court majority, and blinded by that hunger.

"Thanks for the visit, Oliver. We'll see you on the Hill, where I look forward to an uneventful and speedy confirmation process. We have a voting majority in both Houses. I don't see any way for those liberal bastards to prevent your confirmation."

"My pleasure, Senator. I look forward to serving the conservative agenda for decades to come."

"Love the sound of that," MacDonnell cheered, rubbing his hands together.

"It's been a long time coming."

Wilkinson rose, approached each senator, and warmly shook hands with each, exchanging a word or two as he prepared to leave. He nodded and smirked at Martin MacDonnell and walked out the door.

After he was gone, MacDonnell addressed his fellow Republican senators.

"What do you think, ladies and gentlemen?"

"Arrogant prick," Senator Elizabeth Finch sneered.

"We should investigate cannabis and alcohol use in college and beyond," Senator Joseph Manford suggested.

"Indeed. Can't take many risks—we won't have time to confirm a replacement, following a contentious hearing," warned Senator Jack Baldwin.

"How about his answers about women? He strikes me as way too narcissistic to be a 'gentleman,' as he refers to himself. His criminal record or records of complaints should be checked," Senator Alvin Cartwright proposed.

"That's already been handled in the initial vetting process. Nothing came up. As for the rest, I'll get a private investigation started right away. Wilkinson's not my favorite guy, but that's irrelevant. If we want real conservative change in this country, it starts on the Supreme Court, and Oliver Wilkinson is solidly conservative," MacDonnell decided.

"Hear, hear!" Manford affirmed, rising and holding out his coffee mug.

"Hear, hear!" Everyone stood and toasted. A conservative majority on the Supreme Court would soon be a reality.

Chapter Eight

Zachary Blake made Micah Love a rich man, although Zack didn't quite see things that way. Micah's investigative work on the Farmington Hills clergy abuse case was instrumental to its success. In Zack's view, the *case* made both of them rich men.

The two didn't always get along. When Zack was struggling, unable to pay his bills, he stiffed Micah on an invoice. Micah cut him off and wouldn't work for him. When Zack came calling for investigative help on the abuse case, Micah initially refused. Zack Blake could never take no for an answer. He was very persuasive when he wanted something. When Zack told Micah the tragic story of two innocent kids, a predator priest, and a massive church cover-up, Micah not only agreed to investigate, he agreed to payment on contingency.

Micah's decision paid off handsomely. The case hit for the largest verdict in Michigan history—the church settled soon afterward. Micah worked hard for his money but would forever be in debt to Zachary Blake for persuading him to handle the investigation.

Micah viewed this investigation as remarkably similar to the church investigation. Like the church case, this case involved a sexual predator, inappropriate sexual activity, abuse of power, and, most likely, another massive cover-up. Law enforcement officials and politicians, similar to the church hierarchy, chose to cover up an attempted rape for money or political favors. Micah found this repugnant. He would do whatever he could to find the truth and bring down the Wilkinson nomination. In fact, as he pondered similarities, the only difference he could come up with was there would be no pot of gold at the end of this rainbow. He'd be paid well by the hour but would see no multi-million-dollar contingency fee.

On this day, Micah left his Downtown Detroit office, hopped into his new Lincoln MKZ—he only drove *American* luxury cars—and hit the John C. Lodge Freeway north, headed toward West Bloomfield. As he passed through Oak Park and

Southfield, the first two suburbs northwest of the city, the Lodge Freeway turned into Northwestern Highway.

A few miles further north, Northwestern Highway ended at a very confusing and busy traffic circle. These things were cropping up in and around the West Bloomfield/Farmington Hills area. Micah hated them, but this time it was easier as he was only making a right at Orchard Lake Road. He breathed a sigh of relief as he exited the circle.

The West Bloomfield Township Offices were in the middle of an area that featured two synagogues, a church, and multiple residential subdivisions. Multi-cultural co-existence seemed to work in West Bloomfield.

Micah turned right into the Township offices complex, found the police department, parked the car, and strolled into the building. He walked up to the reception desk and inquired where he might locate and discuss a twenty-two-year-old criminal sexual conduct file and investigation. The sergeant invited him to have a seat and swiveled his chair, turning his back to Micah. He dialed a number on his desk telephone and began to talk to someone on the other end of the line. Micah strained to listen but could not hear the sergeant's side of the conversation. The sergeant finally hung up the phone and advised Micah to be patient. A detective would be out to see him.

After twenty minutes of waiting, Micah was becoming agitated. As he stood to give 'Sarge' a piece of his mind, he heard footsteps to his left.

"Mr. Love?"

"That's me," Micah chirped.

"I'm Detective Lacy. What can I do for you?"

Micah flashed his PI license.

"Is there somewhere we can talk?"

"Sure, follow me."

Detective Lacy led Micah through a maze of offices and a lock-up. The detective was a large man, maybe six foot two or three, with white hair and a protruding waistline. He had a ruddy complexion, like someone who spent too much time in the sun or drank too much. Micah hoped a man of his age had been with the West Bloomfield Police for a long time and would remember or know how to locate the fruits of a twenty-two-year-old investigation.

When they reached the detective's bullpen, Lacy led Micah to his cubicle. He offered him a seat and a pop—they don't call it 'soda' in Michigan—and Micah accepted both offers. With the preliminaries out of the way, Micah told Lacy the story about the party, the Wilkinson family, and Hayley Larson Schultz.

I hope he's a Democrat!

Lacy listened carefully to Micah's story. Lacy was a young detective at that time, transitioning from patrol officer the year before the events Micah described. Lacy had a vague recollection of the case because he tagged along with some seasoned detectives as they visited the Wilkinson estate. He remembers this, he advised, because this was the most incredible house he'd ever seen in his life.

"Were you involved in the investigation?" Micah inquired.

"Not even close. I was a raw rookie, present only to learn and keep my mouth shut."

"Do you remember any of the particulars of the case?"

"No, not a thing, other than some young girl accused the Wilkinson boy of attempted rape. It happened at a party at the mansion, as I recall."

"That is correct. The girl's name was Hayley Larson. The accused was Oliver Wilkinson. Does that name ring any bells for you?"

"Sounds familiar. Where have I heard the name?"

"He's President Golding's nominee for the vacant United States Supreme Court seat."

"Holy shit! And he's the guy who was accused twenty-two years ago?"

"Same guy."

"What's your interest in this?"

"I work for an attorney named Zachary Blake."

"I've heard that name, too. He's big shit around here, right? Very successful trial lawyer—didn't he sue the cops for killing a black guy?"

"That's the guy, but that's not why we're here. Besides, the statute of limitations is long gone on any police misconduct in the West Bloomfield case."

"I guess that's true. So, what's your angle?"

"Zachary represents Hayley Larson, the girl who was assaulted twenty-two years ago. She's not trying to do anything to anyone except prevent a sexual predator from becoming a Supreme Court Justice. Zack feels the same way, which is why he's agreed to help her. Where do you stand on these issues?"

"I'm right there with the victim and her attorney. Politically, if that's what you mean, I'm an independent. I vote for the man or the woman, not the party. I *hated* RonJohn—I think he's set our country back fifty years with his divisive crap. I don't like Golding much better. Probably voting for a Dem in the next election."

"Perfect. Then you'll help me find the file?"

"I'll do what I can. Hold the phone while I check the computer and see if there's an archived file and, if so, where it might be kept. Maybe I can locate the detectives on the case—they're probably retired by now. Who were they? Damn! I remember going to that massive castle, but I can't for the life of me, remember who went with me."

"I understand. It was a long time ago. I appreciate whatever you can do."

Lacy pulled out some reading glasses, perched them down at the end of his nose, punched some keys on the keyboard, and stared at a monitor. Micah was seated behind the monitor and could not see the screen. Something hit because Lacy grabbed a pen and took down some information. When he looked down, he used the reading glasses. When he looked up, he didn't. Micah chuckled to himself as Lacy continued this 'eyes up, eyes down' routine.

It's a bitch getting old, isn't it, Detective?

Lacy finished the computer exercise, removed his reading glasses, and studied Micah. He appeared conflicted about whether he should make certain disclosures. He resolved the conflict and spilled his guts.

"The detectives on the case were Jordan Levin and Eric Lorenz. They have both since retired. The file was closed and sealed, which is unusual. The computer entry indicates the investigation revealed the girl was unreliable, perhaps a liar. Finally, she decided to drop the case.

"The mayor got involved and ended up sealing the file. I remember Levin and Lorenz. They were partners. Both good police who taught me a lot. Now that I know who the officers were, I remember it was Levin who I went to the mansion with."

"Is there some way to unseal a sealed file?"

"I'm not sure if there's a procedure for that."

"Can you find out and let me know?"

"Will do."

"Do you have any contact info on Lorenz or Levin?"

"Hang on for a minute. Let me go over to human resources or pension and see where they are sending retirement checks."

"Thanks, Lacy. I really appreciate it. Hey, you got a first name?"

"William H, like the actor, but I'm William H. *Lacy*. He's William H. *Macy*. My friends call me 'Will,' Mr. Love."

"Micah. We're friends now."

"Micah it is then. I'll be right back."

He walked toward the hallway where they entered the bullpen. He was gone ten to fifteen minutes. Micah *heard* his return before he *saw* him.

Probably annoying to work with.

Lacy returned to his desk but did not sit, an indication to Micah that the meeting was over.

"Do you have their addresses or phone numbers?"

"No. I don't have anything. There wasn't anyone at human resources. Maybe I'll check back later."

"Maybe?"

"Look, Micah. I'm a busy man, and this is a busy police station. I've got to cut this short."

His demeanor had completely changed. He started out of the bullpen and expected Micah to follow. Micah stood his ground. Lacy turned back and faced him.

"Love, this is a *police* station. We follow orders here. We don't loiter because we might piss someone off and possibly get arrested. Now let's go. This meeting is over."

Micah followed him out into the hallway. Lacy began looking at the various surveillance cameras lining the corridor. When they passed the Men's Room, Lacy stopped.

"I've got to take a leak," he uttered.

"Is this a public or a private bathroom? I need to wash my hands."

"You can use it. Follow me."

They walked into the bathroom. Lacy stopped, pulled out his cell phone, and turned to Micah. Micah almost ran into him. He jumped back at Lacy's unexpected stop.

"Quick, Micah, what's your cell phone number?" Lacy whispered.

"248-555-7088. Why?"

"I'm going to text you those officers' phone numbers. They're watching us on surveillance cameras. My superiors told me to escort you out of here and give you nothing. The file cannot be unsealed. Those orders don't sit well with me—I'll do what I can to help you and still keep my job. Apparently, the Wilkinson family still has a lot of pull in this town."

"I guess so. I appreciate what you're doing and will protect you. I need you here and working, not fired."

"Me too. Thanks, I guess. A little selfish, but still appreciated."

"I didn't mean it like that, but I understand how it may have sounded."

"We better get out of here before we arouse suspicion."

"Your secrets are safe with me."

"I'll be in touch. I'll do my best to get you whatever information I can."

"Thanks, Will. I appreciate it."

The two men left the bathroom. Lacy escorted Micah to the reception area where he first walked in. They passed the sergeant Micah met earlier. Micah nodded a thank you to him. Micah and Will walked to the front door, shook hands, and Micah walked out into the parking lot. He unlocked the car door with a fob and a chirp and entered the Lincoln. As he did so, his phone vibrated and buzzed. He received a text from an unknown number.

Levin-Commerce Township-248-555-2828

Lorenz-Sylvan-248-555-7234

Couldn't access addresses. Will text with more if I find anything.

Micah chuckled and shook his head, staring at the text. *Thanks, Lacy. You've got one set of balls!*

Chapter Nine

"Good morning."

"Good morning. I have a ten o'clock appointment with Zachary Blake."

"Mrs. Schultz? I'm Kristin. Mr. Blake is expecting you. Would you like something to drink?"

"No, I'm fine, thank you."

Hayley made the appointment at Zack's request. Their mission was to prepare a letter for delivery to Diane Stabler, a Democratic senator from Michigan and ranking member of the Senate Judiciary Committee. Zack knew her, having contributed to her recent successful re-election campaign. While the Dems were the minority party in the Senate, she would be the most valuable asset in Hayley's and Zack's mission to defeat the Wilkinson nomination.

"Hang on, Mrs. Schultz. I'll ring his office."

Hayley looked around the opulent office. It was once a large mansion-type home. It was much more modern than Hayley and Joel's home in Huntington Woods, but Hayley could appreciate the attention to detail.

Apparently, Kristin was told to bring Hayley back because she stood and invited Hayley to follow her. As she walked through the lobby door and into the law office's inner sanctum, Hayley was impressed with Zack's interior design expertise, the conversion of a den to an administrative office, and a great room into a beautiful combination conference room and library. Adjacent to the conference room was what was once a family kitchen. The room was beautifully transformed into a break room/dining room combination. An employee served a wide variety of breakfast and lunch items to hungry employees or guests. Small meeting rooms stood off to the side for any lawyer who wanted to grab something to eat or have a quick private lunch or breakfast meeting with a co-worker or client. Apparently, the lawyers' offices were either upstairs or downstairs.

Kristin walked Hayley into the stunning conference room. She invited Hayley to have a seat and, once again, offered coffee or pop. Hayley, again, declined.

"If you change your mind, help yourself. Mr. Blake will be right with you."

Kristin pointed out a buffet with two pots of coffee, a carafe of fresh-squeezed orange juice, and a spread of bagels, lox, and cream cheese placed professionally on a silver service tray. Mahogany bookshelves, full of law books, surrounded a gorgeous hand-carved mahogany conference room table. Legal themed paintings adorned walls that contained no bookshelves. Hayley was especially fond of two works featuring movie scenes from *To Kill a Mockingbird* and *Twelve Angry Men,* two of her favorite movies. She studied side-by-side courtroom paintings depicting jury trials, one recent, and one from the eighteenth century. The scenes were identical, with intense lawyers delivering oratory to their juries. The difference in the décor of the two courtrooms and their participants' wardrobes was quite fascinating. A fresh bouquet of flowers sat in the middle of the table. Sixteen executive chairs surrounded the table. The opulence was way over the top for one meeting with one person, especially when that person was Hayley Larson Schultz.

Zachary Blake walked into the conference room to find Hayley on her feet, studying the courtroom paintings.

"They are beautiful, aren't they?"

Hayley jumped. "Oh, you startled me. I didn't hear you come in. Yes, they're fascinating. I love the contrast in periods yet the similarity in proceedings."

"Trials and the law haven't changed much. Only issues, wardrobes, and surroundings," Zack observed.

"Welcome to Zachary Blake and Associates. Did Kristin offer you anything to eat or drink?"

"She did. Is all of this for little ole me?" Hayley joked.

"I'd like to say 'yes,' but the truth is we have several conferences and meetings today. We freshen up the tray before each meeting."

"I appreciate the spread and the honesty. Your office is incredible."

"Thanks. The building used to be a residence, but it had already undergone a commercial conversion when we bought it. The décor is vintage Jennifer Tracey Blake."

"I haven't met the lady, but her taste is impeccable. This room is gorgeous. Did she do your personal office, too? It must be stunning."

"I'll take you upstairs later if you'd like. My office is more of a working office, which is why I see people down here in the conference room." He smiled.

"In other words, it's a mess. Papers and files all over the place?" She laughed.

"Astute observation. You're familiar with guys like me?"

"I'm familiar with *women* like you. You should see *my* office!"

"Well, I'll keep your secret if you keep mine," Zack grinned.

"Deal!" Hayley offered her hand.

Zack took her hand and shook it gently. He got down to the business of the meeting.

"I invited you here today so we could talk about your background and draft the letter I plan to write and send to Senator Stabler."

"I understand. What would you like to know?"

"I've been studying up on you. You are quite an accomplished woman."

"Thanks. I've worked very hard for victims of sexual assault. Now you know what's driven me all of these years."

"Not everyone can turn such a horrible negative into a positive. You deserve the accolade."

"Thanks. The praise is nice. It brings attention to my practice and more people to help, but it certainly isn't what drives me. It's not why I do what I do. I've been there. I've felt the pain and unjustified guilt. I've encountered a community's rejection of the truth and the cover-up of crimes and criminals. I decided to make a career of preventing what happened to me from happening to others."

"Personal experience is a tremendous motivator, but you've taken this to a whole new level. Senator Stabler is an old friend. I know she'll appreciate your response to what must have been an awful experience for a young teenager to endure."

"As long as it helps to inform the American people who Oliver Wilkinson really is."

"Let's get down to it then. I'm going to bring in a stenographer to record our conversation if that's all right with you. I don't want to misquote you or forget to include anything. Okay?"

"It's okay with me. Whatever you need to do. I appreciate your willingness to help."

Zack pressed a button on a device in the center of the table, and a voice responded.

"Yes, Mr. Blake?"

"Would you please send Judy in, Keri?"

"Right away, sir."

A few minutes later, Judy walked in carrying her equipment. Greetings were exchanged as she set up. Soon, she nodded her readiness to begin.

"We are now recording, Hayley. With your permission, Judy will record everything you say. Do I have your permission to record our conversation?"

"Yes."

"Great. Shall we start with your personal and educational background?"

"Okay. I was born and raised by two wonderful parents in West Bloomfield. I have an older brother and a younger sister who still live in the area. Both are married, and I have five wonderful nieces and nephews. I've been married for almost twelve years to Dr. Joel Schultz. We have two young children, a boy and a girl.

"I was a straight 'A' student at West Bloomfield High School and was accepted to the University of Michigan, where I graduated with a Bachelor of Science in Social Work. I continued my graduate studies at U of M and obtained a Master's in Social Work. I decided to make counseling victims of sexual assault and domestic violence my life's work . . ."

Hayley continued to describe her education and work experience in detail, explaining her work at the Tri-County Rape

Crisis Center, her focus on education and counseling, and her clinic opening in Pleasant Ridge. She talked about her professional training programs for students interested in going into her field and her professional expertise in grant writing and fundraising in poor communities. She was especially proud of her twenty-four-hour hotline to respond to crisis calls, her participation in the sexual assault response team, and her ability to balance all of this with her role as a wife and mother to two young children.

Zack was impressed with her role in the legal system's response to these tragic incidents. Hayley provided legal advocacy services to survivors and provided rights counseling advice to victims, something sorely needed in the criminal justice system. When interacting with law enforcement or the district attorneys' office, her hands-on work with victims was equally impressive. She was also a visiting professor at Oakland University in Rochester and Oakland Community College in Farmington Hills. Hayley Larson Schultz was a brave and accomplished woman. The more Zack listened, the more honored he was to have her as a client.

"Quite the impressive resume, Mrs. Schultz," Zack marveled, with a wink and a smile.

"Thank you, sir," she nodded, more of a slight bow.

"Are you registered to vote, and for what party?"

"I am a registered independent. I vote, in most elections, for Democrats. Nationally, it's *always* Democratic."

"Are you looking to derail the Wilkinson nomination for any *political* reason?"

"No, I have no political agenda here. Oliver Wilkinson is a sexual predator and a spoiled and entitled narcissist. He is not fit to be a Supreme Court Justice, whatever his politics. *That* is my motivation. It's difficult to believe I'm his only victim. A detailed investigation into his past should expose similar incidents and produce more victims."

"That will happen with or without a committee hearing, Mrs. Schultz. I promise you that."

"Thank you, Mr. Blake."

"Would you please describe for the record, with as much detail as possible, the sexual assault committed against you by Judge Wilkinson approximately twenty-two years ago? I believe you told me the assault happened in the master bathroom of his parent's home when you were a high school student, and he was in college, correct?"

"Correct. Oliver and his brother, Jared, who was my age, liked to throw these wild parties when their parents were out of town. This was my first time at one of these parties. A friend dragged me there."

"Tell me, in your own words, what happened. Try not to leave anything out. I'll try to fill in any blanks from memory of what you told me earlier. Okay?"

"Okay."

Hayley spilled her guts in painstaking detail. She described how, in her search for a bathroom, she stumbled across the most beautiful master bath she'd ever seen, Oliver and Sean's rude bathroom break-in, their drug and alcohol-induced condition, and the terrifying circumstances that followed. Only her screams and the sudden appearance of some concerned party attendees, including Oliver's brother, Jared, saved her from being raped.

"That's quite a story, Mrs. Schultz, and a terrible ordeal. Do you have anything you wish to add to the narrative?"

"No, Mr. Blake. I think I covered it in full. It is very painful to repeat the story over and over again. They say if you talk about traumatic things, you may deaden some of the pain. Unfortunately, it has not been like that for me."

"Everyone's different. Let's talk about the letter. What would you like to communicate to Senator Stabler and the Judiciary Committee?"

"I'd like to call for a comprehensive investigation into this incident and this nominee. I presume that would be done by the FBI or, perhaps, by the Michigan State Police. I'd like that investigation to uncover my original complaint and the West Bloomfield Police Department's response to my complaint. I'd like to know why the complaint was swept under the rug and dismissed, who was responsible for doing the sweeping, and what influences or pressures were brought to bear to cause law enforcement officers to give a free pass to a dangerous sexual predator. Finally, I'd like to know if there have been similar charges brought by other women against Judge Wilkinson."

"Couldn't have said it better myself. Anything else you want to say before we close the record?"

"I wish the truth to come out and for justice, at long last, to be served."

"The politics are rough right now, Mrs. Schultz. I won't lie to you. This will not be easy. The so-called law and order party is far less interested in law and order when one of their own is the accused party. That is especially true when the stakes are this high. Who will shape the court for decades to come? I will do my absolute best to get to the truth and expose this predator to the Judiciary Committee. And I will be by your side for the entire journey. Judy, let's close the record."

Judy stopped recording. Zack ordered two copies of the transcript. Judy packed up her equipment, bid Zack and Hayley goodbye, and walked out of the room. Zack again offered Hayley something to eat, but she declined, alleging a grumbly stomach.

Not surprising given the reason for her visit.

"Here's what I have in mind for the letter. Let me know what you think."

Zack began to recite a sample letter, recounting Hayley's recorded statement, sometimes word for word. The letter would be powerful and hard to ignore, even by the most ardent Wilkinson supporter. Hayley was very pleased with Zack's oral draft and astonished at his memory for detail. When he finished, she voiced her exuberant approval.

"I will dictate and draft the letter and then email it to you for final approval. Will that be sufficient?"

"That's fine, Zack, thanks." She sighed.

"I'm Zack again?"

"I thought we should be more formal for the record."

"I caught on. Good thinking. Is there anything else you want to discuss?"

"No, I think I'm good."

They rose and walked out of the conference room. As promised, Zack gave her a tour of the rest of the mansion.

Hayley was blown away and made Zack promise to arrange a get-together so Hayley and Joel could meet Jennifer. When the tour ended, Zack escorted Hayley to the front entrance. Hayley waved goodbye to Kristin and walked out to the parking lot with Zack.

"Thanks for doing this, Zack. I feel so much better."

"Only a temporary condition, Hayley. This is going to be a tough battle. Republicans have the majority. This guy is extremely conservative and in lockstep with the majority on the committee. They want him approved. They plan to crush anything and anyone who gets in their way. They will try to humiliate you."

"I can be tough, too, Zack. I'll be ready for them. Besides, I have a secret weapon."

"Oh? What's that?"

"I'm represented by Zachary Blake."

"True that, Hayley. True that."

Chapter Ten

The following week, Hayley approved the letter, which was sent to Senator Stabler via the law offices of Zachary Blake & Associates:

The Honorable Diane Stabler
Co-Chair, Senate Judiciary Committee
United States Senate
Washington D.C. 20510

Dear Senator Stabler:

I am writing with information relevant to the Senate Judiciary Committee's upcoming hearings related to Federal Appeals Court Judge Oliver Wilkinson's nomination to the United States Supreme Court. As your constituent, I expect you will maintain this letter's confidentiality until we have an opportunity to discuss its contents.

I regret to inform you that Oliver Wilkinson physically and sexually assaulted me twenty-two years ago at a party at his home in West Bloomfield, Michigan. He perpetrated the assault with his friend's assistance, a young man by the name of Shane Marbury. I was sixteen years old at the time, about to graduate high school. The boys were twenty-two. I believe Oliver graduated from college and was about to enter or had recently entered law school.

On the day in question, I was an attendee at the party and needed to use the bathroom. Oliver's brother, Jared, pointed me to the master bathroom. When I finished in the bathroom, I unlocked and opened the bathroom door to leave. Oliver Wilkinson and Shane Marbury stood at the threshold, blocked my exit, walked in, and closed the door behind them.

They unzipped their pants, exposed themselves, and stood there, apparently admiring my body. They propositioned me. When I refused their advances, Oliver grabbed my blouse and ripped it open. I screamed, but they cornered me, tearing at my clothing until I was clad only in bra and panties.

Shane reached out and tried to rip off my bra. I scratched his face, drawing blood. This and my screaming infuriated Shane and Oliver. They pounced, slammed me to the marble floor, and began tearing at my undergarments. At that point, various partygoers started knocking loudly on the bathroom door and demanded someone open the door.

I continued to scream. Oliver grabbed me, placed his hand over my nose and mouth, and cut off my breathing. I thrashed, kicked, and broke free, knocking Oliver into the whirlpool bath. I ran to the door and opened it. Several classmates, including Oliver's brother, Jared, were standing there.

I was horrified. I remember running out of the bathroom and down the stairs in front of all party guests. I ran out of the front door and home. When I arrived home, my parents were shocked at my appearance and offered to take me to the hospital. I told them everything about the attempted rape. My friends and I prevented Oliver and Shane from completing the crime. I agreed to bag my undergarments, get dressed, and go with my parents to the West Bloomfield Police to file a report of the incident. I never received medical treatment following the assault, but I did receive psychiatric treatment.

The West Bloomfield Police claim to have investigated, but the Wilkinson family was influential in West Bloomfield and somehow persuaded the police not to pursue a vigorous investigation. The police advised that pursuing the case would be an uphill battle and a 'he said—she said' investigation. Eventually, they dropped the case without pursuing charges. I have never spoken to the Wilkinson or Marbury families about these events, nor have I reencountered Oliver or Shane.

Since the incident, I have remained relatively quiet and permitted Oliver to continue his life and career without interference from me. However, a lifetime appointment to the United States Supreme Court is a bridge too far. I cannot permit a known sexual predator to serve on the Supreme Court.

I contacted local attorney Zachary Blake. He suggested I write you this letter. It is unpleasant to rehash these events or

discuss sexual assault and its repercussions in a public forum.
However, I feel compelled as a citizen to speak out in protest of
the nomination of a sexual predator to the United States Supreme
Court.

I am available to speak further with you should you wish to
discuss the matter in greater detail. If you deem it necessary, I
would also be willing to testify about these events to the Senate
Judiciary Committee.

Thank you for your kind attention to this letter.

Very truly yours,

Hayley Larson Schultz, MSW

The letter was sent UPS Next Day Air and arrived in Senator
Stabler's office the following day. All senators and congressmen
and women have multiple people on their staffs that do nothing
but preview and answer mail. The volume of mail pouring into
congressional offices is overwhelming, and a congressperson or
senator seldom personally reads or answers a constituent's letter.

That was not true in the case of Hayley Larson Schultz's
letter to Senator Diane Stabler. A mail clerk named Julia
Kaufman received, opened, and read Hayley's dramatic and
heartfelt letter. Astutely recognizing its urgency, she bypassed
multiple steps in the usual chain of command and raced through
the Capitol Building to the office of Senator Stabler's Chief of
Staff, Kaitlyn Schmidt.

Schmidt hardly knew Kaufman and refused to see her, telling
her assistant to take note of whatever her issue was and to 'get
rid of the kid.' Julia, however, knowing the importance of the
letter, refused to take no for an answer. She also refused to leave
or to give the letter to anyone but Schmidt or Senator Stabler.
She promised to stay all day and into tomorrow, *all week*, if
necessary, until she was granted an audience with Schmidt or
Stabler. She even threatened to go to the press and indicate she
was sitting on an issue of national importance. However, neither
the Senator nor her Chief of Staff would give her the time of day.

The press threat was the last straw for Schmidt. She invited Kaufman in under threat of termination if the to-be-delivered message didn't match the histrionics of her efforts to deliver it.

"Do you have a death wish, young lady?" Schmidt snapped as Kaufman entered her office, accompanied by her terrified assistant.

"No, Chief, but you and the Senator need to see this," muttered an intimidated but determined Julia, waving the letter.

"What's your name again?" Schmidt inquired. "I want to make sure your termination letter spells your name correctly."

Kaufman winced. "Julia Kaufman, Ma'am. I am a letter clerk. You've never seen me before, right?" She braved.

"Right. And I never want to see you again. Now show me what's so damned important and then get out of my face."

"The reason you've never seen me before is that I know what's important and what's not. I'm terrified to be here under these circumstances. I would never have thought to be insubordinate until this moment. Read this. If you disagree it was worth my visit, I'll resign."

Schmidt softened. She was impressed with the kid's moxie and guts.

"Deal. Let's see what you've got."

Kaufman handed her the letter.

Schmidt's eyes bulged as she read. She reached over to an intercom at the end of her desk and pushed a button. The speaker expelled an audible beep; Senator Stabler's voice followed.

"Yes?"

"Senator Stabler! Julia Kaufman and I need a moment of your time." Schmidt smiled and gave Kaufman a 'thumbs up' sign.

"Who's Julia Kaufman?" Senator Stabler wondered.

"Your new best friend."

Chapter Eleven

Senator Diane Stabler picked up her landline and dialed Zachary Blake's office. Kristin answered as usual. She became flustered when the speaker indicated she was a U.S. senator. Kristin immediately placed her on hold without comment.

She transferred the call directly to Zack. As his extension began to ring, Jack glanced at the telephone. This was quite unusual. He had no idea who was calling. Because of the offices' so-called sophisticated, state-of-the-art equipment, Zack could not talk to Kristin without walking down to the reception desk and speaking to her directly. He had two choices: Let the call go to voicemail or pick up the receiver. If he waited much longer, the system would decide for him and send the call to voicemail. He picked up the receiver.

"Zachary Blake, how may I help you?"

"Zack? This is Senator Diane Stabler. How are you? What's going on with your receptionist?"

"Senator, it's an honor. What did Kristin do?"

"When I told her who was calling, the line clicked without a word. I got music until you picked up. I almost hung up."

"I think she got flustered. After all, it is not every day an ordinary constituent gets to talk to her U.S. senator."

"Point taken. Did she vote for me?"

"I don't know. Want me to ask her?"

"No—just kidding. Let's cut her some slack, shall we?"

"We shall. Besides, she's a *great* receptionist, your call notwithstanding."

"I suppose you know why I'm calling."

"My client's letter about the Supreme Court nominee?"

"Bingo. How credible is this woman?"

"I'll send you her curriculum vitae. She is *extremely* credible. I do business with her husband, and he indicates she told him about Wilkinson years ago. They are *both* credible."

"How would you like to play this? If she checks out, I'd like to put her in front of the full committee."

"That's what she wants, a public forum to expose Wilkinson as a sexual predator to the Senate, House, and all voters. She wants everyone to know he is not qualified to sit on the United States Supreme Court."

"The letter describes some pretty nasty conduct. Can anyone back up her story?"

"We're working on that, Senator. We need to find and talk with Shane Marbury to see what he has to say. Wilkinson's brother was one of the people who knocked on the bathroom door. We need to interview him and the others who came to Hayley's rescue. She ran down the stairs in her undergarments in front of a large group of partygoers. We need to track these people down and interview them. It won't be easy.

"Hayley filed a police report. There was an investigation that Wilkinson's parents ended up deep-sixing. We need to interview the investigating detectives, the cops who took the report, and the officials who were persuaded to drop the case. We also need to find out where the file is, why they dropped the case, and what hard evidence they had to pursue charges. This will be difficult and time-consuming. I'm not sure what the committee's timetable is, but I'm sure that the Republicans have the nomination fast-tracked. This is their last best hope for a conservative Justice. Perhaps we can get the FBI involved and shorten this thing? I know some agents in the Detroit Bureau if you can green light an investigation."

"The FBI is a great idea, Zack. I don't know that I have the authority to bring this to them without full committee approval. We have to find a way to corner Chairman Ashley and make him think that the whole investigation was *his* idea. Let me work on that. Would you go to the mat for this lady?"

"I would bet my reputation and my license on Hayley Larson Schultz, Senator."

"How tough is she, Zack? They're going to come at her like a nuclear bomb. Will she be able to handle the pressure? Will she cave?"

"She's tough, smart, determined, and *pissed* that President Golding put politics ahead of common sense. She will make a terrific witness, Senator. I promise you that."

The conversation went on for another ten to fifteen minutes. Senator Stabler continued to ask the same questions repeatedly, apparently looking to see if she could poke holes in the narrative. She didn't want to leave anything to chance. The confirmation hearings were less than a month away. They needed to have all of their ducks in a row. One of the keys to the success of the investigation was the inclusion of the FBI. Stabler was an experienced political operative and had confidence she could manipulate Chairman Ashley into ordering an FBI investigation.

She thanked Zack and his client for the letter, for Hayley's bravery and patriotism. Stabler granted permission for Zack and Micah to begin a private investigation for the time being. Zack agreed to update Senator Stabler as the investigation continued. At the moment of their telephone conversation, Hayley Larson Schultz was completely unknown to anyone but her family, colleagues, and friends. Soon, she would become the most famous woman in America.

Chapter Twelve

When Zachary Blake gives Micah Love an assignment, Micah almost always pawns off his current business slate to his subordinate detectives and handles the Blake assignment himself. The investigation into Hayley Schultz's allegations against Judge Oliver Wilkinson was no exception.

Micah decided to track down and talk to the two ex-cops before tackling the other witnesses at the party. To save valuable time, Micah *did* delegate the task of locating all of the party witnesses to others at Love Investigations. When he finished with the cops, addresses and phone numbers of all of the witnesses were expected to be available. Dividing up the witness visitations and questionings would be done once all contact information was known.

For no particular reason, Micah decided to try Jordan Levin first. He had a telephone number but no address, although he did know Levin lived in Commerce Township. The quickest and easiest way to find someone, especially when the person doesn't know you're looking for him, is to look him up online. As a private investigator, Micah paid for access to more detailed records so he could enter Levin's name and number into the computer. Hopefully, the website would spit out an address and some background information. Micah quickly found Levin's address on Benstein Road in Commerce. It was time for a road trip.

When Micah arrived at the address, a man was kneeling on the front lawn, doing some gardening work. The guy looked to be in his late fifties, early sixties, with thin greying hair. There was a huge bald spot on the back of his head. He was well built but compact, maybe five foot seven or eight. Micah parked the Lincoln, exited the car, and began walking toward the man.

"Jordan Levin?" He called out.

The man did not turn around. He continued to work on his garden.

Micah continued toward him and began to walk up the front walkway.

"Mr. Levin?" Micah repeated, a bit softer because he was now close to his subject.

The man suddenly turned, pulled a gun, and leveled it at Micah. Micah jumped back and raised his hands in the air.

"Whoa," Micah retreated.

"Who's asking, mister?" The man continued to point the gun directly at Micah, center mass.

"My name is Micah Love. I'm a private investigator. Please stop pointing that gun at me." The man had a dark trim beard and mustache with a touch of gray in both. If looks could kill . . .

"When I'm satisfied that you mean me no harm."

"May I reach into my jacket and get my business card?"

"Left hand."

"Left hand it is." Micah reached into his pocket, pulled out a card, and presented it to the man. The man paused a second but took the card.

"Are you Jordan Levin?" Micah repeated, with hands still raised.

The guy continued to point the gun at the private investigator.

"What do you want with Jordan Levin?"

"I want to talk to him about an old case he and his partner, Eric Lorenz, handled in the middle nineties, about twenty-two years ago."

"What case?"

"A young teenager named Hayley Larson filed a complaint against a college student by the name of . . ."

"Oliver Wilkinson." The man finished Micah's sentence.

"Right. You're Levin? May I put my hands down now? Will you please holster the gun?"

"You carrying?"

"I am."

"Do you promise to behave?"

"Scouts' honor." Micah crossed his heart

"You can put'em down." He motioned with the gun to Micah's raised hands and then holstered the gun.

"Where's your gun?"

"Under my jacket."

"No sudden moves. No funny business."

"Got it. I promise. May I ask you a few questions?"

"You can ask but can't say I'll answer. That case was a long time ago."

"Fair enough. I'll make this very simple. Young kid alleges an attempted rape at a party—the cops start an investigation. You and Lorenz are the detectives assigned. Wilkinson looks guilty as hell. He's an adult—she's a minor. Suddenly, the whole thing is deep-sixed. The perp's parents are wealthy and prominent citizens. The case is dismissed; the file is buried. The whole thing smells like someone was paid off to drop the case. Was that someone you or your partner?"

Levin paused. His face twisted in anger, and he turned a shade of red.

"You've got a lot of fucking nerve . . . Love," he snarled. He looked down at the card to recall Micah's name.

"I get that a lot. Why was the case dropped?"

"The complaining witness did not wish to proceed."

"That's not what she says. She claims you guys pulled the rug out from under her when she wanted a full investigation. If she decided against proceeding, how did you feel about her decision? What did the evidence suggest? Was there an attempted rape? Can you get me the file?"

"She's full of shit if she says that. The evidence didn't suggest shit, and why the fuck should I get you anything but the hell off my property?" Levin pulled his gun for a second time.

"These are simple requests, Levin. This isn't going away. Check me out online. I'm very good at what I do; I *will* get to the truth. This guy Wilkinson has been nominated to become the next Supreme Court Justice. Do you want a sexual predator on the United States Supreme Court?"

"I hear he's a law and order candidate. Big on Second Amendment rights, isn't that the word on the streets? I like those things. Why should a misunderstanding at a kids party prevent him from serving on the Supreme Court?"

"A misunderstanding? *That's* what this was? I'm going to keep digging. I won't quit until I prove this was more than a 'misunderstanding.'"

"Good luck with that, asshole." He motioned toward Micah's car with the gun.

"Don't come back here," he warned as he walked Micah backward, down the walk, and toward the car. "I may not be so hospitable if there's a next time. Get my drift?"

"This is you being hospitable?" Micah quipped, continuing to walk backward.

"Real fucking comedian. Have we communicated, Love? I don't want to see your fat face ever again."

"We've communicated; you don't want to see me again. However, I will get to the bottom of this, with or without you. Get *my* drift?"

Micah turned his back on Jordan Levin and walked to the car. He got into the driver's seat, started the car, and looked back at Levin. He was still standing on the walkway, pointing the gun at the car. Micah flipped him the bird and took off.

Chapter Thirteen

Judge Oliver Wilkinson's next hurdle was a meeting with the Chairman of the Senate Judiciary Committee, Chuck Ashley. Ashley was eighty-five years old and looked like he was one hundred. He had a full head of yellow-grey hair, a color only a heavy smoker would have. He was medium height, maybe five foot nine or ten, with a bulbous nose and a forest of hair on his ears and coming out of his nose. He was a Republican, the senior senator from Iowa, and he was in lockstep with his party on all core issues. He was pro-life, anti-environmental protection (it had a detrimental effect on farming), had an 'A' rating from the National Rifle Association, wanted to repeal the estate tax, and was opposed to health care for all.

Some also considered him to be anti-women in politics. He once famously claimed that women should not be permitted to serve on the Judiciary Committee because the committee's workload was too heavy. Privately, he felt women should stay home, give birth to and raise children, tend to their homes and the needs of their men.

Ashley met Oliver Wilkinson for lunch at Charlie Palmer Steakhouse on Capitol Hill. Both men ordered the steak salad. The two men had never met before. A one-page brief on Wilkinson's career and court decisions sat in a folder on the table in front of Ashley. Ashley also called in a favor with the FBI and requested a cursory investigation into Wilkinson's family and the judge's own background, education, criminal record, college and law school activities, and early legal career. There were no red flags. Ashley was very excited.

"So, Oliver—may I call you Oliver?"

"Absolutely, Senator."

"Oliver, you've had quite a mercurial rise to this nomination. To what do you attribute your political and judicial success?"

"Honestly, Senator, it is a combination of things, timing, and luck, for example. I have a reputation for being very conservative. If my record caught a Democratic administration's eye, it would have been viewed as a negative for advancement. I had the good fortune of issuing a few controversial decisions during *Republican* administrations, first in my home state of Michigan, then, later, at the federal level. In both instances, the right people were in place and took notice of my work.

"I'm not controversial. I tow the party line. I am firm but fair, and I do not ruffle anyone's feathers. My rulings are almost one hundred percent in lockstep with the party platform. I surprise no one. My decisions are well-written, well-reasoned, and rarely successfully appealed.

"Finally, I am blessed with a great pedigree. My parents are very well off and were active in the Republican Party, especially in Michigan. Their money and power provided me with an excellent education and introduction to their political ideology. I was literally *born* for this opportunity, Sir. One could say it is my destiny."

"I admire your candor, Oliver. You are confident without being cocky, self-assured without being arrogant. Where do you stand on the issues?"

"Such as?"

"Abortion?"

"Solidly pro-life, except in cases of rape, incest, and health of the mother."

"*Roe v. Wade?*"

"It's the law of the land, but a right to privacy? This was Thurgood Marshall's very creative interpretation or extension of the Constitution. I see life, liberty, and the pursuit of happiness, but nothing in the Constitution about a right to privacy."

"I can live with that. Guns?"

"Solidly behind the Second Amendment and the NRA."

"Environmental issues?"

"The environment is important. Business success and jobs in America are *more* important. Global warming or climate change, whatever the politically correct term for it these days, is nothing but a hoax."

"Criminal Justice?"

"A convicted criminal should be treated fairly but harshly. If you do the crime, you do the time – no exceptions and no leniency."

"Immigration?"

"Follow the law. If you are doing what you should be doing, you should have a path to citizenship. If you did anything illegal along the way, you should be deported. Again, no exceptions and no leniency, I hate this overwhelming need some politicians have to be politically correct."

"*Citizens United*?"

"One of the best First Amendment decisions of all time. God bless Justice Kennedy."

"Patriot Act?"

"A necessary step to protect our citizens' safety. If you polled all American citizens, a huge majority would give up some fundamental freedoms in exchange for safety from terrorism. The Patriot Act does that."

"Tort reform?"

"Junk lawsuits are hurting America's businesses."

"The Constitution?"

"The framers were geniuses. The document lives and breathes on its own and should not be expansively interpreted. That's where we get into trouble. Marshall and his right to privacy on abortion is a good example. The word 'privacy' is nowhere to be found in our Constitution."

"My Republican colleagues are going to love you, Oliver. Do you know of anything, anywhere, any *issue* or person that might derail this nomination? Golding is probably a lame duck. We are looking at an incoming Democratic administration. We cannot get this wrong."

And there it was again—Wilkinson was forced to tell a 'little white lie' during his meeting with MacDonnell. He paused to consider his past. Would anyone have the guts to come forward?

Am I still on their radar screen? Have they moved on with their lives? High school and college are well over twenty years ago. I'm a different person now. People have had numerous opportunities to come forward during previous confirmation hearings. Hayley tried once, but no one else has come forward.

*Do I have a responsibility to the party to let them know there's a
remote possibility someone has something on me? Should I talk
to Dad and hedge my bet, make sure women who have been quiet
stay quiet?*

"Not to my knowledge, Senator."

"No skeletons in your closet of any kind?"

"A lot of people were jealous of my family's wealth and
influence at the time, but I don't know of anything or anyone
who could hurt this nomination."

The salads arrived. Ashley studied Wilkinson, searching his
eyes for any clue of deception. Wilkinson stared right back at
him, confidently, almost *defiantly,* daring Senator Ashley to
challenge his veracity.

"Very good, then, Oliver. Let's eat."

He picked up his wine glass and held it out in front of him.

"To your successful nomination to the United States Supreme
Court, your good health and *very* long life."

"Thank you, Senator. I won't let you down."

"Onward to the hearings."

The two men ate a leisurely and peaceful lunch. Various
House and Senate members stopped by the table for
introductions, congratulations, and encouragement. The hearings
were scheduled for next month, and the Republican majority
expected smooth sailing. What would anti-career woman Chuck
Ashley do when he discovered one of those career women stood
between this pro-life conservative and a precious appointment to
the United States Supreme Court?

Chapter Fourteen

Micah Love had low expectations for his next meeting. Jordan Levin was a trigger-happy asshole, solidly in favor of the so-called blue wall that helped cops, even good ones, shield dirty cops from facing justice for unethical or illegal actions. Micah couldn't help comparing Levin's protectionist behavior to when Dearborn police captain Jack Dylan was accused of murder. Chief Christopher Alexander and his Manistee cops did everything they could to prove his guilt. Levin was the complete opposite of Alexander. Would things be different with Eric Lorenz?

Micah quickly located a last known address on Lorenz in Sylvan Lake, a small lakefront community north of West Bloomfield. He hopped in the Lincoln and drove north on I-75 toward Detroit's northwestern suburbs. Sylvan Lake lined both sides of Orchard Lake Road, just west of Telegraph Road. The Lincoln's navigation system quickly found Avondale Street. The address took Micah to a well-cared for ranch style home. He parked the car on the street directly in front of the home, walked up a short walkway, and knocked on the door.

A tall, late-forties white man answered the door. *Why do these ex-cops all look like they spend too much time in the sun?* The guy's face and ears were bright red. He had a thin mustache and a shaved head. He often wore a hat, Micah figured, because his head was white just over the ears and on the sides of his head. Micah guessed him to be about six foot two, two ten to two hundred twenty pounds, all muscle.

"May I help you?"

He's far more pleasant than Levin.

"Yes, sir, are you Eric Lorenz?"

"Who wants to know?"

Must be a cop thing. "My name is Micah Love. I'm a private investigator working for attorney Zachary Blake. Perhaps you've heard of him."

"I've heard of him, and I've heard of you too. I understand you paid a visit to Jordy Levin a couple of days ago."

"Ah, he told you about my visit—real nice guy, that one. Before I could introduce myself and state my business, he pulled a gun on me."

"Sounds like Jordy. He doesn't like people snooping around our old cases. They're no one's business except the cops and the vics. I understand you had some questions about a case from the late nineties, correct?"

"Yes. And this inquiry *is* on behalf of a victim."

"Oh? Who?"

"Hayley Larson. She's married now. Her name's Hayley Schultz."

"I remember her. I was rather new on the force. Jordy was my rabbi. I was supposed to sit down, shut up, and learn, but Jordy had different ideas about training a rookie detective. He believed in hands-on training, throwing the rook to the wolves, if you know what I mean."

"I used to be a cop. I know *exactly* what you mean."

"Yeah? What department?"

"DPD. Did my tour of duty in Detroit at about the same time you were in West Bloomfield."

"Is it as dangerous as they say?"

"It's not a walk in the park, but the day-to-day danger and the rap Detroit gets are greatly exaggerated."

"I was told not to talk to you, Mr. Love."

"Call me Micah." *This guy is not Levin. He is cut from cleaner cloth. Seems pleasant. If I'm reading the tea leaves correctly, he may be a bit tormented.*

"I'd like to help, *Micah,* but I can't be talking to you."

"Do you always listen to Levin? Aren't you both retired from the force?"

"Yes, we are, but I value my privacy and my good health. Knowing Levin as I do, talking to you is bad for my health, like cigarettes to a lung."

"You sound like someone who is carrying around some things. You seem . . . I don't know . . . *burdened* by something. What if I told you anything you say to me will be kept strictly confidential? If there is criminal activity involved, the first to talk gets a full pass, complete immunity? Zack Blake has that kind of power with the current governor. What do you remember about Hayley Larson?"

Lorenz looked around as if trying to see if he was under surveillance.

Is he?

He hung his head and took a deep breath. He raised his head and looked to the heavens.

"Yeah, Micah, I remember Hayley. She was a nice kid. Scared as hell of the whole Wilkinson family. They had lots of money and power. When old man Wilkinson talked, the mayor and the chief of police listened. Hayley claimed old man Wilkinson's son, the college kid, not the high school boy, trapped her in a bathroom and tried to rape her. I'm trying to remember the two boys' names, but I'm drawing a blank."

"Oliver and Jared. Jared was the high school kid—Oliver was the college boy. Hung with a guy named Shane Marbury."

"That's right. I remember now. Hayley claimed it was Oliver and Shane. Jared was not involved, right?"

"Right. It was Oliver and Shane."

"Why are you digging up this old case now? The statute of limitations is long gone, and Hayley dropped the case. If she's having second thoughts, she's too late."

"The name Oliver Wilkinson doesn't ring any current bells with you, Eric?"

"No. Why? Should it?"

"You don't watch the news?"

"Not if I can help it. I just want to enjoy my retirement and be left alone. Are you going to tell me what the hell is going on?"

"Oliver Wilkinson is President Golding's nomination for a seat on the United States Supreme Court."

Eric Lorenz suddenly looked like he'd seen a ghost. All color drained from his face. He looked like he might faint but quickly regained his composure.

"You've got to be fucking kidding me!"

"I would not kid about something like this. Hayley Larson may have dropped the charges. She may know she can't convict the son-of-a-bitch anymore, but she's not willing to stay silent and allow a sexual predator to serve on the Supreme Court. The question of the day is, are you? Levin is an asshole. He'll never help us. That's why we need *your* help, Eric. What do you say? Blake can get you immunity *and* protection."

Lorenz again looked like he was going to be sick. He paused and contemplated his fate. He was ready to burst; that's how much he wanted to unload. He was also scared; Micah could see the conflict in his eyes.

Do I do what's right, or do I do what's safe?

Eric Lorenz decided to do what was right.

"We were partners, Levin and me. As I indicated earlier, he was my rabbi. Our captain *loved* Levin. He assigned me to him and told me to learn all I could from him. Said he was 'good police.' Well, Jordan was anything but good police. I had issues with his policing style from the get-go. But we were making arrests and getting convictions, so everyone was happy. Who cared how we did it?

"Whenever Levin wanted to bend the rules, the brass would look the other way. A bribe here or there, drug money goes missing, no big deal. Hell, sometimes, the brass was *complicit* in the illegal activity."

"Can you give me some examples?"

"I just gave you one. Follow the money. We would take down a dealer and suddenly be sitting on a wad of cash. The dealer says: 'Keep the money; give me a break.' Suddenly, like magic, the dealer pleads to misdemeanor pot possession, and the money disappears along with all other evidence of a crime.

"They wanted to bring me into this, the whole kit and caboodle. The inner circle, they called it, but I didn't want any part of it. I became a cop to uphold the law and put criminals *away*, not to *become* a criminal.

"I requested a transfer. They busted me back down to patrol. I was *scared*, man. I had no idea how far up the chain this went or what level of bribe-taking or other criminal behavior these guys were capable of. I did my time, kept my nose clean, got my twenty in, and retired with a full pension. Here I am, alive and well, living the dream."

"Why didn't you go to Internal Affairs? Blow the whistle? That's what honest cops do."

"I didn't know how far up the ladder this went or who I could trust. I was a rookie detective. *Everyone* outranked me. I got busted down to patrol for the minor crime of refusing their offer. Can you imagine what would have happened if I blew the whistle on any of them? Besides, I didn't have any hard evidence of corruption to give to IA. I had a career, a solid paycheck, and a family to support. I was young and stupid. I thought you go along to get along."

"And now?"

"Now I'm divorced and retired. I've got a good job as head of cybersecurity for a large real estate company. I have my police pension and a corporate salary. Life was good until you came knocking on my door."

"So, you're going to continue to look the other way, take the safe route? You're going to let this sexual predator be appointed to the United States Supreme Court?"

"That case has always bothered me. Hayley was so sincere and so determined to get justice. She wanted us to charge Wilkinson and Marbury and interview every person at that party. I was ready to do it. I was really *gung-ho* excited to get my feet wet. Levin was letting me run with the case. I promised Hayley I wouldn't rest until these wannabe rapists were brought to justice. For the first time, she had a look of hope . . . of *life* in her eyes. When I first interviewed her, she looked like a conscious dead person. All of that changed when I told her I was on the case."

"What happened?"

"I was at my desk at the precinct when old man Wilkinson walks in and asks to see the Chief. He's immediately ushered in, and they have a rather heated discussion about something or other. I begin my investigation, might even have interviewed a few of the partygoers. I think I spoke to Marbury, and, if I recall correctly, he was pretty remorseful. He told me he was drunk at the time. Apparently, Wilkinson egged him on and did most of the dirty work. I thought this was an auspicious development. I told Jordy about it.

"All of a sudden, Levin and I get called into the Chief's office. The big man tells us to close the case, no explanation and no protest allowed. The Larson girl dropped the charges. The evidence was lacking. Case closed, just like that."

"Sounds like the key to this might be Marbury."

"That would be *my* first move."

"Thanks, Eric. You've been very helpful."

"What can they do to me now? Hayley Larson . . . what's her last name?"

"Schultz."

"Hayley Larson Schultz deserves some closure and some justice. That punk cannot become a Supreme Court Justice. One more thought."

"What's that?"

"In my experience, there is no such thing as a one-time rapist. This guy had the world by the balls with daddy's money and power. He thought his shit didn't stink. Any woman should be proud to be with him, don't you know? If he tried to rape Hayley Larson, he tried to rape other women as well. Carefully track this guy's last twenty-five years. Where has he lived, and who did he interact with? I will bet you a year's salary there are other women."

"I agree, Eric. And thank you. Feel better?"

"I sure fucking do, Micah. Get this asshole. Let me know if there's anything more I can do."

"You don't happen to have a copy of the old file or know where I might find it, do you?"

"I don't. Let me do some digging."

"Be careful, Eric. These guys are more ruthless as adults than they were as kids. And the old man's still alive. He wants to see his son become a Supreme Court Justice."

"I wish all those assholes nothing but the worst. I'll be careful."

"Here's my card, in case you find or think of anything else."

"Thanks, Micah."

"No, Eric, thank *you!*"

Chapter Fifteen

Micah Love was certain Eric Lorenz was the only West Bloomfield cop willing to talk to him. He decided to move on to the witnesses. Hayley Schultz emailed Micah a list of all of the people she could remember being at the party the evening of the assault. Micah was most interested in the people who came to the bathroom door after hearing Hayley's screams.

Although Jared Wilkinson invited Hayley to the party, Micah was confident Jared wouldn't help her. Micah immediately crossed him off the list. Hayley also remembered the names of the girls who came to the door, and Micah would concentrate on locating them.

Probably married with children by now.

Married names would be different than late nineties maiden names. He could track them down the hard way, through public records of marriage licenses, home purchases, mortgage recordings, and birth certificates. However, Micah thought of a clever shortcut. The event happened twenty-two years ago. Hayley and these girls were seniors in high school at the time. Perhaps the high school had a twentieth reunion last year— perhaps these girls attended.

Unfortunately, the city of West Bloomfield supplied students to multiple school districts. Micah presumed the majority of the partygoers lived north of Walnut Lake Road. If so, they probably went to Andover or Lahser in Bloomfield Hills. Micah called both schools and told the receptionists he was once a student at their high school, missed his reunion, and was trying to get in touch with a committee chairperson so his name could be added to the list. Both receptionists put him on hold, and both came back with the names and numbers of the planning chairperson.

Micah telephoned both schools' chairpersons. They were very helpful and friendly. Micah indicated his name was Shane Marbury and that he was trying to get ahold of three former friends, Amy Sanders, Lauren Bortnick, and Sabrina Page. He hit pay dirt with an accommodating woman at Andover High named

Erica Long. Erica had phone numbers, addresses, and married names for all three women. She was eager to reunite friends from the past. After all, isn't that what reunions were all about? Micah gave Erica his address and instructed that all future correspondence intended for Shane Marbury be sent to this address. Erica was more than pleased to add a new name to her growing list of future reunion attendees.

Micah quickly tracked down all three ladies. All were married and still lived in the area. For no particular reason, he decided to begin with Sabrina Page, now known as Sabrina Russell. She lived with her husband and two sons in Northville, a few miles southwest of West Bloomfield. Micah decided to visit without calling. If she had something worthwhile to say, he didn't want to give her time to talk herself out of cooperating.

Using his state-of-the-art navigation system, Micah drove to a relatively new and upscale subdivision of rather large four and five-bedroom colonial homes.

A homeowner needs some coin to live here.

He checked the address and parked in front of a stately brick and aluminum colonial home. The home was well cared for and professionally landscaped. In fact, the whole subdivision was quite impressive and very well maintained. Micah started up the walk as the automatic garage door whirred and began to open. He crossed over the lawn and stood on the driveway. A heavyset late thirty-something woman with platinum blond hair walked out of the garage. She jumped when she saw Micah standing in her driveway.

"Shit! You scared the hell out of me! Are you at the right house?"

"Sorry, I didn't mean to scare you. I think so. I'm looking for Sabrina Russell. Is that you?"

"Who wants to know?" The woman was suspicious and immediately defensive. She didn't appreciate an unannounced visit by an unknown trespasser.

"My name is Micah Love. I'm a private investigator."

"A private investigator? What are you investigating?"

"I can answer that, but only if you're Sabrina Russell."
Micah set the hook. Would Sabrina take the bait? The woman
couldn't resist.

"I'm Sabrina Russell. Now, state your business or get off my
property."

"I'm sorry to drop in on you unannounced," Micah lied. "As
I indicated, my name is Micah Love, a private detective working
on a case for attorney Zachary Blake. You ever hear of him?"

"The guy who took on the church for those two boys and
their mom? *Everybody's* heard of him. What does this have to do
with me?"

"How about Oliver Wilkinson? Does that name ring a bell?"

"I went to high school with his younger brother, Jared. Oliver
is the new Supreme Court nominee, right?" If Sabrina knew why
Micah was there, she was doing a great job of disguising her
feelings.

"That's the guy. How well did you know him?"

"I didn't know him at all. I knew his brother. What is this all
about? I have things to do." Sabrina was getting impatient.

"Did you know a young lady in high school by the name of
Hayley Larson?"

Sabrina's face demonstrated a sudden awareness of the
reason for Micah's visit. However, she decided to make Micah
work for his information.

"Yes, I knew Hayley. Why? Is she okay?"

"She's fine. When did you last speak to her?"

Sabrina paused to reflect. Micah interpreted this pregnant
pause as an attempt to fabricate an answer. He was wrong.

"The last time? We were at a party at Oliver and Jared
Wilkinson's house about twenty-two, twenty-three years ago.
They were famous for throwing wild parties when their parents
were out of town on one of their all too frequent exotic trips. The
Wilkinsons were quite wealthy, you know."

"Yes, I know. Did anything unusual happen to Hayley at that
party?"

"You know it did. That's why you're here, right? What's
your interest in Hayley, Oliver, and that party, if I may ask?"

Micah decided to tell her the truth.

"I'm looking into an incident that took place in the master bathroom on the night of the party. Do you have any knowledge of that?"

"I think I know the incident you're referring to, but I still don't understand why you're here asking about it twenty-two years after it happened."

"Because Hayley Larson Schultz doesn't believe a sexual predator should be rewarded with a seat on the United States Supreme Court."

"I understand," she softened. "Were I in Hayley's shoes, I'd probably feel the same way."

"I have been cautious not to put words in your mouth because I want to hear what you remember happened that day. I have Hayley's statement, but I want to hear yours. Is it okay if I record this?"

"No, it is *not* okay. I will tell you what I remember, but I won't let you record my statement. If I'm subpoenaed or ordered to testify at a hearing under oath, I will do so."

"Fair enough. What do you remember?"

"I was with Hayley that day. She had to go to the bathroom. Hayley was not big on parties, especially the kind the Wilkinson brothers threw, with drugs, sex, and older college boys all over the house. She didn't want to go, but my friends and I talked her into going."

"Your friends would be Amy Sanders and Lauren Bortnick?"

"Yes."

"Please continue," Micah urged.

"Hayley was looking for a bathroom. There was one on the main floor, but it was occupied. She decided to look for one on the upper level. We watched her go up the stairs. Shortly after she went upstairs, we saw Shane Marbury and Oliver Wilkinson follow her."

"Did they actually *follow* her, or did they just happen to go up the stairs after she did?"

"I wasn't sure at the time, but afterward, I *know* they followed her."

"How do you know?"

"Because Hayley didn't return. Neither did Oliver or Shane. I was still with Amy, Lauren, and Jared when I noticed Hayley was gone for quite some time. I pointed it out to the others, and we decided to go up and see if she was okay."

"Was she? What happened next?"

"As we approached the master bathroom, we heard Hayley screaming bloody murder. She sounded terrified."

"What did you do?"

"We knocked on the door and demanded someone open it."

"Did someone open it?"

"Not right away. We heard at least one guy's voice threatening and demanding for Hayley to have sex."

"You actually heard a male voice demanding sex?"

"Yes."

"Did you know who the voice belonged to?"

"Not right away. We kept banging on the door. We heard a splash and a guy scream. The door suddenly opened. Hayley was standing there in her bra and panties, crying, trembling, and hugging herself. I think she was in shock. After she ran past us, I saw her torn clothing on the floor. Shane Marbury was standing in front of a mirror; his face was bleeding. His pants were unzipped, and his penis was hanging out. Oliver Wilkinson was trying to climb out of his parents' whirlpool bath, fully clothed. He was drunk or high, so he was having trouble climbing out of the soapy water. His penis was exposed, too."

"What did you do?"

"We were stunned. Hayley ran past us in her underwear and started down the stairs. Amy and I followed her. Jared stayed behind with the boys. We called out to her, but she dashed down the stairs and out the front door. Everybody on the first floor saw her run out."

"Anything happen after that?"

"We went back to the bathroom. Shane and Oliver were seriously drunk or stoned. They were shouting at Jared for inviting that 'frigid bitch' to the party."

"That's what they called Hayley? 'That frigid bitch?' How is it that you remember that?"

"I could never forget that night. I have never seen a sexual assault before or after. I have never gone to a party since unless I knew the host and all the guests." Sabrina was staring out at the horizon, remembering that day like it was yesterday.

"I understand how you feel. Did the cops ever talk to you?"

"Yes, some cop called on the phone and requested permission to interview me. He left it up to me, and I agreed to come in."

"And did you come in?"

"Yes. I told some cop the same story I just told you."

"You remember the cop's name?"

"No. Wait . . . yes! He was a detective. Jordan something or other."

"Levin?" Micah saw no harm in leading her on this small point since her story was delivered entirely from a twenty-two-year-old memory.

"Levin! That's the guy."

"He took your statement?"

"Yes."

"Was it recorded?"

"Yes."

"With your consent?"

"Yes."

"Do you know whether anyone else gave a statement?"

"No one else gave a statement because after I came in and gave mine, the case was dropped. Hayley refused to press charges. At least, that's what I was told."

"Did you ever ask Hayley about it?"

"No, we never spoke again. She took some time off from school. When Hayley finally came back, she wasn't the same girl. She didn't talk to anyone, didn't hang out, and kept to herself. Soon after the incident, we graduated from high school. She went to Michigan, I think. Amy and I went to State. Lauren went to Western. I still talk to Amy once in a while. Hayley, Lauren, and I have lost touch. Is Hayley okay?"

"She's fine, Sabrina. She graduated from Michigan and got a master's in social work. She owns a clinic and counsels rape victims. In many ways, it has been a struggle for Hayley, but she has turned a horrible negative into a positive."

"Good for her. Please tell her I'm sorry I ever suggested we go to that party, and I'm so sorry for what happened to her."

"You can tell her yourself someday. Let me ask you this, Sabrina. Do you think Oliver Wilkinson should be awarded a seat on the United States Supreme Court?"

"No, absolutely not."

"Would you be willing to come forward and testify in front of the Senate Judiciary Committee and repeat what you've told me today?"

"I would have to ask my husband, but, yes, I would testify. Is Hayley going to testify?"

"Yes."

"She's so brave. I'm so proud of her. I wish we could have remained friends. That night ruined a lot of friendships."

"Sabrina, I have to warn you, this might be dangerous. The Wilkinson's have a lot of power and even more money. They were able to shut down an attempted rape investigation in West Bloomfield. I don't know if they bribed or threatened people, *including* cops, but they were able to quash the investigation. Now, one of them has a chance to be a Supreme Court Justice. Who knows what they're capable of? They won't know we've found and interviewed you. They won't know anything about you until the hearings, but the danger still exists. Will Oliver remember who you guys were?"

"Maybe. Jared certainly would." Sabrina was beginning to have second thoughts.

"I have a husband and small children. I'll have to think about this."

"We can subpoena you and *make* you testify."

"You're threatening me now?"

"No, not at all. I'm telling you we can make it look like you were *forced* to testify and didn't appear voluntarily. Even Oliver Wilkinson can't expect you to lie to Congress after being served with a subpoena."

"Understood. Let me talk to my husband. I'll get back to you. Do you have a card?"

Micah pulled out and handed Sabrina his business card.

"Thanks. Please tell Hayley, 'hi.' for me. And I'm glad she came through this. I've often thought about reaching out, but I didn't want to open old wounds."

"I'll tell her, Sabrina. Thanks for talking to me."

"Thank you isn't necessary. This is my civic duty and my long overdue obligation to an old friend. I'm somewhat overwhelmed by the power Hayley and I have been given. We can bring down a Supreme Court nomination, amazing! Who would have thought?"

"If we aren't careful, Oliver Wilkinson and his family."

"Then, we need to be careful."

"Amen, Sabrina. Amen."

Chapter Sixteen

With the confirmation hearings only a week away, Zack, Micah, Hayley, and Joel set up a meeting in Zack's office. The meeting's purpose was to brief Hayley and Joel on the status of the investigation.

As usual, Zack set the meeting for his office conference room, and, as usual, he served a tray of food fit for a king or, maybe, a bar mitzvah luncheon. Micah was the first to arrive. He advised Zack of the two cop interviews. He reported on the Sabrina Page interview and additional interviews with Amy Sanders and Lauren Bortnick shortly afterward. Their stories were remarkably similar, lending even more credence to their potential testimony. Micah told Zack an off-color joke he heard earlier that day. As soon as Micah delivered the punch line, Kristin entered with Hayley and Joel. Zack was laughing hysterically.

"What's so funny?" Joel questioned, amused and curious.

"It's *Micah*, Joel. I'll tell you when Hayley's not around."

"Hey! I want to hear Micah's joke!" Hayley frowned.

"Sorry, Hayley. I'm too much of a gentleman. I'll tell Joel someday, and if he wants to tell you, that's his business," Zack chuckled, still catching his breath.

"Must be pretty gross," Joel guessed.

"It's Micah, man. Need I say more?"

"Guess not."

"Not fair," Hayley pouted.

"Sorry, that's the way it is. Sue me."

"When this is all over, maybe I will."

"Can we get down to business, please?" Zack changed the subject for two reasons. He was short on time, and he did not want to be forced to divulge Micah's crude joke.

"Alright, I guess." Hayley pouted.

"Good. Micah has made great progress. We have formulated a strategy and have an excellent opportunity to prevent Oliver Wilkinson from surviving the confirmation hearing. With no

further ado, ladies and gentlemen, Micah Love!" Zack turned
toward Micah and directed both hands toward him, palms up.

Joel and Hayley shrugged and applauded.

"Thank you, thank you," Micah smiled and bowed his head.

"Here's the latest—I have interviewed former West
Bloomfield detectives, Jordan Levin and Eric Lorenz. Levin's an
asshole. He wouldn't talk to me. He actually pulled a gun and
ordered me off his property. Lorenz was much more
forthcoming. He gave me some valuable information about how
the cover-up might have happened. He may be willing to testify
at the confirmation hearing. I also tracked down the three
witnesses who came to the bathroom door that evening, Sabrina
Page, Amy Sanders, and Lauren Bortnick.

"They confirmed your story, at least the end of your story.
When you went to the bathroom, they saw Shane Marbury and
Oliver Wilkinson follow you. They were concerned about you
because Shane and Oliver had a reputation. The girls knew you
were inexperienced. They went to look for you because you
didn't come down right away.

"They approached the bathroom, heard screaming, and began
banging on the door. You finally opened it in your underwear
and ran past them hysterical, screaming and crying. You ran
down the stairs and out the front door, in front of everyone at the
party.

"The girls turned back to the bathroom. Marbury was at the
mirror, tending to a wound. When he turned to the girls, excuse
my French, his dick was exposed and hanging out of his open
zipper. Wilkinson was trying to climb out of the whirlpool. He
was fully clothed. One of the ladies reports *his* open zipper and
exposed penis, as well. So, all three ladies appear to confirm an
attempted rape.

"Lorenz and the three ladies will make excellent witnesses in
front of any committee. My recommendation is to disclose their
identities and a summary of their expected testimony to Senator
Stabler. She knows how committees operate. Let her decide how
to proceed."

"Oh my God, Micah! That's wonderful! I feel so . . . so
vindicated! I haven't spoken to Amy, Lauren, or Sabrina since

that evening. Were they cooperative?" Hayley was hopeful her old friends had her back without any prodding from Micah.

"More than that, Hayley. They have almost a photographic memory of these events. They thought there would be an investigation and charges would be filed. They felt *terrible* for you. They wanted to reach out to you back then, but you closed yourself off to all your classmates. The girls couldn't believe the West Bloomfield Police deep-sixed the investigation. They felt guilty they couldn't help you. These ladies have carried the guilt around all these years."

"I *did* shut them out. I thought no one believed me. I figured they were all on Oliver's side or bought off by him. I feel awful. I couldn't have been more wrong. They were good friends who wanted to help, and I turned my back on them." Joel reached out and squeezed her hand.

"Don't be so hard on yourself, honey. You just experienced a serious traumatic event. The cops didn't care, and they dropped the case. It's not hard to understand why you thought everyone was on Oliver's side. Let's look at the bright side. Three old friends still have your back, sweetheart." Joel was *very* comforting.

"You are something else, Joel Schultz. I am so glad you're my husband. I love you so much."

"Love you back." Joel turned to Zack.

"What do we do with these witnesses and their stories? What's the strategy going forward?"

"Good question, Joel, but Micah kind of answered it already. We take the information to Senator Stabler and let her decide what to do. I have some ideas, but I'd like to hear her thoughts before giving her mine," Zack reasoned.

"That's fine, Zack, but I'd like to know what *you* think," Hayley pressed.

Zack paused.

Hayley is the client; it's her case. My job as her attorney is to advise and counsel. The decision on how to move forward belongs to Hayley. But, how can she decide whether to take my advice if she doesn't know what it is?

"If you look at press reports about the nomination, this attempted rape case is on no one's radar. I'm sure Wilkinson met with Chairman Ashley and his Republican committee members. Wilkinson's name is withdrawn if there was even a whiff of anything like this in the vetting process. Then, they pull the next name on the list. This is the Republican's last best chance to seat a Supreme Court Justice for a while.

"We take the information to Stabler. She weighs its credibility and decides the witnesses will testify. She contacts the FBI. The bureau repeats our interviews of the four friendlies. The FBI is wholly independent, not biased, like Micah and me.

"I have friends at the Detroit office of the FBI. If the right people work the investigation, we should be fine. Hayley, you're not going to like what I'm about to say, but it's the truth in today's politics. Republicans on the committee are probably more interested in getting a Constitutional conservative appointed to the Supreme Court than in a twenty-two-year-old attempted rape allegation. The majority will call this some type of unproven youthful indiscretion, and Wilkinson gets the nomination.

"We need to get Wilkinson's testimony on the record . . ."

Zack laid out the strategy in detail. Hayley and Joel were initially confused. *How can the Judiciary Committee ignore an attempted rape?*

However, the more Zack spoke, the more sense the strategy made. The couple began to understand the committee would find new crimes or misconduct much more convincing than an old attempted rape allegation. Zack wanted the attempted rape exposed and for Wilkinson to be ruined. His ultimate goal was to force every senator on the Judiciary Committee to vote 'no' on the nomination.

The group fully endorsed Zack's strategy—the die was cast, and they would proceed. The next step was for Zack to arrange a meeting with Senator Diane Stabler. A roller coaster ride of a Supreme Court nomination process was about to begin.

Chapter Seventeen

Zack caught the morning 7:05 flight on Delta from Detroit Metro Airport to Reagan National for a 10:30 meeting with Stabler. The two spoke on the phone. Zack advised he had important information but didn't want to discuss anything over the phone. Zack told the senator he'd meet her whenever and wherever she wanted, Michigan or D.C., but time was of the essence. The meeting had to take place before the hearings began.

No details were discussed over the phone—Zack was *that* paranoid about Wilkinson's power and reach. Instead, they arranged to meet on Wednesday morning at Stabler's office in the Capitol. The flight was uneventful and landed in D.C. at about 8:35 a.m. As Zack exited the plane and walked to arrivals, a limousine driver stood at the end of the ramp, holding up a 'Zachary Blake' sign.

Nice touch, Senator.

Zack identified himself and shook hands with his driver, who led Zack out to an area reserved for essential vehicles and people. Soon, they were cruising up the Washington Memorial Parkway toward the Capitol. Zack had been to D.C. multiple times and was quite familiar with his surroundings. While the average person might glance around to see the sights, Zack busied himself with the file and documents he was bringing to Senator Stabler.

There were bottles of water, cans of soft drinks, and a carafe of hot coffee set in a cup holder tray opposite his seat. He pulled out an environmentally friendly coffee cup and poured himself some black coffee from the carafe. Then, he settled in and began to read the file.

During rush hour, the trip to the Capitol was a bit longer than the usual ten minutes up the Parkway and I-395 north, but they arrived, safe and sound, in around twenty. One of the nice perks of flying to D.C. was the airport was only five miles from everywhere one needed to be. In Detroit, unless you lived or worked in Romulus or somewhere near Romulus—*no one ever went there*—you had to schlepp a long way from Detroit Metro to your Detroit area destination. *This limo ride is another nice perk.*

Zack exited and generously tipped the limo driver. The man tried to refuse the money—he'd been well taken care of. Zack insisted, and the driver drove off, a very happy man. Zack was an hour early and decided to have breakfast at a local diner.

He ordered a cup of coffee and a bagel with cream cheese. While waiting for the food to arrive, he checked his email and called the office. There was nothing earth-shattering going on in his absence. His bagel arrived—one bite reminded Zack how bland Washington, D.C. bagels were compared to those terrific Detroit area bagels he grew up eating and enjoying.

He continued to check emails as he ate, finished, paid the bill, and walked out. The Capitol was a block away. It was now 10:00 and close enough to the time of his meeting to go directly to Senator Stabler's office. By the time he walked to the Capitol, stated his business, went through security, and took the elevator to Stabler's floor, it was almost 10:20. He entered the Senator's office, gave his name to a man seated in the reception office, sat down, and waited. In less than five minutes, the man at the reception desk rose and walked over to Zack.

"The Senator will see you now."

They walked through a door and into the inner sanctum of the Senate offices. The reception clerk walked up to an ornate mahogany door and knocked lightly. A female voice responded.

"Come in."

The man opened the door as Senator Diane Stabler was approaching the same door from the other side. She met Zack at the threshold, shook his hand, and welcomed him to Washington, D.C.

"Thank you, Jimmy," she addressed the clerk. "That will be all for now. Mr. Blake is a constituent from Michigan. I do not wish to be disturbed until our business is concluded."

When Jimmy left and closed the door, Stabler invited Zack to have a seat. She explained she was less than forthright with Jimmy because this was Washington, and one never knew who the source of a leak might be. No one knew the reason for Zack's visit. For the most part, she trusted her staff, but the reason for the meet was too important to leave to chance.

Zack scanned the large office. There was an old map of Michigan framed and hung over the Senator's side cabinet. Behind her desk chair hung a beautiful painting of John F. Kennedy on a boat at sea. Stabler's desk was gorgeous, made of carved, two-toned wood, with ornate trim. Her chair matched her desk. Out the window was a beautiful view of Washington, D.C.

Senator Stabler reached toward a refrigerator concealed by a cabinet door, pulled out two bottles of water, and handed one to Zack.

"Thanks for coming, Zack. I really appreciate it."

"I am the one who owes thanks, Senator. Blocking this nomination would mean the world to Hayley Schultz."

"How's she holding up? Does her story ring true?"

"That's why I'm here, Senator. The story not only 'rings' true, it *is* true. Multiple witnesses have verified it."

"I'm looking forward to seeing what you have."

"Let's get to it, then."

Zack opened his briefcase and pulled out a file. There were multiple copies of the same documents, mostly transcribed statements of the witnesses who would testify at the confirmation if called upon. Zack handed Senator Stabler a package and sat back, waiting while she read all of the interviews and notes. Her eyes widened at times. At other times, she peered over her reading glasses at Zack, expressing amazement at what she was reading. When she finished, she reclined the back of her executive chair, hands folded behind her, eyes looking toward the ceiling.

"This is *incredible,* Zack. The witnesses back Hayley's version of events almost word for word."

"We don't know exactly what it took to stop the assault investigation, who gave what to whom, but we certainly know an attempted rape occurred, a crime was covered up, and the charges were dropped. Micah is still digging around. Perhaps we can find more smoking guns."

"I'd love to be able to demonstrate the Wilkinson family was behind the cover-up as well as the crime," Stabler preferred.

"Amen to that, Senator."

"You told me over the phone there were things you were uncomfortable talking about on the telephone, some kind of strategy you wanted to discuss. You have my word; this office is bug-free. There are no recording devices or intercoms in here."

"I wanted to discuss my proposed strategy in complete secrecy. That's the reason for the visit. Hopefully, when you hear me out, you'll agree this is the best course of action."

"I'm all ears."

"Here's what I've got in mind . . ."

Zack laid out his plan in detail. He didn't wish to leave anything to chance. He couldn't count on majority Republican senators to deny a Supreme Court nomination based on an old attempted rape allegation that went nowhere in the criminal justice system. He needed fresh evidence. Stabler listened, smiled, and nodded a few times, as she did when she read the file. Zack finished reciting the strategy.

"Brilliant, Zack. This may work, but timing is crucial. We cannot give Ashley and his cronies any wiggle room. They must endorse the idea of an FBI investigation."

"Exactly, Senator. That's where you come in. It's your job to implement the strategy and choose the right time."

"Geez—no pressure on Stabler," she groaned.

Zack laughed. "I'm certain you can handle the pressure, Senator."

"I *live* on pressure. The thought of turning the tables on this nomination and delaying the process for just enough time for the Republicans to be unable to appoint a replacement is priceless."

"Then it's settled."

"Yes. But get me that cover-up information. That will seal the deal."

"We are doing the best we can."

"Forget this water, Zack. It's early, but let's toast the potential destruction of this nomination."

She opened another cabinet and pulled out two small glasses and a bottle of Tito's. She pulled ice from the fridge, dropped the cubes into the glasses, and poured two drinks.

She handed one to Zack and held out the other in a toast.

"To Oliver Wilkinson. May his nomination be withdrawn, his reputation sullied, his license to practice law revoked, and his coming days spent in a cushy white-collar prison."

"Hear, hear," Zack cheered.

They drank down the smooth vodka and continued plotting the demise of the Wilkinson nomination.

Chapter Eighteen

On the morning of the hearings, every morning show, political or otherwise, discussed the Supreme Court Confirmation Hearings. The Strauss Report on MSNBC was one such program. It was hosted by former Michigan newswoman Nancy Strauss. Her guest was a law professor and expert on the Supreme Court.

"This is Nancy Strauss, reporting from Washington. This morning, the Senate Judiciary Committee will commence hearings on the nomination of Sixth Circuit Court of Appeals Judge Oliver Wilkinson to be our next Supreme Court Justice. My guest is University of Michigan Law professor Carl Shipp, a constitutional scholar and an expert on all things Supreme Court. Professor, thanks for joining us. What can we expect today?"

"Barring any last-minute surprises, we can expect some fiery rhetoric from the left, but a rather easy confirmation for Judge Wilkinson. There's a clear Republican majority in the Senate and on the committee. I don't see the Democrats being able to prevent Wilkinson from becoming our next Associate Justice."

"What 'last-minute surprise' might there be?"

"I have no idea. But I've been watching these hearings for a long time. In our current very partisan and divisive political climate, these hearings have become quite contentious. I don't expect the Democrats to go down without a fight. Some senator will have something up his or her sleeve. Judge Wilkinson and his team must prepare for the unexpected."

"What's at stake with this nomination, Professor Shipp?"

"Not much. Just the balance of power on the court for the next few decades," he chuckled.

"Please explain what you mean to our viewers. I'm originally from Michigan. I'm very familiar with Judge Wilkinson's rather extreme conservative record. But the average viewer might not understand what this means for future decision making on our Supreme Court."

"Without Justice Fitzgerald, the High Court is basically divided four to four. Fitz was what I would call a right-leaning moderate, the swing vote on the court. Sometimes his votes and opinions surprised people on the right. A bit more often, he disappointed people on the left. Replacing him with a hardcore conservative like Wilkinson will be a hard pill to swallow for those who value a more expansive or liberal interpretation of the Constitution. Some Justices are of advanced age. There will be more opportunities in the future, but Wilkinson will have an immediate impact on shifting decisions to the right."

"What types of issues are we talking about?"

"Access to abortions is at risk. Affirmative action, civil rights, and LGBTQ+ rights are at risk. Citizen rights vis-à-vis corporate interests are at risk, and an ultra-conservative court has not helped the situation. Majority rulings will, undoubtedly, cause long-lasting harm to tort victims. If Wilkinson is confirmed, trial lawyers might as well hold a funeral for the Seventh Amendment. "

"Criminal justice issues will be hard-lined in favor of law enforcement. Watch out for religious freedoms and immigration issues. We may also see some very conservative decisions about executive power. These could be tough times in America."

"You mentioned the Seventh Amendment, Professor. I'm not sure all of our viewers are familiar with the Seventh. Would you elaborate?"

"Sure. The Seventh Amendment provides for or codifies a citizen's right to a jury trial in civil cases. Trial lawyers have long argued that legislative attempts to restrict people's recoveries in tort cases violate the Seventh Amendment. So-called 'tort reforms' which cap damages or prevent certain lawsuits are examples. We saw an example of this recently, with Barrington Arms and the *Protection of Lawful Commerce in Arms Act of 2005*. This is a law that prevents gun manufacturers from being sued in most cases. Many constitutional scholars believe laws like this violate the Seventh Amendment. President John's presidency was brought down over this issue.

"Many Republicans talk out of both sides of their mouths on constitutional issues. The Second Amendment is sacrosanct—the

Seventh be damned. Tea Party Republicans are the exception. They are strict constitutionalists and, as such, are anti-tort reform and pro-Seventh Amendment. There is an interesting split in the Republican Party—pro-business interests versus constitutional protections. Wilkinson's judicial rulings, state or federal, have been almost one hundred percent in favor of corporations and insurance companies. He is decidedly and hypocritically anti-Seventh Amendment."

"Thanks for the explanation. We'll just have to wait and see. Thanks for joining us, Professor."

"Thank you, Nancy."

Shortly after the Strauss program ended, the hearings officially began. The scheduled star witness, Judge Oliver Wilkinson, was decked out in an expensive gray tweed suit perfectly coordinated with a pink shirt and pink and gray tie. All committee senators were seated on the dais. Senator Ashley swiveled his chair, leaned over, and began a private discussion with Senator Stabler. The mood in the chamber was somber and serious. After all, the Supreme Court is the ultimate check on Congress and the president.

To insulate the high court from political influence, a Supreme Court Justice is appointed for life or until retirement. The impact of Supreme Court decisions is felt long after the president who appointed an individual justice has left office. Senator Ashley completed his business with Senator Stabler, slammed a gavel, and called the hearings to order. Those in attendance settled in and quieted.

Ashley launched into a lengthy and pompous narrative about bipartisanship and the importance of a balanced Supreme Court. He claimed political ideology is unimportant when considering a lifetime appointment because a Justice is accountable to nobody. Of course, this was nonsense since billions in political contributions were responsible for the current Republican majority—thanks to *Citizens United v Federal Election Commission*—and donors fully expected serious bang for their bucks.

Ashley's Republican colleagues on the committee paid careful attention to his opening statement, while Democratic members whispered to each other or effectively ignored him. When Ashley completed his statement, each senator was granted five minutes to welcome Judge Wilkinson or otherwise pontificate. These hearings provided senators with a tremendous opportunity to address their constituents. Following these speeches, several dignitaries were called to 'introduce' Judge Wilkinson to the committee and testify to his attributes as an outstanding man, friend, and judge. This was a tradition at such hearings; much pomp and circumstance before bringing the candidate forward to testify.

After these witnesses concluded their introductory speeches, Ashley called on Judge Oliver Wilkinson to swear-an oath to tell the truth. Wilkinson rose and approached the witness table with his hand raised. He swore to tell the truth, the whole truth, and nothing but the truth. He was then provided an opportunity to deliver an opening statement.

"Thank you, Mr. Chairman, Senator Stabler, and distinguished members of this committee. I'd like to thank my esteemed colleagues for those very generous introductions. They are true patriots; each of them represents the greatness of America. I am grateful for their friendship and humbled by their praise.

"Over the past several weeks, I have met with all of you and a vast majority of the senate body. I've learned about your states and your constituents. I can clearly see each of you is devoted to public service, your state, and your country.

"I am eternally grateful to President Golding for this honor and opportunity to serve. As a judge and citizen, I am deeply impressed with the President's keen interest in this nomination process and the rule of law. The President entertained my family at the White House, and he and Mrs. Golding could not have been more gracious.

"For the past twenty-five years, Justice Noah Fitzgerald has served on the Supreme Court and has been one of the most important and distinguished Justices in our history. The list of his important opinions and dissents is lengthy. I consider him a hero and model of the quintessential Supreme Court Justice."

Wilkinson droned on, thanking his colleagues on the Sixth Circuit Court of Appeals, his parents, particularly his father, and his own young family, his wife and children. Those in attendance chuckled when he joked that his kids were enjoying their 'fifteen minutes of fame,' with a trip to the White House, a meeting with the President of the United States, and a fancy dinner served by the White House Chef. He described his affluent upbringing, almost to the point of bragging about his private school education and other advantages of being the son of well-to-do parents. He recalled being taught equal rights in school and the importance of landmark Supreme Court decisions that solidified equality for all Americans. He claimed he never forgot how lucky he was compared to people involved in decisions like *Brown v Board of Education.*

"As a Justice of the United States Supreme Court, I pledge to always remember the Court decides real cases for real people, and that I must always stand in the shoes of those who come before the Court.

"As a judge in Michigan and on the United States Court of Appeals for the Sixth Circuit, I have made countless rulings and have written hundreds of opinions. I am proud of my service and my body of work."

He described that body of work and suggested his rulings were based exclusively on the law and the Constitution. Some of his criminal rulings went for the prosecution and some for the defense, he alleged. While this statement was technically correct, his criminal rulings favored the prosecution an incredible ninety-seven percent of the time. He made the same claim in deciding cases between citizens and corporations, workers and bosses, and businesses and the environment. However, in those areas of the law, he ruled for business interests over ninety-eight percent of the time. He claimed all of his rulings were 'compelled by adherence to constitutional values.'

He spoke of separation of powers, the Supreme Court's role as politically independent, and how the Constitution guarantees certain rights and liberties.

"There are no aisles on the Supreme Court. Justices do not sit on opposite sides or caucus separately. Our nine Justices are a team, and I will be the ultimate team player for the common good of our constitutional system and our citizens. I have spent my entire legal career in public service. If confirmed, this will be the final chapter of my public service. I plan to commit to the cause of justice for decades to come."

Democratic committee members cringed at the statement. The thought of the partisan Wilkinson serving on the high court for 'decades' was abhorrent.

Wilkinson described his religious Christian upbringing, indicating he was active in his church—a lie—and a tutor and counselor for the poor—technically true, but virtually another lie. Wilkinson volunteered to counsel as a resume builder but never actually accepted an assignment. He also indicated he 'volunteered to serve meals to the homeless.' This was true. He did *volunteer*. However, when called upon to actually serve meals, he always made sure he had another commitment and never served a single meal.

He thanked various teachers, those who taught him, and those who have taught and currently teach his children. He indicated education, more than any other commodity, is the ticket to success in life, especially in America, where we have the 'finest education system in the world.' He thanked his 'multi-cultural staff,' consisting of one Asian woman, one black man, and seventeen white Christians. He thanked his family and friends for their love and support.

His final words were for his wife, Jodie, a graduate of West Bloomfield High School and the University of Michigan, the mother of his children, and a woman's rights advocate in Cincinnati, where the Sixth Circuit Court of Appeals was situated. He thanked her for her unconditional love and support, kindness, and making him a better person. He called on the committee to ask insightful questions, examine his body of work, and consider an independent judiciary's importance. He promised to keep an open mind in every case, thanked the chairman and all committee members. With his opening statement out of the way, he sat back, satisfied with his performance, and awaited questions from the committee.

Chapter Nineteen

The senators began the questioning process. They invited Wilkinson to explain some of his Sixth Circuit opinions and dissents. He testified with bravado, proud of his reasoning and judicial philosophy. Senator Morrie Reader, a Democrat, challenged his judicial record as claimed in his opening statement and compared the 'fabrication' to his actual record. Wilkinson admitted the percentages overwhelmingly favored corporate interests and criminality but explained the issues before the court were decided in accordance with the law and the Constitution.

He pledged to decide cases that came before him as a Justice of the Supreme Court under those same standards. If appointed, he would decide cases without regard to partisanship or special interest, governed only by legal and constitutional standards. Even Democratic pundits had to admit Judge Wilkinson's first hours of testimony were solid, well versed, and well-rehearsed.

Senator Theo Tills, Republican from North Carolina, prompted Wilkinson to comment on the First Amendment. Tills indicated many First Amendment decisions dealt with obscenity and rights of assembly, but these were not key reasons for the Amendment. What did Wilkinson believe the framers had in mind?

"Of course, they had *political* speech in mind. That was what the First Amendment was all about," Wilkinson reported, as rehearsed.

"Thank you for your candor, Judge Wilkinson. Considering First Amendment protections and rights, please explain the *Citizen United* decision to citizens who are watching us now."

"Certainly, Senator Tills. Thanks for the important question," Wilkinson sucked up.

"The case was not about money. It was about the right of any citizen to engage in political speech, which is the foundation of our First Amendment rights."

"You received a private school K through high school education. Is that correct?"

"Yes, sir," Wilkinson grimaced. He didn't understand where Tills was going.

"Do you believe a citizen has a right to use school taxes to pay for private school education?"

"Remember, Senator, it is a judge's responsibility to interpret existing law. Assuming I was deciding a case under current law, the answer would have to be no. I know of no existing law that permits the use of public school funds for private school purposes. However, I do not believe that if written at the state or federal level, such a law would violate the Constitution. I believe one's educational tax dollars should be spent any way the particular taxpayer deems appropriate."

Even committee Democrats who disagreed with the use of public funds for private purposes had to be impressed with the reasoning Wilkinson used to phrase his answer.

The judge was questioned about the Fourth Amendment and what constitutes an illegal search and seizure. He testified that only *unreasonable* searches and seizures were unconstitutional. A balance test between the public interest and the extent of the privacy violation must be conducted in each case.

Democratic Senator Christoff Kunesman challenged the nominee about end-of-life decisions and assisted suicide.

"Senator, actively assisting a suicide is a criminal act. However, any person can decide to end treatment, end the poking and the prodding, and demand release to die in the comforts of home and in the arms of a loved one," Wilkinson reasoned.

Various senators attempted to elicit testimony from the nominee about how he would rule on specific cases or specific issues. Wilkinson declined to answer on the grounds it would violate the principles of an independent judiciary for him to disclose how he would rule on a case or an issue. He promised, again and again, to rule on the law and the Constitution. When pressed on matters of Constitutional *interpretation,* he suggested this would also be done case-by-case and issue-by-issue.

The hearings droned on, discussing prior Supreme Court decisions and potential future decisions. Republicans began to

accuse Democrats of a double standard. It was only relevant for
the Dems to know where a nominee stood on important issues
when the nominee was a conservative Republican. Standards
should be consistent, regardless of party. Wilkinson argued
adherence to the law, the Constitution, and case precedent should
be the standard.

On the third day of questioning, Senator Diane Stabler, as
pre-planned with Zachary Blake, went off script and questioned
Wilkinson about the vetting process and character issues.

"Judge Wilkinson, you have been through a vetting process
related to this nomination, have you not?"

"Yes, Senator."

"And you have been through this process related to other
nominations, including your nomination to the Sixth Circuit
Court of Appeals, correct?"

"Correct."

"And you have been confirmed at each process with flying
colors, correct?"

"Correct."

"Were you queried at any hearing, under oath, as to whether
you have ever been convicted of a crime?"

"I don't recall, Senator."

"Let's clear this up for the record, then, Judge Wilkinson.
Have you ever been convicted of a crime?"

"No, Senator, I have not." Wilkinson glanced at Ashley,
confused.

"I want to place an objection on the record to this line of
questioning," Ashley stammered.

"Noted, Senator. This question and others I intend to ask are
relevant to this proceeding. I would argue *character and fitness*
are the core issues of this proceeding. This is my time, and these
are my questions. I didn't interrupt you, and I would appreciate a
similar courtesy." Ashley huffed and waved at Stabler to
continue.

"Now, Judge Wilkinson, your answer includes misdemeanors
and felonies?"

"It does, Senator. Once again, I have been vetted. I have never been convicted of a misdemeanor or a felony," Wilkinson fumed.

"Thank you, sir." Wilkinson relaxed. Stabler appeared to have concluded her questioning.

"Oh, I almost forgot, Judge Wilkinson. Have you ever committed a crime, misdemeanor, or felony, for which you were accused but not charged?"

Wilkinson rolled his eyes and considered his answer.

Where is this shit coming from?

"I don't know, Senator. I was a teenager at one time in my life. Maybe, in my youth, I smoked pot or drank too much. Maybe I operated a vehicle when I shouldn't have? Maybe? I do like beer—I always liked to throw parties."

"Oh, one more question along these lines, have you ever been charged with or *accused* of a felony?" Stabler appeared to read questions from a document sitting in front of her, reading glasses perched at the end of her nose. The document was actually blank. She looked out over her reading glasses, waiting for the nominee to respond.

Wilkinson paused and considered his answer.

What does she know? Is she referring to something specific? Who or what is saying otherwise? She seems confident. What's she reading from? Is this some sort of trap?

"No, Senator. I have never been charged or accused of a crime of any kind."

"Thank you, Judge Wilkinson. Mr. Chairman, I yield for now but reserve the remainder of my time. There is a matter I would like to discuss in a closed session," she advised.

"Very well, Senator, after today's questioning."

"Thank you, Mr. Chairman."

The gallery, especially press members, began to buzz in anticipation of an interesting closed session. Senator Ashley pounded his gavel and demanded silence and proper decorum. Stabler's line of inquiry usurped the rest of the afternoon's questions. Everyone was focused on the nominee's criminal record and the subject and substance of an upcoming closed-door session.

Press members scattered throughout the Capitol Building were looking around for Stabler's clerks or interns searching for a scoop, but there were no leaks or leakers. The press and the American people would have to wait for the next session to find out what was going on.

When Chairman Ashley finally pounded his gavel to end formal testimony, he temporarily excused the witness until the next morning. Capitol guards cleared the chamber, leaving only committee members and stenographers behind. Senator Ashley turned to Stabler.

"What's going on, Senator?"

"Mr. Chairman, I've received a letter from a constituent, and I would like to read the letter into the official record."

"Without objection, Senator." Ashley was confused but consented.

Senator Stabler donned her reading glasses again and began to read.

"The letter is addressed to me and signed by the constituent, Mrs. Hayley Larson Schultz, MSW. It reads as follows . . ."

Senator Stabler read the letter into the record. A nominee for the United States Supreme Court stood accused of attempted rape for the first time in American history. Committee members on both sides of the aisle listened in stunned silence as the senior senator from Michigan presented the letter's contents.

Many members visibly cringed as Stabler read the parts recalling Wilkinson's alleged conduct. He trapped Hayley in the bathroom, ripped at her clothing until she was clad only in her underwear. He exposed himself and slammed Hayley to the marble floor while ripping at her underwear. She escaped being raped but suffered embarrassment by running through the house, almost naked, in front of dozens of partygoers. Thoughts were flying through various senators' minds:

Must be multiple witnesses . . . What happened to the investigation? How could police let this poor girl down? Why weren't charges pursued? Shit! Can these charges be true? Can they be verified? This nomination is toast. If this is true, it could be characterized as a youthful indiscretion. We can get past this. But what about his testimony—can we get past that?

Eyebrows were raised at the mention of Zachary Blake. Many senators remembered Blake as the lawyer who represented the Dearborn Muslim woman and the Michigan school shooting victims. Blake was the guy who, almost single-handedly, brought down a sitting president of the United States.

Will Blake now bring down a nominee for the Supreme Court? Who the hell is this guy?

Stabler completed her reading, turned to Chairman Ashley, and studied him over her reading glasses. Ashley looked stunned. He silently digested the incredible narrative he just heard.

"Mr. Chairman . . ." Senator Tills shouted, interrupting Ashley's thoughts.

"I must strenuously object to this very late and desperate attempt to disparage our nominee's good name. He has been vetted at three different judicial levels and confirmed as preferred and well qualified each time. Where was this woman, this . . . Ah. . . Hayley Schultz . . on *those* occasions, Mr. Chairman? Why wasn't this letter provided to us before the commencement of these proceedings?" Tills raged. Chairman Ashley was grateful for the bailout.

"Ahem . . . ah . . . yes, Senator Stabler, what about this? And what about the timing?" Ashley stammered.

"Mr. Chairman, as to the timing, I was unable to release the contents of the letter until I received express permission from Mrs. Schultz to do so. Furthermore, I will state for the record Mrs. Schultz *did* level these charges to a local Michigan police department and previous legislative and congressional committees sitting in confirmation of Judge Wilkinson's previous judicial nominations or appointments. Her letters fell on deaf ears at each Republican-controlled hearing. Unless they were whitewashed, Mr. Chairman, these charges should be part of the public record in Judge Wilkinson's previous appointments, especially his Sixth Circuit appointment. However, Judge Wilkinson's powerful reach in Michigan may have prevented public disclosure," Stabler speculated.

"What would this woman have us do at this late stage, Senator Stabler?" Ashley demanded.

"She wants this committee to order the charges be investigated by referral to the FBI. She also wants the opportunity to testify."

"That's impossible, Senator," Ashley shrieked. "These hearings are nearing conclusion. The nominee's confirmation is almost a foregone conclusion."

"I will release this letter to the press if we can't agree privately to investigate this woman's allegations and allow her to be heard." Stabler delivered her coup-de-grâce.

"That's *blackmail*! Uh . . . what do *you* have in mind?"

"I formally move we refer the matter to the Detroit office of the FBI for a non-partisan investigation of these allegations. The alleged incident happened in the Detroit Metropolitan area. Various witnesses and police officers still reside there.

"While the investigation is ongoing, I move we schedule the testimony of Mrs. Schultz and any witnesses uncovered by the FBI's investigation. I'm sure the FBI will conduct a thorough and speedy investigation that won't impede the nomination. That is unless it discovers criminal wrongdoing."

"How do you know that witnesses and cops are still in the area?" Ashley inquired.

"I have been assured that certain witnesses are willing to come forward and be interviewed."

"Where does the assurance you speak of come from?"

"From Mrs. Schultz's attorney."

"Attorney? Who might that be?"

"Zachary Blake."

"Blake? Are we talking about President John's Blake? The guy from the Ay-rab trial and that school shooting case?"

Stabler ignored Ashley's use of slang for 'Arab' or his failure to specify Arya Khan's Muslim heritage.

"Yes, Senator Ashley. He's the same guy from the case where Ronald John and Geoff Parley tried to railroad and make an example of a Muslim woman and her family. He's also the guy who put Barrington Arms out of business and Roland Barrington in prison. Remember, Senator? The case resulted in President John's impeachment."

"Real impartial guy," Ashley mocked, openly disgusted.

"I don't know, Charlie. Oliver Wilkinson just testified all of his decisions were based on the law and the Constitution. Are you suggesting Mr. Blake and I do not hold our conduct to the same standards?"

"Uh . . . well . . . no, I am *not* suggesting anything of the kind, Diane. I have confidence in your integrity," Ashley backpedaled.

"Good. Then, it's settled. Do you want to put this to a committee vote or order the testimony and investigation as a bi-partisan resolution between you and me?"

"We can do it by joint resolution, I guess," Ashley conceded.

"Without objection, Senator Stabler and I move that we proceed as discussed."

"I object, Mr. Chairman. This is nothing more than a late-hour ambush. Senator Stabler has had the letter and failed to disclose its contents for almost four days. Taxpayer money and time wasted," Tills argued.

"Even if I intended to ambush as you say, Senator Tills, your objection makes clear why we need an investigation. If these allegations are proven true, the nominee is not qualified to serve. Have we wasted time if we prove a nominee for the highest court in the land is a felon? Do you plan to vote in favor of an attempted rapist?" Stabler challenged.

"That's . . . uh . . . that's . . . not exactly what I meant," Tills stuttered.

"That's *exactly* what you meant. At least have the stones to admit it," Stabler sniped.

"Must I remind you we are still on the record, Senator Stabler? Language?" Ashley cautioned.

"I'm satisfied with my language and this record. I've heard much worse than 'stones' from you good ole boys," Stabler mocked.

"Are there any other objections?" Ashley moved on.

The room was silent.

"Let's bring the nominee back in to advise him what's going on and what will happen going forward," Ashley declared.

A guard left the chamber and returned with Judge Oliver Wilkinson.

"Judge Wilkinson . . ." Ashley began.

"There has been a last-minute development. We must continue your testimony and this hearing at a later date. By mutual consent, we intend to refer this matter to the FBI so the Bureau may conduct an investigation. When that investigation is complete, we'll bring you back to explain if it revealed any misconduct on your part," Ashley explained.

"What kind of misconduct, Mr. Chairman? What kind of investigation?" Wilkinson demanded, judicial temperament flying out the window.

"A woman has alleged you tried to rape her at a party at your house over twenty-two years ago."

"That's an absurd allegation. Who is this woman?" Wilkinson cried as though deeply offended.

"Her name is Hayley Schultz. She's a rape counselor in the Detroit area," Stabler revealed.

"Am I supposed to know this person? That name is unfamiliar to me." Wilkinson snarled.

"How about Hayley Larson?" Stabler pounced.

Wilkinson paused, ever so slightly.

"Not . . . uh . . . familiar . . . uh . . . with that name either," he lied.

"Judge Wilkinson, sir, with all due respect, she remembers you very well. She also remembers your brother and another boy named Shane Marbury."

Wilkinson struggled to control his emotions. He carefully considered his next words.

"Where do we go from here?"

"We adjourn these proceedings. We refer the matter to the Detroit office of the FBI for a thorough investigation. We immediately schedule the testimony of Mrs. Schultz. Any witnesses made known by virtue of the investigation will have an opportunity to testify under oath. When the investigation is completed, we will give you an opportunity to respond. How does that sound?" Ashley inquired.

"Sounds like a political witch hunt to me," Wilkinson grumbled.

"These are serious allegations, Judge Wilkinson. The timing could have been better, but we cannot confirm your nomination under a cloud of potential criminality," Stabler reasoned.

"This is absurd, Senator. Do you know who I am and who I have been in Michigan? Attempted rape? Me? Why would Oliver Wilkinson ever need to force *anyone* to have sex with him?" Wilkinson continued to demonstrate his pompous arrogance at this crucial moment.

"Interesting, Judge Wilkinson. Your comment speaks volumes to your judicial temperament," Stabler lectured to Wilkinson *and* committee skeptics.

"These histrionics are beneath the esteemed senator from Michigan. You've made your point," argued Senator Tills.

"So has the nominee," Stabler countered.

"Judge Wilkinson, these steps have been approved by majority rule. Your comments are on the record, and your frustration in making them is certainly understandable. But Senator Stabler is quite correct in her analysis. While her timing is suspicious, we cannot confirm a nominee under a cloud of criminality," Ashley concurred.

"I hereby order a referral to the Detroit office of the FBI for an investigation lasting . . . no longer than two weeks?" He glanced around at all members for silent affirmation. All members nodded their heads.

"Let the record reflect all committee members have nodded their assent. We will schedule Mrs. Schultz's testimony forthwith. We're adjourned."

The senators immediately left the dais, and Wilkinson and entourage departed the chamber. As the doors opened, the press corps surged forward and enveloped the nominee.

"Judge Wilkinson—what happened in there just now?" A reporter shouted over other voices. She stuck a microphone in Wilkinson's face.

"No comment," muttered Wilkinson, pushing the microphone aside, bullying past the reporters, and avoiding eye contact.

"Could the issue prevent confirmation?" A reporter shouted.

Wilkinson ignored the question and continued to push his way through the growing press corps. He turned to the guards.

"The judge has no comment," yelled one of the guards.

"Now, let us pass, or I'll call in all of our guards, and we'll start arresting people."

The press corps stepped aside ever so slightly, creating a narrow pathway for Judge Wilkinson. He fast-walked through the opening to temporary freedom from questioning.

What the fuck, Hayley? I never did anything to you—we were drunken kids, for Christ's sake! This was so long ago . . . nothing happened! You weren't hurt. The charges were dropped. Why do you keep raising this incident? When was the last time, at my Sixth Circuit confirmation? What will it take for you to go the fuck away? Money? Is that what you want, bitch? How can you do this to me? This is the fucking Supreme Court! The most important moment of my life! I could go down in history as the longest-serving Justice ever! You'll pay for this . . . you'll pay dearly.

Chapter Twenty

Senator Stabler contacted Zachary Blake immediately after the confirmation hearings bombshell and was pleased to report the strategy was implemented without a hitch. Hayley was now free to testify. Other witnesses, assuming they made themselves available, could testify as well.

Under the leadership of Zack's old friend, Special Agent Clare Gibson, and her first lieutenant, Pete Westmore, the FBI Detroit office was assigned to investigate Hayley's accusations. Unless impeded somehow, the FBI would most likely find enough evidence to demonstrate Wilkinson was, at least, *charged* with attempted rape following the incident twenty-two years ago. Further, the paper trail would likely document an investigation commenced by the West Bloomfield Police Department. Assuming the FBI found Hayley's statement credible and other witnesses backed her story, including the allegations of a cover-up, would this be enough to sink the Wilkinson nomination?

Zack was always comfortable that Wilkinson's criminal behavior could be established once the FBI got involved. He was *never* comfortable with the *politics* of using the incident as the *sole* reason for any Republican to vote against the Wilkinson nomination. Zack was quite fearful the Republican majority was so beholden to the Wilkinson money that even an old *substantiated* attempted rape charge would not bring down the nominee.

He envisioned how it would all play out. The Republican majority would argue that the incident occurred when Wilkinson and Hayley were young. Since that time, Wilkinson went to and completed law school with honors. As a lawyer and a judge, Wilkinson enjoyed remarkable success, rapid legal and judicial career ascension. Part of his success was based on his intelligence, legal, judicial, and *political* ability. However, most of his success was a consequence of his family's wealth and power. *Who* Wilkinson knew and the campaigns he financed were greater precursors to his success than his legal acumen or *what* he knew.

Would the committee's majority, those who most happily accepted Wilkinson money for their campaigns, 'take one for the team' and risk their own re-elections, so a conservative majority would exist on the Supreme Court for years to come? That central question was why Zack and Micah came up with what they now called the 'two crime' strategy.

Zack met in his office with Micah, Hayley, and Joel to discuss the past few days' events. Hayley's testimony was set for early next week, and Zack couldn't be more pleased with the results thus far. His plan was working beautifully.

"Wilkinson behaved exactly as we expected. I'm not even sure he understood the consequences of his testimony. I've long suspected he's too arrogant to admit wrongdoing to the Senate. Thankfully, he didn't let me down. The nomination is now in serious jeopardy." Zack explained.

"How so?" Joel wondered.

"He fell for our 'two crime' strategy, hook, line, and sinker. When Clare Gibson and the FBI prove Wilkinson was *charged* with attempted rape, whether or not they can prove his guilt, they will also demonstrate our distinguished nominee lied under oath to the Senate Judiciary Committee. Regardless of politics, the Senate does not look too kindly upon people who lie under oath in testimony before a committee. If we can't get the Judiciary Committee to reject the nomination on the attempted rape charge, we can get him on perjury or lying to Congress. I think he's toast," Zack boasted.

"Zack, that's wonderful," Hayley Schultz cried. "The 'two crime' strategy, huh? That is brilliant! I'm so pleased, Zack, so glad we decided to come to you for advice."

"Me, too, Hayley. Me too."

"So, what happens now?"

"Now, the Judiciary Committee will schedule your testimony in the next few days. The Detroit office of the FBI will conduct a whirlwind investigation. By next week or the week after, after all of the witnesses have testified, there will be a vote.

"This will not be easy. We do not enjoy a favorable political climate. The majority desperately wishes to confirm this nominee. However, we now have a fighting chance; a better than even chance, Oliver Wilkinson will be denied his seat on the United States Supreme Court. Many of these senators have to face the voters soon, and they can't be seen to support a sexual predator and a liar, now can they?" Zack beamed, convinced the strategy was a success.

"Will I still testify?" Hayley inquired.

"Yes, Hayley. You get to do what was denied you twenty-two years ago. Is this great or what?"

"Just like that, Zack?"

"Just like that, Hayley. But there's more. We aren't leaving anything to chance. Our hope is the FBI will put witness subpoenas in the hands of various people with knowledge of the crime. We expect to have Detective Eric Lorenz, who was busted down to officer, in Washington to testify how the rug was pulled out from under his investigation. We also want to get three of your old girlfriends, Shane Marbury, and even Wilkinson's brother, Jared, to testify under oath. Let's see if they're willing to commit perjury to save Oliver's ass."

"This is so exciting, Zack. Other than the fact that I'm terrified about testifying, I couldn't be more pleased." Hayley beamed.

"You'll be fine, Hayley. And I'll be right there by your side."

"Thanks, Zack. You are amazing!"

"Please don't feed his already enormous ego," Micah smirked, speaking for the first time.

"When you're brilliant, you deserve to be egotistical about it, Micah," Hayley argued.

"Gag me with a spoon." Micah stuck his fingers in his mouth and pretended to gag. Hayley and Joel laughed. Zack rolled his eyes.

"No one uses that old expression anymore. Besides, Micah, *You*, of all people, know she speaks the truth," Zack chuckled.

"You're so humble, Blake. Where's the bathroom? I need to finish vomiting."

"She's the *client,* Micah! We can't argue with a *client,* now can we?"

"I suppose not. Can you take your head out of the clouds for a moment? What would you like me to do, moving forward?"

"Liaison with agents Gibson and Westmore. Offer them the fruits of your investigation and any other help they may need. Clare will be running point for the FBI. She hasn't been given much time to complete her investigation, but this is the FBI. They don't *need* much time, but offer your assistance, anyway. You never know."

"Will do, boss." Micah chirped and saluted.

Zack rolled his eyes again.

"Anything else for us, Zack?" Joel wondered.

"I want to go over Hayley's testimony at least once before the hearings resume, but we don't have a date yet. Let's schedule some time after the hearings resume, and we are closer to the date of her actual testimony."

"Okay by me." Joel glanced over at Hayley, quietly in thought.

"Hayley?" Zack jolted her out of her thoughts.

"Okay by me," she uttered, her mind clearly elsewhere.

"Penny for your thoughts?" Joel turned to her and patted her hand resting on the table.

"Thinking about my testimony. I can't believe this is actually happening after twenty-two years of suppression."

"I would say it's about time, wouldn't you, sweetheart?"

"Okay, Joel—it's about time, sweetheart." Hayley joked.

She immediately retreated to her trance-like state. An opportunity to testify to the crimes of Oliver Wilkinson and Shane Marbury, after twenty-two years of being ignored, was only a few days away.

Chapter Twenty-One

Upon receiving the assignment to investigate the twenty-two-year-old attempted rape charge against Supreme Court candidate Oliver Wilkinson, the first person Special Agent Clare Gibson called was Zachary Blake.

"Zack? Clare Gibson, here."

"Clare! It's so nice to hear from you. How the hell are you? Is this a social call? You miss me that much?"

"Always the clown, Blake. You know why I'm calling," Clare laughed.

"Humor is the way I cope, Gibson. This is some serious shit I've gotten involved in."

"I see by the referral. Attempted rape by a candidate for the United States Supreme Court? Serious shit indeed. What's it all about?"

Zack told her the whole story. He described the incident, the cover-up, and Hayley's desperate and futile attempts to see that justice was done, or Wilkinson's subsequent political and legal appointments were derailed. He indicated Micah Love's agency was investigating the people involved and suggested Clare liaison with Micah before proceeding.

"What kind of person is Hayley Schultz, Zack?"

"She's a terrific young woman, Clare. Her story is true. Micah has interviewed one of the cops who investigated the complaint. The Wilkinson's used their influence to shut down the investigation."

"To be proven."

"To be proven," Zack conceded. *Will she be a problem or part of the solution?*

"You know I'm a straight shooter, Zack. If he attempted to rape this lady and used political clout to cover it up, I will report that."

"That's all Hayley wants, Clare, a fair and impartial investigation into her charges twenty-two years ago. Why did the police back off?"

"I'm on it, Zack. Anything else?"

"Start with Micah, Clare. He has some good background for you. The names and addresses of some of the key players."

"Will do, Zack. I will not be in touch with you as this goes forward, except as it relates to the need for information from your client, understood?" Clare established appropriate investigation boundaries.

"Clear, Agent Gibson. Avoid the appearance of favoritism or impropriety. We want a fair and impartial investigation," Zack repeated. "Just the facts, Ma'am."

"Always the comedian." Clare rolled her eyes and chuckled. Clare ended her call with Zack Blake and called Micah Love.

"Claaaarrrree! How the hell are you?" Micah exclaimed.

"That's almost exactly how Zack reacted to my call," Clare laughed.

"Great minds think alike," Micah joked. "Calling about the Wilkinson thing?"

"Correct. Zack says you are the best place to start."

"Indeed. I've made some *unofficial* headway to get you *officially* started."

Micah recounted his fruitless and dangerous conversation with Detective Jordan Levin. "He might still be on the Wilkinson payroll," Micah speculated. "I had better luck with a former Detective named Eric Lorenz."

Micah recounted his conversation with Lorenz. He described law enforcement's fear of the Wilkinson family's political might, as well as Hayley's description of the events at the party. Lorenz described Hayley as a nice, scared kid, determined to seek justice for Oliver's despicable behavior. However, the Wilkinson power persuaded the cops to back off, and Hayley and her family ultimately deferred. Micah provided addresses for Shane Marbury, Wilkinson's partner in crime, and Jared Wilkinson, Oliver's younger brother, perhaps a witness to specific events.

He told Clare about Lorenz's surprise when he heard Oliver Wilkinson was a Supreme Court nominee and how that revelation caused Lorenz to open up about the case.

"It was hard for Lorenz to talk about the case because Levin was his rabbi and because he was scared of the backlash from the Wilkinsons."

"Go on . . ." Clare urged.

Micah recounted how Levin had the clout to break the rules and get the brass to look the other way. The pair had a solid arrest and conviction record. No one cared if they bent the rules from time to time. Lorenz even speculated but couldn't prove that the brass was involved in or benefited from these rule-bending activities. He talked about bribes and missing money and the quid pro quo resulting from bribes and missing money. Whenever lots of money was involved, evidence and charges would disappear.

"Lorenz was offered a seat at the table to be a part of their inner circle. He told them to pound sand—he became a cop to uphold the law, not become a criminal. In return, the powers that be busted him down from detective to patrol. That scared the shit out of him, so he shut his mouth, put in his time, and retired with a full pension."

"Why didn't he go to Internal Affairs?" Clare wondered.

"Everyone outranked him. He had no idea how far up or out this went and no actual evidence to take to IA. He had a family to support—called himself 'young and stupid.' He has a lot of remorse about how things went down."

"What would happen if the FBI came knocking on his door?"

"He's pissed. He wanted to *prosecute* Oliver Wilkinson. He looked Hayley Larson in the eyes and promised her justice, only to find out the system was corrupt. He certainly doesn't want to see this guy on the Supreme Court."

Micah continued recounting the events through Lorenz's eyes. He was *gung-ho* to prosecute and had the rug pulled out from under him. Oliver's father paid a visit to the chief of police, and, suddenly, the investigation was squelched, insufficient evidence, or some such nonsense. Lorenz did speak with Marbury, who was remorseful but was never permitted to follow up on the conversation.

"Sounds like Lorenz and Marbury are my first moves," Clare decided.

"Marbury was my next visit."

"You'll stand down and let the FBI do its job, right Micah?" This was more of a warning than a request.

"Absolutely. I wouldn't want to show you up like we did the last time," Micah chided. Gibson and Blake were not exactly on the same page during the Jack Dylan murder trial. Zack and Micah eventually persuaded Clare to see the light, and she helped them resolve the case favorably to their client. That's how they became friends.

"You and Blake should become a comedy team," Clare groaned. "Anything else?"

Micah laughed and gave Clare the names, addresses, and phone numbers of the other potential witnesses. He also mentioned Lorenz's speculation that this was no 'hit and run.' Wilkinson probably did this before or after he attacked Hayley Larson.

"Thanks for the background, Micah. This has been very helpful. All kidding aside, you are a terrific investigator."

"High praise coming from you."

"Ever consider joining the FBI?"

"Couldn't afford the pay cut."

"Good point. Thanks for your help on this one. Oh, and Micah, hands-off, now, promise?"

"Scout's honor."

"You were never a scout."

"True. From one terrific investigator to another, then?"

"I'll take that."

"Get this asshole, Clare."

"I promise to get to the *truth,* Micah. Will that suffice?"

"Good enough for me, Clare. The truth will sink this asshole."

Chapter Twenty-Two

Eric Lorenz was an amateur car buff. He recently purchased his latest toy, a classic 2008 Saturn Sky Red Line convertible. While the silver and black sports car was a remnant of GM's good years, it was also a reminder of the company's bankruptcy a year later. The Saturn division and all its models were discontinued as a result, which made this sports car even more special to automobile geeks like Lorenz.

The engine warning system light lit up the last time Eric drove the vehicle, indicating the car was running 'hot.' Perhaps it needed coolant or a radiator flush, or maybe, it leaked somewhere. He was determined to get to the root of the problem and repair it before driving it again. He backed the sports car into his garage and began to work on the vehicle. He faced the interior of his garage with his back turned to any potential visitor.

The stranger watched Eric from her vehicle. She had parked three houses down on the opposite side of the street. Her mandate was clear. Lorenz was to die without any evidence of foul play.

She was an infamous expert in her field, a killing machine. It didn't matter to the stranger whether Lorenz was married, had children, grandchildren, or whether he had his whole life in front of him at the time of the hit. She did what she did for one reason and one reason only—money.

In this case, she'd been promised lots and lots of money. In fact, more money than any pair of sanctions she'd ever accepted, and more than the past ten combined. She could retire after this job and disappear without a trace.

Only the wealthy and powerful could pay this kind of money for two simple sanctions. Who are these guys to them? How can they hurt them? It might be wise to know. Perhaps some other time. For now, it's time to get the first job done.

She exited the vehicle, closed the driver's side door without slamming it, and advanced, cat-like, toward the Lorenz residence. She wore a full-body black spandex workout suit, with thin black gloves on her hands. She would leave no fingerprints. Her long, dark hair was tied in a tight bun and concealed under a form-fitting, stocking hat. She would leave no DNA, no evidence of foul play. Only the most expert medical examiners would be able to identify foul play, and only if they decided to ignore the more obvious cause of death. Most of these people were overworked and underpaid. Mistakes were always made, except on television.

She conducted constant surveillance, glancing up and down the street, peering into homes, and looking around for any signs of homeowners puttering about on their front porch or peering out their windows. She was mindful of pedestrians on the sidewalk and cars going up and down the street. She saw no signs of anything or anyone, so there would likely be no witnesses. Perhaps a camera from someone's alarm system might capture the event. Even so, she wouldn't be identifiable to anyone, nor would anyone be able to recount evidence of foul play.

The stranger had a reputation, but no record appeared on any watch or wanted list. She didn't exist on paper. A witness might say some attractive woman visited Lorenz that morning, and after her visit, my dear neighbor expired. A heart attack, perhaps? The assassin continued her approach in deadly silence. She came within striking distance of Lorenz and whispered.

"Excuse me?"

The startled Lorenz jumped and hit his head on the roof of the Sky. He turned toward the source of the whisper as he reached for the gun in his pants pocket. As he turned, he felt the needle enter the base of his neck. The injection delivered a warm glow feeling that began at the injection site before quickly spreading to his neck, shoulders, back, and arms. As he tried to withdraw his gun, move his arms and hands, his body would not cooperate.

This must be what paralysis feels like.

Eric mustered all of his strength and turned to face the whisperer and saw the most beautiful woman he'd ever laid eyes upon, glaring back at him. *Looks like Catherine Zeta-Jones.*

'Zeta' shrugged and smiled back at him. The warm glow began to penetrate his lower extremities, and his legs began to give way. His systems were completely shutting down.

The stranger reached out and grabbed Eric under his arms, laying him gently over the open front end of his sports car. She glanced behind her, conducted another routine surveillance check, and saw nothing, no one. She calmly walked into the garage, located the automatic garage door button on the back wall, and pushed it. The door began to close with a loud screeching sound until the garage was enveloped in darkness.

What the hell is happening to me?

This was Eric Lorenz's last conscience thought on this earth.

The stranger left Eric draped over the engine, under the hood. She walked to the back of the garage and tried the garage door entrance into the Lorenz home. Eric conveniently left it unlocked. There was a burglar alarm, but, of course, it wasn't armed. She entered the home, walked through a breezeway to the front door, and let herself out, locking the door before she exited.

Again, she perused her surroundings—nothing, no one. Eric Lorenz would soon be found, slumped over his car's engine, the victim of an apparent heart attack. And this sanction paid well, very well.

It's time for act two.

Chapter Twenty-Three

Shane Marbury's parents' wealth and limited political power failed to serve Shane's life and career choices. On the other hand, Oliver Wilkinson's parents' wealth and power served Oliver quite well. In the late 1990s, Shane flunked out of law school, despite his parents' sizeable cash contribution to the school. His parents offered to pay for a master's degree instead, but Shane lost interest in school. Instead, he decided to go into business.

He borrowed more money from his dad and opened a chain of franchised frozen yogurt stores. The stores were profitable for a while, but soon, because of poor management, Michigan's cold winters, and waning public support for ice cream alternatives, the stores failed, forcing Shane's company into Chapter Eleven bankruptcy. The company's principal creditor was Shane's father. He did not take kindly to losing a six-figure investment into his son's business venture after wasting another six figures on Shane's education.

Shane's father demanded repayment from Shane's personal assets, despite the bankruptcy and the absence of Shane's personal guarantee on the investment. When Shane told his dad to pound sand, the elder Marbury disowned and disinherited him. Despite his mother's vehement protests, Shane was left completely on his own with a semi-worthless four-year bachelor's degree in Sociology, dwindling assets, and no job.

Shane reached out to then Michigan Court of Appeals Judge Oliver Wilkinson, and Wilkinson came through. He found Shane a position as a policy analyst for the Michigan Republican Party in Lansing, the State's Capitol. The position required skills Shane didn't possess, but the Party was beholden to Wilkinson's money. When Wilkinson needed a favor, the Party had little choice but to grant one. To his credit, Shane Marbury worked hard for the first time in his life and became an asset. However, Shane was acutely aware the only reason he was able to hang around the Party long enough to become an asset was his relationship with Oliver Wilkinson. Shane owed everything to Oliver—he would never betray him.

The paranoid, narcissistic Wilkinson wanted to rely on Marbury's loyalty. After all, they had been friends for almost thirty years, through good times and bad, through thick and thin. Could he trust Shane to keep his mouth shut? Probably, but 'probably' was not good enough for the likes of Oliver Wilkinson. He wanted to be a Supreme Court Justice, and Shane Marbury knew where the bodies were buried. His loyalty must be unwavering, or he needed to disappear.

***

The beautiful stranger had never been to Lansing. She carried an old picture of Shane Marbury, along with the address of his well-guarded loft apartment complex on Grand Avenue and his downtown office on Capitol Avenue near the State Capitol Building. Surprisingly, apartment complex security was superior to the office building's security, especially at night. The stranger was advised that Marbury worked long hours, often alone, on conservative legislation or policy for local and State Republicans.

As the stranger strolled along Capitol Avenue toward Marbury's office building, a cool breeze blew from west to east and through her nylon turtleneck cover-up and her traditional black spandex workout suit. Her black gloves kept her hands warm; her nylon cap kept her head and ears protected. She was a tropics girl, unaccustomed to these cool Michigan temperatures.

When this is over, it's back to Cabo and retirement. No more killing for the pleasure or protection of others. No more risk-taking for unknown powerful assholes. I'm no better than they are—human life has only one meaning for me—an expendable commodity, a way to use my unique skills to obtain riches the average person only dreams of. But I kill for the simplest of reasons; I have no emotional skin in the game. What motivates the powerful? What have the weak done to deserve death?

She questioned her benefactor for a fleeting moment. As quickly as they entered her mind, those thoughts and questions faded. The stranger had a job to do.

My last sanction . . . Michigan is cold at night, even in late spring . . .

She shivered and continued to walk in the protection of darkness. As usual, she scrutinized her surroundings. Cars driving east and west on Capitol passed her, paying her no attention. Streetlights and other evening lights barely lit the sidewalks. The stranger easily avoided the lights by staying in the shadows and hugging the buildings.

She arrived at her destination and crossed the street to the other side of Capitol Avenue. She watched the office building from a distance across the street. A lone security guard sat in the middle of the lobby in front of a computer screen. In order to complete the sanction, she'd have to distract the guard and disable a Wi-Fi-controlled surveillance camera. If an alarm sounded, perhaps her prey would run out of the building and into her arms. However, there was no precision, skill, or expertise in such an operation. She preferred to enter unnoticed and undetected, complete the sanction, and exit without the guard or surveillance team knowing she was ever there.

The stranger pulled off her backpack and opened the nylon bag to reveal an electronic device. She pointed it at the building and punched a few keys. The device began to make a whirring sound. The assassin began to look, back and forth, from the pack to the security guard. After a long minute, the security guard peered into the computer screen and began to gently tap on the keyboard. When his actions failed to produce results, he foolishly banged on the top of the monitor, forgetting the source of his discontent was the CPU, not the monitor. Realizing his stupidity, he bent over and reached under his desk, checking the CPU and wiring. Everything looked good. He returned to an upright position, confused and frustrated.

The guard picked up the telephone on his desk and was about to make a telephone call when a visitor began pounding on the front door. Attempts to buzz the man in failed for the same unknown reason the surveillance cameras were inoperable.

The guard vacated his desk and walked to the door, where he exchanged words with the guest. The stranger set the device on a ledge and left it pointing directly at the CPU inside the office complex. She calmly walked across the street toward the building, observing the conversation between guard and visitor. When the guard finally pushed open the door to allow the visitor to enter, the stranger pranced to the entrance. The guard and visitor turned toward the lobby, backs to the stranger. She raced to the door as it was closing and inserted a small wedge between the door and the jam, preventing it from locking.

As the pair continued their walk to the security desk, the stranger pulled open the door, ever so slightly, squeezed inside, bent over, and pulled the wedge out of the door. It closed with a slight click, unnoticed by the two men in front of her. Instead of going forward toward the center of the lobby, she dashed to the right, where schematics reviewed the night before displayed an inner stairway and an emergency entrance and exit for safety purposes or elevator malfunction.

She entered the staircase and held the door, slowing it down as it silently closed on the lobby. Her prey was located in an office on the fourth floor, an easy climb for someone in excellent physical shape. She reached the fourth floor and tried the door expecting it to be locked on the inside. She carried expert lock picking equipment in her backpack and fully expected to need those skills to enter. To her great surprise, the door opened with a simple yank on the handle.

According to the information she received from her handlers, her prey worked late almost every night, often alone. She roamed the hallway until she located the office. She again removed the backpack, set it on the carpeted floor in the hallway, and opened it. She pulled out a *Range-R* hand-held radar device used by law enforcement officials to 'see through walls.' The device picks up images, human breathing, and movements within a building.

The assassin activated the device and pointed it at the office. The results determined a sole occupant seated in front of a computer screen located in an office to the suite's far right. She tried the door, but it was locked. She removed lock-picking equipment from the backpack and began to work on the front door. A camera in the hallway pointed directly at her, but she knew it remained deactivated by the device on the ledge outside the building. She made fast work of a routine locking mechanism and stepped inside. She removed a hypodermic identical to the one that claimed the life of Eric Lorenz. Marbury and Lorenz's deaths, from similar causes and at relatively young ages, might arouse suspicion, but that was not her problem. She was told to terminate them and leave no evidence of foul play. This was her preferred 'no evidence of foul play' method.

She soundlessly advanced to the office in question. As she strolled down the hall, she passed numerous dark and empty offices, with nameplates on the outside left of each door she passed. Finally, she came to a slightly illuminated office. The nameplate read:

Shane Marbury
Policy Analyst

She peered around the corner. A forty-something white man sat at a computer monitor. On the monitor, two naked couples were taking turns satisfying each other in unique ways. Marbury's right arm moved rapidly up and down from his lap to his belly and back again. The stranger smiled at the sight.

Heart attack brought on by masturbation and porn addiction—details at eleven.

Marbury's eyes were glued to the screen as the stranger began her silent approach. His hand and arm continued to move up and down. Sweat was beading on the sides of his face. As the predator reached her prey, Marbury sensed her presence, stopped, and began to turn toward her. His face went dark as he turned away from the computer screen. Hers was illuminated by the monitor's light, directly in front of her. She was gorgeous— an ultimate wet dream amid the man's final computer porn fantasy.

Is she real or a figment of my imagination?

The assassin didn't hesitate. She turned the man's chair back toward the screen as she simultaneously plunged the hypodermic into his neck, with similar results to yesterday's sanction of Eric

Lorenz and others she terminated over the years using the 'no foul play' method. The man shook violently. His hands dropped to his side as he pitched forward, face down on the desk in front of the computer screen. No two sanctions were exactly alike, even when the same death delivery method was utilized. Soon, the man heaved his final breath and lay completely still. She did not wish to move him and risk leaving evidence of her visit. She moved to his side and bent forward, still unable to see his face. His exposed penis was now limp outside his pants zipper, his crotch stained with the results of his final orgasm. The assassin smirked.

He died a happy man . . .

The stranger retreated from Shane's office and fast-walked through the hallway out into the fourth-floor lobby. She returned to the emergency stairwell and descended the stairs. She skipped the first floor and ventured down to the basement level where the stairway ended at a door that read:

EMERGENCY EXIT ONLY—ALARM WILL SOUND

Will the alarm sound? Will the suppression device prevent this?

She was uncertain of her next move for the first time in a long time. She didn't wish to risk walking by the guard a second time. She could use the *Range-R,* but the device would only detect the guard's location and not which way he faced. She could wait until he left the lobby again but preferred to get the hell out of there. She glanced at her watch. She'd been at the site for almost forty-five minutes.

She decided not to risk the main lobby exit. Escaping through the emergency exit in the basement was her safest route. From reviewing the schematics, the assassin knew the door led to a long staircase on the north side of the office building, which led to an alley outside the building. A quick trip up the stairs and dash through the alley, she would be gone without a trace and with no evidence a crime was committed.

If the alarm *was* activated when she opened the door, she doubted anyone would know how the alarm tripped. Office management and the clueless guard would assume the alarm was tripped when the system came back on. By then, she'd be long gone.

As she pushed the bar, the door opened with a slight grunt. No alarm sounded. She felt an immediate release of the tension she'd been feeling. She stepped into the outside staircase and stood between the door and the jam.

There was no handle or locking mechanism on the outside of the door. All she could do was wedge her foot between the door and the jam to minimize the sound of the locking mechanism.

She slowly began to remove her foot, dragging it backward until only her toes were wedged in the opening. As the door slid off the tips of her toes, it closed with a slight click.

No one could possibly have heard that!

She glided up the staircase and found herself—as she expected—in the north side alley. She traversed the alley back to the front corner of the building and headed up the sidewalk. As she passed the front door, the guard, a maintenance worker, and a suit—perhaps a computer technician or building manager—were crouched at the reception desk and examining the CPU.

Perfect execution—no one suspected a thing.

The stranger walked to the opposite side of the building. Not wishing to break any law, she crossed Capitol Avenue at the crosswalk and returned to the spot where she'd left the electronic device. She deactivated the device and turned toward the office building across the street.

To the absolute delight of the two men and the guard, the CPU immediately became operational. The monitor buzzed and began to produce multiple rotating images. The alarm and buzzer entry system reset itself.

It was quite obvious the men inside thought this event was some sort of computer glitch, or the technician in the suit did something to repair the problem. In fact, based on the stranger's reading of the three men's body language, the technician was boasting about having remedied the situation. He would probably tender a substantial invoice for services rendered.

She retrieved the device, placed it into the backpack, and began to retrace her steps down Capitol Avenue. The assassin approached the vehicle provided for her use by her handlers. She was to return it to a lot in Detroit near the new Little Caesars Arena downtown and leave the parking ticket in the visor.

   She telephoned her contact and confirmed fulfillment and wire transfer information. She had an early morning flight to Cabo San Lucas from Detroit Metro and wanted assurance the money would be in her account by morning or as soon as her handlers could confirm the two deaths. Satisfied with their quick response, the stranger turned and glanced back toward the office building where Shane Marbury's body would soon be discovered. The Capitol dome was beautifully illuminated in the evening sky. Bills were written. Laws were enacted and broken in Lansing on what looked to be an ordinary night in Michigan history.

Chapter Twenty-Four

Clare Gibson was having difficulty connecting with Eric Lorenz. She tried his cell and landline multiple times over a couple of days. All of her calls were sent to electronic voicemail. She left a couple of messages but had a bad feeling about his refusal or inability to answer his phones. She knew Lorenz lived alone after his divorce. He had a daughter, but she lived with his ex-wife and now attended Eastern Michigan University in Ypsilanti. Telephone calls to both ladies revealed neither spoke to Eric in a couple of weeks.

Perhaps Eric wasn't returning her calls because he didn't recognize the number and thought they were robocalls. Clare persuaded both daughter and ex-wife to place telephone calls to Eric on the theory he'd pick up calls from familiar numbers. Their calls were also sent to voicemail. Thanks to Clare, both women were now quite worried about Eric.

She apologized, promised to locate their ex-husband and father, and notify them as soon as she found him. She telephoned the Sylvan Police Department, gave the desk sergeant Eric's address, and suggested he send a squad car to ensure the former police officer was okay. She deliberately mentioned Eric was former police, so they'd be quicker to assist a brother in blue. The sergeant was very pleasant and agreed to send a car. In this quiet lakefront community, an officer was probably grateful for an assignment. The sergeant indicated an officer would call with an update and invited Clare to wait for his call.

Clare's bad feeling about Eric Lorenz intensified. She'd handled white-collar criminals in her career. Wealthy, entitled, politically connected criminals always considered themselves above the law. She recalled Zack Blake's recent encounter with Roland Barrington of Barrington Arms as a perfect example of this type of criminal. Unlike Barrington, who currently resided in federal prison, many of these rich and famous criminals could buy their way out of trouble. If Oliver Wilkinson was guilty of attempted rape, still an open question, Clare wanted to see justice

done. She could not wait for a call. She hopped in her car and
headed to Sylvan Lake.

As Clare traveled north on 1-75 toward Sylvan, Officer Brad
Polsky parked his squad car at Eric Lorenz's home. He called in
his arrival on the scene and reported all looked quiet. He exited
the vehicle, walked up steps leading to a small porch and the
front door, and rang the doorbell.

No one home . . .

He walked back down the front steps, turned left, and walked
the perimeter of the home toward the backyard. The house
backed up to a canal and had no backyard fence. He continued
along the perimeter, through the backyard, and stepped up onto a
deck. He cupped his hands around his eyes and peered into the
home through a sliding glass door.

No sign of movement . . .

On a whim, he tried the sliding glass door. It was unlocked.

"Hello?" He called out as he pulled the door open. "Anyone
home? Sylvan Police here— your slider wasn't locked—easy
prey for a break-in. Hello?"

No response. Polsky had no warrant and was technically
breaking and entering, but a missing ex-policeman, an open
door-wall, and the deafening quiet of the home were enough
probable cause in Polsky's mind to continue his journey. He
walked through a cluttered family room and into the kitchen. The
microwave was beeping. An LED screen displayed the food
inside was 'ready.' He opened the microwave and saw TV dinner
sitting on a round glass surface. He touched the package.

Cold.

A can of Diet Coke sat open on the counter. He touched it.

Warm.

He continued through the kitchen and came upon a
breezeway leading to the laundry room. He walked past a door
he assumed led to the garage and stuck his head into the laundry
room. Greasy rags lay on the floor. The washer door was open,
but there were no signs of life. He turned and started to walk
back toward the kitchen but stopped at the entrance to the garage.
He opened the door and encountered a glass inner door on the

other side. When he pushed it open, he gagged, immediately overcome by the pungent smell of death.

Polsky reached inside the garage and turned on a light switch. He saw the silver sports car inside with its front hood raised. He felt around for the garage door opener along the back wall and pushed the button. The door slowly screeched open. Polsky pulled his weapon and entered the garage with the gun extended. He walked around the car on the driver's side toward the front of the house. He reached the driver's side door and leaned forward to see behind the open hood. The decomposing body of Eric Lorenz was draped over the engine. Polsky jumped back immediately, dizzy and nauseous. He dry-heaved and willed himself to calm.

He stepped out of the garage and walked down the driveway toward his squad car. He pulled out a cell phone, dialed his precinct sergeant, and reported the yet-to-be-identified body. Multiple squad cars from Sylvan and three small neighboring communities were dispatched to the scene along with a fire truck, ambulance, and the Oakland County Medical Examiner. Numerous emergency vehicles raced down Orchard Lake Road. The sirens could be heard in every home in Sylvan Lake. Something terrible happened in this quiet, peaceful, lakefront community.

Chapter Twenty-Five

Five minutes after Officer Brad Polsky discovered an unknown adult male's body at Eric Lorenz's home, Clare Gibson received the call she was dreading. She immediately telephoned Pete Westmore, who answered on the first ring.

"Pete? Sylvan Police have just found the body of a man who I presume is Eric Lorenz. Where do we stand on the interviews of the other witnesses?"

"Shit! Cause of death?"

"We don't know yet. We're not even sure if the body is Lorenz."

"Maybe we'll catch a break and it's not him. As to the witnesses, I've interviewed all three ladies. They have interesting and *consistent* stories. They didn't actually witness an attempted rape, but they knocked on the bathroom door, and when it finally opened, they saw Hayley, Shane, and Oliver almost immediately after the incident. They were at the scene of the crime. Their stories sure look and sound like attempted rape. I haven't talked with the younger Wilkinson brother, who was also part of the group that knocked on the door. I don't expect much cooperation there.

"The only other direct witness, besides all the partygoers who saw Hayley dash down the stairs and out the door, is Wilkinson's old buddy, Shane Marbury. Who knows how cooperative he'll be? He lives in Lansing and hasn't answered his phone over the past fifteen hours."

"We need to isolate and arrange twenty-four-hour protective custody for our three female witnesses, stat! We also need to find Shane Marbury and get him into protective custody. Contact our Lansing office and have them liaison with Lansing PD. Search Marbury's home and office and get out an APB right now! We must find him! There is no time to lose. It looks like Oliver Wilkinson will resort to *anything* for a seat on the Supreme Court."

"That's a little over the top, Clare. Don't you think? We don't even know if this is Lorenz or how he died."

"Just do it, Pete. I have a gut feeling about all this. I will bet you a month's salary that the body is Lorenz. This stinks to high Heaven."

"I'm on it, Clare. I trust your gut. What are you going to do?"

"I'm heading to Sylvan Lake. Call me with updates, Pete, even the littlest thing. Find Shane Marbury. Shane's definitely next if Eric was a hit."

"Understood. I'll keep in touch."

"Thanks, Pete."

Clare now raced up I-75. She exited at Square Lake Road west and drove to the address she was given. The scene was total chaos. She parked on the street, walked up to the home, and flashed her credentials to a cop installing yellow crime scene tape around the perimeter. Clare requested the person in charge, and the officer pointed her to a well-dressed elderly man. Flashing her badge again, Clare introduced herself to the man.

"Richard Lieberman, Chief of Police here in Sylvan Lake. Glad you're here, Agent Gibson. This is a bit unusual for us."

Clare was pleased with the introduction. It was unusual and very refreshing for a local police department to *welcome* FBI intervention. Clare's recent case with Zack Blake and Jack Dylan in Manistee was a good example of the usual conflict between feds and locals.

"Murder is *always* unusual, Chief. We never expect to see someone murdered."

"Let's not jump to conclusions, Agent Gibson. We have no idea what caused this man to die."

"Acknowledged Chief. Have we confirmed his I.D.?"

"According to the address and his driver's license, his name is Eric Lorenz. He's a former cop on the West Bloomfield police force for over twenty years."

"I'm familiar, Chief. The FBI is investigating. Lorenz was a key witness in that investigation. He's relatively young. His death is very convenient for certain people who are targets of our investigation. Any signs of foul play?"

"No. According to the Oakland County Coroner's Office, the M.E.'s preliminary finding is 'heart attack.'"

"Is the body and the M.E. still here?" Clare looked around at various people as she spoke.

"Yes, Agent Gibson. That's him, over by the garage. The body was found in the closed garage, draped over a car Lorenz was working on."

"Who found the body?"

"Officer Polsky." Lieberman pointed to a young officer sitting on the porch. He was dazed, pale, and staring into space.

"Is he alright? Does he need medical attention?"

"He's never seen a dead body. He's shaken up, but he's young and strong—he'll be okay." The two experienced law enforcement professionals glanced at Polsky with trepidation. Cops everywhere experienced something like this at the beginning of their careers. Polsky lifted his head and acknowledged his superior officer.

"May I see the body? I also need to talk to the M.E. and Officer Polsky."

"Not a problem, Agent Gibson."

"Call me, Clare."

"Clare, it is. I'm Rich."

They walked over to the garage. Lieberman introduced the coroner, a tall, thin, middle-aged man in a white medical smock. Joe Bloom actually worked for the Oakland County Coroner's office. Sylvan Lake was too small to have its own medical examiner.

"What are we looking at, Joe?" Lieberman inquired.

"Natural causes. It looks like he had a coronary while working on his car."

"How long has he been dead?" Gibson wondered.

"Twenty-four, maybe as long as forty-eight hours."

"And nobody noticed him slumped over the car in all that time? What kind of neighborhood is this?"

"He wasn't noticed because the garage door was closed," Bloom explained.

"Closed?" Clare questioned. "Who works on an engine with the garage door closed? He's former police—I'm sure he's worked suicides or murders by carbon monoxide poisoning."

"Interesting point, Agent Gibson. That hadn't occurred to me. Still, my preliminary cause of death is a heart attack."

"How old is Lorenz?"

"According to his driver's license, he's fifty-two, born in 1968."

"Not impossible, but a bit young for a heart attack, wouldn't you say?"

"That would depend on his lifestyle, family history, diet, and exercise regimen. If he was a non-smoker, in good shape with good habits and no family history of heart attack or stroke, yes, it would be unusual."

"When you get the body back to the morgue, would you please very carefully check for any sign of foul play? This is way too coincidental for my taste."

"Sure, Agent. What's this all about?" Bloom and every cop within range stopped what they were doing and waited for Clare's response.

"Well, gentlemen, this is not public knowledge, but we are investigating Oliver Wilkinson, the Supreme Court nominee. He was accused of attempted rape in West Bloomfield about twenty-two years ago. Lorenz was one of the detectives assigned to the case."

"Holy shit!" One officer exclaimed. He quickly covered his mouth in embarrassment.

"Indeed," offered Bloom. "That certainly *is* a coincidence. I will proceed on the assumption of foul play and examine every inch of this poor man's body."

"Thanks, Doc. That's all I can ask for."

"Back to the garage. Where's Polsky?"

Polsky wandered over and was listening to the conversation. He raised his hand at the mention of his name.

"Officer Polsky? Nice to meet you—I'm Clare Gibson, special agent with the FBI. You found the body?"

"I-I did," Polsky stammered.

"And I understand the garage door was closed when you found the body, true?"

Polsky methodically explained his visit, finding the door wall unlocked, entering the house, and eventually finding the garage and the body. He indicated the garage door was closed, and he opened it because of the strong odor and because he could not see around the hood of the car. He was extremely defensive.

"You're not in trouble, Polsky," Clare assured. "You did nothing wrong. We'll need to dust the whole place and your elimination prints, but what you did was totally understandable under the circumstances."

Polsky breathed a huge sigh of relief. "Thanks, Agent Gibson," he muttered.

Clare addressed her entire audience.

"What experienced police officer would work on a car's engine with the garage door closed?"

At what was now officially a crime scene, the officers began to ponder the question, shaking their heads and murmuring to one another. Every cop's consensus on the premises was that no police officer would work on a car engine in a closed garage due to every officer's experience with carbon monoxide poisoning. The Wilkinson investigation, coupled with the closed garage, created a whole new slant on the situation. What seemed like a death from natural causes now seemed like a murder to every officer on the scene.

Chapter Twenty-Six

Clare Gibson left Eric Lorenz to the locals and offered Lieberman and Bloom FBI assistance for autopsy or any other issues they encountered in their investigation. She also indicated that Micah Love, a high-profile private investigator, was involved in the case. His office possessed state-of-the-art equipment and access to tremendous crime-solving technology. If stumped on anything, they were to telephone Clare or Micah. She gave the locals Micah's private cell phone number.

As she drove south on I-75 back toward Detroit, she ordered her Bluetooth to dial Zachary Blake. Zack's receptionist answered and promised to connect her right away. In less than thirty seconds, Zack picked up his extension.

"Hey, Clare, nice to hear from you. Everything okay?"

"No, Zack, everything is *not* okay. You sitting down?"

"Clare, what's wrong?" Zack groaned.

"Sylvan Lake police just found the body of Eric Lorenz."

"He's dead? Oh my God, Clare. Wilkinson killed a cop?"

"Preliminary findings are that he died of natural causes."

"You don't believe that for a second, do you?"

Clare told Zack the whole story, which buttressed their belief that foul play was involved. However, they preferred *forensic* proof to mere speculation or coincidence. Zack put Clare on hold and conferenced in Micah Love. Clare repeated the story to Micah.

"This is all hands on deck, Micah," Zack ordered. "Whatever you can do to help prove that this was murder, I want you to do. No expense is too high. Understand?"

"I read you loud and clear, good buddy. I'll call Sylvan and Oakland County as soon as we hang up. Clare, will you grease the skids for me?"

"Already taken care of, Micah. The local FBI crime lab is also at their disposal."

"I will mention that too. Anything else?"

"No, Micah. Cause of death is of vital importance. We must prove this was murder. I guarantee it will lead us right to that son-of-a-bitch Wilkinson."

"It's possible he died of natural causes, Zack," Micah cautioned. "Don't let your hatred for Wilkinson blind the truth."

"Bullshit, Micah. The man is an attempted rapist and a murderer. He will stop at nothing to claim the power he covets. He must be stopped by any means necessary."

"I read you loud and clear, Zack, but we must tread carefully. Wilkinson's aligned with some very powerful people. We do not know who they are or how far up they go," Clare warned.

"Don't need the warning, Clare. You can't go much further than the President of the United States and the United States Supreme Court."

"You're suggesting President Golding is involved?"

"No. Stephen Golding is no Ronald John. But he vetted this man and appointed him anyway. Who are the people who made that happen? *That's* how high this goes. The FBI can't investigate without a mandate to do so." Zack reasoned.

"We're going to have to blow the lid off this thing ourselves, Micah. And we start by finding out who led the team vetting Wilkinson for Golding."

"As Clare suggested, these guys are pros, I'll do my best, but this is not Detroit. It's D.C.—I may be out of my league."

"Nonsense. We brought down a crooked president; we can do this. We have tremendous resources at our disposal. Use them— you have carte blanche. Find out who's responsible for this cover-up. Who stands to gain the most from a Wilkinson on the Supreme Court? I'd start with the old man."

"Orville Wilkinson?"

"Why not? He's the source of Oliver's power."

"Worth a look, I guess, but I don't see it."

"My two cents?" Clare offered. "It seems like a good starting point."

"I suppose . . . but what does the old man have to gain worth committing murder over?"

"He orchestrated the cover-up of the attempted rape. We know that much," Zack pointed out. "Perhaps he's still trying to cover up it up."

"Never thought of it that way, Zack," Micah admitted. "Either way it goes, I'm on it."

"Thanks, Micah. Hayley is counting on you."

The three professionals were silent for a while. Zack suddenly appeared panicked.

"What about the other witnesses?"

"I have a team rounding them up as we speak. We will be providing twenty-four-seven protection," Clare reassured.

"Great, Clare. Thank you. I guess that's one thing we don't have to worry about. You need to track down Jordan Levin. Let him know what happened to Lorenz. He'll need protection, too. Maybe Lorenz's death will persuade him to open up, be a human being."

"Great point, Zack. Forgot about him. I'll take care of it."

Clare's cell phone began to bark.

"What's that?" Zack wondered, amused.

"My company cell phone. This guy I work with is always barking at me, so I thought I'd choose an appropriate warning system for his telephone calls."

The two men were still laughing when Clare answered the phone with a giggle. She put the company phone on speaker so Zack and Micah could hear the conversation.

"Clare Gibson."

"Clare? Barry Miller here. I have news."

"What's going on, Barry?"

"There's been another death, this time in Lansing with similar circumstances as Lorenz."

"Shit! Marbury?"

Both Zack and Micah shook their heads from side to side.

"He died in his office. He was looking at a porn site, Clare. I don't know how to sugar coat this, so I'll just say it. His dick was literally hanging out. His pants were stained with semen. The coroner says he had a heart attack in the middle of some, shall we say, vigorous activity."

"Bullshit!" Zack shouted.

"Who's that?" Miller inquired.

"Zack Blake, Barry."

"The attorney? Why is he listening to this? This is an official investigation," Miller barked.

"Because all of this started when his client accused a United States Supreme Court nominee of attempted rape. He's good people Barry."

"I'll take your word for it, Clare. I don't like lawyers. They always fuck things up."

"Your feelings aside, Barry, Zack has been very helpful with this and previous FBI investigations. He's on the team for this one."

"Again, I'll defer. It's your case."

"Who do we have handling this in Lansing?"

"Westmore's heading there now. The point of contact in the Lansing office is Donald Hoff.

"I know Donny well. Good guy. I'll reach out. Thanks, Barry. Oh . . . Barry?"

"Yes, Clare."

"There was another ex-cop on the Wilkinson attempted rape case. His name is Jordan Levin. He lives in Commerce. We need to get him to talk to us and consent to a protective detail. Tell him about Lorenz and convince him his life may be in danger."

"He's kind of an asshole," Micah opined over the personal phone's speaker.

"Who the hell is that, Clare? What is this, a party?"

"That was Micah Love, Barry. He's Zack's PI."

"Another private citizen copied in on a federal investigation of a Supreme Court nominee? What is wrong with this picture, Clare?"

"These men can and will help us, Barry. You promised. This is *my* case. Right or wrong?" She challenged.

"Your case, Clare. Be careful who you trust, that's all."

"Thanks for the advice, Barry. We good?"

"We're good, Clare."

Clare ended the call. The three fell silent again, commiserating.

"Sorry about Barry, guys. Now you know why I use that ring tone."

"I've been dealing with guys like Barry my whole career," Zack growled. "Not important. What *is* important is I don't believe in coincidences when it comes to death. Do you, Clare?"

"Two heart attacks with two key witnesses in the same case, within twenty-four hours of each other? No, Zack, I have to agree. This is no coincidence."

"So, what do we do about it?"

"We prove these were not isolated, unconnected heart attacks. We prove they were murders. Hopefully, autopsies and forensics will find the truth."

"What if they don't?"

"We cross that bridge when we get to it, Zack. Let's hope for the best, shall we?"

"For now, Clare. What's the next step?"

"I'm going to Lansing."

"I'm going with you. Meet you somewhere along I-96, Twelve Oaks Mall, perhaps?" Zack suggested.

"Suit yourself, Zack. Twelve Oaks works for me. Micah?"

"You don't need me in Lansing. I'll start looking into Wilkinson's appointment and vetting process to see if old man Wilkinson played a role."

"Great, Micah. Thanks," Zack concurred.

"No problem, Buddy. We'll get these guys."

"Sure, we will, Micah," Zack sighed. "Sure, we will."

Chapter Twenty-Seven

As Zack and Clare sped down I-96 toward Lansing, Clare called Pete Westmore. She hoped he was already in Lansing, learning things about the death of Shane Marbury. Westmore answered on the first ring.

"Hey, Clare. I just got here, but I've spoken to the locals in charge."

"You're on speaker with me and Zack Blake, Pete."

"Hi, Zack. This really sucks, doesn't it?"

"Hey, Pete. Sure does. What's going on out there?"

"It looks like this guy literally died with his dick in his hand—heart attack while masturbating. If this wasn't so tragic, I suppose some would consider it funny."

"I don't think it's funny at all," Zack grumbled, a bit more biting than he intended.

"Sorry, Zack," Pete whimpered.

"Make sure Lansing law enforcement knows about Sylvan Lake and the connection to Wilkinson. The medical examiner should flyspeck that body for signs of foul play," Clare instructed.

"I'll convey your message, Clare. Anything else?"

"We are on our way to you, Pete. Keep us posted if you discover anything new."

"Will do."

"This happened in an office building that housed an office of the Michigan Republican Party. Was there security? Surveillance cameras?" Clare continued to talk and think at the same time.

"Apparently, there was a security guard and cameras in the building where the incident occurred. The cameras and the CPU that controls them were out at the time of death. The guard says only one person entered the building during that time, and he was with that guy the whole time. Well . . . two . . . I guess. A tech guy came to repair the CPU."

"Very convenient malfunction for death by natural causes. When did the tech guy arrive?"

"About twenty-five minutes to a half-hour after the monitors went dark."

"Is the tech guy within the window of time of death?"

"I guess he is."

"Check him out, Pete."

"Will do."

"Was anyone else in the building?"

"The guard says no."

"Does he know Marbury?"

"I don't know."

"Find out."

"I will."

"What about other buildings, other cameras? If someone snuck into the building and offed our vic, could he have been picked up on another surveillance camera somewhere?"

"I'll check that out as well. What's your ETA?"

"We're in . . ." She looked up at the nearest road sign. "Wixom. Be there in an hour or less."

"Hopefully, I'll have some answers for you when you get here."

Clare disconnected the call and turned to Zack.

"What do you think?"

"I think we have two murders to cover up an attempted rape by a United States Supreme Court nominee. Can you believe this? The country is going to hell in a handbasket," Zack grumbled.

"Two deaths of two witnesses within twenty-four hours is too coincidental for me too. We still need evidence of foul play to lock it down. Hopefully, the coroners or the forensics guys will discover something."

"Hopefully so. These guys are good. We need to catch a break . . ."

Clare's cell phone rang on the car's speakers. Clare banged on the display screen.

"Yes, Pete? What's up?"

"Big news, Clare. The victim is *not* Shane Marbury. The guard confirmed this. The dead guy is his legislative assistant.

Guy's name is Ira Gallant. He's about the same age, height, and build as Marbury."

"Wow, Pete. That *is* big news! If this *was* an assassination attempt, it's a colossal fuck-up by the bad guys." Clare paused, thinking, turning to Zack, back to the lit display screen, then back to the road ahead. She sped up.

"Pete? Here's what I want you to do. Contact the DMV and get me driver's license photos on Gallant and Marbury. Have Lansing police pay a visit to Marbury's home. I doubt they'll find him there, but maybe they'll find evidence leading to his whereabouts.

"When the bad guys find out they terminated the wrong person, Marbury will become the most hunted person in America. Put a BOLO out on Marbury, stat. Zack and I are turning around. You handle Lansing. I'm going to quarterback the rest of the investigation from Detroit. Get the Ingham County M.E. to step up the autopsy in Lansing. I'll do the same in Oakland. We've got to protect these witnesses and find Marbury. Do you read me?"

"Loud and clear, boss."

"Keep me posted, Pete. Stay on these people. Make sure they appreciate the urgency of this."

"I read you, Clare, talk soon."

Westmore disconnected the call. Clare glanced at Zachary Blake, who was rubbing his chin and staring out the windshield.

"What's on your mind, Zack?"

"Marbury's alive. He and Levin and some West Bloomfield bigwigs could blow the lid off this whole conspiracy, Clare! How do we find them, protect them, and get them to talk?"

"Leave the details to me, Zack. After all, my friend, I *do* work for the FBI."

***

Clare returned to the Twelve Oaks Mall in Novi and dropped Zack off at his car. She promised to protect the witnesses whose whereabouts were known and locate the witnesses whose whereabouts were in question. Zack promised to share the fruits of any of Micah's labors.

Zack cruised east on Maple Road through Walled Lake, West Bloomfield, Bloomfield Township, and Birmingham. He made a Michigan left on Woodward Avenue and drove north to his Bloomfield Hills office. He hadn't been in for a while. Kristin gave him a warm welcome, then rewarded his return with a large stack of phone messages.

As he pranced through the office, administrative staff members and associates waved or verbalized their own warm welcomes. Zachary Blake was a kind, generous, and well-liked employer. As he approached his office, he was greeted by his personal paralegal, Phyllis, who was advised of his arrival. Phyllis had several files to discuss with him and offered to go through the stack of phone messages to determine which she could handle now or in the future and which could only be handled by the boss.

Zack wanted no part of any of what Phyllis was suggesting. He wanted to discuss and plan a strategy for the upcoming trip to Washington D.C. and Hayley Schultz's testimony before the Senate Judiciary Committee. Phyllis knew who was in charge, but she also knew if Zack concentrated on the upcoming D.C. trip, the files and calls he neglected while working on the Schultz matter would be neglected for another week or two.

"Can we at least discuss who you want to handle these calls and files while you work and travel on the Schultz thing?"

"Sure." Zack smiled as if he never offered opposition in the first instance. He displayed an unintentional but nonetheless condescending attitude that enraged paralegals and secretaries in law offices all across America. By way of example, paralegals or secretaries *always* found 'missing files' for rushed, impatient, ill-tempered, and frustrated lawyers in those lawyers' own offices or automobiles.

Phyllis rolled her eyes, took a deep breath, calmed, and one-half hour later, a plan to handle the files and messages while Zack concentrated on Schultz emerged.

Was that so difficult?

"Happy now? Can we discuss strategy on Schultz?" Zack smirked.

She loved him. He was a great boss, especially when there was no pressure, which was not often in a busy, successful law office. But sometimes . . .

Should I smack him now or wait till later?

"Yes, sir, we can discuss Schultz," she conceded.

"We need to arrange an office meeting with Hayley and Joel. Hayley's testimony is scheduled for the end of this week, and we must prepare. We've got to discuss talking points for Senator Stabler to use when questioning Wilkinson on rebuttal. I want no stone left unturned. Stabler's got to unload on this guy. Two people related to this nomination have been killed in a twenty-four-hour period. Too coincidental, wouldn't you say?"

"Died," Phyllis corrected him.

"Huh?"

"No one has proven they were killed, Zack."

"Potato, potahto," Zack grumbled.

"No, it's not. You can say they mysteriously died in one twenty-four-hour period, but you'll look terrible if you say 'murder' without proof of foul play," Phyllis argued.

Zack relaxed. "You're right, of course. What would I do without you?" He smiled.

"You don't want to even consider that possibility, Mr. Blake."

"Oh, now we're formal? Suddenly, I'm *Mr. Blake*?"

"Only when you're grouchy."

"I'm sorry, Phyllis, truly I am. This case is getting to me. How did we reach a point in this country where a guy like Wilkinson stands to be nominated to the Supreme Court? Have the rich and powerful completely taken over? When will politicians return to their constitutional roots? When do we reclaim our nation governed by the people and for the people."

Phyllis admired Zack's passion for justice and the law.

"Those are great talking points for the hearing, Zack. Let's start there. I've written them down," she offered.

"I'm so glad I have you by my side."

"Always, sir."

"Thanks, Phyllis. We also need to call Micah and get him in on the 'find and protect all witnesses' sweepstakes."

"I'll take care of it. Let's get back to the talking points."

Chapter Twenty-Eight

Two days later, Zack, Hayley, and Joel boarded a flight for Washington D.C. Hayley was scheduled to testify that morning. Wilkinson would offer rebuttal testimony that afternoon or, if Hayley's testimony ran long, first thing the following morning.

The three exchanged light banter on the plane. There was no talk about Hayley's testimony; Zack's goal at this juncture was to calm her nerves. An obscure and ordinary citizen a short while ago, Hayley Larson Schultz was suddenly the most talked about woman in a deeply divided America.

To conservatives, pro-Golding or pro-Wilkinson, Hayley was a lying scoundrel and a progressive plant. She concocted an attempted rape story to deny conservatives their rightful seat on the Supreme Court. To progressives, Hayley was a brave hero who would have to endure the pain of rehashing a vicious sexual assault for the good of the country, the Constitution, and the United States Supreme Court. There was little or no middle ground.

The threesome arrived in Washington. As she had when Zack visited earlier, Senator Stabler arranged limousine transportation. A driver met them with a Zachary Blake sign as they deplaned in D.C. They engaged in minimal conversation during the ride to the Capitol Building.

When the limo arrived at the Capitol, all hell broke loose. There were demonstrations, protesters, counter-protestors, press members, and a significant police presence controlling all of the various participants exercising their First Amendment rights. As Hayley and Zack exited the limo, the swarm descended upon them, shouting words of encouragement and damnation at the same time. Amid these protester chants, the press corps shouted questions.

Hayley could not make out any of the comments or questions because everyone was shouting at the same time, effectively drowning each other out. The crowd was scaring the hell out of her. Zack and Joel took turns pushing Hayley through the anxious crowd while the police tried to provide an escort and create a narrow pathway to the Capitol steps.

They finally reached the steps. Zack Blake stopped, turned, and faced the crowd. Shocked a participant would actually address the maddening crowd, the protestors and the press quieted to listen.

"Ladies and gentlemen, my client, Hayley Larson Schultz, has come to Washington, at tremendous personal sacrifice, to tell the truth about an incident from twenty-two years ago. She could have stayed silent and remained an ordinary citizen, but she chose not to because she is an extraordinary person. If you're here today in support of Hayley's brave efforts to enlighten the committee about a particular Supreme Court nominee, we thank you for your support. If you're here in support of the nominee, we support your exercise of First Amendment rights but not your right to harass and intimidate. If you are members of the press, we have no comment other than Hayley Larson Schultz plans to tell the truth, the whole truth, and nothing but the truth.

"If all of you behave yourselves and allow us the courtesy of entering the building unencumbered, providing testimony, and leaving without being assaulted, we may have a statement for you, then allow questions after the hearing is concluded. That's all for now. Please let us pass."

The police created a narrow pathway up the steps, but protesters and press members continued to shout until Hayley entered the Capitol. The three visitors were led to security and then ushered into a waiting room adjacent to the chamber where the hearing was to occur.

"Wow!" a shaken Hayley Schultz remarked.

"Not surprising, really, sweetheart." Joel tried to 'matter of fact' the uprising.

"I suppose not," Hayley admitted.

"Are you ready?" Zack changed the subject.

"As ready as I'll ever be." Hayley inhaled deeply and slowly exhaled.

Someone knocked on the door, and Zack invited whoever it was to enter. Senator Diane Stabler and Chairman Charles Ashley walked into the room and greeted their guests. They made a great show of unity even though they were on opposite sides of the Wilkinson debate.

"Welcome to Washington and the Capitol, Mrs. Schultz," Ashley schmoozed.

"Ditto," Stabler chimed. "Ready?"

"As I just told Zack, ready as I'll ever be."

"Do you understand the protocol, Hayley?" Stabler inquired.

"I'm not sure what you mean."

"You'll be permitted to make a ten-minute opening statement. Chairman Ashley will be the first to question you. Then it will be *my* turn. In order of rank, ranking Republicans and Democrats will be permitted ten minutes for questions until everyone's had an opportunity to ask questions. After the questioning, the chairman and I will offer concluding remarks, and you will also have an opportunity to offer a closing statement of sorts. Sound good?" Stabler was calm, gentle, and reassuring. Hayley was appreciative. She actually calmed a bit.

"We're going in, Mrs. Schultz. Someone will come and retrieve you when the time comes. Your husband and your attorney may sit at your side or directly behind you in the room," Ashley advised.

"Thank you, Mr. Chairman," Hayley acknowledged.

The two senators left the room. Hayley poured a glass of water, then held the pitcher up to Zack and Joel, who declined her offer. They sat in relative silence, sometimes making small talk. A half-hour later, there was another knock on the door. A Capitol Policeman entered to announce it was time for Hayley's testimony. The three stood, exited the room, and were escorted to the packed hearing room. Hayley was instantly nervous and claustrophobic.

An assistant showed Hayley where to sit while Zack was invited to sit by her side. Joel took the seat directly behind Hayley. He reached out and patted her on the shoulder. Hayley placed her hand on top of his, turned, and smiled. She was grateful for his love and support.

Ashley pounded a gavel, called the hearing to order, and began his opening statement:

"This morning, we continue our confirmation hearings on the nomination of Sixth Circuit Court of Appeals Judge Oliver Wilkinson to serve as the next Associate Justice of the United States Supreme Court. We will hear from two witnesses today and tomorrow, if necessary, Mrs. Hayley Larson Schultz and Judge Oliver Wilkinson. We thank both witnesses for accepting this committee's invitation to testify.

"This hearing has become contentious. Mrs. Schultz's allegations against Judge Wilkinson have been controversial and explosive. Both witnesses have endured a terrible couple of weeks. Citizens and politicians have chosen sides and dug in for a battle royal. Both witnesses and their families have received vile threats and an unacceptable level of contempt, which is a terrible reflection on the state of civility in our democracy.

"So, Mrs. Schultz and Judge Wilkinson, on behalf of the Judiciary Committee, I want to publicly apologize to both of you for the way you've been treated. My committee members and I pledge to you that today's hearing will be safe, respectful and dignified . . ."

Ashley went on to give committee members and the audience a history lesson in what brought everyone to the hearing today. President Golding nominated Wilkinson to a lifetime appointment on the United States Supreme Court. The hearings commenced, and the senators were sailing along toward confirming a new justice. A background check was conducted, and no allegations of any kind were discovered in the investigation. There was nothing in any bipartisan review to indicate Judge Oliver Wilkinson ever engaged in inappropriate sexual behavior.

Ashley indicated Hayley first raised her allegations in what he called a 'secret letter' addressed to Senator Stabler, but the Senator initially took no action. She sat on the letter, deciding not to share it with the committee. He charged that Stabler's actions prevented these allegations from being investigated in the ordinary course of committee business. While Senator Stabler's excuse was Mrs. Schultz called the shots and did not want the contents of the letter released out of fear of retaliation, Ashley maintained the committee could have acted in confidence, same

as Stabler. Late disclosure of the letter, Ashley charged, was
unfair to the nominee.

The nominee answered over one thousand written questions
submitted by the senators, and not one question dealt with this
secret evidence. 'At the eleventh hour,' Senator Stabler
published the allegations contained in the letter and demanded an
FBI investigation into Hayley's charges. Shortly after that, her
letter was leaked to the press. The witnesses have been inundated
with mistreatment and threats ever since.

Ashley called their treatment 'shameful,' the aftermath of a
'media circus,'' and accused Senator Stabler of conducting a
partisan witch-hunt. Stabler remained silent during this partisan
assault on her character and her calculated actions. Wilkinson
submitted to follow-up questions under oath and categorically
denied the new allegations.

"After Mrs. Schultz's identity became public, the Detroit
office of the FBI conducted an investigation. The committee staff
has personally contacted all of the individuals it could locate who
attended this party twenty-two years ago. My own staff has
reached out to Jared Wilkinson, Amy Sanders, Lauren Bortnick,
Sabrina Page, and Shane Marbury. While we could not locate
Mr. Marbury, we did locate the others, and all of them denied
having witnessed a sexual assault . . ."

Ashley was telling *his* truth. Congressional investigators and
the FBI discovered all three witnesses reported seeing an
indecently exposed and inebriated Wilkinson in the bathroom as
Hayley ran out of the bathroom and then the house wearing only
a bra and panties. Apparently, this wasn't enough for the
Republican majority on the committee. This was exactly what
Stabler and Zack feared and why Zack devised the perjury trap.
Ashley also lied when he remarked the committee made repeated
attempts to interview Hayley Schultz, but her attorney refused
their requests. Zack stood and interrupted the Senator, a highly
unusual breach of protocol.

"Excuse me, Senator, but that statement is inaccurate. I
request it be stricken from the record. Not only were there no
'repeated requests' made to my office for an interview with my

client, but there was not a *single* request to interview my client by *anyone* on this committee."

"Mr. Blake, you and your client will have ample time to make your presentation . . ."

Zack remained standing and interrupted the chairman again.

"I'm not referring to our presentation, Mr. Chairman. I am talking about an accurate record and a true account of events. I challenge you and your staff to name one attempt to interview my client, the date and time of the attempt, and anything that might demonstrate that this attempt, if proven, was denied by my office, myself, or my client."

Ashley put his hand over the microphone and turned back to his chief assistant. A heated discussion took place between the two, and the assistant kept shaking his head from side to side. Ashley was clearly angry. He looked bewildered and embarrassed. The conversation ended in a huff—Ashley turned back to the witness and audience.

"Mr. Blake, I apologize to you, sir. My chief assistant advises you are absolutely correct. No one on this committee reached out for an interview with your client. I was misinformed. I apologize to your client and my colleagues on the committee. Without objection, I order my comments regarding any request to interview Mrs. Schultz be stricken from the record."

"Thank you, Mr. Chairman," Zack responded respectfully. He sat down and patted Hayley on the hand—victory number one.

Ashley may have been temporarily embarrassed, but he had an agenda and a constituency to represent. He continued his attack on the minority party.

"Some of my committee colleagues, consistent with their stated intent to obstruct Judge Wilkinson's nomination by any means possible, have demanded the FBI continue its investigation until the Bureau pronounces the investigation complete. I will not force such an investigation, especially since the allegations are now public and the witnesses available to this committee . . ."

"Sorry, Senator, I acknowledge the breach of protocol and apologize, but your statement is, again, inaccurate." Zack objected, rising to his feet.

Ashley was utterly confused. "What statement? What inaccuracy?"

"Shane Marbury is missing. Another witness has died. While this committee might be able to conduct an investigation, all witnesses are not 'available,' as you suggest, and the FBI is far more able to locate and protect prospective witnesses than your committee is, Mr. Chairman," Zack argued.

Again, Zack caught Ashley by surprise. Apparently, Ashley was not aware of Lorenz or Gallant's deaths, nor was he aware of Marbury's disappearance. Ashley again turned and engaged in a second heated conversation with his chief assistant. When he finished, he turned back and addressed Zack's arguments.

"I was unaware of the status of the witnesses you mentioned, Mr. Blake. I must apologize to you and your client one more time. Let's table the discussion about continuing the FBI investigation until after the conclusion of these two witnesses' testimony, shall we?"

"That is your prerogative, Mr. Chairman. I formally request that you withdraw your statement about the availability of witnesses, as well as the accusation that committee members have requested an extension from the FBI out of an intent to obstruct," Zack demanded.

His statement was not only accurate, but it was also the first time some committee and press members became aware that certain witnesses were either dead or missing. This effectively planted seeds of doubt about the process and the nominee, precisely Zack's intent.

"Your request shall be taken under advisement, Mr. Blake," the chairman grunted. "I will state for the record the FBI does not perform credibility assessments—"

"Hold the phone, Mr. Chairman," Senator Stabler interrupted. "I must object. Mr. Blake has correctly alerted you to an issue. I will afford you the benefit of the doubt and presume you were unaware of these occurrences. One witness is dead; another is missing. This is highly suspicious. Taking this under advisement is not sufficient. I do not want this issue tabled. I want you to order the FBI to continue to investigate the death of Eric Lorenz and the disappearance of Shane Marbury, key witnesses in this investigation and confirmation."

Ashley turned red. He again covered the microphone and turned to his assistant. Conservative Senator Jack Baldwin, Ashley's right-hand man on the committee, joined the conversation. This controversy was exactly why Baldwin was concerned about the nomination of Wilkinson in the first place. This was not only embarrassing, but it created the appearance that committee Republicans were hiding something and trying to thwart a legitimate investigation into missing and deceased witnesses. They had little choice but to order the investigation to continue. Baldwin called over other conservative members, and the conversation continued in earnest. When the confab was concluded, Ashley addressed Senator Stabler and the gallery.

"I have conferred with my colleagues, and we agree that the FBI investigation shall continue for the time being. Let's take a ten-minute recess."

Ashley pounded his gavel and walked out in heated conversation with his colleagues. This was the best Zack and Stabler could have hoped for—victory number two. To the press and independent observers, the tide was turning. Before this hearing, word on the street accused frustrated Democrats of concocting this entire attempted rape plot to obstruct a too-conservative, alt-right nominee. Now, Hayley hadn't even testified, and critics were whispering about a cover-up conspiracy by the Republicans and their sinister nominee.

Chapter Twenty-Nine

Senator Ashley reconvened the committee and completed his opening remarks. He promised Hayley a fair and respectful hearing and announced that committee Republicans would not ask her a single question. Each senator agreed to defer ten minutes to Andrea Gartner, a Southeastern Lower Michigan prosecutor who specialized in sex crimes and family violence cases.

Ashley warned that the hearing dealt with allegations of sexual assault and was 'R-rated.' He advised children and those who could not handle these topics to tune out. Zachary was stunned by this development.

Politicians willing to give up their soapbox and ten minutes on national television? These alta-cocker conservatives are too squeamish to ask a woman questions of a sexual nature. Incredible!

Ashley completed his opening remarks with a reminder for all witnesses—Wilkinson and Hayley—under Senate Rule 26.5. The witnesses could request that the committee goes into a closed session if a question required an answer that invaded their privacy. He called for opening remarks from Senator Stabler, and she didn't disappoint her followers. She offered a clear and cogent explanation of why Hayley Schultz had to testify and why the FBI and other law enforcement officials were investigating the disappearance and death of two witnesses.

Senator Stabler more than ably defended her actions and deliberate inactions. She apologized to Hayley Schultz and argued that the way the system and this body treated Hayley Schultz is precisely why victims of sexual assault are reluctant to come forward in other law enforcement settings. She accused the majority of stifling the process and failing to allow witnesses to be interviewed or to come forward to give testimony. She claimed she virtually had to beg for Hayley Larson Schultz to be permitted to appear before the committee and threaten to leak Hayley's story to the press to get the majority to take this seriously. Ashley and others were fuming over her stinging, albeit true, accusations. She reminded the committee that Hayley Larson Schultz was not on trial today. The purpose of the hearing was to conduct Oliver Wilkinson's 'job interview.'

Following Stabler's remarks, each Senate Judiciary Committee member delivered his or her opening remarks along party lines, political theatre of the absurd. By the time the last senator delivered his oratory, it was well past lunchtime. Ashley adjourned for lunch—promising Hayley's opening remarks were next on the agenda.

Zack took Hayley and Joel for a light lunch at a restaurant near the Capitol. Zack wondered if Hayley had any questions about the morning session; she did not. He told her Senator Stabler would introduce her in the afternoon and read her curriculum vitae into the record. Zack also made sure Hayley understood Democratic senators would be asking their own questions, but Republican senators would defer to Andrea Gartner, who Zack knew and respected.

"She's tough, but she's fair, and she is normally a victim's advocate. It's kind of strange she took this assignment. I must presume she has an anti-Hayley and pro-Wilkinson agenda, which I find surprising. She's not your friend. Don't let her lull you into a false sense of security. She'll probably try to get you to admit you didn't pursue a case and dropped the charges. We discussed this—let her have it with both barrels." Zack counseled.

The rest of their lunch was spent discussing Hayley's career, Zack's strong Democratic roots, Joel's independence, the recent fortunes of Detroit, and the misfortunes of its sports teams. It was showtime!

They returned to the hearing room at the appointed time, despite being again accosted by the gathering crowd outside the Capitol. The police had the whole morning to tame the crowd. Entrance into the committee room was a relative breeze.

Members of the committee filed in, and Ashley called the committee to order. Senator Stabler read Hayley's impressive curriculum vitae into the record and introduced her to her fellow committee members. With introductions out of the way, Hayley Larson Schultz was invited to give her opening remarks.

Her remarks were substantially consistent with her letter and conversations with Zack, Joel, and the select few others she shared her tragic story. The crowd and the committee were mesmerized. The incident was twenty-two years ago but so traumatic and so compelling it sounded as if it happened yesterday. Hayley Larson Schultz was no political plant. She experienced a profound, life-changing trauma, and those in attendance were hanging on her every word.

When she completed her opening remarks, it was Ashley's turn to ask questions. He swore the witness and deferred to Andrea Gartner.

Her independence or lack thereof is about to be revealed. Still, she's a strange choice. Zack was puzzled.

"Mrs. Schultz, coming here and testifying about events like these is very difficult. You and I both counsel rape victims for a living. We *know* how hard this is. So, I am very grateful to you for your strength and bravery in coming forward," Gartner began.

Hayley started to relax. *So far, so good.*

Stay on your guard, Hayley, Zack silently urged.

"Sexual violence is a serious problem in our country, which, unfortunately, goes largely unreported. According to the Center for Disease Control, one in three women will experience some form of sexual violence in her lifetime, and of those, about sixty percent go unreported. I do not want this hearing to deter the reporting of these types of crimes. No woman wants to be victimized twice. Most of us are old enough to remember Anita Hill. We will try not to repeat that process here today, so thank you, Mrs. Schultz, for being here."

"Thank you for inviting me," Hayley responded.

"I have read your letter to Senator Stabler and a transcript of your recorded statement to your attorney, Zachary Blake. Mr. Blake, do we have your permission to place those two items into the record to shorten things here today?"

"I have no objection, Ms. Gartner," Zack concurred.

"Without objection, Mr. Chairman?" Gartner requested.

Mark M. Bello   167

"The letter and recorded statement are hereby admitted without objection." Ashley ruled.

"Thank you, Mr. Chairman. Now, in your recorded statement to Mr. Blake, you indicate Judge Wilkinson engaged in inappropriate sexual behavior at a party twenty-two years ago, is that correct?"

"Yes."

"And does that statement and your letter to Senator Stabler accurately detail the behavior we are here to discuss?"

"Yes, but this is not only about sexual assault," Hayley charged.

Gartner appeared surprised by Hayley's answer. She glanced at Senator Ashley, who shrugged and turned to his assistant again.

"Let's focus on sexual assault for a moment. How old were you at the time of this alleged assault?"

"Sixteen."

"And you were at this party without your parents' knowledge, correct?"

"Correct." *Where is she getting this stuff?* Hayley glanced over to Zack, who motioned for her to relax.

"Were you intoxicated that evening?"

"I had a few drinks, I guess."

"Even though you were underage?"

"Yes."

"Did you drink a lot back then?"

"Certainly not."

"Do any drugs?"

"No."

"Would it be fair to say your experience with alcohol and drugs was, shall we say, experimental at that time?"

"I didn't do drugs," Hayley repeated.

"Alcohol, then."

"Alcohol, then, what?"

"Experimental?"

Hayley shook her head in frustration.

"I suppose."

"Yes or no?"

"Yes."

"You went up to the master bathroom that night?"

"Yes."

"You drank some alcoholic beverages and did not have complete control of your faculties. Is that correct?"

"No, that is *not* correct. I testified I drank some—I was in control of my faculties and have not testified otherwise."

Way to go, Hayley, Zack smiled. *Keep it up, kid!*

Gartner continued to test her resolve and her memory of the events of that evening. Gartner got Hayley to admit she was not raped, her genitalia were not touched, and she ingested at least three alcoholic beverages. Gartner also questioned whether it was possible someone at the party spiked her drink, making her more intoxicated than she realized. This was not a trial. The question was highly speculative, but neither Hayley nor Zack could do much about it. The rules of evidence did not apply to a congressional hearing. Gartner knew this and took advantage of the lax standards.

The questions droned on, forcing Hayley to discuss how she came to be at the party, how she knew Marbury and Wilkinson, her trip to the bathroom, and the attack itself, in agonizing detail. She displayed a remarkable memory, a mostly calm demeanor, but there were also moments of confusion where she couldn't remember if Shane did this or if Oliver did that. Apparently, Gartner's strategy, orchestrated by Ashley, was to blame most of the bad stuff on Marbury. Wilkinson was depicted as too inebriated to participate or to have a conscience memory of the attack. While this strategy might embarrass the candidate, it would not subject him to criminal charges and might not be enough to deny him the nomination. His lack of recall might even justify his testimony he'd never been charged with a crime. Stabler was not pleased. Zack was not familiar with the protocol, but he decided protocol be damned.

"Mr. Chairman, you promised not to repeat the mistakes of past committees and provide Mrs. Schultz with a fair and respectful hearing. She is not on trial here. This is a hearing intended to assess the qualifications and credibility of Oliver Wilkinson for a seat on the Supreme Court. These questions are starting to sound like a criminal trial cross-examination. I would like to place my objection on the record."

"This is not a court of law, Mr. Blake. Your objection is noted for the record, but I see no harm in examining Mrs. Schultz's mental state on the evening in question or her memory of events. Please continue, Ms. Gartner," Ashley ruled.

Hayley testified she was terrified in that bathroom as Shane and Oliver entered, locked the door behind them, confronted, and terrorized her. She was a minor, certain she was about to be gang-raped by two wealthy, entitled adults who wouldn't take no for an answer. Oliver and Shane both groped her, ripped off articles of her clothing, and exposed themselves. She claimed she was not drunk, but Shane and Oliver were visibly intoxicated and may have been on drugs. When she tried to scream for help, they turned up the volume on the music playing over the home's sound system or put their hands over her mouth and nose to cut off her breathing. Most of all, she recalled their taunting, maniacal laughter.

She indicated she was testifying, not out of vengeance, but out of civic duty to tell this committee what happened twenty-two years ago. She was ashamed and embarrassed that she put herself in that position.

When the Wilkinson family used its influence to persuade the West Bloomfield Police not to prosecute, Hayley convinced herself this was for the best. She tried to move on and pretend the assault didn't happen. That proved impossible, though, as the incident haunted her through her college days and afterward and substantially impacted her career, marriage, and sex life.

Hayley provided the names of several partygoers to be invited to testify, including Shane Marbury, Jared Wilkinson, Sabrina Page, Lauren Bortnick, and Amy Sanders. She invited the committee to ask her husband or parents to testify, as they had also known about Oliver Wilkinson for years. Committee members and the audience were spellbound. Gartner ran out of questions, failing to rattle the irrepressible Hayley Schultz.

Each Democratic senator lobbed a few softball questions and enjoyed his or her moment in the limelight. Finally, Hayley requested the opportunity to make a few closing remarks, which Chairman Ashley readily granted.

"Once the media discovered my identity, I've had many sleepless nights. Reporters have camped out at our residence, forcing us to temporarily move out. There have been death threats and protests. But, I have also received a tremendous outpour of support. My life has been picked apart by the media. People I don't even know have judged, criticized, and accused me of some sort of political bias. I want this committee and everyone in America to understand that no one can buy my silence or perjury. I am no politician's pawn. I have and will continue to speak the truth about that incident.

"Thousands of people whose lives have been impacted by sexual violence have come forward to share their experiences and to thank me for coming forward. Aside from the events I described from twenty-two years ago, these past few weeks have been the most difficult of my life. I want to thank my attorney, Zachary Blake, for his advice and counsel. I especially want to thank my husband, Joel, for his unwavering love and support. I could not have gotten through this without them.

"My motives for coming forward are pure. Decision-makers should know who Oliver Wilkinson is before they put him on the United States Supreme Court. My goal in coming forward was to provide facts, hopefully leading to a serious discussion about sexual assault and whether people guilty of predatory behavior should be appointed to high political or judicial office.

"It is not my duty to answer this important question as it relates to Oliver Wilkinson; it is yours. My duty is to be truthful in my statements and responses before this committee, and I have done my duty. Thank you for the opportunity to be heard, Mr. Chairman."

"You are welcome, Mrs. Schultz. By the way, the questioning is over, but I have one more question or issue to ask you about. Would that be okay?"

Hayley turned to Zack, who shrugged and signaled it was up to her.

"Yes, Mr. Chairman. What is it?"

"Would you be willing to submit to a polygraph exam if submitted by professionals chosen by this committee?"

Hayley turned back to Zack. He placed his hand on the microphone, and a sharp shrill filled the Senate chamber.

"Sorry, Mr. Chairman."

"That's all right, Mr. Blake. Hard on the ears but happens all the time," Ashley smiled.

Hayley and Zack discussed the request. Polygraphs are not admissible in court because they can be beaten and are not entirely reliable. However, if Hayley told the truth, the test would be likely to confirm that truth. They agreed to permit the test.

"Yes, Mr. Chairman, I would be willing to submit to a polygraph examination. I would also invite Judge Wilkinson to do so as well," Hayley ad-libbed, to Zack's considerable delight.

What a remarkable woman!

Chairman Ashley grimaced at the suggestion. "Thank you for your appearance and candor here today, Mrs. Schultz. The witness is excused." Ashley checked his watch.

"Due to the lateness in the hour, I suggest we adjourn and pick up with Judge Wilkinson's opening remarks and rebuttal testimony in the morning. Does that work for everyone? I hear no objection, so we are adjourned until tomorrow morning at nine o'clock sharp."

Chapter Thirty

Oliver Wilkinson grabbed the remote control, turned off the television, and flung the remote across the hotel room. It hit the far wall, putting a serious dent in the drywall and shattering the remote.

"That's a mature and intelligent response. Want to discuss your judicial temperament?" Leo Lenard sniped. Lenard, Dan McGinnis, and Judge Wilkinson were holed up in a posh hotel room at the Watergate. They just watched Hayley Larson's testimony.

"Softballs! They lobbed her softballs! I thought this prosecutor . . . what's her name? Gardner?" Wilkinson fumed.

"Gartner," McGinnis corrected.

"Who the fuck cares? I thought she was supposed to be a barracuda! She was too fucking soft on that bitch. All that shit about attempted rape, cover-ups, and being rich and entitled— our so-called 'friends' on the committee made me look like a total asshole!" .

"We don't care if you look like an asshole, Oliver. In fact, admit it, man, you *are* an asshole. All we care about is that no one proves you're an attempted rapist or a perjurer. So far, no one has. Once you're a Supreme Court Justice, *if* that happens, this will go away." Lenard speculated.

Wilkinson calmed. "All right, I guess. I suppose you're right about that. So, what's the plan—another *murder*? Who came up with *that* lame idea? If they tie this to the nomination, you're looking at the *fall* guy!

"What were you thinking? On top of that, your guy fucked the whole thing up. I can't believe this shit!"

"Gal," McGinnis corrected.

"Huh?"

"The assassin is a lady and one of the best in the business. She has no record, no blueprint of any kind. On paper, she doesn't even exist. They will never prove the two deaths resulted from anything but natural causes." McGinnis explained.

"Does she know she fucked up? You know, executed the wrong guy? Does she come with a fucking money-back guarantee?"

"We haven't been able to reach her yet. I'm sure she'll correct her mistake if we choose to have her do so."

"*If*? Why wouldn't we want her to fix this? In for a penny, in for a pound, no?"

"No. We are now sitting on two heart attack deaths within twenty-four hours of each other. One was a witness, and the other a friend of a witness to the investigation. Another death is extremely risky." Lenard opined.

"So is Marbury's mouth," Wilkinson cackled. "What about some type of undetectable accident? Can't he disappear or some such shit?"

"We have no evidence Marbury planned to talk in the first place. And he *has* disappeared. He's in the wind. We can't find him, which means they can't find him either. There is a very short window before the committee votes. I say we lay low and let sleeping dogs lie. You testify tomorrow. You can deny all of the Schultz woman's allegations, or you can have some remote memory of an incident and blame the whole thing on Marbury." Lenard was pacing and rubbing his hands together as he concocted strategy.

"I like that idea, I guess. But what if he's watching? He won't take kindly to me blaming him for everything. Maybe it will draw him to the committee."

"And into our assassin's waiting arms?" McGinnis sneered.

"That's a chicken-egg situation, dammit! It's extremely risky, arrogant, and dangerous to think we can get to him before he contacts someone to offer testimony." Wilkinson barked. "I vote for deaf, dumb, and blind. I wasn't there. I don't know what the hell Hayley is talking about."

"And if they ask you about a polygraph?"

"There are ways to train to beat those—that's why they're not admissible in court." Wilkinson showboated his judicial knowledge.

"Are you familiar with techniques to take them and beat them?" Lenard had a germ of an idea.

"No, but I know people who can help with countermeasures and the like."

Lenard began to re-think his idea.

"That would involve bringing in one more co-conspirator to the party."

"The guy I'm thinking of is reliable," Oliver countered.

"Even if he's looking at federal conspiracy charges?"

"Well . . ."

"Let's see if Schultz takes a polygraph and passes. We won't need this unless that happens," McGinnis suggested.

"True. I agree with that. Oliver?"

"Whatever . . ." Wilkinson groused. "What about Marbury? I don't like loose ends."

"Our people will continue to search for him. He hasn't used a credit card, purchased an airplane or train ticket. He's around here somewhere. We'll find him and deal with him," McGinnis promised. He blustered for Wilkinson's sake. He needed the judge to keep his wits about him.

"Anything else?" Lenard studied the two men.

"Yeah. Call down to the front desk and order a new television remote. Tell them we had an accident. I'll pay for the repairs," Wilkinson offered.

"Will do. Good luck tomorrow, Oliver. Knock'em dead!" Lenard cheered.

"Funny guy."

Chapter Thirty-One

The following morning, Hayley, Joel, and Zack walked to the Capitol. They flashed their temporary credentials and were granted passage. Some reporters recognized them and tried to get a statement but were rebuffed by Capitol security.

Zack retired early the night before. Hayley and Joel enjoyed a quiet supper in the sanctuary of their hotel room. Hayley was exhausted, and they, too, retired early. None of the three discussed Hayley's testimony following the hearing, nor did they watch television to view pundits' reactions. Hayley told the truth. She knew commentators would be divided along party lines. None of them had any credibility. She didn't care what any of them reported.

Hayley hoped for assigned, prominent seating. She wanted to see and be seen by Oliver Wilkinson, theorizing it would be more difficult for him to lie to her face. Hayley Schultz was the only person present who knew that Wilkinson would lie to the committee. Zack decided not to burst her bubble by telling her a criminal and pathological liar wouldn't care who was standing in front of him as he spun his deceitful tales. As it turned out, they *were* given priority seating, courtesy of Senator Diane Stabler.

As they sat down, committee members began to meander in. Some acknowledged Hayley with a wave or nod of the head. Senator Stabler walked up and greeted them before engaging in conversation with Zack. The crowd began to stir and murmur. Hayley turned to see Oliver Wilkinson enter the chamber. He smiled and waved to his enduring followers, conservatives who were willing to sacrifice any spiritual, ethical, and moral issue they cherished to appoint a right-winger like Wilkinson to the United States Supreme Court. The irony was completely lost on these people.

The crowd settled, committee members ended their light banter, and everyone took their seats. Chairman Ashley called the confirmation hearing to order with a slam of his gavel and addressed Wilkinson.

"Would you please rise, sir?" Wilkinson pushed out of his chair and stood. He raised his right hand without a request to do so.

"Do you solemnly swear or affirm your testimony before this committee will be the truth, the whole truth, and nothing but the truth, so help you God?"

"I do," Wilkinson muttered.

"You may be seated, sir. I understand you have some opening remarks to share?"

"I do."

"Proceed."

"Mr. Chairman, members of the committee, and Mrs. Schultz. This is my statement. No one has read it—no one has helped me write it. It is mine and mine alone. It comes from my heart and my memory.

"Following Hayley Larson Schultz's public allegations against me, I searched my soul and my memory, trying to recall an event even close to the one she alleges. I can think of no such incident and no reason for her to accuse me of such behavior. It was a long time ago, but her accusations against me are not true. Maybe something happened to her that evening. Perhaps it was Mr. Marbury; the man alleged to be my so-called co-actor. I cannot speak to anyone else's conduct, but I know that I did not sexually assault Mrs. Schultz. In fact, I have never sexually assaulted *any* woman, ever.

"Did I throw wild parties when I was young? Yes. Did I drink or have consensual sex at those parties? Yes. I was a college student. College students do dumb things. They like to party and drink, sometimes, excessively. They like the ladies, too, but most men I knew treated them with respect. I know I did.

"In my youth, I liked to drink. I drank mostly beer—I like beer. On a few occasions back in the day, I drank so much I blacked out. However, I would *never* disrespect or sexually assault a woman, no matter how drunk I was. Like most college students, as I grew older, I became more responsible. I studied law, became a lawyer, and then a judge. Such behavior ended. I became an adult and a responsible citizen.

"Since these allegations surfaced, my good name has been dragged through the mud. I have been labeled a sexual predator. Additional false and vicious accusations have damaged my reputation. Where do I go to reclaim my good name and my reputation, Mr. Chairman?

"I may have known Hayley Larson when she was in high school. I believe she was friendly with my brother. Talk to him. Talk to people who know me now and knew me then. Listen to the people who I grew up with, worked with, or who were friends and acquaintances. Even if I threw the party Hayley references, I never engaged in inappropriate sexual conduct with her or any other woman. I understand some of the partygoers were located and gave statements to investigators or the FBI. No one can testify they saw Oliver Wilkinson sexually assault Hayley Larson. No one!"

This statement was technically correct because Shane Marbury was never interviewed by the police and never gave a statement to the committee, the FBI, Micah Love, or anyone else investigating the incident. Oliver Wilkinson was now one hundred percent invested in the silence of Shane Marbury. Wilkinson continued.

"Since my nomination a few months ago, the extreme left-wing of the Democratic Party has engaged in a political hit job, a massive smear campaign to undermine my record as a judge and destroy my credibility. They needed to do something and were willing to do *anything* to derail my nomination. While I acknowledge this body has an obligation to advise and consent, it does not have the right to distort, lie, cheat, or *steal* a nomination. This process has engaged in gross partisanship, and this committee no longer has any credibility. All of you should be *embarrassed*.

"This proceeding has sullied my good name and my impeccable legal and judicial credentials, built through two decades of hard work and public service at the highest judiciary levels in state and federal governments. The consequences of these proceedings will extend long past this hearing, whether I am confirmed or not. This orchestrated character assassination will have a chilling effect on future candidates for judicial, legislative, and executive positions, regardless of political party. Good people will not wish to undergo this type of life examination, this level of scrutiny, and that is sad for our country. Hear my message, loud and clear: I will not withdraw my name. I will not quit. You've tried hard to defeat me, but I am still here, still standing, and I will defend my record and my good name until my dying day.

"Sexual assault is a serious issue. People who allege sexual assault deserve due process. They deserve to be heard. By the same token, due process also means giving a voice to those who must defend themselves from false accusations and charges. I come from good stock, strong stock. My parents are self-made, and so am I. They taught me the value of respect for the law, a good education, and hard work. I have tried to live by the fine example they have set for me . . ."

Zack rolled his eyes. *What an asshole! His parents set no example. They made their money the old-fashioned way—they inherited it! Everyone knows that! Who is this guy trying to kid? His folks were so busy living life in the fast lane they had no time for their kids. They threw money instead of offering love and kindness. That's how you create an Oliver Wilkinson.*

Wilkinson was finishing up his opening remarks.

"I have an unblemished twenty-year career without anything, not a single charge even remotely mimicking the charges levied here. This last-second ambush speaks for and smells of itself. It stinks to high heaven. I am innocent of this charge. It is not who I was, nor who I am. I have been appointed to multiple state and federal courts at all levels, with no mention of these twenty-two-year-old allegations. Where was Hayley Larson during those appointments and promotions? What's changed? I'll tell you — *politics* have changed!

"I have been a good judge and a good person my whole career. I did not do this to Hayley Larson or anyone else. Perhaps something happened to her. Perhaps in her own drunken stupor, she's confused. Hayley, I am not angry with you. I'm sure that something happened to you, but, for the record, Hayley Larson Schultz is confused if she truly believes I was involved.

"I had many female friends in high school and college. Thirty of these women have submitted letters attesting to my character. I demand they be made part of the record. Furthermore, the majority of my staff members are female. Some have been with me since the beginning of my legal and judicial careers. Not one female employee has lodged even a whiff of a claim of sexual harassment or misconduct. Think about that, ladies and gentlemen. Thank you, Mr. Chairman, members of this committee. I am ready to answer your questions."

"Thank you, Judge Wilkinson, for that stirring opening. I'm sorry you must submit to this, but these are serious charges. As we did with Mrs. Schultz, the Republican members will be yielding their time and referring their questions to Ms. Gartner."

Ashley invited the seasoned prosecutor to come forward and question the witness.

"Ms. Gartner, if you please?"

"Thank you, Mr. Chairman. Judge Wilkinson, good morning."

"Good morning."

"Before I question the witness, I want to make sure all of the committee members have received a copy of the definition of sexual behavior."

All committee members nodded their heads.

"Judge? Do you have a copy?"

Wilkinson began to sort through papers sitting on the table in front of him.

"I believe it's here somewhere . . . here it is! Yes, I have it."

"I'd like you to review the definition and tell me when you're ready. While you're doing that, Judge Wilkinson, I'd like to ask you, has anyone told you or provided you with a copy of the questions I plan to ask you today?"

"No, and I've finished reviewing the definition."

"If this is embarrassing to you, Judge, I apologize. However, I assure you, these questions are necessary. They go to the crux of this matter."

"I'll be fine."

"I'd like to refer to two specific references in the definition before you. Examples of sexual behavior include rubbing or grinding your genitals against someone, whether clothed or unclothed. The definition does not require sexual motivation— the behavior could include a person who might be joking, but the other doesn't take it that way. Understood?"

"Yes." Wilkinson lowered his head. He remembered well his time in the bathroom with the beautiful Hayley Larson. He remembered pushing up against her and grinding her, fully dressed. He remembered how aroused he got and how much he wanted her.

"Judge Wilkinson?" Gartner interrupted his thoughts. "Did you hear the question?"

"I'm sorry about the definition? I already answered."

"No. Perhaps you didn't hear me. I'll ask again. Did you hear or review Mrs. Schultz's testimony?"

"Yes, I did."

"Do you remember the party she referred to?"

"As I indicated in my opening remarks, I liked to party in those days. My brother was in high school, and I attended a local college. Our parents traveled a lot. When they did, it was party time. We threw *lots* of parties, I'm afraid. I don't recall specifics," he lied with the straightest face he could muster.

"Were there regulars at these parties? People who came to them all the time?"

"There were some. Names do not come to mind. My best friend was Shane Marbury. He was at most of the parties."

"Speaking of Shane Marbury, have you seen him recently? Do you know his whereabouts?"

"I haven't seen Shane in a while." This was another lie.

"What is your relationship with Shane now? Are you still friends?"

"I have not seen him in a while. Shane did not go to law school. Once I became a lawyer, we kind of drifted apart. Our lives and careers went in different directions."

"Do you know Sabrina Page?"

"I believe she was friends with my brother, Jared."

"Lauren Bortnick?"

"Same answer."

"Amy Sanders?"

"Same answer."

"Do you recall a specific party your brother, Shane Marbury, Sabrina, Amy, Lauren, and Hayley all attended?"

Whose side is she on?

"No. As I indicated, I have no specific recollection of specific parties. I believe all of those people have, at one time or another, attended a party at our house." Wilkinson decided a little harmless volunteerism might be a nice touch.

"How well did you know Hayley Larson?"

"I believe she was friendly with my brother, Jared. I didn't know her at all. I hardly remembered her or thought of her until I became aware of these allegations," Wilkinson's third lie.

"Judge Wilkinson, would you have a problem delaying these hearings so all of these people can testify?"

"Ms. Gartner, I have been vetted multiple times for multiple public services and judicial appointments and promotions. No one has ever uttered a peep about bad conduct or what you referred to earlier as 'sexual behavior' in high school, college, law school, or at any position I have ever held. I cannot imagine what any of these people might say, but I will defer to the committee about any further delays in this process. I am here. I am well-qualified and ready to serve."

"Certain members on this committee would like a full investigation of these charges, a detailed statement, and perhaps testimony from all of the witnesses."

"That is not for me to decide. The committee decides, and the FBI investigates. I will defer a response to them. I am here defending my good name against these baseless charges. This committee can and will do whatever it wants. This inquiry is a disgrace."

The best defense is a good offense . . .

"And if any of these witnesses testified you were guilty of any behavior that fits the definition of sexual behavior, those witnesses would be lying?"

"Non-consensual, you mean?"

"Yes, I'm sorry, non-consensual."

"Yes, they would be lying. If they are saying non-consensual, then they are lying, wrong, mistaken, or whatever word you choose. This thing is a farce."

"Mrs. Schultz and others have indicated you were extremely drunk at the party at issue. Did you often drink at these parties? Did you get drunk?"

"Yes. I drank. I liked to drink back then. I was a college kid. College kids liked to drink at parties—still do, don't they? Drinking at a party or getting drunk at one is not a crime."

"Did you get drunk?"

"I don't know. There are tests for that sort of thing, but I was never tested. I partied, drank, and felt pretty damned good. Can't say whether I was drunk."

"Ever fall into a whirlpool bath?"

"I don't recall that. I heard Hayley mention it, but I don't recall that."

"Have you ever passed out or blacked out from drinking?"

"I don't remember. I don't think so."

"Are you saying the whirlpool thing didn't happen, or you don't remember it?"

*Shit! Who is this broad working for? They **know** it happened. Jared and those three bitches gave statements to the FBI. How do I answer this?*

"I am aware people have given statements about this whirlpool incident. I don't remember it. I can't say it didn't happen, but I don't remember it. All I can say is I have never sexually assaulted anyone. Not Hayley Larson, not *anyone!*"

Gartner's time expired. Ashley turned the questioning over to Diane Stabler. She immediately went on the attack.

"You've never passed out from drinking? What do you call being pulled out of a whirlpool, totally plowed, and having no memory of the incident?" Stabler was astounded by his declaration.

"I didn't say I don't remember it twenty-two years later because I was drunk. It was a long time ago, that's all. I don't remember it. You are twisting my words to fit your agenda."

"So, you are claiming, under oath, for the record, you have *never* passed out from drinking?"

"Never is a long time. My testimony is that I don't recall ever passing out from drinking."

"Ever wake up in a strange bed, with missing clothes?"

"What? No . . . no . . . what a ridiculous question!" He appeared to search his memory. In reality, the question scared the crap out of him.

Do they have a witness who says otherwise?

"Do you remember any party at any time in your life fitting the description of the party Mrs. Schultz described for this committee?"

"Yes. I already testified to that."

"Judge Wilkinson, doesn't it follow that everything that Mrs. Schultz is telling the truth, and you don't remember it because you were heavily intoxicated?"

"No, dammit! This is a-a-a . . . sham . . . a witch-hunt! I resent these accusations, Mr. Chairman. My record and reputation speak for themselves." Stabler achieved her goal. She rattled him and got him off his game. She pounced.

"Let's discuss specific allegations, shall we? Remember, please, the definition of sexual behavior. Did you grind your body into Mrs. Schultz's body?"

"No—I never did that!"

"Did you put your hands over her face to prevent her from breathing?"

"No, dammit."

"Did you and Shane Marbury rip off her blouse?"

"Not me. I can't speak for Marbury. Maybe something happened between those two, and Hayley is transferring Shane's behavior to me. You'd have to ask him."

"Did you pull off her dress or pants and leave her dressed only in her undergarments?"

"I understand people gave statements that Hayley ran out of a party at my house wearing only her underwear. But I had nothing to do with that. Shane, maybe . . . I really don't recall." Wilkinson looked up at the roof of the chamber.

"Have you ever engaged in sexual behavior with Mrs. Schultz, consensual or non-consensual?"

"No—never!"

"Where is Shane Marbury, Judge Wilkinson?"

"I have no idea."

"Did you have anything to do with his disappearance?"

"I will not dignify that question. Of course not!"

"Are you aware that a good police officer who investigated this incident has suddenly died?"

"I've heard a former West Bloomfield cop died of a heart attack. Is that the officer you're referring to, Senator?"

"Within twenty-four hours of Eric Lorenz's death, a legislative assistant to Shane Marbury also died of a heart attack. Familiar with that story?"

"I saw it on the news."

"Did you have anything to do with either of those deaths?"

"Mr. Chairman!" Wilkinson snapped.

"Senator Stabler, your time has expired. Ms. Gartner?" Ashley sighed.

Back and forth, the questioning continued, with Gartner and Democratic Senate committee members punching and counter-punching. The hearing droned on. Wilkinson alternated between frustrated, calm, angry, and exasperated. He desperately attempted to maintain a level of temperament befitting a federal appeals judge but often failed to do so. The last senator to ask questions was Kristoff Kunesman.

"Judge Wilkinson, twenty-two years ago, did you or any family member move to quash an investigation into the incident that Mrs. Schultz testified about?"

"I know of no such investigation, Senator."

"Are you telling this committee the West Bloomfield Police never investigated Mrs. Schultz's charges?"

"Not to my knowledge."

"If someone completed and executed a sworn statement stating otherwise, would that person be telling the truth?"

"Again, Senator, I have no knowledge of an investigation."

"As a sitting court of appeals judge, would you agree attempted rape and acting to cover up attempted rape are disqualifying actions for a Supreme Court nominee?"

"Yes, Senator. I would."

"Would lying to Congress also be a disqualifying event for the same nominee?"

"It would, yes."

"Mr. Chairman, that's all I have. However, I demand this committee request a full FBI investigation into Mrs. Schultz's allegations and the West Bloomfield Police cover-up. Also, the two deaths and disappearance of a person associated with these hearings."

"Senator, we've been over and over this. Whatever happened twenty-two years ago, Mrs. Schultz requested an opportunity to address the committee. The committee granted her request and gave her considerable latitude and respect. The whole country has now heard her side of the story. Due process required Judge Wilkinson to be allowed to respond. He has now testified he had nothing to do with any of Mrs. Schultz's allegations. She is either mistaken or a liar. I see no reason for further investigations or any delay in voting. I plan to call for a vote in the morning," Senator Ashley pronounced.

This pronouncement buoyed judge Oliver Wilkinson. The Republicans were the majority party and had the votes to confirm, even if every Democrat on the committee voted against him. Tomorrow morning, despite his rendezvous with Hayley Larson now and twenty-two years ago, he would be an Associate Justice of the United States Supreme Court.

I've won! Nothing and no one can stop me now! Hayley, try as you might, you have failed again, bitch!

Everyone in attendance was stunned by Ashley's call for a vote. Democratic senators shouted in protest. Everyone began shouting at once. Ashley, to no avail, pounded his gavel for order. Partisan cheers and jeers erupted from the audience.

The senators broke off into sub-groups as Ashley tried to restore order. Groups of four or six engaged in vigorous debate behind the committee table. In a far corner, two moderate Republican committee members, Senator Jerome Drake from Arizona and Senator Sharon Cousins from Maine, were engaged in a serious conversation. When they finished, they walked over to Ashley and engaged him in a heated debate. A look of surprise crossed Ashley's face, followed by angst and harsh words. For their part, the two moderates took Ashley's best punches and were still standing, side-by-side, arguing their position, whatever it was.

Their discussion suddenly ended, with Ashley noticeably upset. He slammed his gavel a few more times and covered the microphone, which caused another shrill feedback, worse than the last one. The trick worked, and the room quieted.

"Ladies and gentlemen, I have a damn announcement to make! Quiet, please."

A tense hush filled the room as everyone awaited the chairman's announcement.

"A few minutes ago, I announced that tomorrow morning I would call for a vote on the Wilkinson nomination. I have decided my announcement was a bit hasty. Certain senators on this committee feel there is no harm in delaying the vote to allow the FBI time to complete its investigation. Upon completion, if the investigation reveals relevant information or witnesses, these senators believe the committee should consider the information and invite any witnesses revealed to testify before this committee. While I am opposed to such an investigation, the waste of taxpayer dollars, and this committee's time, I am only one senator and one vote. At this time, I am forced to poll the senators and ask for their 'yes' or 'no' votes on a resolution to table this hearing for two weeks while the FBI investigates. The clerk can record my 'nay' vote," Ashley grimaced.

"Senator Stabler?"

"Aye."

"Senator Finch?"

"Nay."

"Senator Kunesman?"

"Aye."

"Senator Drake?"

"Aye."

The Republican senators on the committee and conservatives in the audience were stunned.

Did he say 'Aye?'

Pandemonium erupted again. Oliver Wilkinson sat forward in his chair and cradled his head in his hands, shaking it in frustration. He was devastated. His certain victory was suddenly snatched away. The Democrats needed one more Republican 'Aye.' Seven votes later, they got a deciding "Aye" from Senator Sharon Cousins of Maine.

Again, the audience broke out in conflicting shouts of glee and anger. Neither Chairman Ashley nor the Capitol Police could restore order. Above the uproar, Ashley called for a voice vote to adjourn, and the hearing was closed. Reporters rushed the podium, shouting out questions, focusing upon Drake and Cousins.

Reporters unable to reach Drake and Cousins descended upon Oliver Wilkinson and bombarded him with questions. He uttered a terse 'no comment' to every question thrown his way and slowly exited the chamber.

Hayley, Zack, and Joel engaged the audience and press members, answering as many questions as possible. All of them heaped praise on Cousins and Drake for their courage, common sense, and for simply acknowledging the importance of this nomination and the seriousness of Hayley's allegations. Thanks to these brave senators, there would be no rush to judgment in Judge Oliver Wilkinson's confirmation process to the United States Supreme Court.

Chapter Thirty-Two

Hayley, Joel, and Zack returned to Detroit in triumph. They achieved what many pundits believed was impossible. While they hadn't yet defeated Wilkinson's nomination before a conservative majority committee, they succeeded in delaying the hearing. Furthermore, the Judiciary Committee ordered a comprehensive investigation into Hayley's allegations of attempted rape and subsequent police department cover-up. Zack expressed confidence justice would prevail if investigators were given sufficient time to conduct a thorough inquiry.

Two days after his return from Washington, Zack was burning the midnight oil, playing catch up on several important cases that the Schultz situation caused him to neglect. He was the only person left in the office. A buzzer sounded.

Someone is at the front door.

Zack looked at his watch—ten o'clock in the evening.

Who'd knock on a law office door at ten o'clock in the evening?

Zack walked to his wall safe, turned the knob, and pulled out a small pistol. He was not a huge Second Amendment advocate. However, when you're Zachary Blake, you're a target, and you're often alone in your office at ten o'clock in the evening.

Zack stepped out of his office and ventured over to the front entrance. A dim porch light lit the entrance, permitting Zack to make out a solitary man standing at the door. He couldn't make out the man's face.

The lobby lights were illuminated, leaving Zack was visible and vulnerable. The man waved. Zack, instinctively, waved back and ventured closer to the door. The man's face became visible. Clare once showed him a fax of a driver's license photo Pete Westmore transmitted to her in the car. Shane Marbury was standing at the front entrance of Zachary Blake and Associates, LLC.

Marbury looked like a homeless person. His clothes were disheveled, his hair a mess and oily. He hadn't shaved in days.

Zack opened the front door of his office. Marbury's body odor was almost overpowering, but Zack invited him in anyway.

"Shane Marbury?" Zack stated the obvious.

"Yes, sir, and I recognize you from all those press photos. You're Zachary Blake. Just the man I want to see. We need to talk."

"Yes, we do, but let's get you cleaned up first."

"Thanks. I appreciate it. I must reek."

Zack squeezed his nose with his thumb and index finger and waved his other hand through the air, fanning the odor. He smiled and led Marbury through his office and into his private bathroom. The bathroom was large and well-appointed, with mahogany cabinets, stone tile, granite counters, and a large shower with multiple showerheads.

"You look about my size. I might be a bit smaller, but there should be a decent change of clothing in that closet over there." Zack pointed to a door on the opposite side of the commode.

"I just want to talk, Mr. Blake. I'm in deep trouble. I need your help."

"With all due respect, Mr. Marbury. You are ripe, sir. How long has it been since you've had a bath or a change of clothes?"

"I've been on the run and in hiding, Mr. Blake. It's been a while."

"Well, I'm not going anywhere until we talk. No one but me knows you're here, and no one would have expected you to come here of all places. You're safe with me. While you're in the shower, I'll call home to let my wife know I'll be late. I'll order some carryout, and we'll get you cleaned up and fed. What's your preference? Deli, pizza, or Chinese?"

"Thank you for your kindness and hospitality, Mr. Blake. This is unexpected and unnecessary. If you insist, pizza, I guess."

"Pizza it is," Zack chirped. "Go get cleaned up. I'll be in the next room, my office, by the way. What do you like on your pizza?"

"Pepperoni? Thanks again."

"Pepperoni is fine. No thanks necessary." Zack closed the door, telephoned Little Caesars, and ordered a large pepperoni pizza, an order of chicken wings, and a two-liter bottle of Diet

Coke for delivery to his office address. He thought about calling
Micah Love or Clare Gibson but decided to hold off until he had
a chance to grill Marbury. He sat down and combed through a
couple of files.

Twenty minutes later, Marbury came out of the bathroom,
wearing an old jogging suit. Zack recalled the suit, a bit large for
him but a perfect fit for Marbury.

Good choice.

"Feel better?"

"Much, thank you, Mr. Blake. We need to talk."

"Call me Zack, and yes, we do."

The front door buzzed. Marbury tensed. Zack pressed the
intercom.

"Yes?"

"Delivery for Mr. Blake," came the electronic reply.

"It's just the pizza, Mr. Marbury. Relax." Shane Marbury
drew a breath and let it out.

"I'm very jumpy these days," Marbury managed.

"I'll bet you are. Stay here. I'll be right back." Zack walked
out of the office, let the delivery man in, and took care of
business, leaving the guy a large tip. Zack returned to his office
with a large pizza box, the wings, and a large bottle of Diet
Coke. He set the food and drinks on a small conference table in
his office and reached above the table for some paper plates,
plastic cups, knives, and forks.

"I don't know about you, Mr. Marbury, but I'm starving.
Let's eat and talk at the same time."

"Call me Shane, Mr. Blake."

"Only if you call me Zack."

"Zack, it is, then. I don't know where to begin."

"Take your time. Let's get some food into you. You can start
wherever you want."

Marbury took a plate and a slice of pizza, then dug into a
chicken wing. Next, he took a cup and poured some Diet Coke.
Zack did the same, and the two men began to eat and drink.
Marbury was starving. He scarfed down several pieces of pizza
and most of the wings in less than ten minutes. With his hunger
satisfied, he was ready to talk.

"Shane, you mind if I record our discussion?" Zack pulled out his phone, hit the record app, and started to record their discussion.

"No, I don't mind if you record this. I think I am in serious trouble, Zack. Someone is trying to kill me."

"What makes you think that, Shane?"

"My legislative assistant, Ira Gallant, was murdered in my office last week. I believe the murderer was looking to kill *me*. I was the target."

"I'm aware of Mr. Gallant's misfortune, Shane, but according to the coroner's office, he died of natural causes, a heart attack, I believe." Zack was testing his knowledge.

"I was *there*, Zack. I *witnessed* the murder."

"You were where Shane?" Zack was officially intrigued. Shane had his complete attention.

"At my office. Ira and I were working on a presentation for the following morning. I was tired and decided to go home. Ira promised to put the finishing touches on the project. We're on the fourth floor. I took the elevator down to the lobby and realized I'd forgotten my keys. I went back up, returned to our office suite, and heard some voices and sounds coming from my office. Frankly, it sounded like someone was having sex in my office.

"I got pissed. I wanted to catch these guys in the act. I walked across the hall and entered the opposite office from a back entrance. You can see into my office from there.

"Ira was at my desk. He was watching porn on my computer. I don't know how else to say this, but he was masturbating at my desk. I was furious. I was about to walk in, embarrass the hell out of him, and give him a piece of my mind. Suddenly, this gorgeous chick shows up, sneaks up behind him, and sticks a hypodermic needle in his neck. Ira starts convulsing.

"I duck under the desk, pull out my phone, and start videoing. The woman holds him from behind until he stops convulsing, turns around to face me, which scared the shit out of me because I thought she saw me, and then she calmly walks out of the office like murdering a person was *nothing*. A walk in the park, Zack! She had to be some sort of paid *assassin!*

"I was terrified. I couldn't move. Shit, I couldn't *breathe*. I just stayed put for several minutes. Finally, I got up the nerve to walk toward my office and around Ira. He was dead—I think the woman mistook Ira for me."

"Why do you think that, Shane?" Zack wanted the story to come from Marbury. He did not want to put words in his mouth.

"Because of Hayley Larson, Oliver Wilkinson and the Supreme Court, Zack. Come on, are you *kidding* me? You're Hayley's lawyer, right? You know exactly why I'm terrified and why I think this killer was after me."

"I do, Shane, but I need to hear *you* say it. I can't put the words in your mouth. If this woman was an assassin, who do you think hired her?"

"*Seriously,* Zack? It was *Wilkinson,* Dammit, Wilkinson, or someone working to make sure he becomes the next Justice of the Supreme Court."

"But, why, Shane? Why would he or they want to kill *you*?" Zack probed. This was like pulling teeth. *Out with it, you piece of shit!*

Marbury hesitated, then instantly understood. *He wants me to admit the attempted rape of Hayley Larson.*

"You *know* why, Zack. It's because I am the only one in the world, besides Hayley Larson and Oliver Wilkinson, who knows what happened in that bathroom twenty-two years ago."

"What bathroom? What happened twenty-two years ago?"

"So, we're going to play games? Okay, I'll play along. You want this to come from me, is that it? Okay, here it is. Oliver and I were extremely drunk and frisky twenty-two years ago. We were at a party at his parents' house. We saw Hayley go up the stairs and followed her into Ollie's parents' bathroom. We trapped her in the room, ripped off her clothes, and tried to fuck her. We hoped she wanted to have some fun. Instead, I think she was terrified.

"We were *plastered* Zack—I didn't think about what I was doing. Nothing bad happened, though—a bunch of kids came to the door and prevented things from getting worse—saved Hayley and saved our asses too. Here we are, twenty-two years later, and

Oliver wants to be a Supreme Court Justice. Me, Hayley, and a twenty-two-year-old incident stand in his way.

"That night has haunted me ever since—affected every aspect of my life. Now, it might *cost* me my life. Oliver Wilkinson is trying to *kill* me to shut me up. Hayley Larson is in danger, too. We need protection, Zack."

"All right, Shane. Thanks for being so candid. Are you willing to talk to the FBI? Testify at the confirmation hearing if we protect you?"

Marbury hesitated, sorting things out in his mind.

"Yes, I am," he concluded. "Will I get witness protection or some such shit?"

"You'll have to talk to the FBI about that. I know people there, though. I can try to negotiate witness protection."

"You would do that for me?"

"Frankly? No, I *wouldn't* do that for you. But I *would* do it for Hayley Larson Schultz. And I'd do it to prevent Oliver Wilkinson from ever being considered for the Supreme Court."

"Same thing, I guess."

"Hardly the same thing, Shane, but the same *result*," Zack grumbled.

"So, what now?"

"May I call my contact at the FBI?"

"I guess that would be okay. It's for the immunity?"

"Who promised you immunity?"

"Isn't that part of a witness protection deal?"

"It can be. I have a conflict here, Shane. I can't be negotiating an immunity deal for you. I represent Hayley Schultz."

"Can't you make an exception, this one time?"

"It is not for me to decide. It's Hayley's decision."

"She probably hates my guts."

"Who would blame her? I'm willing to talk with her, though, and try to get her to waive the conflict. Do you want me to talk with her, or would you rather I refer you to another attorney?"

"Talk to her."

"First things first. Finish eating while I call the FBI."

"It's your rodeo, Zack. Thanks."

Chapter Thirty-Three

The Oakland and Ingham County Medical Examiners, with assists from the FBI crime lab, completed and issued their reports. The causes of death in both the Sylvan and Lansing cases were identical. Eric Lorenz and Ira Gallant died from advanced coronary artery disease, resulting in a heart attack.

While the fact that two young men, with no family history of heart disease and no previous symptoms, died of the same cause within twenty-four hours of each other was suspicious, none of the professionals could find a sign of foul play. Furthermore, no drug or substance was known to either medical examiner that could cause advanced coronary artery disease and a heart attack. The official ruling of the medical examiners was listed as "natural causes, coronary artery disease."

Lenard and McGinnis delivered this bit of good news to Oliver Wilkinson.

"What the fuck do I care? I didn't have them killed. That was *your* fucking brainstorm. Any luck with Marbury?"

"We have not been able to locate him. We have operatives in the field, combing the Lansing and West Bloomfield communities," Lenard reported.

"West Bloomfield?"

"He has family there. It's the next logical place," McGinnis surmised.

"Are the old cops going to be a problem?"

"They've been well-paid, and they know what kind of power they are dealing with. I think we're safe," Lenard surmised.

"Unless Shane comes forward." Oliver shivered at the thought.

"He also knows what kind of power he's dealing with," Lenard smirked.

"So, what do we do now? Sit and wait for the FBI to find Shane and nail my ass to the wall?"

"No, I told you, we'll take care of things. By the way, our lady friend, the one who causes heart attacks, is on her way back to Michigan to correct certain mistakes," Lenard smiled.

"It's time to go on offense. We have arranged a media blitz. You have interviews on Fox News, Bloomberg, and CNN. Republican senators, President Golding, Leo, and I will be crisscrossing networks screaming about the crazy Democrats and their obstructionist tactics.

"It is time to get our base worked up and put some serious pressure on these people to vote. There's a lot of bullshit floating around, but without Marbury, it's your word against Hayley's. In the end, her word won't be enough to prevent the nomination from going forward," McGinnis concluded.

"From your mouth to God's ears—that's the best idea I've heard yet."

Over the next several days, the Republicans implemented their media blitz strategy while the Democrats struggled for equal airtime. Wilkinson, Lenard, McGinnis, and their ace in the hole, President Stephen Golding, were everywhere. They didn't care about the venue. They ventured into the lion's den with CNN, MSNBC, and all the cable news stations and shows, regardless of their constituency.

Wilkinson granted a no-holds-barred interview to Marsha McCall at Fox News. He appeared with his wife and children and repeated his charge that these hearings were nothing more than a partisan political hit job, and Hayley Larson was a pawn in this vast left-wing conspiracy. He turned to his wife and children and told McCall and the audience how embarrassing and traumatic things have been for them, especially for the children in school.

Jodie Wilkinson referred to Oliver as 'the perfect gentleman' while they were dating, engaged, and ultimately married. The man she knew and loved was incapable of the accused behavior. Multiple female friends, employees, and colleagues were interviewed, singing Oliver's praises as a man of integrity, courage, and someone who always supported women's rights. His kids described how tough things were at school. Bullies were out in full force, taunting them, accusing them of being the children of a sexual predator.

"Leave my family out of this," Wilkinson demanded, looking directly into the camera. "This confirmation process is a farce, a political hit, and I am nothing more than the latest target of the left-wing lynch mob. These hoodlums will stop at nothing to maintain their slim majority on the Supreme Court. I'm a veteran of these wars. Nothing in politics surprises me anymore. But leave my wife and children alone, dammit!"

It was tremendous theatre, and the tide of public opinion against the Wilkinson nomination following Hayley's testimony began to swing back in favor of confirmation. Impassioned public appearances by the president, the vice president, and Republican Congress members complemented mass media appearances by the Wilkinson family, Lenard, and McGinnis. The usual conservative talk show hosts and guests were also having an impact. The media blitz strategy was working and working well.

While the Republican strategy was effectively swaying public opinion, it could not sway Zack Blake or the Detroit office of the Federal Bureau of Investigation. Zack contacted Clare Gibson the morning after Shane Marbury rang the buzzer of his office. He told Clare that Marbury was sitting in his office, enjoying his morning coffee. Clare was ecstatic—she was certain Marbury was a third victim of this horrible conspiracy to cover up Wilkinson's past and assure his appointment to the Supreme Court. She hopped in her car and raced out to Bloomfield Hills.

Clare was aware of the criticism leveled at the Democrats, and especially Diane Stabler, for sitting on Hayley's letter and springing Hayley on the committee at the last minute. Clare was a Federal law enforcement official and an apolitical officer, sworn to uphold the law and the United States Constitution. She had no skin in the game except to prevent a criminal from ascending to a position as an associate justice on the highest court in America.

As she drove to Zack's office, she wrestled with how to handle Marbury's sudden appearance.

Should I take him into protective custody and notify the committee?

If she did that, despite FBI protection, Marbury would remain a target for assassination. Despite the findings of two medical examiners, Clare and every other FBI agent knew Lorenz and Gallant were murdered. Perhaps she should notify Stabler, continue to shelter Marbury privately, and wait for Stabler to decide upon the opportune time to notify the committee. *Let's see what Zack has to say,* she finally determined.

She arrived at Zack's office, parked the unmarked federal vehicle in the front lot, and entered the office building. The law office was buzzing. People were rushing everywhere, trying to meet deadlines, preparing for court, complete assignments, or get papers filed.

Kristin was on the telephone. Other lines were ringing as Clare looked around the office. Kristin smiled at her visitor as she multi-tasked the telephone calls and held up a finger, signaling for Clare to wait. Kristin must have secretly summoned someone because Zack's paralegal entered the lobby and invited Clare to enter the office. While Kristin continued on the phone, she smiled and waved to Clare as she disappeared into the law office's inner sanctum.

Phyllis led Clare to a small conference room, offered her coffee and something to eat, bagels, pastries, etc. Clare accepted the coffee, black, and declined the rest. Phyllis left the room and closed the door. It wasn't long before Zack walked in with Shane Marbury.

"Clare Gibson, FBI—meet Shane Marbury, missing person," Zack smirked.

"Nice to meet you, Agent Gibson." Marbury extended his hand. Clare took it and shook it.

"It is *very* nice to meet *you,* Mr. Marbury. We thought you were dead."

"I should be. Fortunately for me and unfortunately for poor Ira Gallant, someone thought he was me."

"I am aware, Zack told me. Let's get right down to business. Tell me what happened, please."

"Micah's on his way, Clare. Can we wait for him?"

The door opened, and Micah Love walked into the conference room.

"Wait for what?" Micah muttered.

"You," Zack laughed. "Welcome to the party."

"Shane Marbury, I presume?" Micah eyeballed Shane and extending his hand. "I've been looking all over for you. Glad you're alive."

"Me, too—pleasure to meet you. Zack says nice things."

"Sure, he does. Don't you believe a word of it," Micah joked. "I see coffee. Where are the bagels, lox, and usual assortment of goodies? You got *kichel*?"

Zack laughed and buzzed Phyllis with Micah's order. "Your breakfast is on its way, your highness. Can we get down to business now?"

"Absolutely."

Phyllis walked in with a carafe of coffee and a tray that included fresh bagels and pastries, lox, cream cheese, and several pieces of *kichel,* a Jewish pastry that resembles a doughy bow tie with kernels of sugar on top. Micah was pacified.

Zack turned to Marbury.

"Shane, will you please tell Clare and Micah everything you told me yesterday evening? You can trust them. They're good people."

Marbury turned to Clare and then to Micah, sizing them up. Satisfied, he spilled his guts. He recounted the events at a particular party twenty-two years ago and the hard times he'd experienced following those events. He talked about the different life paths he and Oliver traveled after that party.

Marbury remained loyal to Wilkinson, despite Marbury's own misfortunes. Wilkinson rewarded his loyalty by securing a position for him with the Republican Party. As a result, Shane remained Oliver's loyal soldier. He would never have ratted him out. But everything changed one night when Shane forgot his keys and accidentally witnessed the murder of his friend and associate, Ira Gallant.

"Show them the video, Shane," Zack prodded.

Marbury pulled out his cellular telephone, hit a few buttons, and turned the phone around for Micah and Clare to view. The murder of Ira Gallant played out on the small screen.

"How did you get this without being seen?" Clare was intrigued.

"All of our offices are glass. Ira was in my office, and I had just walked into the opposite office. Luckily, the woman didn't see me. Otherwise, I'd be dead, too."

"Have you ever seen this woman before?" Micah froze the video on the woman's face.

"No."

"She's gorgeous! Looks like Catherine Zeta-Jones," Micah drooled.

Zack rolled his eyes. "Clare? Does she look familiar to you? FBI wanted list or anything like that?"

"I can run this through facial recognition. I've never seen her before. She's stunning. Hard to believe she's a stone-cold assassin," Clare stared at Zeta's frozen image.

"Mr. Marbury?" Clare turned to Marbury.

"Shane," Marbury corrected her.

"Shane it is. Shane, would you please text the video to this number?" Clare flashed her number and handed Shane her cell phone. Marbury took the phone, entered the number in a text box, and texted Clare the video.

"I'll get this to the office and run it through facial recognition. Zack, how do you want to play this? Obviously, Senator Stabler and other ranking Democrats would love to have Shane testify in front of the Judiciary Committee."

"In my mind, the issues are timing and trust," Zack explained. "If we publicly disclose that we've found Shane Marbury, Wilkinson and his cronies or whoever is trying to eliminate witnesses will be on notice. Shane will be a marked man. Maybe we reveal this privately to the right people, Chairman Ashley, Senators Stabler, Drake, or Cousins, perhaps? Who can we trust, and when should we do the reveal?"

"I agree," Micah opined. "We can't be too careful. Two people are already dead. This woman no one has ever seen before is still in the wind. She's smart and deadly, a lethal combination."

"We can put Shane in protective custody and make public the fact we found him. He's ready to testify. The committee can't help but allow him to testify," Clare suggested.

"All due respect, Clare, the FBI would have to transport him to Washington and then to the Capitol. A lot can go wrong with these types of transports. I'm not suggesting the FBI isn't up to the job, but I like the fact nobody knows we have him a lot better than making it public.

"I trust everyone in this room. In Washington, the only person I trust right now is Senator Diane Stabler. These hits have been made at the direction of Wilkinson or people friendly to Wilkinson. That's pretty clear to everyone, right?" Zack probed. Everyone nodded his or her head.

"That's how important this seat is to the Republicans. After everything we've gone through with Ronald John and now Wilkinson, who knows who can be trusted? For now, I suggest we have a conversation with Senator Stabler and no one else."

"How do you feel about all of this, Shane? Any thoughts you wish to share? After all, it's your ass on the line." Clare turned to Shane, who appeared to be weighing the pros and cons of the discussion thus far.

"I'm with Zack. Anyone who is loyal to this nomination and this nominee is a threat. The same might be true for anyone on the fence. I'd go with Stabler and let her decide who to share this information with and when to share it."

"All agreed?" Zack polled. Everyone raised a hand.

"Good. Glad that's settled. Now, let's talk about protection. I continue to believe we do not arrange for formal witness protection. Perhaps we close the circle at everyone in this room, perhaps we add Pete Westmore to our little group, but I think we should keep this as quiet and unassuming as possible. No planes, trains, or public transportation. Maybe Micah and I *drive* Shane to Washington when the time comes. I don't want credit card swipes or travel manifests. There are Wilkinson supporters everywhere," Zack concluded.

You're not paranoid if they're really out to get you . . .

"I agree we do this quietly, Zack. How tight a circle do we want?" Micah inquired.

"Who knows who is loyal to whom in the FBI? Normally, I would absolutely trust the FBI or the U.S. Marshals Service to take care of this. It is what they do. They are experts at protection. However, the stakes are so high with this nomination, and with the election looming, it is probably too late for the Republicans to name a replacement candidate. The Dems are likely to win in November, and a new president will be making the pick. Thus, for Republicans, it is Wilkinson or a Democratic appointee. As revolting as Wilkinson is, many Republicans would prefer a right-wing *criminal* to a left-leaning jurist with integrity. Is it beyond the realm to speculate some agent or supervisor might be loyal to the Wilkinson campaign and is waiting for an agent like Clare to announce she has Marbury?"

"That's pretty far-fetched, Zack. The FBI and the Marshal's office are apolitical, but I concede your point. At this stage of the game, it is certainly *possible*," Micah agreed.

"Let's get Westmore involved and close the loop there. Pete and I will ride shotgun with you and Micah," Clare suggested. "Sound good to everyone?"

"I'll defer to the experts," Marbury smiled.

"Sounds like we have a plan. Clare, what is the timetable on the FBI's current investigation of these issues? For instance, I know that Micah has shared Jordan Levin's whereabouts and his interview material on the party's three female witnesses. What about Wilkinson's brother, Jared?"

"I believe everyone from the party has been interviewed. Pete and others are circling the wagons on current and former police professionals in West Bloomfield. Pete's also trying to get his hands on the original files and reports. Did Wilkinson or his family deep-six an ongoing investigation? We have not been able to get Levin in for an interview. He might be in danger and hiding. Who could blame him after Lorenz?"

"Who's Lorenz?" Marbury wondered.

"He's the cop who investigated Hayley's case. He died the same way Ira died."

"They killed a cop?" Marbury was incredulous.

"It sure looks that way."

"Clare? The timetable?" Zack was impatient.

"Right. I think Pete and the others should wrap this up by week's end."

"Talk to Pete. When the investigation has been completed, Pete notifies Ashley the committee is ready to deliver the FBI's report. Maybe we get to Levin; maybe we don't. It really doesn't matter at this point. I'd also like to find other women out there. I still find it hard to believe Wilkinson only did this the one time. In fact . . ." Zack turned to Shane.

"Shane, do you know whether Wilkinson ever did this to any other woman? Did *you* ever do this to any other woman?"

"The answer to both questions is, embarrassingly, yes. Hayley's the only one who didn't eventually consent to sex. Oliver was charming and had a shitload of money. If a woman squawked about his behavior, he gave them money or gifts. He even bought one girl a car."

"Do you remember her name?"

"No. I was drunk or stoned most of the time back then."

"Search your memory and come up with some names."

"I'll try."

"Ashley announces the hearing will be reconvened on a specific date, probably early next week, to publish the report. Before publication, perhaps afterward, the report is supplemented with Shane's statement and a copy of the murder video. That evidence is too compelling to ignore.

"The FBI opines there has been foul play in the deaths of the two witnesses, and it strains the imagination that friends of the Wilkinson for Supreme Court campaign are not behind these deaths. As Ashley delivers the report, I walk in with Shane Marbury in tow. I offer his testimony to the committee in support of the FBI's report and Wilkinson's false testimony about his conduct at the party.

"If Ashley rejects the offer, it stinks like a cover-up. Even if Ashley could somehow get away with a cover-up for the sake of the nomination or to appease right-wingers, Drake and Cousins would never go along with it. What do you think?" Zack had a good handle on things going forward.

"I think it's brilliant, Zack," Clare exclaimed. "Micah and his people or Pete and I will stay with Shane the whole time. They won't be able to get to him."

"Especially if they don't know we have him."

"I've got to get back to the office, run facial rec on the video image, and talk to Pete. We'll talk soon," Clair rose and headed for the door. "Shane, it was very nice meeting you. Hope to see you in Washington. Zack and Micah, are you sure you want to take responsibility for Shane for now?"

"We've got this, Clare. Besides, nobody knows he's here, right? Who would guess he'd come to Hayley Larson's attorney, of all people?"

"I suppose that's true. I'll get back to you as soon as I talk to Pete, and we'll coordinate shifts. Bye." Clare walked out the door.

Micah grabbed a cup of coffee and a piece of *kichel.* "What now, your highness?" He bowed to Zack. Shane laughed, enjoying Micah's *schtick.*

"Now, we continue to lay low and wait for the right time or at least until the FBI finishes its work."

"I'll get some of my men over to . . . where is our friend Shane staying?"

"My house, I guess," Zack shrugged.

"Have you discussed this with Jennifer and the boys? Might be risky."

"Why? I repeat, no one knows where Shane is."

"These are really powerful people, Zack. Remember the Coalition and the Church? Those people knew what you were doing before you even thought to do it. They were cunning and powerful. So are these Wilkinson dudes. Don't underestimate these people. I'll round up some of my finest people and send them over in shifts until the hearing, but *please,* be careful," Micah warned.

"Aye, Aye, sir." Zack saluted with a smirk.

"Mock me if you want, but heed my warning."

"Thanks for your concern, Micah. Consider the warning heeded."

The three men rose, and Shane and Zack escorted Micah to the lobby. They engaged in light banter all the way. As Micah walked to his car, he turned and walked backward, conversing with Shane and Zack, standing on the front porch.

The stranger watched from a distance and took photographs with her cell phone. She decided to follow Clare Gibson to see what the Detroit office was up to. There wasn't much time, and there were no leads.

Wilkinson's people have had surveillance on Blake's office since he announced he represented Hayley Larson Schultz. The stocky, shorthaired woman is FBI, the fat guy is the investigator, and the grey fox is the lawyer. Who's the other guy?

She pulled out the photos she had of Eric Lorenz and Shane Marbury, comparing them to the man on the porch.

Son-of-a-bitch!

Chapter Thirty-Four

The stranger considered her options. It was broad daylight, with multiple people going in and out of the law office.

Too dangerous—too many innocents, unprofessional, she decided. *Stay put, keep an eye on these guys, and make your move when no one's around.*

She texted the porch photos to the number her handlers gave her.

Leo Lenard's cell phone buzzed a moment after the stranger hit 'send.'

One of these guys is the lawyer, Zachary Blake—who's the other guy?

Lenard texted the photo to Oliver Wilkinson along with a message:

Who's this?

He waited about fifteen minutes for a response. His phone buzzed again.

Shit! That's Marbury! The text screen on his phone advised.

Lenard felt like he'd been punched in the gut. His was a visceral reaction, a feeling of impending doom. *Shit is right!*

He dialed the usual number he dialed when he needed certain stuff done. A man answered, and Lenard uttered a password. He was put on hold and transferred to a woman.

"That man's the target, isn't he?"

"Yes," Lenard confirmed.

"Thank you. I've got it from here."

"No more fuck-ups, no cases of mistaken identity," Lenard commanded. He was terrified, but his desperation trumped his fear.

"I've got it from here," Zeta repeated.

"Sure, but did you hear my orders?"

"He's a dead man. I owe you one."

"You sure do," Lenard huffed, growing a set. "We're counting on you."

"I've got it from here. Hang up and let me do my work."

"Good luck."

"Luck has nothing to do with this."

***

Zeta sat in the rental in a parking lot across Woodward, opposite Zack's office. People continued to go in and out all day long.

Does Blake know all these people? Any clients come in off the street? Perhaps I could wander in . . .

She decided against the idea. What would she do when she got inside? How many people would see her face? Did the office have surveillance cameras? She could disable them as she did in Lansing, but then what?

Blake's too smart not to realize why the cameras went out. All hell would break loose.

Were any of these people witness protection or FBI? There were too many questions and not enough answers. She would wait for Marbury to leave the office and see whom he left with and where they went. As it turned out, she was forced to wait into the evening hours. The crowd of people dwindled, both in and out of the law office, as dusk descended on Bloomfield Hills. There was no sign of Shane Marbury.

He can't stay in there forever.

After dark, automatic lights came on and dramatically lit up the mansion.

How convenient! Night vision!

One-half hour later, Zeta watched as Zachary Blake and Shane Marbury walked out the front door. Zack seemed to do some amateur reconnaissance of the area around the office before heading to the parking lot, motioning Shane to follow. Zeta laughed to herself.

He's a rookie—doesn't have a clue how to do this.

The headlights of a small two-seat BMW flashed on and off, as Zack must have engaged a key fob. The two men got into the car and drove off down Woodward Avenue. Zeta followed them out at a safe distance. About a mile south of the office, the BMW turned right onto a residential dead-end street. Zeta slowed down,

counted to five, turned off her car lights, and followed them onto
the dead-end street. She stopped at the corner and observed her
surroundings. Tucked away in a forest of trees, just a short
distance from Woodward Avenue, were several estate-sized lots.
Some were empty, some contained homes under construction,
and some were home to beautiful, multi-million-dollar mansions.

Zeta continued to watch the little BMW. It was about five
lots in front of her. The brake lights engaged, and the BMW
disappeared.

He must have turned into his home.

She edged the car forward. Her speed did not register on the
odometer. She counted the houses or lots she passed, one, two,
three, four . . . until she came to a beautiful mansion standing
majestically on a circle at the end of the road. Neither the BMW
nor the two men were anywhere to be seen. A sign in front of the
mansion warned of protection by Brinks home security. All
activities would be monitored by video camera.

She paused, uneasy, trying to decide what to do.

*This must be the lawyer's home. He might have a family. He
might have weapons. I can disable the security system, but I
won't kill someone's wife and kids to get to a target. Disable the
system, sneak in, locate the target, and eliminate him? How do I
identify the target if there are multiple people inside? What if I
choose the wrong person? Better to monitor and follow until a
better opportunity presents itself. I have time . . . they still have
to get to Washington . . .*

Zeta decided to be patient and wait until the lawyer left with
the target. However, she couldn't stay where she was. This was a
watched neighborhood. These mega-wealthy residents must have
a private security service patrolling at night. A rental parked
overnight on this block would be noticed. She decided to return
to Woodward Avenue and find a location that would allow her to
monitor traffic flowing in and out of the lawyer's neighborhood.

The following morning, Zeta watched from an office building
across Woodward. The BMW Roadster left the residential
neighborhood and made a Michigan left to travel north on
Woodward. The vehicle passed Blake's office building and
stopped at Little Daddy's Restaurant, a diner located at

Woodward and Long Lake Road. Zeta followed at a safe distance and turned into the restaurant parking lot. She parked her rental and donned a Detroit Pistons cap. She tugged the cap down over her forehead, almost totally blocking her facial features, and walked into the restaurant.

A hostess greeted her at the entrance and told her to 'sit anywhere.' Surveying the diner, Zeta saw Blake and Marbury seated in a booth against the back window, across from the bathrooms. She wandered toward the back but abruptly turned toward the restrooms when the lawyer stopped mid-conversation and glanced her way.

Zeta walked into the ladies' room and washed and dried her hands. Exiting, she ventured to and sat down in the booth directly in front of the one where Zack and Shane were seated, back to back with her target.

Zack Blake noticed the woman with the ponytail and the Pistons hat when she walked in. He watched her walk in and out of the bathroom and over to the booth directly behind Shane.

Have I seen her before?

Zack tilted his body right and leaned to look past Shane at the booth behind him. He could see the woman was seated in the booth, but he could not see anything beyond her right shoulder. As he recalled from her entrance, she wore some type of athletic warm-up suit. He motioned to Shane to move to his right. As Shane started to turn to look behind him, Zack motioned him a second time to stop and move right. Shane slid a bit to the right, revealing the shoulders and back of a woman's head, the backside of a Detroit Pistons cap with a long, dark-haired ponytail coming through the opening in the back.

The woman seemed to be minding her own business, but Zack couldn't shake the feeling he'd seen her somewhere before. He shrugged, squared himself in the booth, and prepared to resume his conversation with Shane Marbury. Before he could do that, a server arrived and took their breakfast order. After taking their order, the server moved back and waited on the woman in the booth behind Shane.

"Twenty-four-hour protection will be provided in three eight-hour shifts. Pete Westmore and a junior agent have one shift,

Clare and another agent have the second shift, and Micah and his men have the third. They'll rotate until it's time to get you to Washington. Micah will also provide a twenty-four/seven backup detail, just in case."

"Sounds like a plan, for now, but the key is to find a safe way to get to D.C."

"Witness protection and safety are what these guys do. Put yourself in their capable hands."

"Nothing is one hundred percent, Zack, but I've come this far. I really have no choice. Until I actually give my testimony, my life isn't worth shit."

Zeta listened in the next booth.

No, but your death is worth a ton of money.

Subtly and unconsciously, she tilted her head, straining to hear. Zack thought he saw an almost imperceptible movement by the woman in the booth in front.

Did she just turn her head and ear, slightly to the left, trying to hear our conversation? Who is she?

Suddenly, it dawned on him. The picture Shane took of Ira Gallant's assassin! Did Shane have his phone?

Zack got Shane's attention and mimed the use of a phone, gesturing to Marbury about his mobile telephone. Marbury first looked at him like he was nuts, then recognition crossed his face. He reached into his pocket and pulled out his mobile phone. Zack put his fingers to his lips, mimed taking a photograph, and pointed to Marbury's phone.

Marbury hit a few buttons and handed the phone to Zack. Zack scrolled through the pictures until he reached the full-face photograph of Ira Gallant's killer. The assassin was, indeed, beautiful. She had dark hair, pulled back into a ponytail, and wore a baseball cap pulled down over her face.

Same woman? Am I being paranoid?

Zack pulled out his own phone and texted Micah Love:

911—Little Daddy's Parthenon on Woodward at Long Lake. Now—booth behind Shane?

One of Micah's teams was following Zack and Shane everywhere they went. The team was currently camped out in the restaurant parking lot. Micah texted the team the moment he received Zack's text. He sent his operatives into the diner, guns blazing. Restaurant patrons scurried for cover, believing the restaurant was about to experience a terrorist attack.

The team leader immediately identified Zack and Shane and looked into Zack's eyes. Zack motioned him toward the booth directly behind Shane. The team leader looked befuddled. Zack leaned to his right again and pointed directly at the booth. The team leader shrugged. The shoulders and head were gone—the booth was empty.

Chapter Thirty-Five

Stupid, stupid, stupid! What was I thinking? Of course, there was surveillance, but what tipped them off? Who spotted the tail? I was so careful. Am I slipping?

Suddenly and for the first time in her career, the stranger doubted herself. Shane Marbury took a video still of her face, the only such photograph in the world. 'Zeta,' infamous assassin, had no idea she was now unmasked.

She hunkered down in the residential bushes behind Little Daddy's. The rental car sat in the restaurant parking lot. She'd take no chances—the car would stay in the lot until her handlers decided to retrieve it. She needed extraction. If she stayed put, perhaps the lawyer and the target would leave the restaurant and take the surveillance team with them. That would be her signal that it was safe to leave her bush and shrubbery cover. She looked around, studying her surroundings, looking to see if any residents noticed her crouched in a neighbor's bushes.

So far, so good . . .

***

Zack telephoned Clare Gibson and told her the story. He and Shane remained in the restaurant with Micah's surveillance operatives. He sought guidance from Clare about what to do next. Should they leave and increase surveillance? Should they stay and wait for Clare to dispatch agents to the scene? Clare opted for a casual extraction.

"She now knows we have Shane and that he is being protected. She doesn't know the FBI is involved. How good is this protection team?"

"I'm no expert on protection teams, but they'd make me run the other way if they weren't on my side. Besides, they're Micah's handpicked guys. That's good enough for me."

"Where do you plan to go from here?"

"I was going to go to my office, but I can't do that and put my people at risk. We need some kind of safe place . . . what do you guys call those? We need a *safe house.*"

"We have to assume she or people she works with will be watching from a safe distance. She has no idea we know what she looks like. Maybe we can set a trap . . ." Clare tailed off, thinking as she talked.

"What kind of trap? Who's the bait?" Zack didn't like the sound of this.

"Stay in the restaurant. Let's get your office evacuated and your staff replaced with FBI agents. You go back there with Shane, and maybe the lady makes her move on the office."

"I thought you didn't trust anyone but Pete Westmore."

"That's not true. Pete is the one I trust without hesitation. I can't vouch for everyone, but it is extremely rare for an FBI agent to be compromised. Besides, I don't think we have a choice anymore. We have to trust more people."

"It's your show, Clare. What do you want us to do?"

"Stay there. Let me get some agents to your office. Call over there and let your people know what's going on. I'll call you when we're ready. Shouldn't be too long if everyone is on board."

"They'll do what I tell them, especially if it involves a day off."

"I'll call you back."

Clare assembled a meeting of her best people and quickly dispatched a group of men and women to Zack's Bloomfield Hills office. Micah offered some of his private duty team. Under normal circumstances, she wouldn't put civilians at risk in an FBI operation, but she knew Micah, and she knew these guys would be top-notch operatives like those protecting Zack and Shane.

A combined force of fifteen men and women met at the law office and evacuated all personnel. Employee cars and trucks were left in the parking lot for show. The bewildered staff was evacuated to several commercial vans while staff replacement operatives entered the building. Each carried weapons and manned individual workstations. Some assumed executive

offices or associate offices, some assumed administrative
stations. At least from a distance, a woman with a remote
resemblance to Kristin occupied the reception desk. When
everyone was in place, Clare called Zack.

Zack, Shane, and Micah's team left the restaurant together.
Zeta made her way to a Woodward office building south of the
restaurant where she could watch the parking lot. She saw the
men exit Little Daddy's. They checked their surroundings and
engaged in a brief conversation. Everyone got into their cars and
left the premises.

Get the rental and follow? Again, Zeta doubted herself. This
was not a good trend for an international assassin. *Snap out of it.*
She altered her earlier plans and decided to get the rental and
follow the caravan. She raced to her car, started it, and drove off.
The caravan was headed south on Woodward toward Zack's
office. She memorized the vehicles, and, of course, the lawyer
drove that beautiful little roadster.

She drove down Woodward for less than a mile to the office
mansion. The men were exiting their vehicles and heading inside.
Again, they stopped to evaluate their surroundings. Zeta drove by
as the team leader looked up and down Woodward Avenue. She
quickly turned her head away from the office as she drove by.
She would park the car at a neighboring office complex and
double back on foot to find a spot where she could safely watch
the office.

She thought about calling for help or, possibly, abandoning
the sanction and returning the money. Her career could survive
the backlash. Things were getting complicated. She was only one
person, risking her greatest asset – her anonymity. However,
Zeta was a *professional*. She could not abandon this sanction.
She had already assassinated the wrong man during this
operation. True, it was an understandable accident. Her handlers
and clients were okay with it as long as she repaired the damage,
but Zeta rarely made mistakes. She *had* to make things right.

As she left the car and crept along the walls of neighboring
buildings and toward the law office, she wondered if the damage
was irreparable and whether Wilkinson was worth the risk.

Who wants this rapist to be a Supreme Court justice anyway?

Inside the law office, all of the new 'staff members' assembled in the conference room with Zack and Shane. State-of-the-art conference call equipment sat in the center of the huge marble table. The team leader placed calls to Clare Gibson and Micah Love and put them on speaker.

"Does anyone believe this woman will risk a direct move on the law office?" Clare inquired.

"No," the team leader decided. "It's way too risky and too much potential collateral damage for a pro. I think she'll wait until we try to move him."

"The good news is she still thinks she's anonymous. We can use that," another observed.

"Good point. What do we do in the meantime?"

"How about a decoy?" Micah suggested.

"Interesting . . ." Clare seemed to debate the idea in her mind. "What do you have in mind?"

"When everyone leaves tonight, they leave in three or four groups. We pick guys who are about the same size as Zack and Shane for each group. We cover their heads and faces. If Zeta is watching, she doesn't know which group to follow."

"Zeta?" Clare didn't understand the reference.

"She looks like Catherine Zeta-Jones. Don't you think? Anyway, we head for different safe houses—Zeta would have a one in three or four chance to pick the correct safe house. Maybe she tries something, maybe she doesn't, but she'll never know whether she's got the right house or the right target. She doesn't want to miss again, so she can't make a move on Shane. Hopefully, this whole experience has her off her game."

"I like most of that," Clare agreed.

"What part don't you like?" Micah wondered.

"The 'one in three, one in four' part. I'd like longer odds. I also don't like giving away the fact that the employees have been replaced, which your plan does."

"So, what's your idea, Clare?"

"That's just it, Micah. I don't have anything better. Everyone stays at the law office until it's time to go to Washington?"

"Doable, but not very practical . . ." Zack ruminated. "How about . . ."

"How about what?"

"How about we use *live* bait instead of a decoy? Of course, it's your decision, Shane, but why not start for Washington tonight? Shane, me, Micah, and Clare are in the lead vehicle accompanied by one or two tail vehicles? This 'Zeta' lady makes a move, and we have plenty of experience and firepower against one woman, working alone. She likes to work alone, right?" Zack speculated.

"Yes, she does. I guess the question is, do we want to force her to make a move or not?" Clare plotted. "Shane, what do you think of Zack's idea?" Everyone in the room turned to Shane Marbury.

"I'm tired of allowing Oliver Wilkinson to define who I am and what I can or cannot do. I'm tired of him using his wealth and power to manipulate and control the system. The thought of this maniacal narcissist on the Supreme Court is as revolting as President Ronald John was to most Americans. I will do whatever is necessary to stop this madness. I owe it to Hayley Larson and the country."

"Okay, then, let's refine the plan," Clare decided.

Chapter Thirty-Six

As darkness descended on Bloomfield Hills and the law office mansion on Woodward Avenue, a black unmarked commercial van turned into the office parking lot, pulled up to the front door, and sounded its horn. Zeta watched from an office complex across Woodward.

What the . . . Are they making their move?

The front door opened. The lawyer and the target walked out and climbed into the van in the front lot. Three undistinguishable vans pulled up from behind the mansion and parked parallel to the other. It was difficult for the assassin to distinguish them apart. The four vans began to circle the lot until, suddenly, one bolted into Woodward Avenue traffic and slammed on its brakes. Oncoming cars swerved, sounding angry horns. Drivers rolled down windows, cursed, and issued middle-finger salutes, but the van stood its ground. The other three vans joined in, forming a caravan, before heading northbound on Woodward.

Zeta left her hiding spot, hopped into the rental, and took off in pursuit. She lost a little ground because she had to go south, turn around at the next left turn opportunity and proceed north on Woodward. She also lost track of which van carried her precious cargo. As she began her trek northbound, the vans were nowhere to be seen. She breezed by Little Daddy's again and passed Long Lake Road.

Should I have turned on Long Lake? Shit!

She checked her navigation. Square Lake Road was one mile north. She could access I-75 by heading east on Square Lake. If the caravan was heading to Washington D.C., I-75 South toward Detroit would be a logical starting point. The trip to D.C. was almost nine hours. The caravan would have to stop at least once for gas and would probably stop somewhere for the night. Perhaps she could strike at some rural hotel-motel.

She floored the accelerator and sped up Woodward Avenue to Square Lake Road. She made a sharp right turn on a red light, prompting another series of horns and swerves from pissed off Square Lake Road drivers. Zeta smirked and waved.

She zoomed east on Square Lake and followed some signs and a curve to I-75 south. As she merged onto I-75 off the exit, she saw the four vans up ahead, traveling the speed limit, back to back to back to back. She had no clue which van carried her intended prey. Would she have to devise a plan to eliminate vans one by one? She never liked to kill innocent bystanders, but this was different. These people were not innocents. They were paid operatives or part of a plot to protect her intended victim. They knew and accepted the risk.

Fair game . . .

I-75 from Bloomfield Hills to downtown Detroit was a major southbound freeway. Although it was evening, there was medium traffic all the way into the downtown district. Zeta followed at a safe distance. She'd wait for traffic to thin and for her surroundings to become more rural. The caravan skirted past the downtown exits and continued south. Several miles south of the city, they crossed the Ohio line and drove past Toledo. A few miles further south, the vans exited at I-280 and then I-80, the Ohio Turnpike, heading east toward I-76, the Pennsylvania Turnpike.

Zeta was now yawning, yearning for a cup of coffee, hoping the caravan would at least stop for gas. Shortly after crossing the Ohio-Pennsylvania Border, the caravan decided to stop in Sharon, PA for the night. The four vans pulled into a Hampton Inn and Suites.

Zeta turned off her headlights, pulled into the Hampton parking lot, and waited. She had a good view of the lobby and saw several men hovering at the reception desk, presumably trying to rent rooms. She could not make out faces or whether they carried weapons. The vans sat side by side in the lot.

I can easily pick the locks, but to what end?

She had tracking devices and could place one on each van, but she knew where they were going. She also carried a limited supply of explosives but not enough to rig all four vehicles. What if she chose the wrong vans? She decided to place the explosives randomly. Eliminating protective vehicles would eventually expose the target vehicle, or she might get lucky and explode the target vehicle.

She waited until everyone retired for the night. She exited her vehicle and approached the vans. A single guard stood watch, facing the opposite way. Left to right, without a sound, she attached explosives to three of the four vehicles. Her limited supply reduced their lethality, but she would maim the fleet, injure the operatives, and, with some luck, help capture and kill the target.

After she completed placing the explosives, she entered the hotel and looked around—no one in sight except for the night reception clerk. At 1:30 a.m., she approached the reception desk with a credit card, booked a one-night stay for Sharon Jarvis— one of her many aliases—and requested a 5:00 a.m. wake-up call. She didn't plan to sleep. She planned to keep watch but wanted the call just in case she fell asleep.

Can't be too careful . . .

Clare Gibson watched Zeta operate from Clare's own surveillance perch on the west side of the hotel. The superlative FBI agent spotted the tail as far back as Detroit and instructed all of her operatives to keep a sharp watch on the vehicle as they drove along. She was concerned the assassin might try something on the road, like shooting at tires or running a van off the road.

After retiring to her room, Clare exited the hotel out the back exit and walked around the hotel perimeter to a concealed spot on the building's west side. The group pre-arranged this hotel stop because of its location off the turnpike, only twenty-four miles from Wetzl Airport, in North Jackson, Ohio.

After noticing the tail, Clare called headquarters and arranged air transportation from Wetzl to Washington, D.C. The group would board a Gulfstream IV (GIV) 12 seat plane from Jet Vizor, a small charter jet company. The company was more than happy to assist an FBI operation and provide one of its larger, more comfortable, and well-appointed planes.

Clare hunkered down and watched Zeta plant explosive devices on three vans. She again notified headquarters for instructions. Should they attempt to take her down at the hotel tonight or wait until morning? Allow the vans to detonate to give

Zeta false confidence or deactivate the explosives for safety reasons?

They decided to wait. The three vans would 'explode' in the morning; however, the agents would first need to rig the explosives to delay detonation until each vehicle was safely on its way along a rural highway leading to North Jackson. A single bomb squad member in protective gear and safely behind a protective barrier would operate the vehicles and ensure the plans went off safely and without a hitch. They knew Zeta would be watching and wondering why the delay, but any doubts would eventually be alleviated.

Zack, Shane, Micah, and Clare would occupy the only explosive free van. Chase vehicles would follow closely, manned by additional FBI operatives and those left behind at the hotel. The strategy was to lure Zeta to Wetzl, apprehend her at the airport, and fly aboard a charter to Dulles Airport in Washington, D.C., where a team of agents would stand by to take her to FBI headquarters.

Clare watched Zeta register and disappear into the hotel. She emerged from her hiding place, returned to the pre-propped back door, and back to her room. She notified all operatives and participants the plan was now a go. The bomb squad went to work rigging the vehicles while the FBI and private operatives coordinated equipment, ammunition, hotel reentry strategy, and new vehicle arrival strategy needed after the to-be-exploded vehicles left the scene. The terrified but cooperative night clerk advised Clare that 'Sharon Jarvis' requested a 5:00 a.m. wake-up call. Clare decided to make 'Sharon' wait, opting for a 7:00 a.m. wake-up call for the others.

Zack and Shane shared a room. Both were terrified, but Zack tried to be the brave, reassuring one. They were discussing Clare's proposed operation.

"What could possibly go wrong?" Zack pondered.

"Everything, Zack. You need to check out of here right now. Go home to that beautiful family of yours. Thanks for all of your help, and please accept my apology for getting you into this. What was I thinking? I should have disappeared *permanently*. You can't fight powerful people like the Wilkinson family. We should call this off before someone else gets hurt or killed. Agreed?"

"Maybe you can't fight power, Shane, but you don't know unless you try. As to someone getting hurt, these people have been trained and retrained. They know the risk. They know what they are doing. They are elite experts at this, the best of the best.

"Once upon a time, I gave up—I lost my practice. I lost my family. I turned to the bottle to escape. I almost lost my license to practice law. A wonderful woman and her two terrific boys believed in me, for some strange reason, and brought me back from the brink. Since that time, I have never taken responsibility, freedom, democracy, justice, or even *life* for granted.

"I look at you and see myself about five years ago. You can't give up, man! You have to fight the Oliver Wilkinson's of the world, not only for yourself but also for your *country*. You didn't serve in the armed forces, but there are many ways to serve. Look at the work Clare and Micah are doing. Wilkinson may have won some battles to get where he is today, but we must not let him win the ultimate war."

"I hear you, Zack, and I appreciate where you're coming from. I'm sorry you had to go through a lot of shit to become the man you are today. Someday, I hope to learn from your example. As my first step toward redemption, I am declaring this is *my* fight, not yours.

"Oliver Wilkinson and I assaulted Hayley Larson. Instead of standing up like a man, admitting my guilt, and taking my punishment, I let Wilkinson use his power to game and beat the system, and Hayley became a victim a second time. I have been in personal purgatory ever since. You, on the other hand, have no reason to put yourself in harm's way. This is *my* shame and my responsibility. I've got this. *Please*, Zack," Shane retorted.

"I have *every* reason, Shane! Hayley Larson Schultz is *my* client! That's another of my life-changing vows from several years ago. I will *never* let a client down. A client will *never* receive anything but one hundred percent from me or my office."

"Please let me do this, Zack. I cannot be responsible for hurting another innocent person."

"My eyes are wide open. This is my decision and mine alone. *You* are not responsible. I'm doing it to get you to D.C. for *Hayley.* I don't give a *shit* about *you*, Marbury! There, feel better?" Zack snarled.

Shane smiled and then chuckled. "Yes. And fuck you very much."

"Back at you, asshole."

Chapter Thirty-Seven

Zeta was awake when she received an electronic wake-up call. A single night's bill was slipped under her door sometime during the evening and charged to the phony Susan Jarvis credit card. Despite being awake all night, Zeta didn't notice or hear the bill delivery.

I am slipping . . .

She shook off doldrums and self-doubt and decided the ultimate remedy for whatever she was going through was to complete a successful sanction. The hotel served free breakfast and coffee. Zeta was very hungry and needed a boost that only morning coffee provides. She threw on her traditional black spandex and baseball cap. The cap was tilted low over her face as she ventured out of her room.

Carefully scanning for the protective detail, she inched around the hallway leading to the lobby. The place was virtually abandoned, except for a kitchen attendant and the night clerk who checked her in. Their eyes met for a brief moment, and Zeta caught a glimpse of fear in the clerk's eyes. She looked up at him a second time, caught him staring at her, and then quickly looked away.

He knows something. Do they know I'm here?

She walked up to the desk and handed him her room key. His hand trembled, and beads of sweat appeared on his forehead.

"I'd like to check out of fourteen," she stared him down. The clerk refused to look up.

"Did you get the bill under your door?" He managed.

"Yes. So what?" She bent over and leaned in, trying to meet his eyes. He turned his back on her.

"You're all set then. Have a great day," he muttered, his back to Zeta.

"Turn around," she ordered. He couldn't move.

"Turn around, dammit," she snarled.

The clerk forced himself to face her. Sweat was dripping from his forehead and temples. His head was bowed toward the ground.

"Look at me," Zeta commanded.

The clerk tilted his eyes upward and looked at Zeta over his glasses.

"What's going on this morning? What's your problem?" She leaned over the counter and got into his face. "And don't lie to me." She looked over to the breakfast area. The attendant went into the kitchen.

"There is a whole group of police people here. They are guarding someone, taking him somewhere," he muttered, barely perceptible.

"Tell me something I don't know. I'm part of their team," she lied, continuing to get in his face.

"No, you're not. You're the woman they're protecting the guy from."

"Do I look like a person who would hurt someone? Who told you that?"

"The lady from the FBI," he whispered, looking around, searching desperately for assistance.

The FBI is here? The government knows who I am and where? Shit!

"You have me confused with someone else. I'm going to get some breakfast to go and get out of here. Is that all right with you?"

"Yes, fine, whatever you'd like."

"That's a good boy. By the way, did the FBI lady ask for a wake-up call?"

"Seven o'clock."

"Late riser."

"Huh?"

"Nothing."

"Did she say where they were going?"

"No."

Zeta meandered over to the breakfast area and puttered about, only to annoy the clerk. She poured two cups of coffee, grabbed a breakfast sandwich, and walked out the door.

The panicked clerk picked up the house phone to dial Clare's room. Zeta walked back into the hotel lobby with a large gun and pointed it at the clerk, shaking her head and pointing her gun at the receiver, silently ordering the clerk to hang up the phone. He did as she ordered.

"Do not pick up that phone again. Do you understand me?"

"Yes, ma'am."

"I've got people in the hotel, watching you. Understand?"

"Yes, ma'am."

"You're a young guy, right? College student?"

"Yes, ma'am."

"You'd like to live long enough to graduate and get out of this dump, wouldn't you?"

"Yes, ma'am." Sweat poured from his body as he quivered violently.

"When these people come down at seven, tell them 'hello' for me, okay? Not a word until then."

"Yes, ma'am."

"Were you in the service?" She chuckled.

"No, ma'am."

"Hello at seven?"

He nodded vigorously and looked down at the ground. Zeta left the hotel. About forty-five minutes later, the terrified clerk worked up the nerve to alert Clare about his conversation with Zeta.

This changes everything. She knows that we know she's here.

Clare called every one of her rooms and assembled everyone in the breakfast area.

"We need a change of plans," she suggested. "Zeta knows we're on to her. Does anyone have any ideas?"

"Decoy. Send everyone back toward Ohio and Wetzl. The four of you stay here for a couple of hours. Order a rental for transport and head east to D.C. We let Zeta follow the caravan and implement whatever plan she has for when the vans explode. She gets the drop on us and thinks she's won. She'll be pissed when she finds out you guys aren't with us, but she's a pro. She won't harm us. She'll bail and go after you. By then, it will be too late. Even if she was able to catch up to you guys, she wouldn't know what type of vehicle you're driving." An FBI operative laid out the plan.

"Not bad, but what if she doesn't take the bait? What if she figures it out and goes after Shane and Zack's vehicle?" Someone speculated.

"I don't see much chance for that, the way Ben lays it all out. Besides, if it comes to that, Micah and I know how to protect witnesses," Clare remarked. "Hopefully, it doesn't come to that."

"She's only one person, Clare. Aren't we safer together? What's she going to do? Kill us all? Is she that talented?" Zack exclaimed.

"I'm not sure, but my gut tells me *yes*, she is *that* talented. I would prefer to create a situation where this woman never discharges her weapon. I like the decoy idea even though it creates its own set of concerns."

"You're the boss. It's your show," Micah acknowledged.

"Let's coordinate this. Pete—call Enterprise. Have them deliver a rental to the hotel in about an hour or so. We'll grab our gear and meet down here in twenty. Where are our look-alikes?" As Clare looked around the table, two men raised their hands. She looked over at Zack and Shane.

"You guys give these guys the clothes you're wearing. Shane and Zack wear these fatigues. If Zeta's watching us, and I'll bet she is, hopefully, she thinks you two left with the first shift."

"Got it," Zack assented. "Let's go change, Shane."

Twenty minutes later, everyone met in the kitchen area. A group of men in combat fatigues and side weapons drew frightened stares from hotel guests. Clare continued to bark out commands until each operative or agent understood and was ready to implement his assignment. The decoy group left the hotel. Two of them were dressed in casual clothing, jeans, and a sweater. They lined up all of the vans. The third van was Zack and Shane's original explosive free transport van. The decoys entered the third van; the others entered their assigned vehicles. The caravan took off west toward the Ohio border and Wetzl Airport.

Zeta watched from a perch behind a thick oak tree about fifty yards to the north of the hotel. She was confused.

Why are they doubling back?

She pulled out her cell phone and opened her navigation. There was the answer—Wetzl Airport was about twenty miles west of the hotel.

They're going to fly this guy to D.C.!

Zeta knew she had to stop the caravan and execute the sanction before they reached the airport.

The explosives will stop them—I'll handle the rest.

She waited until all of the vans disappeared. She left her perch behind the tree and walked toward the hotel. Something was bothering her, but she couldn't put her finger on what it was. She continued fast walking to the rental. She had to catch up to the caravan as the explosives ignited. She suddenly realized what was missing. The clerk talked with the 'FBI lady.' A woman was in charge of the operation. All of the operatives in the caravan were men.

Where's the woman?

Zeta stopped in her tracks and wondered if she should chase after the caravan, return to her tree perch and continue surveillance, return to the hotel and confront the woman, or hop in the rental and continue surveillance from the parking lot. She decided that she was tired of surveillance. It was time to act. By her count, the woman and maybe one agent or protection operative remained behind. She presumed that the target and the lawyer also stayed behind. It was dangerous to assume that two out of the four were skilled with a weapon and that the other two were not, but it was late in the game. A gamble was necessary.

Zeta pulled out her iPhone and asked Siri to provide the location of the nearest cell tower. Zeta then raced back to the hotel parking lot, hopped into the rental, and took off for the tower two miles from the hotel. Upon arrival, she removed some equipment from the trunk and set it on the ground, aimed at the tower. Upon activation, the tower lights shut down. With everything in place, she sped back to the hotel, parked the car, and headed for the hotel lobby. Suddenly, she heard a series of explosions off to the west.

A shift change was taking place. The frightened night clerk was chatting nervously with his replacement when he observed

Zeta walk through the front door. Panic and fear registered on his face. He pointed at Zeta and yelled something to the day clerk. Both men ducked under the desk.

Zeta pulled her gun and walked up to the counter. She jumped up on the counter, peered over it at the two cowering men, and pointed her gun at them. Hotel patrons scattered for cover.

"Get up," Zeta ordered. The two men rose nervously, hands raised in the air.

"What room is the FBI lady in?"

"They all checked out," the night clerk lied.

"*Most* of them checked out. *She's* still here. Lie to me again, and it will be the last lie you ever tell. What *room* is she in?"

"T-two s-seventeen," he stuttered.

"Is anyone else in her party still here?"

"T-two guys—t-two n-nineteen."

"Anyone else?"

"Another guy—t-two t-twenty-one."

"See how easy that was? Now, hand me your cell phones."

The men complied. Zeta violently pulled the landline out of the wall and addressed all of the hotel guests within earshot. She realized she might not have every guest, but she sought to minimize exposure.

"Attention, everyone. I am in law enforcement, here to apprehend a dangerous criminal. These nice hotel clerks are going to walk around collecting cell phones. Give them up, cause no problems, and you will get them back. Refuse or otherwise cause problems, and you will be arrested for hindering an FBI investigation. Does everyone understand? Say 'yes' if you understand."

A chorus of 'yes' came from all corners of the lobby. The two frightened clerks walked around collecting phones.

"I want everyone to get up and walk over to the kitchen— *now.*"

Everyone left their respective hiding places and walked with the clerks toward the kitchen area.

"Everyone inside the kitchen," Zeta commanded.

"Is there a telephone extension in there?" Zeta addressed the frightened day clerk.

"No."

"Does the kitchen attendant have a cell?"

"I don't know."

"Go in there and ask—bring it to me if she has one. And don't fuck with me," she warned.

The clerk went into the kitchen and returned with an old flip phone.

"Haven't seen one of these in a while," Zeta laughed. She immediately returned to serious command mode.

"Everyone inside." She motioned with her gun toward the kitchen. All hotel guests and clerks meandered into the kitchen, cowering, hands raised.

"Stay there. Anyone seen in the lobby will be arrested or shot on sight. This is a terror alert. I have people all over this hotel." Zeta broke a lobby chair and shoved a broken chair leg through the door handle, trapping everyone in the kitchen.

She walked to the staircase at the end of the lobby and climbed the stairs to the second floor. As she opened the door to enter the long-hallway leading to second-floor rooms, Clare Gibson, Micah Love, Zachary Blake, and Shane Marbury were walking toward her. Clare saw the door open and immediately pulled her service revolver. She saw Zeta and fired a shot. Zeta retreated into the staircase. Clare motioned to Micah to usher Zack and Shane out of the hallway. The three men turned and ran to the opposite stairwell. Clare slowly backed out of the hall with her gun pointed at the stairway exit door. Zeta pushed open the door a second time. Clare fired another shot dead center into the door.

The lady can shoot . . .

Zeta raced down the stairs to the empty lobby and ran to the staircase on the opposite side. She opened the door. Shots reigned down from the stairs above. She quickly slammed the door, grabbed another broken chair leg, and wedged it into the door handle.

The group now only had one exit. Zeta would wait by the exit and take each of them out, one by one, if necessary.

On the second floor, Clare and Micah considered their options. A terrified black woman poked her head out of an empty room, then quickly retreated into the room. Clare walked to the room, knocked, and shouted:

"FBI, open up."

The horrified woman, apparently a room attendant, opened the door with her hands raised.

"Do you speak English?"

"I'm American," she whispered.

"Good. My name is Clare Gibson, supervising agent of the Detroit office of the FBI." Clare flashed her badge. "Hang on a second; need to make a call."

Clare pulled out her cell phone to call the local police and the nearest FBI office, probably Pittsburgh.

No service.

"Zack, Shane, Micah, do you guys have a cell signal?" The three men checked their phones.

"No," they chimed.

"Zeta must be jamming the nearest cell tower. *God,* she's good! We've got to get out of here."

Clare turned back to the frightened room attendant.

"What's your name, hon?"

"Lois."

"Lois? I need you to do something for me. Use your master key and go into as many rooms as you can. If there are people still in the rooms, tell them to stay there and open the door for no one until we say it's safe to come out. Take all of the sheets off of the bed in every room and bring them to me. Understood? My associate, Micah, will help you. Do all of the second-floor windows open from the rooms?"

The woman nodded affirmatively.

"Good. Get going, please—this is a matter of life and death."

Clare turned to the shocked and frightened Zack Blake and Shane Marbury.

"I need you guys to start tying these sheets together. We need to make ropes to climb down from the second-floor windows to the ground. We can't stay here. I'm not getting into a shootout with civilians in the crossfire."

"Understood and appreciated," Zack acknowledged. Shane nodded his assent. He was happy to assist.

This whole thing is my fault . . .

Micah and the room attendant returned to the hallway with several sheets and pillowcases. Zack and Shane went right to work, tearing them into long thick strips and tying them together. The men soon constructed three solid sheet ropes long enough to get them from the second floor down to the first. Clare instructed Lois to barricade herself into one of the empty rooms and promised the terrified woman she would contact local police as soon as she regained cell service.

Clare gazed out the back window. Behind the hotel and to the south was a deeply wooded area. Clare had no idea how far the woods extended, but she knew Ohio and the Wetzl Airport were located in that direction. Clare and Micah secured the three ropes to a bedpost. Clare opened the window and tore out the screen. The men dropped the sheet ropes down the backside of the hotel. The ropes ended about two feet from the ground.

Perfect. "Okay, guys. It's time. Micah, you go first. When you get to the bottom, wait there for Zack and Shane. The minute they get to the ground, you guys head for those woods. Do not wait for me. Run like hell! 'Zeta' is a sharpshooter. If she sees you in the open, she'll pick you off like a kid playing a video game. I'll be right behind you. If she shows up, I will try to provide some cover. As soon as you get cell service, call 9-1-1. Got it?"

"Got it, boss. Good luck," Micah beseeched.

"You too. Now get the hell out of here."

The three men climbed to the window ledge, looked back at Clare to acknowledge her bravery, and began to climb out the window. The men reached the ground in seconds. When they looked back up to the second-floor windowsill, Clare was gone. Shots rang out.

Chapter Thirty-Eight

Clare Gibson abandoned the window ledge and returned to the stairwell. When she pushed open the door, Zeta immediately opened fire. Clare returned the fire and slammed the door.

That should get the boys to the woods. Time to go . . .

Clare raced back to the room and ran to the window. She grabbed a sheet rope, climbed up on the windowsill, and quickly traversed down the rope. As she did this, Zeta decided to boldly sneak up the stairs. She planned to confront Clare if she dared to push open the stairwell door again. Zeta pressed her ear to the door and listened.

Nothing. Is this a trap?

She slowly and carefully pushed the door open a crack. No one stood at the door. She pushed it open all the way and jumped into the hallway with her gun extended toward the hall. There was no one there.

Where are they?

She began to tiptoe down the hallway. As she passed the laundry room, she noticed movement from an outside window. She ran to the window and saw the FBI lady running across a clearing toward the woods behind the hotel. The woman was alone.

Is this a diversion? Where are the others?

Zeta dashed through the hallway, trying various room doors as she passed them. She heard no sound from the rooms and saw no sign of the target. She returned to the stairway and raced down to the first floor. She pushed open the first-floor exit door and looked to her right and left. She saw three sets of sheet ropes leading from a second-floor window to the ground below. She looked up at the woods and saw the female FBI agent disappear into the woods. She presumed her prey was with the agent. She immediately set off for the woods.

As Clare Gibson entered the woods, she turned back and saw Zeta racing toward her. Clare turned and ran deeper into the woods. Somewhere, up ahead, she hoped the three civilians were headed west toward Ohio. As she continued further into the woods, she wondered what to do next.

Should I stop, hide, and confront? Or should I continue on and try to hook up with Micah, Zack, and Shane? She decided to continue. If Zeta got the best of her, only Micah stood between Zeta and her mission. Micah was undoubtedly capable, but he was a civilian. He had no obligation to protect and serve. If they were going to go toe to toe with Zeta, they were better off together.

Micah, Zack, and Shane raced through the woods, grateful the brush and trees were not so thick as to prevent easy travel but thick enough to provide cover. They were hopeful these woods continued for miles without a clearing. Micah and Zack constantly looked back, hoping for Clare to catch up. Both feared the worst—they might turn back and see *Zeta* rather than Clare. That possibility kept them moving as fast as they could.

Micah was a well-trained field operative with terrific survival instincts. However, he was not in great physical shape and was the first to tire to the point of exhaustion. He tried valiantly to press on but eventually needed to stop to catch his breath.

Zack was in excellent physical shape but understood and tolerated Micah's physical limitations. They were good friends and experienced multiple perilous situations together. Marbury was also in good physical shape. As Zeta's intended target, he was far less understanding of Micah's need to stop and rest. He had little choice other than to proceed alone without professional protection. He wisely chose to stick it out with Zack and Micah.

After a five-minute break, they were on the run again. As they tore through the woods, they heard footsteps behind them. Micah repeatedly turned as he ran, trying to decide what to do.

Clare or Zeta? Wait or run?

He decided to do both. He'd have to take another break soon, meaning whoever was back there would catch up. He turned west and ran as fast as he could, ten to fifteen feet behind Zack and Shane.

Clare Gibson thought she heard footsteps up ahead.
Is it one or all three?
She raced to the sound and caught a glimpse of Micah Love
running about thirty feet ahead of her. She did not see and could
not hear Zack or Shane running fifteen to twenty feet ahead of
Micah. She turned on the gas.

Zeta dashed through the woods at top speed. She estimated
Clare had a five-minute head start with the target somewhere up
ahead of Clare. She thought about terminating the race and
returning to the car. She'd drive to Wetzl Airport, where she was
sure they were heading. She also thought about calling for
assistance but remembered she disabled the nearby cell tower.
She decided to continue the chase.

Fifteen minutes later, Zack and Shane came to a one-
hundred-yard clearing with dense woods on the other side. They
stopped at the edge of the eastern side of this meadow and stared
out at the clearing. Zack considered his next move. *The one-
hundred-yard-dash—what was my time in high school?*
He knew top athletes ran the hundred in less than ten
seconds. He figured he and Shane could do it in fifteen. They had
two choices—wait for Micah or Clare or take off right now. As
Zack decided to make a run for it, Micah appeared out of the
brush. He frantically waved his arms for them to continue. The
three men took off for the other side of the meadow.

Clare Gibson could faintly make out an image of Micah Love
waving his arms and running for his life. She increased her speed
and took off after him. As she reached a clearing, the hundred-
yard meadow, she saw the three men disappear into the woods on
the west side. *Should I follow or create a diversion and force
Zeta to follow me?*
Clare decided she could not leave three citizens to defend
against an internationally famous assassin. She dashed into the
clearing. In a matter of seconds, Clare reached the west side
wooded area. There was no sign of the assassin. Suddenly, Clare

had an idea. She would create a diversion *and* follow the boys. She crouched behind a tree and waited.

A few minutes later, Zeta appeared at the edge of the east woods. She surveyed the clearing in front of her and realized how exposed she'd be if she tried to cross. Clare watched her as she calculated her next move.

Is someone on the other side waiting to ambush me? If she wanted to complete the sanction, she had no choice but to cross the clearing. She started to cross, gun drawn, turning three hundred sixty degrees several times as she approached the west woods. She walked about halfway through the clearing when Clare opened fire. Zeta hit the deck and belly crawled back toward the east woods. More shots rang out. Dust and weeds were flying around her. She reached the eastern woods and jumped for cover behind a tree. As she jumped, three more shots whizzed by her head and torso. She was pinned behind the tree. Worse, the shooter knew where she was, while Zeta had no idea where the shots came from, other than somewhere on the western side of the clearing. The shooting stopped. Insect and animal noises were the only sounds Zeta heard for the next ten minutes.

Should I try again? She meandered out into the clearing while hugging the edge of the east woods, waiting for shots and ready to dive back for cover. Nothing happened. She ventured west, inching forward ever so slowly—no noise, no shots—no nothing.

Clare watched Zeta brave the clearing. She admired the woman's guts and tenacity. Her job was not finished, and she was determined to complete the sanction. *She's got balls. I'll give her that—too bad she's a ruthless, stone-cold killer . . .*

Clare opened fire, and once again, Zeta jumped back for cover. This time she saw the muzzle flashes. She belly-crawled in a circle, aimed, and fired in the direction of the muzzle flashes. A lucky bullet tore at the flesh of Clare Gibson's left arm. She recoiled in pain, expelling a grunt. Zeta heard her reaction to the shooting and took the opportunity to run back to the east woods for cover. *It's the woman. She's hit. How bad is it?*

Clare glanced at her left arm. It was bleeding. She tore off a piece of her blouse and wrapped it tight around the wound.
No big deal, unless I bleed to death . . .

Back in the east woods, Zeta was buoyed by the fact the woman was hit by a bullet and was over in the west woods, probably writhing in pain. Where were the men? Where was the target? Zeta suddenly realized this standoff was an attempt to increase the distance between Zeta and her target. The woman knew Zeta was a pro. She also knew Zeta would only kill her if her own life was threatened or if she stood between Zeta and her target. Right this minute, in these woods, the woman stood between Zeta and her target – while the target was getting closer to the airport.

Zeta decided to brave the clearing one more time. *If I were shot, wounded, and facing a trained assassin, I'd get the hell out of here.* She belly-crawled across the clearing. It was not the fastest means of transportation, but it was the safest. No sounds came from the west side, and no shots were fired. Zeta finally reached the other side.

She pulled her weapon and ventured toward the direction of the muzzle fire. There was no one there, only a piece of torn cloth and a five-foot trail of blood. Zeta followed the blood trail into the west woods. She lost valuable time in the gun battle. Her mission and her reputation hinged upon getting to Wetzl Airport before a plane bound for Washington D.C. took off with the target safely on board.

Micah, Zack, and Shane heard multiple shots and stopped dead in their tracks. Clare was engaged in a shooting match with an internationally infamous assassin. What chance did a local FBI agent have against a notorious killer? The three once again pondered whether they should turn back and render assistance.

Micah had faith in Clare Gibson. He opined she'd be pissed as hell if they didn't make a beeline for the plane in Ohio. Clare's mission was to transport Shane to Washington D.C. to give testimony to back up Hayley Larson's story and prevent an asshole from becoming a Supreme Court Justice. With Clare out there, somewhere east of the men's current location, perhaps still engaged in a gun battle with an assassin, it was Micah's job to do what Clare would do. Micah needed to get Shane and Zack safely to D.C. by any means possible.

He motioned for Shane and Zack to follow. They all took off west, deeper into the woods.

Clare could not let little things like a bullet wound and blood loss get in the way of her mission. She was making good time heading west toward Ohio. She had no idea how long it might have taken Zeta to realize she could cross the clearing in safety. She only knew what Clare Gibson would have done. Assuming Zeta thought like Clare, Clare estimated Zeta was now five to seven minutes behind her. Clare's brave stand at the clearing brought her some time. *Better still, I probably bought the men fifteen to twenty minutes. But will it be enough?*

Hopefully, her FBI colleagues secured a plane and were ready and waiting to whisk everyone to the safety of FBI headquarters in Washington. Clare checked her cell phone—still no service. She estimated she was now ten to twelve miles from the hotel with another ten to twelve miles to go. The makeshift tourniquet controlled the bleeding to a trickle. Still, she was losing blood, which meant a loss of energy as she attempted to stay ahead of Zeta and avoid a deadly confrontation. She estimated the boys were a mile or two ahead of her, with maybe eight miles to go. She wished there was some way to communicate with Wetzl and the three men running for their lives a mile or two ahead.

Twenty minutes later, Zachary Blake checked his cell phone. *One bar—we must be heading toward a working cell tower.*

Zack slowed his pace and tried to call his office. The phone rang, cut off, and rang again. Kristin answered, but her voice kept cutting out. Finally, the call disconnected. He picked up the pace and caught up with Micah and Shane. He'd wait a few minutes and try again.

Zeta was in top physical shape. She didn't know it at the time, but she was gaining on the wounded Clare Gibson. With ten or so miles to go to North Jackson, Zeta began to wonder whether she could overtake her prey. Even if she caught the FBI agent, she'd have to stop for the battle, win it, and still have time to catch up to her target. She was losing hope but pressed on.

Several minutes later, Zack checked his cell a second time—three bars now. He tried the office again. Kristin started to answer with her usual professional introduction, but Zack cut her off.

"Kristin! Thank God! I need you to dial 9-1-1 and get them to connect you with the North Jackson, Ohio Police Department right now!"

Kristin was quite familiar with Zack Blake's emergency tone.

"Doing it now, boss. Hang on. Are you okay?"

"I'm running for my life, Kristin. I've got Micah and Shane with me, but I have no idea where Clare is—she's back there somewhere dealing with an assassin!" Zack shouted. He was panting—talking made him even more breathless.

A 9-1-1 operator answered the line, and Kristin repeated her instructions. She told the operator this was a matter of life and death. A shooter was gunning for a client who was scheduled to give testimony in Washington. The operator maintained a calm demeanor and promised to handle the call with the urgency it demanded. Less than a minute later, Kristin was connected with Captain Arlene Ringer of the North Jackson Police. Kristin repeated what Zack told her to say, placed both of them on conference hold, and conferenced them into the call.

"Hello? Captain Ringer here. To whom am I speaking?"

"Captain, this is Zachary Blake. I'm an attorney from Detroit. I was escorting a witness to Washington D.C. with a partner and an FBI agent when a female assassin attacked us. She disabled a cell tower and has been chasing us through the woods, east of you, near the Ohio-Pennsylvania border. Clare Gibson, the FBI agent, engaged her in a firefight. I have no idea if either of them was hurt or killed. If she got past Clare, I have to believe she's gaining on us. We need help now!" Zack urged.

"I need you to remain calm, Mr. Blake. I know the area very well. You should be coming out of the woods soon. The fact you were able to make this call means you are somewhere near the cell tower near Youngstown. Have you passed any highways?"

"Yes, but we were afraid to run along the highway out in the open. We felt safer in the woods. We are probably ten miles or so west of the border. We're trying to get to Wetzl Airport. There's supposed to be a plane waiting to take us to D.C."

"Keep running west. I want you to tell me the next highway you come to, and we'll come and get you. I'm sending some cars out your way now. You mentioned an FBI agent. Any idea how far back she is?"

"Not sure. We heard shots and then nothing. It's probably been an hour or so. She's a friend. I'm worried about her."

"Agents are well trained and in great condition. She can take care of herself. Do you know her cell phone number?"

"Yes, but I just got service. If she's a few miles back, she may not have service yet."

"May I have the number?"

Zack gave her Clare's number.

"I have your number tracked, sir. I am going to get my people to work on tracking Agent Gibson's. For now, keep running and don't stop. When you get to the next highway, go north. That's the direction of the Turnpike. We'll be tracking you. Call me to confirm what highway you're on. Got it?"

"Got it."

"Good luck. I'll keep this line open for you."

"Thanks." Zack disconnected the call and took off to catch up to Shane and Micah.

Captain Ringer dialed Clare Gibson. The phone rang but was immediately disconnected. She would try again in a few minutes.

Clare Gibson was slowing down. Her arm ached, and blood continued to trickle from her wound. She couldn't keep up this pace for very much longer. She might have to stop and force a last stand with Zeta. At least she would accomplish her mission. Suddenly, her phone rang. After one short ring, the line went dead. She looked to see if a number registered, but none appeared on her screen. She checked her reception status and noticed it now displayed two bars. She was running toward a cell tower. This revelation gave her restored energy, and she took off with a renewed burst.

Zeta thought she heard a soft ringtone up ahead. She checked her phone. *Two bars. Call my handlers? What can they do at this point?* She dialed the phone and reached her intended party. She told the boss about the hotel, the cell tower, and the chase thus far.

"They're on the run and headed for Wetzl Airport where a plane is waiting to take them to D.C. If they board that plane, it's game over. I need to get to the airport stat."

"Understood. Keep up the chase. Engage if you catch up. We'll send one team to the airport and another to fetch you. Hang in there. Good work."

"Not so good. It's my fault we're in this mess to begin with."

"Not true. The target has been well protected."

"Only because I missed him the first time."

"Honest mistake. Anyone could have made it—stop beating yourself up. Let's try to correct the mistake here and now. There's a huge bonus waiting for the successful operative."

"I think the FBI agent is just up ahead. I heard a phone ring. I clipped her. She's bleeding."

"Good. She'll be easier to catch and kill."

"I've got no beef with her unless she gets in my way."

"She's a witness."

"They all seem to know who I am. That ship has sailed. It's not a reason to kill her."

"You sound impressed with her."

"She's a capable and tough competitor. It's hard not to be impressed. I'll do my job if it comes to it."

"Don't let her slow you down. Do you know where you are?"

"No. I just leaped over a highway, but there were no signs."

"How do you know they didn't take off down the highway?"

"Because there's no cover, and they want to keep heading west. That's what I'd do, and I know that's what she'll do. Don't ask me how I know. I just know."

"I trust your instincts. You say you just got reception? You must be somewhere near Youngstown."

"How far from Wetzl?"

"About twelve miles."

"Shit!"

"We'll track your phone and come get you."

"Good. We need to set up the ambush at the airport. Tell your team not to engage at the airport. There will be too many innocents. My one chance is to take out the target from a safe distance."

"You're sure that's where they're going?"

"Damn sure."

"Good enough for me."

"I'll need an M24." The M24 Sniper Rifle is the military and police version of a Remington 700 rifle, a highly effective long-range weapon.

"We'll have one waiting for you."

Zeta abruptly cut the man off. She wasn't one for small talk.

Clare Gibson's phone rang a second time. She hit the 'accept call' button on her screen.

"Agent Gibson?"

"Who's asking?"

"This is Captain Arlene Ringer of the North Jackson Police. Are you okay?"

"I've been shot in the arm. I don't think it's too bad, but it's slowing me down."

"Do you know where you are?"

"About ten miles or so west of the Ohio-Pennsylvania border. How did you get this number?"

"From an attorney named Blake. He's worried about you."

"Yeah? Well, I'm worried about *him*. What's his status?"

"We are sending cars your way. So is Youngstown PD. Keep your phone on. We're tracking you. Blake is about to reach Highway Eleven in Mineral Ridge. If he heads north, he'll hit the Turnpike. We can intercept somewhere near there."

"Wonderful! I'm a few steps ahead of a trained assassin— perhaps I should engage and give the target more time?"

"Negative Agent Gibson. You aren't far from Highway Eleven yourself. Keep going. Do you copy? Keep going! Do not engage."

"You're breaking up. Not sure I heard you," Clare lied and disconnected the call. She hadn't made the decision to engage or not, but she wasn't going to be told what to do by a stranger. She appreciated the information about her location. She would head for Highway Eleven and go north to I-80.

Chapter Thirty-Nine

Captain Ringer called Zack to report Clare was alive but injured. Patrol cars were closing in on their location, maybe ten to fifteen minutes away. Ringer's team was tracking Zack's cell phone and reported he was less than a mile from Highway Eleven near Mineral Ridge. She reminded Zack to head north when he reached the highway. She also reported she was tracking Clare's phone. The FBI agent was about a mile or so behind Zack. Clare would also be heading for Highway Eleven.

Zack caught up with Micah and Shane and told them about his telephone call with Captain Arlene Ringer. He reported Clare Gibson was still alive but shot in the arm by Zeta. They were about a mile behind. Micah wanted to turn back and render assistance. Zack told him their first responsibility was to the case and the target. They had to get Shane to safety and Washington. That was their first and only priority.

Zack repeated Clare would do the same thing. He reminded Shane and Micah that Clare was a trained agent and could take care of herself. Part of him wanted to do exactly what Micah suggested. Every instinct except duty told him to turn around and help Clare. They continued west.

The men reached Highway Eleven and headed north. Zack and Micah kept turning around to look south, half expecting some goons with machine guns to come barreling up the highway to try to take out Shane Marbury and anyone protecting him. As they were about to reach I-80, they heard sirens coming from the west. They looked west and saw several police cars zooming east on the Turnpike. The squad cars reached the Highway Eleven exit. Zack and Shane were jumping up and down, waving at the police and flagging them down. Micah was more sedate. He worried Zeta might burst from the woods behind them, determined to complete her mission. Instinctually, despite the fact they appeared to have been rescued, Micah turned south and pointed his gun.

A squad car pulled up alongside the men. Captain Ringer, the only female on the scene, exited the vehicle. She pulled her weapon and ordered Micah to put down his gun. Micah obeyed her command, and Ringer holstered her weapon. She invited her guests into an armored SWAT-type vehicle. Shane, the star witness, entered first, followed by Zack and then Micah. Captain Ringer climbed into the driver's seat and advised all occupants to buckle up. Zack and Micah began to protest.

"What about Agent Gibson?" Zack demanded.

"What's her status?" Micah inquired.

"I've got squad cars heading south on Highway Eleven as we speak. As soon as she hits the highway, we'll pick her up. There's nothing to worry about."

"We prefer to wait if you don't mind." Zack insisted.

"This isn't your call, Mr. Blake. I've got orders from Agent Gibson's superiors to take Mr. Marbury into protective custody so he can testify in D.C."

"Tell them he's not testifying unless he's certain Agent Gibson is safe and in police custody," Shane advised.

Zack glanced over to Marbury and grinned. He was impressed with his newfound moxie.

This guy's come a long way . . .

"I suppose we can tail the squad. But if there's any danger, we get the hell out of there. Does that work for you guys?"

"Yes, Ma'am." Zack smiled and saluted.

"Cut the shit, Blake. Let's go." Captain Ringer radioed the lead vehicle. She would be a follow car. Four cars headed south on Highway Eleven.

"How far down did you guys reach the highway?" Ringer inquired.

"Not too far. Less than a mile, I'd say," Micah estimated.

"Let me know if you can pinpoint the spot when you see it. My guess is, Agent Gibson will hit the highway close to where you came out."

At that moment, Clare Gibson emerged from the woods and jumped into a ditch alongside the highway. She turned and fired several shots into the woods. Someone in the woods fired back.

Three squad cars pulled up to the ditch. Six officers jumped from their vehicles and started shooting blindly into the woods.

Ringer hit the brakes, threw the armored vehicle into reverse, and took off backward, squealing the tires and laying rubber. Her orders were not to put Shane Marbury in harm's way, and she meant to follow orders. The three amigos in her back seat were not happy about this development, but they certainly understood what was happening and why. They promised to 'get the hell out of there' at the first sign of danger. Multiple gunshots coming from the protection of the woods were, absolutely, a sign of danger.

Ringer continued driving backwards until she reached I-80. She passed the exit ramp going west on the Turnpike and slammed on the brakes again. She put the armored vehicle in drive, turned on her flashers and siren, and took off west down the ramp and onto the Turnpike.

Back at the highway, officers were helping Clare Gibson to safety. Several of them charged the woods, chasing a ghost. It was dark, making it difficult to see. They weren't even sure who they were pursuing. After a short time, they abandoned the pursuit.

Zeta ran through the woods back the way she'd come. She was shocked to see multiple squads of police officers as the FBI agent burst out of the woods. Bullets whizzed by her. One almost hit her in the face. Her calf burned—may have been grazed by a bullet. Police scoured the area for a half-hour or so and then gave up the search. The fight was over. The good guys won – for now.

Maybe we can get him at the airport . . .

Chapter Forty

Captain Ringer briefed her squad. The FBI agent was safe. She glanced at her three passengers in the rearview mirror.

"Agent Gibson has been rescued and is on her way to a local hospital. My orders are to take you guys to Wetzl Airport."

The three men were relieved at the news. They cheered and high-fived each other in the back seat of the impressive vehicle. They were disappointed that Clare Gibson, the only reason they were alive, would not accompany them to Washington.

"Can we go to the hospital first, Captain?" Zack wondered.

"Yes, Captain, or do I have to threaten the feds again?" Marbury added.

"Come on, guys! Give a gal a break. I have my orders. She's fine. As I understand things, the prize package here is *you,* Mr. Marbury. The sooner we get you on a plane to D.C., the better."

"We won't go without Gibson," Shane protested.

"Jesus H. Christ! What the hell? I have my orders. I told you that."

"Can't you call and get those orders rescinded?" Micah prodded.

Ringer sighed. "I can *call.* I have no control over whether anyone will listen."

"That's all we ask. Thanks, Captain," Zack sighed.

"You must be great in court."

"I have my moments."

Captain Ringer made the call. The response surprised her.

"The feds are still working on your travel arrangements. They see no reason why you can't visit Agent Gibson. She's over at St. Elizabeth in Boardman about ten minutes from here. I can do it in eight with siren and flashers. Hold on, boys!"

Ringer turned on the flashers and siren and did a three-sixty. When the vehicle righted itself, she took off in the opposite direction. They reached the hospital in seven minutes. Captain Ringer called ahead and arranged to have them immediately taken to Clare. She was being stitched up as they entered her treatment room. Her face first registered pleasant surprise, then anger when they walked in.

"What the hell are you three doing here? Why aren't you at the airport?" Clare growled.

"And we are so happy to see you alive and well, Agent Gibson." Zack cracked.

Clare softened. "I'm very happy you guys made it out of the woods safe and sound. But, my orders and our priorities for the country are to get Shane to Washington. Those orders did not account for a detour and a hospital visit. My understanding was the local police were going to transport you. What happened?"

Captain Ringer stepped forward. "I can answer that. Captain Arlene Ringer of the North Jackson Police."

"A pleasure, Captain. I'm Special Agent Clare Gibson of the FBI's Detroit office. These studs give you any trouble?"

"Nothing I can't handle. They seem very attached to *you,* Agent Gibson."

"Call me Clare—as to the boys here. They do grow on you after a while."

"Like a fungus?"

Clare burst out laughing and then grimaced in pain. "That's a good one, Ringer. Shit! It really hurts when I laugh." She moaned in pain.

"No more jokes, please. Anyway—you were about to tell me what happened?"

"Their plane isn't ready. They want more officers in place at the airport in case the bad guys are planning another attack. They need more time. So, when these guys begged to see you, it seemed like a logical diversion while we wait for a green light on the D.C. mission."

"Understood." Clare studied the three men who were filthy but otherwise in good shape. She was the only casualty. Despite the pain, she knew her injury was minor. "How long do you think it will be?" Clare was hopeful for a release and a chance to accompany the three men to D.C.

"Air traffic controls promises an hour or two. Why? You think you can get out of here in time?"

"Great minds think alike. By the way, does anyone else know you guys are here?" Clare looked worried.

"No, why?"

"This woman has a nasty habit of showing up when and where you least expect her."

"What woman?"

"The assassin trying to take out Mr. Marbury over there is a *woman*—a very dangerous and *infamous* woman."

"Wow, an FBI agent, a police captain, and an infamous assassin. Woman's lib is alive and well. Our gender is certainly making gains in the job market," Ringer giggled.

Clare burst out laughing a second time, and again her laughter terminated with a wince of pain.

"I told you . . . no jokes," she whined with a smile.

"Sorry. I'll behave. As to your assassin, unless someone followed my siren and flashers, I don't see her showing up here. Do you want me to notify Boardman P.D.?"

"No, but I would like you to stay and transport us to the airport when the time comes. Does that work?"

"At your service, Madam. Oops—don't laugh."

Clare chuckled, then scowled in jest at Ringer.

"We have a contingent of agents heading for Wetzl Airport in anticipation of trouble. Can we also get every cop in the area to assist?"

"You can count on North Jackson. That's *my* domain. As to neighboring community police, I'll call around."

"Thanks, Ringer. It's nice to know you. Keep that sense of humor. You need it in this line of work."

"True that—I'll be back in a minute."

When Ringer left the room, the men immediately began to dote over Clare.

"We're so happy you're all right. We were terrified when we heard those shots," Zack gasped.

"I needed to delay Zeta any way I could. It's my job. It's *still* my job to get Shane to D.C."

"Well, I don't think I'd be alive if it weren't for you, Agent Gibson," Marbury gushed.

"Just doing my job. You're a citizen trying to do the right thing for the country in the face of great danger. You're pretty heroic yourself."

"A hero doesn't do the things I've done."

"I'd have to agree with Clare on this one. When a guy puts his life on the line to correct his past mistakes, he's something of a hero," Zack chimed in.

"I third it. Stop beating yourself up. Let's go beat up Wilkinson instead." Micah demanded.

Chapter Forty-One

Zeta's recovery team arrived at Highway Eleven in Mineral Ridge. Multiple police vehicles blocked traffic southbound. The driver had little choice but to head north and wait for the cops to leave. Upon orders from his superior in the passenger seat, the driver headed north for a half-mile, made a U-turn, and retreated south.

As he approached I-80, he killed the headlights and pulled off to the side of the road. A quarter-mile ahead, south of the turnpike, police vehicles were still present. They were searching for Zeta and wasting the recovery team's precious time.

A half-hour later, the driver and passenger were still at the side of the road. Passersby tried to breach the contingent on the south side but were turned back and told to take the next exit. Another fifteen minutes went by before there were signs of movement. Someone was ordering the others, but neither man could make out the words. Officers began to enter squad cars and leave the area. The coast was finally clear, but the passenger was taking no chances. He ordered the driver to stay put for another ten minutes. His eyes darted this way and that, scouring the area for any sign of police presence.

Finally, he instructed the driver to start the car and head for the spot where the police conducted their search. Before the driver could put the car in drive, there was a knock on the passenger side window. The passenger turned to the window and came face to face with the muzzle of a Ruger SR 22 with a silent-SR sound suppressor. The gun motioned the passenger to open the door. The man opened the door, raised his hands, and kicked the door until it opened all the way.

The gun backed away as the man stepped out of the vehicle with his hands still raised. He turned toward the gun and observed a woman dressed head to toe in black spandex. She was filthy, bleeding in some spots, but was otherwise okay. The men dropped their arms.

"You really *do* look like the actress. Glad to see you survived the onslaught. That was quite the show of force by the cops. We saw most of it. Those guys were no match for you."

"I *don't* look like her, *got it*? Thanks for coming. Sorry about the gun, can't be too careful. Until you exited the vehicle, I couldn't be sure it was you."

"Understood. Apology accepted. What now?"

"Now we get to the airport. Did you bring the M24?"

"Back seat. Hop in. There's a first aid kit back there too."

Zeta hopped into the back seat and immediately tore at the first aid kit.

"You're welcome!" The man smirked as he climbed into the passenger seat. The driver put the car in drive and slowly pulled out into the road.

"Not one for small talk or gratitude. We all have jobs to do. How about we get to the airport?"

"Your wish is my command, lovely lady."

"Cut the sexist crap. Want me to call the EEOC?"

The man laughed. "Why madam—was that an attempt at humor?"

"Go fuck yourself. Now get me to the airport."

The driver gunned the accelerator. Soon they were traveling west on I-80 toward North Jackson and Wetzl Airport.

***

Clare Gibson drove the hospital staff crazy until they finally cleared her for discharge. The friendly staff invited Clare never to get hurt in the Youngstown area again. Five minutes after her release, Clare, Arlene, Zack, Micah, and Shane were headed for the airport, unbeknown that they were on a collision course with an infamous assassin and her colleagues.

Chapter Forty-Two

Zeta and her men arrived on the outskirts of Wetzl Airport in ten minutes. They scanned the area and crept to an area east of the terminal building. Zeta rescanned the area with the scope of her M24.

Suddenly, multiple squad vehicles appeared from all directions and swarmed the terminal building entrance on the north side. Others assumed positions on the west and south sides of the building. Another contingent of cops took up positions directly in front of Zeta's position on the building's east side. Zeta chuckled to herself.

*They've got things covered from every direction. They have no idea the distance from which I can nail a target. I can keep an eye on the cops **and** the plane from here. And there are no cops behind me, which should permit an easy escape.*

There was no sign of the target, though. Zeta wondered if he was already in the terminal and under heavy police protection. The other good thing about the late arrival and placement of police officers was it helped Zeta identify which plane would be used to transport the witness to Washington D.C. The target jet stood alone on a short runway of the tiny airport. It was gassed and ready to go. It was the only flight taking off that evening because all other planes were either garaged or pulled adjacent to the terminal building.

Zeta always flew commercial under one alias or another. She considered airports and jets like these to be 'rinky-dink' airlines. In this case, however, she was pleased the feds chose to fly the witness by private chartered jet. She stood a good chance of picking off her target without the type of commotion that would have resulted if she attempted to execute the sanction at a major airport with a commercial jetliner. All she needed now was a good perch and a clear shot.

She continued to study the lone Gulfstream IV through the scope. Marbury and guests would enter the plane through a door located just south of the cockpit. The target would have to ascend a portable multi-step ladder adjacent to the entrance to the cabin. Assuming her perch was not detected in time, a head shot to Marbury would be a relatively easy task. Given the current police presence and the fact the FBI, especially the woman, had yet to arrive, she expected the worst and hoped for the best. If she failed again, it would not be due to a lack of effort. While her occupation left little room for fuck-up, and her reputation would undoubtedly be tarnished, Zeta was satisfied she did all she could do to honor her contract and complete the sanction.

Her companions studied her and marveled at her calm, skill, and intensity. Even though one of the men was technically her superior, he awaited her instructions. Zeta looked to camp out on the east side of the plane, an ample distance behind the police. She suggested the others set up shop on the west side and warned that there was to be no shooting by anyone but her. They were green-lighted only if they were in mortal danger.

Secretly, she hoped that someone would ignore her orders at the last minute. If others decided to engage, they would be blamed for the missed opportunity. More importantly, a commotion on the west side would help Zeta escape on the east side. She suggested the two men walk to a waiting companion or walk to the rendezvous point because she would need the escape vehicle. The men saluted her and wished her luck. They turned and walked into the darkness.

Clare, Arlene, and the men arrived at the airport on the east side. Ringer immediately observed two men walking in the darkness on the northeast side of the terminal. Ringer gunned the engine and drove straight at them. The men pulled weapons and took off running for the terminal building. Arlene cut them off. She and Clare hopped out of the SWAT vehicle with guns drawn. The men had little time to react to Ringer's sudden appearance. They dropped their guns and raised their hands in surrender.

Ringer handcuffed the two men and returned with them to the vehicle. She backed out of the area and drove to the other side of the terminal building. Clare held a gun on the men the whole time and ordered them to talk if they wanted a lighter sentence.

The men scoffed at the suggestion and sneered at Shane Marbury. *Two down; how many to go? And where's Zeta?* Clare wondered.

Zeta crouched down behind a group of luggage carts with a clear view of the plane. She waited with no idea her companions were arrested. She was not privy to the size of her companion operatives' additional force nestled in on the west side of the runway. She wished she'd inquired about the size of the force and their arsenal.

Nothing I can do about that now. I hope they open fire. I'll need the diversion.

There was no sign of the three men from the woods. She was especially anxious to set her sights on the target one last time. There was no sign of the FBI agent either. There was nothing Zeta could do now but wait, identify the target when he finally arrived, and shoot to kill.

The SWAT vehicle pulled up to the front of the terminal building on the north side of the building. All occupants exited the vehicle and started for the terminal building. There were multiple officers stationed at the entrance. They hopped to ready position when they saw Clare and Arlene. Some were FBI; others were North Jackson and neighboring police. It was quite the show of force.

They engaged in a brief conversation, and Clare advised the officers where she and Ringer captured the two outlaws. She suggested a small force of men and women return to their vehicles, head east and west, and widen the perimeter around the terminal. Arlene was convinced there were more operatives and, perhaps, even the assassin over on the terminal building's east side. She volunteered to lead a small contingent of cops to cover the wider area and search for the criminals. Clare turned to Zack, Shane, and Micah.

"Guys, I know you want me to board with you, but I need to do something first. It might be a matter of life and death. Do you mind if some of my agents assist you in boarding the jet? I'll board later, Okay?"

"Absolutely. Whatever you decide," Zack assented.

"We agree," Shane chirped, speaking for Micah, who opened his mouth but was usurped by Shane. Micah scowled but remained silent.

"Glad that's settled." She turned to Arlene, who read Clare's thoughts.

"You want to come with us, right?"

"Yes, I do. This is my detail. These guys are my responsibility."

"Acknowledged Agent Gibson, let's go."

A small contingent ventured out on foot into the darkness. They headed in the direction where Arlene and Clare first saw the two men. They looked to their left and observed a large number of police officers from different communities, in position and ready for action. These were small-town police officers whose normal day-to-day activities were to return lost pets to their rightful owners, help old people across streets, and direct traffic or issue citations.

They must be scared out of their wits. Clare surmised. Perhaps she was underestimating the force. The competent and professional Captain Arlene Ringer was their leader.

She must have trained most of these guys.

Clare concluded she was pleased they were stationed there. The group hugged the terminal building and silently moved past the officers camped out on the east side. They widened their paths after they passed the building. It was quite dark on that side. Most of the action took place at or west of the terminal building. The east side was more of a storage and warehouse side. They separated into groups of two and continued heading east. Some broke off at Arlene's command and headed north and south once they established the wider perimeter distance.

Clare and Arlene paired up and took the middle position, flanked on both sides by the other officers. As they took positions behind a large commercial waste container, Clare noticed movement directly ahead of them. She tapped Arlene on the shoulder and motioned with her hands and eyes. Something or someone was up ahead. Clare pulled night vision glasses out of her fatigues and pulled them on over her face. Directly in front of them and perched behind a luggage carrier was a woman with a high-powered sniper's rifle. Clare could not make out her features, but she was positive that this was the infamous Zeta—in the flesh. She silently mouthed 'Zeta,' removed the goggles, and handed them to Arlene. Arlene donned the goggles, looked out at the luggage bin, and nodded her head.

At that moment, a group of police officers, FBI agents, and Shane, Zack, and Micah emerged from the terminal building. Clare again looked to the luggage bin and observed the woman shift positions, lean forward, and ready the rifle for a shot. There was no time to lose. Clare abandoned her post, pointed to Arlene to stay put and cover her, and ventured out toward the woman's perch.

Officers and agents began ascending the jet steps backwards and forwards while looking out in every direction. They lined up on the stairway, providing full coverage from the north and south. The jet provided full protection from west to east. Unfortunately, the only place where the show of force was vulnerable was from east to west, where Zeta was perched waiting to complete her assignment. She crouched over the carrier and pointed the rifle west. She looked through the scope. Marbury was at the bottom surrounded by a contingent of cops and his two companions—the lawyer and the fat guy.

Zeta wiped sweat from her brow, inhaled, and then exhaled. The men started up the stairs. Zack went first, followed by Shane and Micah, seeking to give a little more cover from the west and the east. But it was no use. Zeta focused and placed Shane Marbury's head directly into the crosshairs of the rifle. She took another deep breath and put her finger on the trigger.

Before she could pull the trigger, Clare Gibson yelled and jumped out at her.

"Hold it right there, lady!"

Clare was too late to prevent the shot. It rang out, but Clare's actions startled Zeta as she got the shot off. It zoomed slightly off target, grazed Marbury's scalp, and hit an officer on the leg. The man went down, writhing in pain. The officers stationed on the steps looked east and mindlessly began to fire, forgetting there were many cops stationed east, including Clare and Arlene. They all hit the deck and scattered for cover, barely escaping the friendly fire. The cops quickly realized their error and ceased fire. Clare and Arlene looked over at the luggage bin. There was no one there. Clare looked back to the east and saw her, perhaps fifty yards in front of her, heading east. She took off after the assassin and watched helplessly as Zeta raced to a car, opened it with a fob, and took off into the night. No one could follow her because all of the police cars were parked over in the north lot. This was a colossal blunder by everyone involved.

Gunshots suddenly erupted from the west side of the terminal building as Zeta's operatives opened fire on the police stationed to the west. There was a much larger force on the west side, however. After a fierce gun battle, all of the operatives were either wounded or surrendered. One bad guy lay dead. Two cops were wounded.

Zeta's gunshot caused only cosmetic damage to the Gulfstream. The jet was totally operational. When the hostilities were over, Clare and Arlene joined Zack, Shane, Micah, and two terrified flight attendants aboard the Gulfstream. Clare thanked Arlene and her police force for their bravery. The men thanked both women for saving their lives *again.* Zack and Micah would owe Clare Gibson a variety of favors when they returned to Detroit.

Payback is a bitch but worth it in this case. Zack reasoned.

Arlene waved goodbye and exited the plane. Officers spread out around the plane and beyond began to applaud. The embarrassed Arlene motioned vigorously for them to stop, but the applause grew louder. Finally, she acknowledged and thanked her fellow officers for their courage and actions in protecting a vital witness.

Clare and the three men stood at the entrance to the plane and waved thanks to the officers. Clare turned and noticed Shane had followed her. He was exposed at the entrance, and Clare violently pushed him back into the plane. Shane staggered backward and fell into a plush executive chair, shocked at the force of the shove.

"Sorry, Mr. Marbury. But after all of this turmoil and danger, you left yourself completely exposed to the assassin. Are you nuts?"

Shane was in a virtual state of shock, but Zack and Micah broke out in hysterical laughter. Shane joined in, probably from relief, as did Clare and the flight attendant. The captain flashed a seat belt sign and announced the plane was ready for takeoff. The flight attendant secured the entry door and instructed all passengers to fasten their seatbelts. With that completed, the plane started to roll, roared, and took off down the runway. Soon, it began its ascent into the evening sky. Shane Marbury was on his way to Washington, D.C., and a date with destiny.

Chapter Forty-Three

Oliver Wilkinson met with Leo Lenard and Dan McGinnis at a quiet Washington restaurant to discuss recent developments. The FBI and local police in Ohio thwarted the assassin's last-ditch effort to silence Shane Marbury. If Marbury testified and barring a miracle, he would, the new strategy was to persuade key senators loyal to the president and the party, to trash Marbury's reputation, and accuse him of attempted rape and perjury. Their ultimate accusation would be Marbury, not Wilkinson, who assaulted Hayley twenty-two years ago. Wilkinson, like Hayley, was an innocent victim of a twisted criminal mind.

Oliver was furious. Marbury's sanction cost a fortune, with nothing to show for it except an empty promise his money would be refunded. He was dubious about this new plan. Hayley had specific memory of the events of the infamous party. When Shane backed her story, who would believe this mistaken identity nonsense? Maybe he could arrange a meeting with Marbury and talk some sense in him. After all, Marbury *owed* him.

Lenard and McGinnis quickly nixed the idea. There was no way a cooperative Democratic witness would meet privately with the nominee, especially when he believes the nominee tried to have him killed. Alternative facts were the best and only strategy under the existing circumstances.

The Party was running out of time on this nomination. The election was coming up, and the Democrats were going to win. If a new nominee was necessary, that nominee had to be chosen 'yesterday.' If Wilkinson was voted down, Lenard, McGinnis, and others decided to support Amanda Paget, the Ninth Circuit Court of Appeals Judge from Arizona. The choice was confirmed in a secret meeting of the top brass in the FedRight Society.

Paget had solid credentials and no skeletons in her closet. And . . . she was a *woman*. Lenard reasoned the feminist card might be appealing to some of the more centrist female

Democrats. On the other hand, gender might not help her because her record was even more conservative than Wilkinson's. The Republicans still retained a majority. Lenard was determined to get a candidate vetted, appointed, and confirmed before the next election.

Wilkinson continued to whine throughout the evening at the unfairness and betrayal. Lenard and McGinnis pretended to be sympathetic, but they believed Wilkinson—for the good of the party—should have fessed up to the original crime at the time of his nomination. Lenard, especially, felt all of this unpleasantness could have been avoided.

All three men completely ignored the fact they were guilty of murder under the Felony Murder Statute. While they didn't inject Lorenz and Gallant with lethal poison or kill cops at the airport, they conspired to solicit or commit these murders. The Felony Murder Statute considered them murderers.

This was Lenard and McGinnis's most pressing concern. If Wilkinson lost the nomination and was indicted for murder, he would no doubt turn state's evidence against his co-conspirators in an effort to save his own ass. Lenard and McGinnis decided to cross that bridge if and when they came to it.

Wilkinson continued to rant, rave, and express his displeasure with the plan. The hearing was tomorrow. The Party was hanging him out to dry, and there little he could do about it. He demanded the opportunity to rebut Marbury's testimony. The pair assured him Ashley would grant him that opportunity. However, Wilkinson continued to rant about his superlative record of success and entitlement to fulfill his destiny. He slammed his hand down on the table and made a spectacle of himself to startled diners. Oliver Wilkinson, once the proud nominee for Associate Justice of the Supreme Court, began to cry. He was a sexual predator, a murderer, a perjurer, and a *crybaby*.

Lenard and McGinnis eyed each other.

What were we thinking? Lenard pondered.

If I go down, they go down, Wilkinson decided.

Chapter Forty-Four

Shane, Micah, and Zack spent the night at an FBI safe house guarded by the best of the best of the FBI. Clare Gibson picked them up in the morning. They were in the second limousine of a four-limousine caravan bound for the United States Capitol. The streets were blocked and deserted. The feds were taking no chances, fearful of one last Zeta ambush.

Zack and Shane had a chance to discuss Shane's testimony over a meal generously provided by the taxpayers. Zack believed Senate questions would probably focus on three areas.

The first was the attempted rape incident itself. Shane faced possible charges if he admitted the crime, but Hayley would have to press charges. After all of this time, she was unlikely to do so. He reminded Shane he was *Hayley's* lawyer, and his advice was for Hayley's benefit. He wanted Shane to testify fully and truthfully about the incident and face whatever consequences resulted. Once Hayley's case was over, Zack would help Shane if criminal representation was required.

The second area of inquiry and perhaps more important than the first—assuming Shane decided to talk about the attempted rape—would be Oliver's culpability for the same crime and the cover-up conspiracy in concert with the West Bloomfield Police. Zack advised Shane to testify fully and honestly about Oliver and the cover-up because it buttressed the perjury charge as well as the sexual assault.

Shane was testy. His recollection was faulty. What he remembered was mostly hearsay. Zack told him this was not a court of law. Hearsay testimony was permitted.

The third area of inquiry would be Shane's recent brush with death. Both men were convinced that Oliver Wilkinson or people working in concert with or on behalf of Wilkinson orchestrated the attempts on Shane's life. Zack advised Shane to testify about the attempted murder, the murder of Ira Gallant, and Shane's suspicions linking Wilkinson and company to the attacks.

Someone killed two people and tried to make things look like an accident. The only connection between these two victims, the only person who benefitted from their deaths, was Oliver Wilkinson. While the causes of death were officially listed as 'heart attacks,' Shane's video of Ira Gallant's injection would overcome that finding. The committee would presume murder from the video—the only issue for the committee's discretion or adjudication was whether Wilkinson was involved. The injuries and deaths of police officers in the Wetzl Airport standoff were aftermaths of the Lansing and Sylvan Lake crimes, making those Wilkinson's responsibility too.

In Zack's opinion, the committee would have to be deaf, dumb, and blind to conclude Wilkinson was innocent. Zack hoped Oliver would not only be denied a seat on the Supreme Court but also be charged and convicted of Felony Murder. Perhaps he'd roll on his co-conspirators. To purge his conscience, Shane needed to testify to *all* of it and testify truthfully. Shane promised to do just that.

They arrived at the Capitol. As the group exited the vehicle, one of the limousines backfired, sending everyone running for cover. If tensions weren't so high and everyone wasn't so stressed, all would have seen the comedy of this occurrence. Everyone was terrified Zeta was at it again.

They walked into the Capitol together, waltzed through security, and entered an almost empty chamber. In less than half an hour, this chamber would be full of tension and people. Micah took a prime seat in the gallery. Zack assumed a seat reserved for witnesses' attorneys.

Senator Diane Stabler appeared through a door toward the front of the chamber, waved and caught Zack's attention, and motioned him to enter the inner sanctum through the open door. Zack stood and walked over to Micah. He instructed him to keep an eye on Shane, walked over to Stabler, shook her hand warmly, and stepped inside.

"I hear you had quite the adventure getting here, Zack. From the bottom of my heart, thank you for your brave service."

"It was harrowing, Senator. I'm still in a state of shock."

"You should be, Zack. After all, as I understand things, you were almost killed."

"Senator, that's not it. This is the seat of our American Democracy. A federal appeals court judge and candidate for the Supreme Court ordered a hit on witnesses! He lied under oath! That same candidate tried to rape a woman twenty-two years ago and used his family's wealth and power to cover up his crime. Is this the best our country can do?"

"We are a deeply divided nation right now, Zack. In our nation's history, there have always been peaks and valleys. This is one of those valleys. It will pass, and the country will remain strong. This is still the greatest democracy in the history of the world. By the way, I have a surprise for you."

"A surprise? I'm not sure I can handle any more surprises."

"While you were away, several women stepped forward. They have agreed to testify against Wilkinson about additional sexual assaults and cover-ups similar to Hayley's incident. We have them on standby, and we have notified Wilkinson and his cronies. Your theory that this was no 'one and done' turned out to be correct."

"That's a pleasant surprise. Not that he did this before or after Hayley, I was sure of that. However, I *am* surprised these women finally came forward."

"As I told you earlier, our country remains strong. We, the people, still crave justice. Oh! I almost forgot. I have another surprise for you."

"*Another* surprise? I can't take much more," Zack laughed.

"I have requested, and Chairman Ashley has approved with consent, that Zachary Blake will be the principal interrogator of Shane Marbury on behalf of the committee."

Zack was stunned. A United States senator tapped him to conduct the direct examination of a witness before the Senate Judiciary Committee. He was honored and touched by the gesture.

I have to call Jennifer and the boys!

"I am deeply honored, Senator Stabler, but I haven't prepared anything. Perhaps this is a mistake? You should get someone else."

"You have a lot of experience. I'm confident you'll know
what to ask when the time comes. Besides, Shane Marbury
virtually *demanded* you conduct the inquiry. He all but
conditioned his testimony on that demand."

"Shane did? Amazing. When Hayley Schultz first told me
about Marbury, I hated the guy for what he and Wilkinson did to
her. However, where Wilkinson went low, Marbury went high.
I'm proud of him, proud of his transformation from a selfish,
entitled punk to a hero."

"A bit strong, don't you think? 'Hero?'"

"With all due respect, Senator, you weren't with him in the
trenches."

"True enough, and he obviously feels the same about you.
Ready?"

"I suppose I'll have to be."

"Go out there and do America proud."

"I will try my best, Senator. Thank you for everything you
did for Hayley and our country."

"Just doing my job, Zack, same as you."

"You've earned my vote—that's for sure."

"That is the ultimate compliment for a public servant. Thank
you. Let's get these hearings back on track."

***

Zack returned to the chamber the way he went out. The
atmosphere was night and day. When he left for his chat with
Stabler, the room was virtually empty. Now, it was packed,
noisy, and bursting with anticipation. Shane Marbury sat at the
witness table, chin resting in his hands, contemplating his fate.
Potential questions were running through Zack's head.

Where do I start?

Zachary Blake was not prone to panic, but this awesome
responsibility was almost overwhelming. The committee
wandered in. Ashley was the last to arrive. As they did before,
senators began to engage in non-partisan banter. Partisan politics
are tossed aside when the cameras and microphones are disabled.

One of the senators must have told some of the others a joke because three senators began to laugh hysterically. Shortly after Ashley arrived, he assumed his chair in the center of the dais and slammed his gavel for order. The United States Senate Judiciary Committee deciding whether to advance Oliver Wilkinson to the Supreme Court was now in session.

Chapter Forty-Five

Ashley formally called the hearings to order. He announced Shane Marbury as the day's first witness and indicated a report of the FBI's investigation. Interviews from various witnesses would also be presented. If necessary, Hayley Larson Schultz or Oliver Wilkinson would be given an opportunity to rebut Marbury's testimony, depending upon which of the two was harmed most by the testimony. If both needed to testify, arrangements would be made. Ashley was now bending over backwards in order to be fair. Zack and Stabler glared at each other and wrinkled their noses—they didn't like the smell of this.

Ashley thanked Shane Marbury for appearing to provide testimony. He invited Shane to be seated, swore him in, and offered him an opportunity to make an opening statement. Per previous discussions with Zack, Shane declined to address the committee. With the preliminaries out of the way, Ashley introduced Zachary Blake to the committee and the gallery.

"Ladies and gentlemen, we are going to shake things up a bit today. Zachary Blake, Hayley Larson Schultz's attorney, is here with us today. We have invited him to question Mr. Marbury on behalf of the committee. Mr. Blake has accepted our invitation.

"If any member feels compelled to ask a question after Mr. Blake has examined the witness, please write it down and present it to a page. He or she will pass that request along to me. My goal is to get to the truth and to give everyone a chance to tell their story. Mr. Blake, if you please?" He gestured to Zack to begin his examination of the witness.

"Thank you, Mr. Chairman. I am honored." He turned to Shane.

"Mr. Marbury—let's start at the beginning. Do you know Hayley Larson Schultz?"

"Yes."

Zack took Shane slowly and methodically through his high school years, his friendship with Oliver Wilkinson, the parties that Wilkinson threw, and the young ladies who often attended.

One of those young ladies was Hayley Larson, the victim of a twenty-two-year-old crime committed against her by Oliver Wilkinson and Shane Marbury. Both men were acquainted with Hayley. She was a high school student and a friend of Jared Wilkinson, Oliver's younger brother.

Shane testified to facts remarkably similar to those testified to by Hayley Larson Schultz. He described trapping the terrified teenager in the bathroom and about his and Oliver's indecent exposure and sexual gyrations. Oliver suddenly ripped at Hayley's clothing and tore off her outer garments, leaving her scantily clad in her bra and panties. Both boys mocked and threatened to rape Hayley while trying to convince her to give herself to them willingly. Luckily for Hayley, and before the two boys could consummate their intentions, some guests intervened. They knocked on the bathroom door and eventually gained entrance. Hayley escaped down the stairs, running partially naked out the front door, in front of all the party guests.

Hayley decided to press charges, which scared the hell out of Shane. He was afraid he was going to jail for attempted rape. He contacted Oliver. Oliver told him not to worry—his dad was well connected in the West Bloomfield community. The senior Wilkinson knew the chief of police and paid lots of money to have the police bury the charges. The police conducted what Shane called a sham investigation, and eventually, the cops discontinued the so-called investigation altogether. They leaned on and ultimately convinced Hayley's parents to drop all charges.

Shane Marbury never forgot that day twenty-two years ago, a fact evident to everyone in the committee chamber. The incident had consumed and tortured him for over twenty years. He testified how it affected his life going forward. He had little interest in school and was going nowhere.

Years later, Shane was struggling to find a job and contacted Oliver Wilkinson. Oliver arranged for Shane's current job with the Michigan Republican Party. Shane was extremely grateful and very loyal to Oliver. It never occurred to Shane that Oliver granted him favors to assure his loyalty and prevent him from telling the truth about the original crime and cover-up.

"Did it work, Shane?" Zack began to focus on recent events.

"I don't understand the question."

"Did Oliver Wilkinson successfully buy your complete loyalty?"

"Yes."

"What caused you to re-think your loyalty to Oliver? Why are you here today?"

"Because I am convinced Oliver Wilkinson hired the assassin who killed Ira Gallant."

The gallery buzzed. Spectators were shocked by this accusation.

"Why? Did he know Gallant? Did he think Ira could hurt him in some way?"

"No. Ira didn't know Oliver. Ira couldn't have hurt Oliver. Oliver Wilkinson put a hit out on *me,* and the assassin mistook Ira for *me.* An assassin's mistake, Mr. Blake, is the only reason I'm alive to testify today."

The gallery buzz increased at this revelation. Ashley slammed the gavel and demanded silence. The crowd quieted, and Ashley invited Zack to continue.

"What makes you think you were the subject of a hit?"

"Because I witnessed Ira's murder."

The crowd reacted with an even louder buzz. People were shocked by the allegation. Ashley again slammed his gavel and demanded quiet. He threatened to have the room cleared.

"That's very interesting, Shane. How did you happen to witness Ira's murder?"

"I just left the office for the night. Apparently, the assassin slipped by the guard in the lobby and entered our office immediately after I left. Ira was in my office, watching a video on my computer. The video was, shall we say, inappropriate. I presume Ira was using my office and my computer to avoid anyone knowing he watched pornography in the Party's office."

"The Party?" Zack couldn't resist the dig. He pre-planned this with Shane.

"The Michigan Republican Party. As I testified, Oliver got me a job with the Republican Party. Ira and I worked in the Party's Michigan headquarters."

The crowd, especially the anti-Wilkinson group, began to buzz again. Democrats were euphoric.

"Please continue. I don't want to lead you, Shane."

"I forgot my keys and returned to the office. I heard voices and noise coming from my office. Because I had no idea what was going on, I used the parallel hallway and the office opposite mine. I was looking to sneak up on whoever was in there and catch them doing something inappropriate. I looked into my office from the office across the hall, and I observed Ira. His back was to me, and he was watching a pornographic video. I pulled out my iPhone and began to record what he was doing in case *I* got in trouble for *his* bad behavior."

"What happened next?"

"Before I could really react to what was happening, this woman appeared in the hallway and snuck up behind Ira. She plunged a needle into his neck. Ira started to shake and convulse, then became completely still. I was certain he was dead. I read where the coroner determined Ira died of a heart attack, but I know the truth because I witnessed his murder."

"If the coroner called his death a heart attack, why should we believe it was murder?"

Republicans loved that question. How could members of the committee take a layperson's word over the word of the coroner? They had no idea what was coming until Shane dropped the bombshell.

"If you recall my previous testimony, Mr. Blake, I activated the record function on my iPhone to catch Ira watching an inappropriate video in my office." Shane stopped. He thought the rest was obvious, but Zack wanted him to feed the committee the full story for the sake of the historical record.

"Yes, Mr. Marbury? Please continue . . ." Zack prodded.

"I have the entire murder recorded on my iPhone. There is irrefutable proof Ira Gallant was murdered that evening. He didn't die of a heart attack."

The gallery expelled a loud roar. Anti-Wilkinson citizens and politicians started cheering and whooping. Pro-Wilkinson supporters began to boo and shout 'liar.' Everyone in attendance, including committee members, broke out in animated conversation, shocked by this revelation.

Ashley slammed his gavel and repeatedly demanded order until some semblance of order was restored. A permanent buzz would continue throughout the balance of Shane Marbury's testimony.

"Mr. Chairman? I have linked Mr. Marbury's iPhone to a computer and projection system. With your permission, I'd like to show the committee the recording."

"Without objection. Please proceed, Mr. Blake."

"May we please dim the lights and start the presentation?"

A Senate page stepped forward and began pressing keys on a CPU computer keyboard linked to Shane's iPhone. Another walked over to a wall and hit a button, dimming the lights. The committee and the gallery watched the entire video. Shocked silence followed the presentation. Zack continued with the witness.

"Mr. Marbury, does the video we've just watched accurately depict the events you witnessed on the evening of Ira Gallant's death?"

"Yes, it does."

"Has the video been altered in any way? Is this the complete video? Is it the same one you recorded on the evening of Ira Gallant's death?"

"Yes, it is."

"Mr. Chairman, I move the video to be admitted into the record."

"Without objection," muttered a frustrated Ashley. His dream of a conservative majority on the Supreme Court was rapidly fading. Zack continued.

"Have you ever seen the woman in the video before?"

"No."

"How do you know Wilkinson was involved in the murder plot?"

"Because Oliver was the only person who stood to gain anything from my silence."

"That's a stretch. How do you make that connection?"

"Shortly after Ira was killed and I went into hiding, I discovered another person died of a heart attack within twenty-four hours of Ira's murder."

"Lots of people die of heart attacks every day, Shane. What's the big deal?"

The crowd was now on the edge of their seats, hanging on every word, expecting another big revelation. Still, they were shocked by what came next.

"The big deal, Mr. Blake, is this: The other victim was a West Bloomfield detective, the guy who investigated the attempted rape of Hayley Larson."

Again, the crowd went wild, pro and con, with a mix of boos, cheers, and loud conversation. Shane's testimony sent shockwaves through the political establishment. Oliver Wilkinson, nominee for the United States Supreme Court, now stood accused, in sworn Senate testimony, of murdering two people, one of them a police officer. To make matters worse for the nominee, his accuser was, until these recent murders, a good friend of the nominee and a loyal *Republican*. The crowd and committee members were stunned.

Shane completed his testimony and delivered a closing statement. He apologized to Hayley Larson and her family and the families of Ira Gallant and the slain police officer. He reasoned both would be alive today but for his actions twenty-two years ago. Zack was quite pleased with Shane's testimony, proud of the redeemed man who delivered it. Shane Marbury hit a grand slam in front of the Senate Judiciary Committee. Ashley called for a recess.

***

A half-hour later, the committee reconvened. The FBI report was read into the record. The report delivery was monotonous but contained several witness statements corroborating Hayley's and Shane's testimony. While Jared Wilkinson refused to cooperate and retained counsel, the girls who stormed the bathroom testified to the indecent exposure, as well as to Hayley's terrifying demeanor and torn-off clothing. Several other

witnesses testified to Hayley running down the stairs and out the
front door in her bra and panties, hysterical, screaming, and
crying.

The coup de grâce of this section of the report, however, was
the affidavit of Jordan Levin and a recorded statement he gave to
the FBI. Zack Blake, Oliver Wilkinson, and his evil companions
had all forgotten about Levin, but the FBI had not. In truth, the
bureau didn't have to do much to track Levin down.

Following Eric Lorenz's death, a pissed off Levin contacted
the FBI and spilled his guts to Agent Pete Westmore, who
recorded the entire conversation. Levin confirmed the cover-up
and corroborated Shane's story about Wilkinson's parents, their
cozy relationship with the West Bloomfield Chief of Police, and
the arrangement to drop the attempted rape charges. The Chief of
Police was now named as a co-conspirator on the obstruction of
justice charge.

The report also contained brief vignettes from multiple
women who were victims of similar predatory acts perpetrated
by Oliver Wilkinson. Multiple witnesses delivered sworn
statements or Senate committee testimony of numerous crimes
committed by Wilkinson. If arrested and charged, most witnesses
were confident a jury or a judge would find Oliver Wilkinson
guilty of attempted rape, obstruction of justice, conspiracy to
commit murder, and felony murder. This was quite a day for the
anti-Wilkinson crowd.

Chapter Forty-Six

When the hearing was over, Zachary Blake called Hayley Larson Schultz.

"Did you see it?"

"It was amazing, Zack. You were amazing. I can almost turn the page with Shane and accept his apology. I'll work on it."

"I'm glad you feel that way, Hayley. I never thought I'd say this, but Shane deserves forgiveness. I know what he did to you and how it affected your life, but what Shane went through to get to Washington and testify was epic. He risked death multiple times and persevered. It may sound strange, but you should not only forgive him, but you might even consider thanking him for his bravery. I will understand if you can't do this, but please understand what we've been through."

"I will certainly entertain the possibility."

"He'd like to come over and apologize to you and Joel personally."

"Whoa, Zack. I'm not ready for anything like that."

"Consider it, Hayley. That's all I ask."

"I will."

"Good. Let's talk about Oliver Wilkinson. His nomination is toast."

"Are you sure? He specializes in using his power and influence to pull off miracles."

"I don't see how any senator who seeks re-election can vote 'yes' on Wilkinson. They're already facing landslide losses because of RonJohn and Golding. 'Yes' on Wilkinson might turn the whole country democratic."

"Mm . . . interesting. Maybe we should support a 'yes' vote." Hayley joked. Zack paused. *Is she nuts?* He instantly understood the joke and began to laugh.

"Just kidding," Hayley chuckled.

"I *love* your sense of humor. It's nice to 'hear' you smile."

"How do you know I'm smiling? Anyway, it's nice to feel like smiling. So, what happens now?"

"Wilkinson might want one more shot at the committee. He might want to tell them it was all Marbury—Shane did it and is covering up his own crime."

"But Shane merely corroborated my testimony. It was *both* of them. *Oliver* was the major aggressor."

"I'm just trying to answer your question about what might happen. I presume Oliver might also try to convince the committee he had nothing to do with the murders."

"That's a stretch. Who else would benefit? The tape makes it clear Shane's associate was murdered, and the two deaths are related. Levin's testimony about the cover-up can't be ignored either. And how about an assassin chasing you guys through the woods?"

"Maybe he can get the West Bloomfield Chief of Police to come and testify on his behalf? How knows? Maybe he can demonstrate he wasn't involved with the hit on Marbury. He also has to get by the statements of all of those other women who came forward. He's got a lot of influence, but at the end of the day, his nomination has to be toast. I just don't see him giving up without a fight. This is all speculation. Let's see what happens over the next couple of days and weeks. One thing is certain. If Wilkinson continues this fight, the Republicans won't have enough time to put forward another candidate. His arrogance may actually work in our favor."

"Wow! I never thought of it that way. Fight on, Oliver! As long as you lose!"

"Amen, Hayley. I'll keep you posted. I get daily updates from Senator Stabler."

They bid each other goodbye. Zack promised to update Hayley every time Stabler updated him.

***

Zack's comments to Hayley proved prophetic as Wilkinson refused to concede the nomination. He requested additional testimonial time before the committee and eventually appeared.

As conservative as he was, Ashley could not condone having a criminal on the Supreme Court, even a staunchly conservative criminal like Wilkinson. He informally turned the committee over to the Democrats. They raked Wilkinson through the coals. Witnesses with no motive to lie came forward in droves to refute Wilkinson's version of facts. Ever the narcissist, Oliver insisted on repeating lie after lie to the committee.

One senator promised multiple prosecutions if Wilkinson persisted. However, Wilkinson ignored her because it was his last chance to realize his dreams. He was going to take it no matter what it cost him.

In the end, it cost him everything. He made a fool of himself and was indicted on several counts of felony murder and conspiracy to commit murder, multiple counts of sexual assault, and multiple counts of perjury. Congress began impeachment proceedings because Wilkinson was still a sitting Sixth Circuit Federal Court of Appeals Judge. The State Bar of Michigan opened an investigation and sought to revoke Wilkinson's law license. Oliver Wilkinson's legal and judicial careers were over. He would need a miracle to avoid a lengthy federal prison sentence.

When he finally realized his predicament, Wilkinson played the only card he could. He promised to cooperate with federal authorities and name names in exchange for leniency. He retained high-profile attorney Lee Bernstein, who publicly proclaimed he would seek a cooperation agreement with federal authorities. His client maintained he was a minor pawn in a vast right-wing conspiracy. Wilkinson and Bernstein had the press and the public eating out of the palms of their hands. Political pundits waited for his next explosive allegation and for the other proverbial shoe to drop.

Oliver was indicted. However, because of his stature, federal authorities offered him the courtesy of surrendering voluntarily. He arranged to turn himself in, was booked, seated for a mug shot, fingerprinted, and arraigned before a federal district court judge in Detroit. He pleaded not guilty to all charges and was released on his own recognizance, again, in deference to his judicial status and stellar career. The angry judge insisted on a tether.

As he and Bernstein exited the courtroom and out the courthouse doors, they were greeted by a mass of reporters. They shouted multiple questions at the same time. The lawyer stepped to a makeshift podium for a post-hearing statement. Reporters continued to shout questions, simultaneously, effectively drowning each other out.

"Whoa, whoa, Judge Wilkinson will speak to you. He's well versed in the law and more than capable of addressing the charges and speaking for himself. We have already met with the committee. Oliver Wilkinson is an innocent victim, will defend this case vigorously, cooperate with authorities, and be vindicated in the end." Bernstein orated.

"I also want to comment on the spectacle this morning. Federal prosecutors did not need to leak Judge Wilkinson's surrender and indictment to the press. They knew where he was and when he was coming. A telephone call with a private arraignment and release would have been sufficient. This was an unfortunate side-show, designed to cause Judge Wilkinson pain and embarrassment. The prosecution's behavior is shameful, a blight on our Judeo-Christian values.

"Judge Wilkinson has nothing to hide. So, without further ado, here is Judge Oliver Wilkinson."

Bernstein moved to the side, and Wilkinson stepped to the podium. A supporter shouted:

"We stand with you, Your Honor."

"Thanks for your support, my friend; I appreciate it," Wilkinson began. Anti-Wilkinson protestors started to boo and jeer.

"Thank you, Lee. After what was an *inquisition* rather than a confirmation hearing in front of the Senate Judiciary Committee, I stand accused of crimes that have nothing to do with a crazy and vindictive woman's accusations from twenty-three years ago. Hayley Larson's failure to pursue charges, in that case, vindicates me and speaks for itself."

Again, the large, anti-Wilkinson contingent began to boo. After the contentious hearing, where witness testimony, video evidence, and thousands of documents proved his crimes,

Wilkinson still had the stones to deny the entire criminal chain of events. He continued.

"Two people tragically died of heart attacks. Someone captured a video of an incident where one of them is seen being injected with a hypodermic needle shortly before his death. Even if this video depicts a murder, it is clear the murderer is a *woman*. Last I checked, I am not a woman.

"I am a student of the law. How can prosecutors justify indicting a man for murder when a video clearly shows someone else committed the crime? Perjury charges resulted when I denied my involvement during my confirmation hearings. America is a nation where one is innocent until *proven* guilty. An accused must not be tried and convicted in the *press*. He is entitled to face his accusers and receive a fair trial by a jury of his peers. I look forward to my trial and total vindication."

The crowd began to chant: "Lock him up! Lock him up! Lock him up!"

Wilkinson held up his hands and signaled for quiet. The noise receded.

"If I erred in giving testimony, it was not material to this indictment and was made without intent. I have offered my cooperation to investigators to help bring to justice anyone responsible for another's death, especially if that death or murder is related to my confirmation hearing. There is not much more I can do. The U.S. Attorney's office issued a press release about my surrender and indictment this morning before notifying my learned counsel of that fact. This process is a carnival and a sham. I look forward to clearing my name.

"I have pleaded not guilty to all charges. I will defeat the government in court. I am deeply troubled by the political motivations of these prosecutors in pursuing this investigation and indictment. I have been a judge for over twenty years and would never bear false witness in testimony for *any* reason. My oath of office requires the truth, the whole truth, and nothing but the truth. The truth will ultimately prevail. As I mentioned earlier, I am looking forward to total and complete vindication."

"Judge Wilkinson? Do you intend to cooperate with the investigation?" A reporter shouted above the noise.

"I have offered my cooperation, but my attorney has not yet spoken in specifics with federal prosecutors. I will let him do his job. I continue to profess my innocence of these charges. I have information that will help these inept prosecutors get to the truth."

"What information is that? Can you share the details? How do you know these things?" Reporters shouted.

"I will have more to say as the case progresses. I intend to tell the truth. I have always told the truth. Throughout my confirmation hearing, I told the truth. I am innocent, and I intend to prove my innocence in a court of law."

"How strong is your allegiance to President Golding? After all, he appointed you to the position," a reporter inquired.

"My allegiance to the president is strong."

"Do you plan to ask him for a pardon?" The crowd stopped chanting to listen to Wilkinson's response. They never considered this possibility.

"The president is a friend. I have not requested a pardon, nor has he offered one. We shall see. I thanked him for the opportunity to be considered for a seat on the Supreme Court. I appreciate his confidence in me. I did not let him down. The Senate Judiciary Committee let him down by allowing its members to get bogged down in phony narratives and ancient histories from crazy left-wing zealots. I'm sure the president knows this and will take this whole charade into account when or if the time comes."

"Did you attempt to rape Hayley Larson Schultz?"

"I addressed that before. No, I did not. This alleged crime is not part of this indictment. Isn't that interesting?"

"How about the other women who have come forward?"

"Copycats looking for fifteen minutes of fame," Wilkinson growled.

"We've got your back, Judge Wilkinson!" Someone shouted from the bottom of the step.

"Thank you!" Wilkinson shouted back.

"Judge Wilkinson, you have now been indicted. Have you seen the evidence against you?"

"No, I haven't. My attorney has seen some of the so-called proofs, but I have not. I haven't even read the indictment. There is a meeting scheduled for tomorrow to discuss my cooperation into an ongoing investigation of these murders—if that's what they were."

"If you've done nothing wrong, Judge Wilkinson, then why are we here?" A reporter got in the judge's face.

"That's all for now." Wilkinson pushed the reporter away.

Wilkinson flashed a victory sign to the crowd and continued down the steps. Reporters blocked his travel and shouted questions as the mob crowded in, creating an almost claustrophobic atmosphere. A woman closed in, then Oliver felt a slight prick in his neck. He continued pushing through the crowd, attempting to reach the bottom of the steps.

Wilkinson began to feel dizzy and nauseous. His legs stiffened and began to give way. He tried to walk, but his legs gave out. He reached out to reporters for support and balance as his arms lost power and control. His body began to convulse, and his eyes rolled behind his eyelids. He stumbled forward directly into a mass of reporters. When they backed out of his way, Wilkinson fell flat on his face and tumbled down the courthouse steps.

"Call 9-1-1!" Bernstein shouted to the crowd. Wilkinson's body lay twitching uncontrollably at the bottom of the steps. Drool dripped down the sides of his mouth. As all eyes were glued to Wilkinson, his body went completely lifeless. Hardly anyone noticed the woman, dressed in black spandex, with a stocking cap pulled over her forehead. A couple of witnesses remembered such a woman. *She was beautiful*, they recalled. *She resembled the actress Catherine Zeta-Jones.*

END

Thank you for reading, and I sincerely hope you enjoyed *Supreme Betrayal*. As an independently published author, I rely on you, the reader, to spread the word. So, if you enjoyed this book, please tell your friends and family, and I would appreciate a brief review. Thanks again.

Mark

Other Books in the Series

L'DOR V'DOR – From Generation to Generation (A Novella)

Betrayal of Faith (Book 1)
Betrayal of Justice (Book 2)
Betrayal in Blue (Book 3)
Betrayal in Black (Book 4)
Betrayal High (Book 5)

The **Zachary Blake Legal Thriller Series** are also available in audiobook format, brilliantly narrated by Detroit's own legendary radio and television personality **Lee Alan.**

About the Author

Mark M. Bello is an attorney and award-winning legal thriller author. After handling high profile legal cases for 42 years, Mark now treats readers to a front-row seat in the courtroom. His ripped from the headlines Zachary Blake Legal Thrillers are inspired by actual cases or Bello's take on current legal or sociopolitical issues. Mark lives in Michigan with his wife, Tobye. They have four children and 8 grandchildren.

Connect with Mark

Website: www.markmbello.com
Email: info@markmbello.com
Facebook: MarkMBelloBooks
Twitter: @JusticeFellow
YouTube: Mark M. Bello
Goodreads: Mark M. Bello

To request a speaking engagement, interview, or appearance, please email info@markmbello.com